Fierce Loyalty
A Toni Brazil Story

by
Scott A. Rezendes

PublishAmerica
Baltimore

© 2003 by Scott A. Rezendes.
All rights reserved. No part of this book may be reproduced, stored in a retrieval system, or transmitted in any form or by any means without the prior written permission of the publishers, except by a reviewer who may quote brief passages in a review to be printed in a newspaper, magazine, or journal.

First printing

This story is a work of fiction. Although some historical facts are true and locations described in this story exist, names, characters, and incidents are either the product of the author's imagination or used fictitiously. Any resemblance to actual persons living or dead, business establishments, events, or locales is entirely coincidental.

ISBN: 1-4137-0328-3
PUBLISHED BY PUBLISHAMERICA, LLLP
www.publishamerica.com

ACKNOWLEDGEMENTS

I'd like to thank those of you who read this novel and gave me your kind thoughts and feedback. Thanks to my family, friends, and colleagues who supported me in writing this story.

Special thanks to Roberta for putting up with me while working on this creature for the past three years. But thanks for being there when I was sick, and really needed you. I love you! To my mother and father, who have supported me in whatever I do. My brothers, Larry and Troy, who give me the fodder for conversation. And finally, to Carla, Jimmy, Lilly, Georgio, and Valarie for all your support and encouragement.

Thanks to A-1 Editing, especially Dr. Bruce Coggins. I learned a lot from your comments. Thank you for your straight-forwardness. This story is a lot better because of you.

I'd also like to thank the doctors and nurses at Stanford Medical Center's Onchology Clinic for everything they've done for me. You do a tough job and see what really goes on behind the lives of so many. I really don't know how you do it, day after day. I found real people fighting and living life in that clinic everyday I was there. Having cancer doesn't mean life is over, it just becomes more urgent.

Finally, I'd like to thank all the veterans who have and will protect our freedom. Truly, freedom is not free at all, and takes the most precious of commodities – human life.

This book is dedicated to the life of Christina Comfort, and her parents Steve and Gloria Comfort. You are the strongest people I know, and Christina was truly a child of God. Rest in Peace, Christina.

"The most difficult of God's demands is compassion for our enemies."
   - S.A. Rezendes

PROLOGUE

One Week Later

I took another swig of beer that cooled my hand, savoring its coldness at the back of my throat. The taste was sweet and made me want more to alleviate the pain I felt. The beer left my gut raw and queasy - not quite a stomachache, more like a nervous twist just before something bad happens. But what could happen now? The past week was bad enough. Maybe I was feeling the residual effects.

I'd just come home, tired from the long week of non-stop traveling, alone in the living room, waiting for my parents and watching a football game on television. Bored, I wondered when I lost my love for the Sunday ritual that replaced godly worship so long ago. Maybe I just hadn't settled back into life yet. My mind and body exhausted.

I looked toward the blank labeled book on the coffee table. I put it there as soon as I came home, and it seemed to have eyes or a voice. Perhaps my own conscious was calling me – or guilt. I wanted to wait a few days before reading it, get situated, but the damn thing stared at me, calling me by name.

I picked the book up and stared at its blank cover, remembering the events of the last week. I felt its rugged leather-embroidered texture, wondering what made me loathe the thought of reading it. I couldn't change what happened, even if I wanted too, but I wanted to forget and just sleep through the night, one night. I noticed the dust that settled on the tan cover and lightly brushed off a layer. I watched as the particles floated upward into the sunlight beaming through the window. I wondered where the dust would settle - not just in the room, but in my life.

The book cover bore no title, just blankness, as if telling its own story. A loud noise came from the television, and I saw the celebration as the game ended. I wished I could smile, but nothing seemed to matter anymore. A groan from across the room caught my attention. Bailey, my dog, looked back at me. She was a sight for the weary when I came home. Just knowing she'd be here when I returned was comforting. I looked away and opened the book to the first page.

There was a picture of a man and a woman, smiles ear to ear. At first I thought the picture was of my ex-wife and me. I looked again, and realized I was seeing what I wanted to see - happiness in my life. I focused on the picture and saw it was my brother and his wife on their wedding day. I wondered what he wrote about his own life, so I began reading.

Journal Entry April 8, 2001

It's 2:30 A.M. and I'm wide-awake from a dream that invades my sleep once or twice every week for as many years as I can remember, since I returned from Nam. Its like my companion in the night, it comes so frequently. Sometimes when I wake in the morning and I don't remember my dream, I wonder if I had the dream again, or I've just forgotten. Always the same dream. I've come to believe its shame that I must feel for not fulfilling the promise I made that day, and so it haunts me over and over again. I'm tired of the violence it brings to my sleep. I had believed that sleep was a time to forget – to be free of my past that seems like someone else's life now. It was so long ago when it happened, why can't I forget? It's as if God has sentenced me to relive it night after night, especially on the days before the day, September 19, 1967.

"Sergeant! Get over here now!" screamed Lt. Steven Yardley, from the door of a large green camouflage tent about a hundred feet from where Bobby sat. Bobby grimaced at the sound of Yardley's voice. He sat on a hill overlooking a mixed green shaded jungle, and golden tall grass terrain dotting the hillsides. It was hot, over a hundred degrees.

"Just another day in hell," he whispered to himself. That's what Vietnam was to him, killing fields of hell, a no-man's land of jungle and swamps, mountains and tough, bush filled trails.

He stood, but the sun's heat pushed him back down toward the rock he used as a chair. Bobby felt his lieutenant scowling at him as he picked up his

FIERCE LOYALTY

rucksack and M-16 rifle and slowly began walking towards the tent. He took his cigarette from between his lips and threw it to the ground in disgust, stepping on it as he glared back at Yardley. He knew if he didn't follow the order, Yardley would probably bust his butt down another rank from sergeant.

That Bobby and Lt. Yardley didn't like each other one bit was no secret. Bobby, a stubborn, stubble faced, stocky, blue-collar type, saw Yardley as just some college dick-head who pretended he was a leader.

"Where was the jerk during the fighting?" he thought to himself. Like many in the company, Bobby believed Yardley was scared to get his hands dirty when the fighting started, but most of all, Bobby didn't like anyone who tried to get him killed. Yardley had almost succeeded a week earlier, in the jungle surrounding the base camp.

Bobby never took his eyes off Yardley as he meandered over and entered the tent, giving Yardley his "savage killer look" all the while Yardley held the entrance flap open.

"Leaves revoked Sergeant!" Yardley said to Bobby, after he had passed by him.

Bobby didn't say a word as he looked around the room at his peers and his captain. "You'll get yours, you shit," he whispered under his breath.

Bobby had waited for leave for over a month and planned it for his twenty-second birthday. He was glad to have made it this far, after being assigned to night patrol the past four weeks, looking for snipers, troop movement, and whatever else moved. It was stressful as hell, but it was his life right now, and Bobby had three more months to go on his tour. He thought about re-upping for another tour, but after the last month, he decided against it. The fighting was heating up, the North was gaining ground despite America's superior technology, and Bobby thought we might lose the war. The war was different from the one his father fought in Europe twenty-five years earlier, a jungle war they weren't prepared for. His friends were dying around him, two of his best friends in the last month. They got soft, let down their guard. Simon ended up with his throat cut, and then it was Johnny – "Good old Johnny Rotten," Bobby thought – who got hit by a sniper right outside the camp perimeter. He was drunk – "Just going for a walk to take a piss" – and that was it. He never came back. A secondary night patrol found his body on the trail. They found the sniper too, but the sniper got Johnny Rotten.

Lt. Yardley followed Bobby into the tent. In the command post were five other sergeants – Johnson, Cooper, Beasley, Seymour, and Gonzalez. Standing at the map board where operations were planned was the captain, a man

Bobby looked up to because he had come through the ranks, fought like the grunts, and earned a promotion. Bobby thought Captain Powell knew what he was doing. He was a real leader, a man he could trust.

"Sergeant, glad you could join us," said Captain Powell, as Bobby walked into the room.

"Yes Sir!" Bobby said, as he saluted his superior and nodded at him. Bobby's friend Freddie "Gonzo" Gonzalez staring at him with his usual jovial look. Bobby didn't know how Gonzo stayed so happy all the time.

"Hey, Gonzo," Bobby said, "and girls, what's up here?" Bobby knew them all. They were the best the company had of what was left.

"Hey, screw you Bobby," Sgt. Cooper said.

"Oh, sorry, Coop, you da man! Ain't ya …" Bobby said, and everyone laughed.

"Shut the hell up Sergeant!" Lt. Yardley commanded. "Everyone's here. Okay look we got a mission to do here. All leave is canceled, and that means you Sergeant." He looked directly at Bobby.

"A mission?" Bobby asked. "I hope you ain't going to get me killed on this one, Yardley," he said, and again the group of young soldiers laughed and shook their heads up and down.

"Hey, fuck you, Sergeant," said Lt. Yardley. "You'll be on point for this one if you push it. After all, I know your tour is up in what? Two, three months?" he finished, looking at Bobby with red churning in his eyes.

"That's enough, boys," interrupted Captain Powell in his usual casual tone. "We got some dirty work to do here, serious shit, and no one, and I mean no one, will get anyone killed here. The lieutenants' going to brief us now. Let's just listen up."

Bobby looked back at Yardley, who at twenty-seven looked like he hadn't hit puberty. He had the face of a fourteen-year old boy who hadn't begun to shave. He was tall and lanky, maybe 6'5", with straight black hair and thick eyebrows that crossed the bridge of his nose. He towered over every one else, and although he wasn't a good fighter, he was a college graduate, which the military liked.

"What's this mission about, Lieutenant?" asked Sgt. Tim Beasley in his deep Southern Louisiana voice. "Why we all here?"

"This came down from command in Saigon," Yardley began. "Some human rights group gave a French diplomat here in Vietnam some pictures of alleged North Vietnamese atrocities. They claimed the North Vietnamese army was coming down to these villages, here," he said, as he pointed to a map on a

FIERCE LOYALTY

large board. "The Cong believe the Vietnamese villages are helping us, so the North is slaughtering them, burning them at the stake. Stories like that. Anyway, the diplomat wants to go to a site, to a village here." He pointed at another location on the map. "He wants to check it out for a possible burial site, where the atrocities were supposed to have happened. Our mission is to protect the diplomat from here to the site, which is somewhere here."

"You outta of your mind, Lieutenant?" said Sgt. Jesse Cooper, a light skinned African American from Harlem. Drafted at age twenty-eight, Cooper was now thirty-two and half way through his second tour. He was a fighter, Bobby thought, reliable, trustworthy, and most of all, a great shot. "That's gook territory, man. We found that out last week. Three of our own got it. No wonder people gettin' killed in there. Shit, man, don't command know any better? They're going to find atrocities all right, us gettin' chopped and diced."

"Stow it Sergeant," said Yardley. "Command said we'd have all the air and ground support needed. They're hoping we find something up there."

"Yeah, they're hoping to find something all right," started Sgt. Stanley Seymour, the youngest in the group at twenty, with his rust colored hair, white skin, and dark rimmed glasses, "so they can start moving us in for more fighting. Shit, man, we got are hands tied around here keeping it clean."

"Yeah. Keepin' it clean," said Cooper and Gonzalez in unison.

"Look, these are our orders, and we're going to follow them!" Yardley started again. "We're here, about ten clicks from the site. The trail is clear. It should be a clean hike. Now, we got two hours before they get here. I want the six of you to pick five of your best and take them with us. It's 10:00 A.M. Brief your men, eat something. We hump out of here ASAP." Yardley looked at Bobby coolly. "Bobby, you'll take point."

Bobby stood, looked around the room at his remaining friends, then at Yardley and said, "You get one of us killed, so help me, I'll take you out myself, Yardley. When you don't expect it. Understand?"

He left the room, taking a copy of the board map off the table. As he walked out of the tent, Yardley yelled at him, "Is that a threat to a superior officer? I'll have your stripes, you piece of shit. I'll have you court marshaled for that!" All Bobby could think about was getting home – alive.

The French diplomat, Dr. Jerome Picard, arrived only five minutes after Yardley's briefing, two hours early. He brought a woman and two young children with him, his wife and two sons. Two journalists, the U.S. Ambassador to South Vietnam, Henry Turgeon, and two of his staff also came. Bobby ate his chow, watching the two boys. They looked scared and he thought, a little meek for boys their age, which he guessed to be about five and eight. They spoke French to each other and Bobby surmised that the French ambassador's wife was not happy to be there. In fact, Bobby agreed with her. She was pretty for a woman in her early forties, but whatever her concerns, her husband was definitely the boss.

Bobby saw the older boy staring at him from about ten feet away. His younger brother had kicked the ball past him, and as he ran over to fetch the ball, he came across Bobby.

"You scared, boy?" Bobby asked, in a gravelly smoker's voice. He blew out the smoke from the cigarette he'd just inhaled while he chewed his food.

"Nah. No," the boy mumbled in a high-pitched voice.

"Oh," Bobby said, "you understand English?"

"Yes."

"Whatcha want?" Bobby asked gently.

"Nothing. My mummy says smoking is bad. Is it really bad?"

Bobby smirked. "Yeah kid, it's bad. You otta listen to your mother."

The boy smiled and looked down in a shy manner. "Are you taking my father into the jungle?" He pointed to the French diplomat standing with Captain Powell and Lt. Yardley.

"That your father over there?"

"Yes," the boy answered.

"Well, I'm not supposed to tell anyone because it's Top Secret, but yeah, I'm the one whose taking him in," Bobby answered, serious but playful.

"Wow," the boy said, with an enamored look. "Have you ever killed anybody?"

"What's your name boy?" Bobby asked.

"Simon."

"Simon, well then. I had a good friend named Simon once. It's a good name, son," Bobby said, pondering the coincidence of his friends' death and the kid showing up with the same name.

"Thanks, mister."

"Simon, killing is the worst thing a person can do to another person," Bobby said.

"I know. I just wondered what it would feel like," Simon answered.

"Simon!" the younger boy across the yard yelled. "Come back!"

"I'm coming," he yelled to his brother, then turned back to Bobby. "That's my brother Thomas. He's eight. I'm ten. Is that old?"

"Simon, ten is very young." Bobby answered.

12

FIERCE LOYALTY

"That's what my mummy says, too. I wanted to go with my father to the jungle, but she wouldn't let me. She says I'm too young."

"You're better off staying behind. But I promise you, I'll protect your dad real good. Okay?"

"Okay," Simon answered. "My mummy is worried, and she doesn't like it here. I'll tell her not to worry, because you're protecting my father."

"There you go. Now, I think you ought to go back to your brother and take care of him, you understand?"

Simon cocked his head at Bobby. "What do mean? Why should I take care of my brother?"

"Because you might need him to take care of you some day. You never know. It's called a brother's keeper. It means you got to take care of your own blood, a fierce loyalty to protect your family, at any cost. No one else will." Bobby lectured Simon like a teacher.

"Oh," Simon answered. "I think I understand. Sometimes I don't like my brother, though. He's a baby."

"Well, we all were once," Bobby said, his three younger brother's faces flashing through his mind like a television screen, wondering if he'd ever see them again.

"We all were, what?"

"Babies, Simon. We were all babies, just like your brother and mine," Bobby replied.

"Oh, yeah. I guess. Well, I better go then," he said, almost disappointed.

"All right. Nice meeting you Simon." Bobby held out his hand to shake Simon's.

"Oh, um. What was your name, mister?" Simon held out his hand to Bobby, and then they shook.

"Bobby."

"Nice to meet you too, Mr. Bobby," Simon answered, then turned and ran back across the yard to his brother, and excitedly told him about meeting a real soldier.

The village was directly off the main trail about ten miles from base camp, in enemy territory. They had a name for the trail, the Ho Chi Minh, and venturing on it was a dangerous gamble. The site wasn't far from camp, but far enough that if the enemy was watching, they knew something was going on. The group took four hours to reach the site, and it would take another four to get back to base camp. Bobby entered the remains of a burned out village with his lead group of five men. The jungle was thick all the way to the site,

13

but just to the west of the village was a huge open field, a rice paddy approximately five acres square, Bobby guessed.

The plan called for Bobby and his men, group one, to hike directly through the trail, flanked on both sides by group two and group three, Gonzo's and Cooper's groups. They would secure the site, and then radio a message to base camp to fly in the diplomats. It was simple enough, yet Bobby thought it was ridiculous. People die in war, and whether by gun, hand or disease, war always created atrocities. The risk to his men however, was unwarranted, which he would make clear to his superiors, later. Being a soldier meant following orders, whether he agreed with them or not.

Bobby threw his left arm up at a ninety-degree angle, his hand balled in a fist, as they approached the village. Jutted fingers signaled his men to spread out through the village and clear it. They moved like shadows in the dust of their footprints, rushing half collapsed huts without a sound. There would be no bullets if they found anything, just a simple bayonet thrust. Bobby waited. A kid named Franklin from Boise, Idaho, came around holding his fist up and outward, signaling nothing found, his sector clear. Within seconds, the four other men appeared all with fists, nothing found. Bobby heard a sound behind him, turned and pointed his weapon ready to fire. Gonzo came through the jungle from a north position.

"Hey, hey, hey, BB! It's just me, Gonzo!" Gonzalez yelled.

"Fuck, Gonzo! You ain't supposed to come out until I give the signal. I almost shot your ass off. I mean your face. I keep mixing them up." Bobby laughed.

"BB, you one funny mother fucker. You need to take a chill pill, my boy. Coop's comin' up the trail behind us. The camp clear?" Gonzo asked.

Bobby waved his hand in a circular motion above his head, "Clear. You see anything that looks like a burial site?"

"Maybe they're buried in the rice fields! Fuckin' gooks, anyway. Why we out here riskin' everything for some political bullshit?"

"I know, Gonzo, but these are the orders," Bobby replied.

"Orders, Bobby. That's not all that's important, my brother."

"Can it, Gonzo! I want to get back tonight, know what I mean? Get your men out there in the fields, and pop the color cans so the choppers can find us. I'm calling base to let em' know we're here," Bobby ordered.

"Yeah, all right," he said harshly, then yelled at his team. "Lets go mutts, we got to clear that field over there." Gonzo took his men into the field to secure positions around a landing site.

FIERCE LOYALTY

Bobby informed base camp they had arrived, and the village was secure for the time being. As soon as the choppers arrived, they'd be open targets to a Viet Cong attack. The journey in was too easy, Bobby thought, and the village was too quiet. He had a gut feeling something wasn't right. The sooner they found a burial site, the sooner they could mark it, photograph it and get back to camp. The summer day was long, but time was getting short that afternoon. Rain was forecast, and when it rained, things got wet fast.

Coop arrived with his group, and Bobby asked them to cover the south end of the village. Bobby's senses became hyper. He heard every noise and felt his skin start to tingle. His hair stood up. It happened every time he was on a mission. He called his men over to discuss a search pattern around the village to look for the burial site. The five searched from within the village spiraling out beyond the perimeter. They were looking for something like freshly moved dirt. Bobby wanted them to be swift, but thorough.

His senses were heightened, buzzing like a grasshopper. Three choppers filled with political brass were on the way to the village. They'd arrive in less than twenty minutes.

"Sergeant! Over here!" yelled Jason Strong, an eighteen-year old from Portland, Oregon. Bobby began a slow jog to his position on the village outskirts near the jungle line opposite the rice field.

"Whatcha find Corporal?" Bobby asked.

Strong reached down into a hole with the tip of his rifle and brought up a severed finger. "Looks like a finger, Sarge, and by the look of it, it's female."

"Female? How can you tell?"

"I don't know, Sarge, just looks like it. It's small I guess," Strong replied.

"All right Strong. Good job. Keep digging." Then Bobby saw what they had come for. "Holy shit!"

"I see it too Sarge," Strong said, looking at the decomposed face of a young Vietnamese female buried in the soft dirt about a foot from where he found the finger. "Geez, she couldn't be more than twelve-years old, maybe thirteen."

"Okay, Corporal. Stay here. I'm getting the rest of the guys over here." Bobby called the other men who hurried to the location and began digging in a circle around the mutilated body of the young girl.

He heard the choppers coming. Bobby turned toward the noise and saw green smoke rising from the smokers Gonzo stationed around a hard surface near the rice field. Two choppers hovered and landed one by one, the first unloaded a squad of eight men who jumped and took positions around the village and the landing site. The chopper took off quickly after it unloaded and took up a defensive air position with two other choppers. The second chopper swooped down to drop off the brass. As it landed, Bobby saw the French diplomat unbuckling his strap.

"He's taking too long," Bobby said out loud. He was holding up the others and Bobby saw the nervous pilot speaking animated. The blades were loud, and no one could hear a thing.

As Bobby watched the confusion inside the chopper, something in the air caught his eye. In an instant, he realized what it was and yelled, "Get down! Get Down!" No one heard him.

He screamed again, but it was too late. At the last possible moment Bobby jumped just as the explosion hit, blowing him off his feet into a hole dug by his own men. Metal and chopper pieces flew everywhere, and gunfire erupted all around. Disoriented and sick, he struggled to his feet, and found his M-16. Another explosion lit the sky, and Bobby fell back into the hole. Dirt hit his face, his eyes closed. When the dirt stopped covering him, he opened his eyes and saw what he believed was up.

There was no blue sky, just streaming clouds of smoke. He lay in the hole, waiting for the enemy to find him. He found the ground with his feet again and heard groans and yelling in English. He peeked from the dirt filled hole and what he saw filled him with distress. Simon's face flashed before him like a ghost. The artillery shell that found the helicopter ripped it apart. Nothing was left. More gunfire erupted around him. He found a pair of legs behind him slumped over the side of the hole. He pulled them down, but there was no upper half. He realized his arm and shirtsleeve were torn and wet. He was bleeding. His thoughts turned to the legs covered in camouflaged pants. He read the name "Strong" painted on the pocket.

Bobby's eyes flinched. "No! Shit! Motherfuckers! No! No!" he screamed and screamed. Everything became blurry. Another explosion hit nearby and dirt flew into the hole. The trousers stared back at him as if they had eyes.

Bobby's senses rushed back like liquid pulled back into a bottle by a suction cup. He realized where he was, and the thought of death hit him. He poked his head up again, looked around and found a second chopper blown apart and burning thirty feet behind him. He heard the other choppers flying in circles above, guns blazing into the surrounding jungle with deadly implication. The second chopper hit had crashed right where Coop and his men dug in. Just where he'd asked them to go. He could only hope they got out before the chopper fell to the ground, engulfed in flames.

FIERCE LOYALTY

"Bobby!" A scream came from behind. He saw the blur of a scared soldier running and jumping into the hole with him.

"Gonzo!" Bobby started, when he recognized the face. "What the hell happened?"

"I don't know, man. The gooks hit us with small artillery and shoulder fired missiles. The choppers covered the noise. Shit!" Gonzo said looking at the burning chopper. "They never knew what hit em', eh?" He looked at Bobby. "Shit, man, you're bleedin'."

"Yeah, I know. It's my shoulder. I'm Okay," he answered. "Strong's dead, man. He was cut in half. I got blown into the hole and it missed."

"I know man. I know."

"He was just a kid, Gonz," Bobby pleaded.

"We gotta get outta here, Bobby, and now. They have us dialed in real good. Must've had us under watch the whole time. Coop and four of his guys bit it." Gonzo was out of breath.

"Coop? Shit! Who's left, Gonz?"

"Me, you, Martinez, Gypsy, Jake, and Jackson. All of Beasley's and Seymour's outfit. That's eighteen of us," Gonzo replied. "We gotta go Bobby. Choppers can't land with the gooks around us like this. Lets go man. We gotta hump outta here."

"I want to stay. Strong, someone's got to take care of him," Bobby mumbled.

"Fuck, Bobby! Strong's dead, man. We gotta go and I mean right now, brother." "But."

"No buts, Bobby," Gonzo grabbed Bobby's arm and began his ascent from the hole. "You're coming' with me."

They left the village together, Gonzo pulling Bobby with him. Within a few minutes, they entered the jungle together. Bobby came back to reality, although he still hurt inside when he thought about leaving Strong cut in half in the jungle. He couldn't find his dog tags and decided he'd have to write the letter to his family. He was responsible for him. He'd never forget it and maybe never forgive himself. They came in with thirty men and six brass. They left with eighteen. Then Simon's face came to him again like a flash of a camera. Simon would be without his father for the rest of his life. It seemed unfair, his promise unfulfilled.

I'll never forget the look on that little boy's face when I returned without his father. The kid just looked at me, stunned, that I failed to protect his father. He did not cry. He just stared at me.

BB

1

The tires screeched as the plane lurched, tossing the passengers forward and back lightly as if a car hit a bump on the road. The plane landed safely as Father John O'Brien silently offered a short prayer, a ritual he performed every time he boarded a plane. Some might say he was paranoid, but the thought of flying in such a large machine daunted Father O'Brien. He did not understand how something so big and heavy could fly, and as a man of the cloth, he thought best to thank the man upstairs for creating such technology.

Father John O'Brien departed Rome an hour before. For reasons he couldn't put his finger on, he didn't feel right when he boarded the plane. He shuddered and laughed when he thought about the extra prayer and clenching his eyes shut when the plane took off. He didn't want to admit it, but he was afraid of dying. A priest afraid of dying, he thought shaking his head. What made him uneasy though, was that he didn't know what was bothering him, unusual for a man in his line of work. He was supposed to know what was wrong, if anything. Was it nothing? Or was his intuition telling him something? Rather than dwelling on it, John put it aside. After all, they landed safe in Venice. Whatever was bothering him, he'd figure it out later.

Father John traveled to Rome every summer on church business. It was July, and Venice was hot, as he expected before leaving Vatican City and Rome, where he spent the weekend. He felt relieved to leave this time. His task every July was to pick up a list of parishes where newly ordained priests from seminaries all over the world were to be sent, even from his own seminary in Dublin. After the usual formalities in Rome, John would fly to Venice, his favorite city, and hand off the list for northern Italy, France, Germany, Switzerland, and Austria to another priest. From Venice, he would fly to Spain,

FIERCE LOYALTY

London, and finally back home to Dublin, all within five days.

Although the job looked easy, the Catholic Church took the task seriously. The pope himself and the cardinals prayed for the souls of the new priests in a daily ritual for three months before their ordination, in the belief that God would tell them where each new priest should go. But this time, John felt like he was under Cardinal Francis McKenney's microscope. John had known Cardinal McKenney for over twenty-five years, since before he was made cardinal, and before John became a priest. They got along well, but this year the cardinal was not himself. He told John he had been ill. John knew better and believed Cardinal McKenney was withholding information. Every time John asked what was bothering his friend, the cardinal said nothing and walked away. They usually had dinner together one night while John was in Rome, but not this time. Cardinal McKenney's behavior bothered John to say the least, but he apologized before he left for Venice.

Father O'Brien was considered the messenger for the newly ordained priests, a job he was specially picked for and enjoyed. John loved to travel and the job allowed him to see a world he probably wouldn't otherwise see. He was one of only fifty or so hand picked messengers, and the duty was easy compared to others he'd performed over the years.

Father O'Brien was one hundred percent Irish and became a priest at the age of twenty-nine. He was 6'2" and weighed 200 pounds, with dark, unreadable eyes that were easy to look at, but could pierce the soul when he looked at you. At fifty-two he'd lost nothing of his shape and was as well muscled and intimidating as he was thirty years before, and with his dark wavy hair streaked with gray; the women in his parish wished he weren't a priest.

The church recruited Father O'Brien for a specific purpose, something the church wanted kept secret, to revive the ancient military orders. In 1972, John O'Brien was a member of the Irish Republican Army. At twenty-three, he was the youngest and maybe the brightest IRA military commander. The church, very aware of the fighting in Northern Ireland, had considered reviving the military orders for as long as five years, but had not found the right priest to head the program.

In October 1972, John's younger brother, Paul, was killed in a British ambush in a border area of Belfast, and John witnessed it first hand. Although wounded in the ensuing battle, John escaped the ambush and retreated to Dublin to recover, where a sympathetic catholic priest named Father Francis McKenney, who taught at Maynooth University and seminary, took him in.

John went into hiding at the seminary as a student, even from the IRA. He had seen his younger brother killed, and for the first time in his life, he felt out of control, confused, and lost. Recovered from his wounds, John started the recovery from his brother's death with Father McKenney's help. He knew of the church's hope to revive the military orders. During his recovery, Father McKenney recruited John for the priesthood, and later the church approached him about reviving the military orders.

The church authorities decided to revive the Knights of St. Michael's Wing, founded by King Alfonzo I of Portugal at the Cistercian monastery of Alcobaza in 1171. Pope Paul VI revived it in 1978, after his friend, Aldo Moro, was kidnapped and killed. The pope himself was almost assassinated in 1970, and had become increasingly concerned about the fate of the world. He decided to prepare the church for the coming millennium by reviving the military orders to protect the church.

Father O'Brien fit the new orders perfectly, and he accepted the appointment to lead, train, and prepare selected new priests to be the churches protector's. He knew how to fight and was good at it. Over the years, Father O'Brien and his trainee's became suitable for various missions the church referred to as messenger duties or missions. The church used John's pupils to investigate such things as archeological sites and digs for ancient scripts. The messengers determined if the explorations were related to church doctrine, or the location of the Ark of the Covenant, even doctrine potentially detrimental to the church. They secured the documents or treasure, copied, photographed the find, or turned it over to the church for further research. It was a dangerous job, and Father O'Brien became the most successful messenger.

At times John had to protect himself. The IRA trained him in hand-to-hand combat, but that training included the intent to kill, which the church did not tolerate. To get around the church's restrictions, John learned and taught Tae Kwon Do and Karate, meant for protection, not killing.

John reported directly to his mentor Cardinal McKenney, who assigned the missions directly to each messenger. He was the only person within the churches higher authority that knew the mission and its plans. The method limited the knowledge of a mission to as few as two people and gave the church deniability if anything went wrong.

Today, Father O'Brien was to deliver the documents to his good friend and former student, Father Giovanni Corvo, in Venice. Over the years, John had found peace within the city walls of Venice. It had become his favorite city, so each year he met Father Corvo there, passed on the usual documents,

FIERCE LOYALTY

and spent a few days visiting. Of course, John ate what he considered the best food in the world.

As the plane finished its taxi to the terminal, the passengers got up to gather their belongings and leave the plane. Father O'Brien stood and reached into the overhead luggage compartment for his carry-on clothes bag. He turned and looked left to enter the aisle, and noticed a Middle Eastern man about his size staring at him. The man seemed glum, so John gave him a quick smile and a nod. The man did not smile or nod in return, but rather looked away. John turned away, stepped into the aisle and walked into the airport terminal where Father Corvo waited for him.

"Gino!" Father O'Brien smiled at his friend and hugged him. Father Corvo was forty-eight, John's first handpicked student for military training twenty years earlier. Also a messenger, Father Corvo was an American born Italian whom John found on a mission. Giovanni Corvo was one of last to return from Vietnam in 1975 after a four-year tour of duty. A Catholic, Giovanni came home lost. He had seen ruthless killing, and had done some of it himself. He spent four years working odd jobs, and drinking his life away. He was a mess, but he wanted to change, so one day he found himself at the local church in his Brooklyn neighborhood. He'd gone to confession like so many times before, to seek absolution. But this day would be different, his confession heard by a visiting priest: Father John O'Brien.

John followed Giovanni after his confession that day, and found him at a local bar. They talked, shared stories, drank till the next morning, and became friends. John took Giovanni under his wing, recruited him to the priesthood, and brought him to Ireland to heal and to train.

Gino helped train new recruits for five years, until the church had approximately fifty messengers. Gino was then transferred to a seminary in Belluno, a small town located at the foot of the Italian Alps. He spoke the language and had visited there with his parents when he was child. He had remembered the area fondly and had requested to be sent there.

"John! It's so good to see you, my friend. Do you have another bag with you?"

"No. No, this is it, I'm ready to go," John said, smiling broadly.

"Good then, I have a water taxi waiting for us. I'll bet you're starving, so let's go eat," Gino said smiling too, since he knew his friend starved himself in preparation for their usual feast at Harry's, John's favorite restaurant in Venice. "I made reservations for 6:30."

"At Harry's, I hope," John replied.

"Where else my friend? Where else could we have such a feast as you are preparing for?" Gino laughed.

As John and Gino turned and left the airport terminal, they didn't notice two Middle Eastern men watching them from a distance – or that the same men followed discretely behind them.

2

The water taxi arrived at Madonna Dell' Orto, the drop-off for the hotel, the Palazzo Dei Dogi. They paid and stepped off the boat to the walkway, watching momentarily as a second water taxi arrived behind them, waiting for an opening. John didn't see who was inside the waiting taxi; the sun's glare too strong for his eyes. He looked at his watch.

"Four-thirty. Perfect timing Gino," he said. "God, thank you. Here we are again. I love this place." He turned to look at Gino. "When do you have to return to Belluno, Gino?"

"They expect me back in two days, but it may be a few days longer," Gino replied.

"Good. Lets get to our business, my friend, and enjoy the time we have here." John paused to take off his collar, with Gino following his every move, and side-by-side they entered the hotel.

The Palazzo Dei Dogi inside is not what it looks like from the outside. The lobby's expensive oriental rugs cover the gold marble floor highlighted by luxurious red velvet furniture with scrolled gold legs. Large paintings of Italian royalty hang from the walls and Murano glass chandeliers dropped from the twenty-five foot ceilings. At the far end of the lobby, glass doors open to a large garden area with tables, chairs, and umbrellas. A pebbled walking trail circled a water fountain featuring a cast bronze angel. The hotel looked expensive for two priests, but O'Brien and Corvo were not ordinary priests, and today they were two ordinary men on business.

John walked through the front lobby to approach the front desk. The overweight desk clerk dressed in a blue-dawned uniform looked at the guest and smiled.

"Buon giorno. May I help you?"

"Yes, young man you can help me. I have a reservation for John O'Brien."

"Yes, Mr. O'Brien. One minute please," the clerk said. "Ah, yes, I see you here. We have you here for two nights? Is that correct?"

"Yes, that is all, unfortunately," John replied.

"Please sign here, sir. Your room is 215. Have a nice stay."

"Thank you. I'm sure I will," John replied.

The clerk curtly smiled and jabbed the bell on the counter. The porter ran to the counter, and the clerk whispered something John could not hear, pointed to John's bags, and handed the porter a key. The porter, a short, thin black man, picked up the bags and turned to John.

"Sir! This way please. 215? Is correct, no?"

John watched the exchange between the clerk and the porter. "Yes, 215." He turned to Gino and said, "I'm in 215. Meet me there in ten minutes."

At the same time, Gino stood at the counter and nodded to John's instruction. Both had reservations under their real names without their titles. If anything happened, the church did not want it known that they were involved in a secret church mission or espionage.

Gino and John walked away from the counter, turned, and went up the stairs. As they did, the two middle-eastern men in business suits who followed Father O'Brien from Rome to Venice walked through the front door.

John was in his room less than ten minutes when a knock came at the door.

"Who is it?"

"It's Gino!"

John opened the door, "Come in my friend." Letting Gino pass, John leaned forward to look into the hallway, but saw nothing. He stepped back inside the room and closed the door, locking both the bolt and the hook and ball. The room, which was a studio with marble floors, a velveteen couch and chair, a marble top coffee table, and a large queen size bed opposite the couch and chair. Two windows opened at each corner onto the main walkway and the canal at the front of the hotel. Gino took a seat on the chair and John sat on the couch. He looked at Gino who looked serious and focused, his dark eyebrows furrowed. In private quarters now, they could talk frankly, not to be inhibited by Church piety.

"Gino, what's so important that you had to meet me two days early? What happened?"

"There are rumors John, rumors of a man from Megiddo calling himself

FIERCE LOYALTY

Gideon. It is rumored he is planning attacks in the U.S., Europe, and Israel," Gino said sternly.

"A rumor?" John asked. "I hope you have more than a rumor to discuss."

"One of our messenger's in the former Yugoslavia heard a rumor of a terrorist plot by a group working out of Megiddo. He called Cardinal McKenney. The mission was given to our man in Israel, Father Michael. When he called in for his usual check-in, his message had few details, and he sounded scared. We haven't heard from him since he left that message five days ago," Gino said.

"Five days ago? Why didn't you tell me sooner? Who do we have nearby, who can find Father Michael?" John asked.

"John, you know the rules. You made them, for god's sake. Only those in the chain know about a mission. You weren't in the chain. And I've already thought of whom we know in the region. I called Yuri," Gino explained.

"You called Yuri?" John exclaimed. "Without asking me first? I hope you have a good reason."

"Michael's message sounded desperate," Gino responded, "and I wasn't able to reach him through normal channels, or the coded ones we set up." He paused, then went on. "You know how it is. If the messenger doesn't call back within twenty-four hours of contact, you have to consider the worst. I called Yuri. He was the only one to call. You would have called him, too!"

"Yes, yes, Gino you're right," John said, "but we have to get permission to call on the Israelis to help us and the Mossad. You could have compromised our mission."

"I understand that. I got permission, and besides, Yuri owes me. I thought it was urgent enough to call in my marker. Forget about it anyway. Father Michael is dead."

"What?" John exclaimed, and made the sign of the cross.

"Yuri called me yesterday and told me Michael was found dead at the safe house in Jerusalem," Gino explained. "He knew the risks, John."

"I know. Who found him?" John asked, in a vengeful tone.

"Yuri said the Israeli police found him. They're saying it was a suicide," Gino replied, "but I know better. He got caught. His mission was to investigate a rumor that large amounts of the smallpox virus had been bought by a terrorist group linked to Bin Laden."

"Where would they get small pox?" John asked.

"They bought it from a renegade Russian general," Gino replied, "then brought the merchandise to Megiddo to this Gideon. The terrorist group has split off from Bin Ladens network, and Gideon is radical. John, we have a mission. I received our orders yesterday from McKenney."

John took papers from Gino and read the orders signed by the pope himself. He thought a moment about the significance of the mission. What if the rumors were true?

"Gino, do you believe the rumor? Smallpox, I mean. Do we know for sure the Russians have it? They were supposed to destroy the virus in 1999, weren't they?"

"Well, yes. The Russians and the Americans were supposed to destroy the virus, but a few months ago, a Russian scientist defected to the United States. He claimed the Russians not only kept the virus, but also continued manufacturing enough smallpox to infect all the major cities in the United States. The Russians have it, and with the meltdown there at the end of the Cold War, it's possible a renegade military commander or the Russian mob could have gotten their hands on it, and put it up for sale to the highest bidder," Gino said coolly.

"Well, I hope Yuri can help us," John said with a sigh.

"I've already asked him. He's here."

"He's here? Here now?"

"He's staying at the Danieli, and he's meeting us at Harry's," Gino said.

"It's no wonder you survived Vietnam. You're always a step ahead, aren't you?" John said, with a sad smile.

"It's how I think when I'm on a mission," Gino replied, making the sign of the cross as he usually did after a meeting. "May God protect us."

"Yes, may God protect us all, and help us find the truth, and Father Michael's killers," John replied, making the sign of the cross, too. He looked at his watch. Almost six o'clock. "It's time to go Gino, are you ready?"

"I was born ready, John. You've known me long enough to know that," Gino said. "It's been too long, John. I mean you and me on a mission. I don't have a good feeling about this one."

"Yes," John agreed. "Let's go meet Yuri, and at least enjoy a good meal before we go to Israel."

Gino reached for his briefcase, then stopped and stared at it.

"What's wrong?" John asked.

"I have something for you. I almost forgot. We have orders to wear this stuff everywhere we go," Gino said. He pulled a small box from his briefcase and handed it to John.

John opened the box. He couldn't believe what he saw. A sudden memory

FIERCE LOYALTY

hit him of his brother Paul being shot, his head ripped apart, his body slumping to the ground. He took out a 9-millimeter Berretta, a holster, two full ammo clips, and spare box of ammo. He hadn't carried a firearm since his brother was killed, thirty years before.

"Are you wearing this now?" John asked.

"Orders, John, I'm following orders," Gino replied. "Put it on. We're trained on these weapons. Remember, you require all of us to fire a weapon, twice a year."

"Yes, I know what my own rules are," John said, "but this seems drastic. I know Israel is not the safest place. Is this why Yuri is meeting us? Because we can bypass Yuri, and get weapons in Israel ourselves."

"He said you might not like it, but he told me to tell you this. Remember what Revelation says about the end times. Megiddo, where the fight begins and ends."

"McKenney," John muttered, considering the message Gino relayed from Cardinal McKenney. He remembered what McKenney said to him before he left Rome: "Enjoy Venice while you're there. Don't get lost. Remember who your friends are." Was that a message? He couldn't think. His brain whirled like a merry-go-round. He stopped himself from over thinking the situation, and refocused on Gino.

"Yes, John," Gino began, "he was the messenger for Michael's mission. Now he's our messenger. Put the gun on. It's getting late. We have to meet Yuri, and we'll have to leave Venice tomorrow. We have to make a stop in Avignon to give the list you have to Father Chantilly. He'll take over your duties. Then we're on to Jerusalem."

Resigned, John put on his gun. In no time, they were on their way to Harry's Bar.

Harry's was busy, but any place close to the Piazza San Marco was busy, except in the winter. They went in and were shown to a reserved table on the second floor. The table was near a window, in the corner, overlooking the plaza, and the water. The mid-July late sun reflected off the glistening water. Yuri had not arrived, and John and Gino sat in silence until the waiter came. They ordered a Peroni. The waiter hurried away just as abruptly as he had arrived and returned with the beer.

"Salute, Gino!" John said. "Here's to Father Mike." He raised his glass and as he touched it to his lips, the man he dreaded seeing, Yuri, appeared at the top of the stairs.

"Salute!" Gino returned.

SCOTT A. REZENDES

"I see you have started without me, as I expected," Yuri Bahrak said, as he ambled up to the table smiling from ear to ear. Short, bald, fiftyish with a barrel chest, he did not seem dangerous at first glance. But Bahrak was intelligent, cunning, and ruthless. He belonged to the Mossad, the Israeli secret police. His accent sounded something between German and Saudi. John had seen Yuri's handiwork some years earlier, when they first met at an archeological dig in Egypt. John was investigating some ancient scrolls and had gone into the main tent late one night to look at them. Unfortunately, Yuri beat him to the punch. He watched in horror as Yuri killed a guard, knifing him through the back of the neck at the base of the skull. John confronted Yuri seconds later, and they wrestled until the noise of the fight brought the camp to life. Other guards chased them both through the camp and into the city streets, where both hid together.

Yuri considered killing John, until he realized John was a priest, but it was anyone's guess who would have killed whom. John made sure Yuri was aware of that. Circumstances had brought them together for a reason, and they stayed together until their escape from Egypt, a day later. John believed Yuri did not have to kill the guard. In fact, he knew he didn't, but Yuri said he did it to make sure he was not seen. It was an ordeal John would not forget. They had to trust each other to get out of Egypt. It was survival. Over the years, they kept in touch and learned to like each other. Both were chess enthusiasts and played by e-mail.

Yuri's involvement in any mission raised the stakes, and John knew it. He wasn't happy to see Yuri, because he thought this new mission would be different. He had a sinking feeling about it. The same feeling Gino had confided to him earlier.

Gino turned in surprise. "Yuri! Welcome! Please sit," Gino motioned Yuri to sit between him and John.

"Thank you, Gino, and thank you for the Cuban cigars," Yuri said with a wink.

"You're welcome," Gino replied, glancing at John. He knew John would question him about the cigars later.

"Well," Yuri said to John, "you are looking good these days, although your last chess move… Have you checked your e-mail lately? It only took me three days to counter."

John smiled. "Well, yes, I did check my e-mail, and I have to say, Yuri, three days to make the move you did." He shook his head. "You must be losing some of your steam. If I've told you once, I've told you a million times,

FIERCE LOYALTY

you must consider your opponents moves in advance. When was the last time you checked your e-mail?"

Yuri's confident smile faded on his now ashen face. He snapped his fingers for the waiter, then took out a cigar and lit the Cuban monster with a match. He looked back at John. "I see you're as cunning as ever O'Brien. We have business to attend to!" he said, gazing heavily at John.

The waiter returned, and all three ordered. The waiter returned quickly, opened the wine, and poured 3 glasses. Yuri picked up his glass to toast. "What is it you priests say? This is my blood, the blood of the everlasting Christ. Drink the blood of Christ, and you shall live forever and ever! Salute!"

"You should have become a priest, Yuri. You drinking to Jesus," John commented.

"It's not the only thing I might believe in these days," Yuri said, looking John straight in the eyes.

"What else do you have for us?" John asked. "We really don't have a lot of time for games. What have the Israeli police found out about Father Michael?"

"Right to the point as always. Gino, what I told you wasn't exactly the truth."

Gino looked at Yuri in surprise.

"What do you mean, you didn't tell me the truth! You lied to me? Tell me what's going on!" Gino exclaimed.

"Please, Gino, calm down," Yuri barked. "I had no choice but to tell you what I told you on the phone!"

"No choice? What the hell are you talking about?" Gino retorted angrily.

"Calm down, Gino!" John said. The three men huddled closer so no one else could hear the conversation.

"I'll calm down when he tells us what's going on!" said Gino, through clenched teeth, his face red in anger.

"You priests sure have bad tempers!" Yuri looked at both men seriously, "I had to tell you that. When you gave me the address of the safe house, I went there alone. What I found wasn't exactly what I expected."

John and Gino sat forward, engaged to every word Yuri spoke.

"I found a desecration."

"Yuri, you're not making sense. What did you find?" John asked.

Yuri took a deep breath. "It wasn't pretty. I found your friend nailed to a cross, hanging upside down from the ceiling."

Gino sat back and looked down, "My God," he said, and took a drink of

29

wine.

"Are you sure you want to hear this?"

John nodded for Yuri to continue.

"His hands and feet had been nailed to the cross, like your savior. His mouth gagged. He'd been beaten and tortured. There was space between the skin and his fingernails. They used some type of bamboo strip. It was terrible. I can't believe one human being could do that to another."

John lowered his eyes at Yuri.

"Don't say a word John. I was never like that. I couldn't do that. I've only done what was necessary for safety."

Gino intervened. "Why did you tell me the police found him, and said it was a suicide?"

"If the police found him like I did there would be a lengthy investigation with news coverage every day. Besides, I believe my people listen to our phones, and I take no chances. I called you from my home. God only knows who's listening on that line. I had to be careful. Look, whoever tortured and killed your friend left everything behind, except for whatever they were looking for. It was murder. I called in a friend I could trust, and we cleaned up, setting it up to look like a suicide, covering your asses. That house could have been traced back to you or the Catholic Church. It was not easy! I think you owe me one Gino!" Yuri said.

"We'll assess who owes whom what later," John said, putting his hand up to stop Gino from responding to Yuri's challenge. "What did you find Yuri?"

"Why do you think I found something?"

"Yuri, we've known each other fifteen years too long. I know when you're setting us up, so you'll look like a hero and we'll get on our knees and give thanks to King Yuri. Now tell me!"

"Well then," Yuri said. "I found a piece of paper in your man's personal belongings. It was in his prayer box, hidden in his Bible."

"What was it?" John asked, as Gino looked on.

"It was a label from a box of some sort," Yuri said. "It had Russian writing on it."

"Smallpox?" asked John, as he looked from Gino to Yuri.

"Yes. I had a friend look at it that night. He confirmed it was Russian. It said smallpox," Yuri finished his cigar. He stared curiously at his two Catholic friends and wondered how they knew what the label said.

"Shit," John said and sat back in his chair. "Yuri, what do you know about this Gideon?"

FIERCE LOYALTY

"You know about him, too? You Catholics don't fool around. I think I've under estimated you."

"We know very little," Gino said. "Only what Father Mike reported to me."

"And what did he report to you?" Yuri asked.

"Look Yuri, we know nothing about the group or Gideon, other than that he's Bin Laden trained, and probably supported. What have you heard?" Gino asked.

John peered curiously at Gino, considering what a master of deception he was, knowing Gino was trying to substantiate Michael's last report.

"Some things should not be shared, but since I confess my sins to you, it is kept confidential, correct?" Yuri asked.

"That's our code, Yuri, we are priests, after all," John retorted, grinning.

"Well, I trust you two, so you didn't hear it from me." Yuri poured more wine in his glass. "Gideon exists. It seems Father Michael found something, something terrible that confirms the smallpox to be Russian. If Gideon has the virus, then we're in trouble."

"What about Gideon? Who is he, Yuri?" John prodded.

"Sadly, we do not know. Our sources report that the leader is a man with the means to support several thousand others, but his background is unknown. He's an unknown." Yuri said, pausing to puff his cigar. "We don't know his nationality, only that he is connected and rumored to be a close confidant of Bin Laden. Some say they parted ways due to differences in opinion."

"Differences of opinion?" Gino questioned. "They're both terrorists. What difference of opinion could they have?"

"Our sources say the man is extremely radical," Yuri began. "They say his face has never been seen, not even by his own men. I find that hard to believe. Someone, somewhere has seen him, and knows who he is."

John sipped his wine, and contemplated what Yuri said. The waiter brought their food. "Buon appetito," John said, just as his eye caught someone in a far corner behind Gino, a man. The restaurant was dark and John couldn't see who he was – but he looked familiar. His head was down. His finger circling the glass. John thought he'd seen him before, but couldn't place him. He looked to the other patrons sitting at their tables, talking, laughing, and drinking. He considered what each person would think, if they had just been confronted with what Yuri had told him and Gino.

Yuri took a bite, then looked up at John. "What is your plan, John?"

"Gino and I will go to Israel and pick up Michael's remains. We'll try to

31

retrace his footsteps the last week or so. With any luck, we'll pick up his trail."

Gino added, "If we pick up the trail, we'll have to call you. Can you help us?"

"I'll do what I can for you," Yuri said, "but I can't be seen with you in Israel. He took out a pen and paper. "Here's a number. If you find anything, call and leave your usual coded message, and I'll come to you. You find trouble; you take care of it yourself. I'll be busy myself on this case, but it will be impossible for me to contact you. Now, enough is enough, let's enjoy this meal. It may be our last!"

After dinner, Gino and John parted with Yuri. John liked Yuri, but he didn't like to be around him. To John, Yuri was Mossad, ruthless people who tortured and killed when it suited their needs, although Yuri would not admit it. Something about Yuri intrigued John. He believed that Yuri had a good heart and wasn't entirely ruthless. But John was on his mission. He would find out who killed Father Michael and track down Gideon. He'd give him the last rights of absolution.

3

John and Gino took in a Vivaldi concert at Santo Stefano, a church a short walk from Harry's Bar. After the concert, they decided to walk back to the hotel – a forty-five minute stroll in the dark. The walkways were quiet, except near the few after dinner bars that remained open. There wasn't too much excitement on a Monday night. John and Gino walked quietly together through the alleys of Venice. They chatted about what Ireland was like that time of year, or what direction the church was headed in the new millennium. Although quiet, neither was uncomfortable, though neither looked forward to the journey that awaited them the next morning.

At the hotel, they entered the lobby, where no one attended the desk. The Murano chandeliers shone brightly. John and Gino walked up to the second floor and reached John's room first.

"I'll wake you at seven for breakfast. Then we'll go to Avignon to see Father Chantilly," John suggested.

"Sounds good. I'm tired, John. See you in the morning. God bless you," Gino said, and turned to walk to his room.

"God bless you too, Gino." John put his key card in the slot, opened the door, and walked in. He was tired, too, and wanted to fall on the bed into a deep sleep. He closed the door, flicked on the light, and started to turn around.

As he turned, someone grabbed him from behind, clenching his neck with an arm. John knew his attacker was trying to stop the air to his brain, and knew if he didn't do something, he'd be out in twenty seconds. He pulled at the man's forearm with all the force he could muster. The death grip around his neck tightened. He and his attacker twisted and turned in a circle in the narrow entry, and John's head hit hard against a wall. A warm stinging gush hit his left eye. He hit the wall again and began to turn and turn, still held firmly around the neck from behind. He was dizzy. He tried to open his eyes, but could only open the right one, just in time to see the knife come up under his chin. He felt suddenly cold as the knife cut through his skin.

The attacker released him and he was suddenly warm, as he fell to his knees, holding his neck. He felt his blood on his hands, but no pain. His left eye stung, but he could see there were two men. He recognized one, a flash of memory, the man on the plane and at the restaurant. But who was he? They looked at him as if waiting for him to die.

The second man pointed something at him. What was it? John tried to think what it was – a long cylinder with a hole at the end. A flash, and then another. John closed his eyes. His body jumped. Something pushed him to the floor. Darkness began to surround him. He opened his eyes. The men were going through his bag, looking at papers. His mind raced uncontrollably. What were they looking for? One looked back. He's saying something. Can't understand him. What was he saying? What language was it? Who were they?

He took his hands from his neck. They were red with blood, his blood. The men paid him no attention. He reached his hand over his head with his index finger and scribbled *my plane* on the wall. John reached in his jacket, pulled his gun and tried to point it. The two men looked at him and laughed. He was too weak to lift the gun. Another flash hit his eyes. His body lurched and contorted. Blood spurt upward and spotted the wall. He saw only darkness, and wondered, had death found him?

His eyes opened. He felt no pain. His eyes drifted, where he saw a bright light from a distance. He stood, felt his neck, but found no wound. He felt his forehead, but found no lump or blood. Someone was coming. A shadowy figure danced toward him. He squinted, then lifted his hand to shade his eyes as the light became brighter. He found the figure with his eyes. More than one figure approached, their feet not touching the ground. The light so bright it surrounded and engulfed him. John felt the warmth of the light come over him. He knew at that moment where he was.

4

Toni woke suddenly, startled by something, a sound he didn't know. He closed his eyes, then opened them one at a time and shook himself awake. He checked his watch. "Two in the morning." Bailey, his three year-old blond lab, raised her head, staring at him as he pushed up from the couch. He wasn't sure what woke him, but he was dreaming of a phone ringing, and his own voice speaking in the distance. He peered around the living room. His eyes fell on the five empty beer bottles. He understood why his mouth was dry, and his head wrapped in a dull ache.

Toni walked gingerly on creaky feet across the cold hardwood floor, through the living room to the spiral staircase and climbed to his office. He looked at his answering machine. Five blinking messages waited. He hadn't checked his messages when he got home. He was just too tired and didn't want to deal with creditors pestering him to pay bills. More awake, Toni sat at his desk, picked up a pen, and balled his other hand in a fist against his cheek, held up only by the pressure of his elbow on his desk. He pushed the button. The familiar voice of his boss, Alex Fox. He was happy it was Alex and not the bill collectors calling non-stop lately. He spoke to Alex earlier on his cell phone, and they had discussed what needed to be discussed. Two messages down, three to go.

Toni hit the third message, and felt a sudden flush slither through his whole body, as he heard the voice of his brother Bobby for the first time in over ten years.

"Toni? It's Bobby. I need your help, man. I can't talk now, I'll call you later."

Toni rubbed his hands over his face, wiping away the remaining grogginess,

35

wondering what his brother wanted. He'd rather have heard the bill collectors voice than his brother's. He hit the next message. Nothing but hang-ups and figured it was probably either the bill collectors or Bobby calling again. Why had Bobby called him after all this time? Ten years was a long time. Had it been that long ago already? Life was passing him by, he thought.

His thoughts returned to Bobby. He was the last person Toni wanted to deal with right now. Ten years before, he and Bobby had it out. Turning his back on his brother and his drug and alcohol problems was the hardest thing Toni had ever done, but Bobby had left him no choice. Toni tried to help his brother get his life back in order after a motorcycle accident 12 years earlier, an accident that killed Bobby's wife, Sabrina. Bobby took it hard and blamed himself.

Toni thought he understood what Bobby felt. The accident itself left Bobby partially paralyzed, his lower right leg and his left hand. He lost feeling in his index and middle fingers, which crippled his career as an auto mechanic. Six months of recuperation left him depressed, addicted to painkillers, and using alcohol as a crutch when he couldn't get his hands on prescription pills. Toni understood the effect of Sabrina's death on Bobby, but after two years, Bobby was no better. He stole from his own family to support his drug habit. He could not keep a job and eventually ended up homeless, living out of a 1975 Chevy Impala, his last possession.

Toni remembered how Bobby used to call him in the middle of the night, drunk, asking for money. He hated being alone. Maybe that's why Bobby called. His last words to his brother over ten years ago rang in his head.

"Goddammit Bobby, this is it! No more! If you don't have a job in a week, don't call me again. I can't do this any more. I won't watch you kill yourself."

Toni recalled Bobby's anger as he took his last $50 offering and walked off.

"Screw you! You don't know nothing, you little shit. Who the hell you think you are, huh? You don't know nothing."

Bobby later moved to Oregon to live with friends. Guilt hit Toni like a brick as he replayed Bobby's message twice. Why had Bobby called him after all these years? How did he get his phone number? What did Bobby mean that he needs *his* help? Bobby hadn't left a phone number, so Toni pushed Caller ID and scratched down the number it displayed. Toni wondered where the 514 area code belonged and contemplated calling the number, but thought better of it and decided the last thing he wanted was to deal with Bobby. No one in his right mind would be awake at that time of the morning.

FIERCE LOYALTY

Toni decided to call his dad the next day to talk about Bobby. He pushed himself to his feet, made his way to the stairs, and then walked tiredly toward his bedroom where he found his bottle of water and aspirin. He flopped down on the bed in exhaustion. He stared at the ceiling. A thousand thoughts crowded his mind. Bailey jumped on the bed and startled him awake. She lay next to Toni and sighed, as if relieved. Toni tried to clear his thoughts, but Bobby crept in repeatedly. Where had he been the last ten years? Why did he need his help? His voice sounded scared, not drunk. Bailey sighed again. He peeked at her as she snored and he knew she was asleep. He closed his eyes, sleep not far away.

5

The phone rang three times before Toni picked it up. He wrenched his right eye open and put the phone to his ear while, peering at the window. It was still dark outside.

"Hello," Toni answered.

"Gee, did I wake you?" asked FBI Special Agent Lynn Fiero.

Toni licked his parched lips, "What time is it? Is that you Lynn?" He looked at the clock and saw a five. "This better be good."

"Oh, it's only five in the morning," Lynn said in a voice too cheery for that time of the morning, "and it's as good as it gets. Jeff called half an hour ago, said the lights were on in Villegas' apartment for the last hour. Just thought you'd want to know, after what happened with your last case."

The memory of six months ago shot through Toni's head like a lightning bolt.

"Yeah, yeah, I see your point. Jeff say what else was happening, or did Villegas just get up to take a piss?" Toni asked, irritated by Lynn's comment.

"Gonna be a funny guy this morning, are we?" Lynn returned. "No, he's seen someone walking around for the last hour or so. Villegas is up, its' early, but I got a feeling something's up. I called the duty AUSA, Randy Black. He agreed I should wake your lazy ass up, and we should pick Villegas up this morning. RB gave the go ahead," Lynn said excitedly.

"All right, all right! Half an hour. I'll pick you up."

"Are you sure that's enough time? Remember it's your turn to bring the coffee and doughnuts for the morning crew," Lynn chided.

Toni now sat up in bed. "I think they'll just have to tough it out this morning, Lynn. We've got our instructions from Randy, so forget the coffee and

FIERCE LOYALTY

doughnuts. Their asses can do without, for one morning," Toni replied, knowing Lynn would have picked them up on her way home the night before.

"All right, I'll bring em' again, but you owe me three times now!"

"Yeah, okay. Whatever you say Lynn," Toni said, and hung up so he didn't have to listen to Lynn bark back at him.

Toni worked with Lynn Fiero, a forty-five year old, red haired, bureau agent assigned to the San Francisco office. Lynn, tall at 5'10", took shit from no one. They had worked together on four cases, all health care frauds, and both Toni and Lynn had good reputations. Each knew how the other liked to work, and they infrequently called each other's house early in the morning. Toni, a Senior Special Agent and ten year veteran at the Federal Health Administration's Criminal Investigation Division in San Francisco, called Lynn whenever a big case came up. He knew Lynn wanted the high profile cases.

Toni and Lynn had been working on this case for two years. Both spent hours reviewing mounds of paper, health care claim forms, and bank records to prove fraudulent billing and the laundering of five million dollars. Because it was a big case, Toni did not want this guy to slip away in the night.

Toni sat up. Bailey stared at him from her position next to him on the bed. He smiled at her and thought he saw tears in her sad dark eyes.

"Good morning girl," Toni said, as he ran his hands around Bailey's head, face and shoulders. "Don't worry girl, Dana's coming to walk you today, Okay?"

Bailey put her head back down on the pillow giving out her usual morning grumble, "GrrrrRRRRrrrr."

Toni looked hard at Bailey. He wasn't sure if Bailey liked Dana, a veterinarian and Toni's neighbor for five years, who loved animals and offered to help after Veronica, his wife, left six months before taking their daughter, Chloe.

Toni climbed out of bed, stopping briefly to look at a family picture of himself, his former wife, Veronica, and their five-year old daughter Chloe.

"I'll get you back," he said quietly.

Toni walked towards the shower. He remembered the phone call and message from his brother. He wanted to believe Bobby's call was a dream, but he knew it wasn't. He didn't want to dwell on it now. He turned to face the bedroom where his dog lay on the bed. She never slept on the bed until Veronica had left him.

He stared at Bailey for what seemed like ten minutes, while Veronica and Chloe churned in his head.

39

"I better get going," Toni said, and grabbed some clothes. He grabbed his equipment bag on the floor and walked out the door.

Toni picked Lynn up right on time, and they arrived at the home of Dr. Jose Villegas just before six. Toni pulled up next to Special Agent Jeff Graves and his partner Steven Woods. As they approached the car from behind, Toni saw Steve's head tilted back on the headrest and Jeff looking straight ahead at Villegas' apartment.

"Steve's asleep again," Toni said, and turned to Lynn with a smart-ass look on his face.

"They're shifting it Toni. When's the last time you worked the all night shift?" Lynn asked.

"Okay, didn't mean to hit a sore spot," Toni replied. "Just don't want anything to come of it especially, if they have to testify. Tell the truth in front of a judge and jury!"

Lynn shot a nasty look at Toni. "See my finger Toni? What's it telling you?"

Toni laughed, "I got the message tough guy."

As they pulled up to the dark blue Ford Taurus, Lynn rolled down her window. "Anything happening, boys?"

Jeff looked over casually. "Nothing new. You bring any coffee? Maybe breakfast?" he asked, sheepishly.

Lynn handed two coffees and two doughnuts to Jeff. "Drink up boys. We got the go ahead to bring him in. Wake Steve up and let's get ready," Lynn said, rolling the window up. "Damn rookies," she whispered, under her breath.

Everyone in the office was looking at Toni to see if he handled the case right. He could feel the eyes over his shoulder from three thousand miles away at FHA-CID headquarters. Just six months earlier, a physician, Dr. Henry Mateo, who Toni investigated for defrauding the government of more than ten million dollars, drove off in the night and disappeared. Toni and the United States Attorney's office in San Francisco had been working on a plea bargain with Mateo's attorney. The negotiations appeared to be going good, maybe too good in retrospect. Neither Toni nor the Assistant United States Attorney considered Mateo a flight risk, a miscalculation he regretted.

Mateo was a celebrity of sorts with his own twice-weekly three-hour afternoon radio program, and a Saturday evening news spot on the ABC affiliate in the Bay Area. With his high profile and popularity, Mateo's disappearance was highlighted on every prime time news show. The story reached nationwide status when CNN picked up the story and ran it all day

FIERCE LOYALTY

long. It was a nightmare for Toni. His superiors considered Mateo's disappearance with an estimated three million in cash an embarrassment.

The FHA Agency Director wanted Toni's head on a platter and his career for dessert. He'd never forget watching Director Chambers's news conference in Washington horrified at his comments. But matter's got worse when Toni's wife up and left with their daughter without warning, leaving a note telling him there was someone else. He didn't see it coming. She moved to Southern California. Toni couldn't talk to his daughter for weeks because he didn't know where they were. His life was a sudden mess.

When the divorce papers were served a month later, he learned where they moved, and who she moved with: Thomas Morehart, a man who'd been in his house many times. Veronica, a real estate agent, had been having an affair with Morehart, the regional director of the Maximillion Real Estate Group. Toni remembered Morehart telling them both at a dinner party celebrating the sale of a multi-million dollar property in San Francisco, that he was being relocated to Los Angeles. The son–of–a-bitch was screwing his wife and he didn't see it. Tied up in his work as usual and now work was all he had, except for Bailey, another relationship on the rocks.

Toni looked at Lynn, who read the faxed arrest warrant for Villegas. He knew he had to snap out of it, and concentrate on the arrest they were about to make. Something had to change and soon. He wasn't sure how much longer he could put up the front. He peered up to Villegas' apartment, considering a plan.

Dr. Villegas lived in a new apartment complex near the Sunset District of San Francisco. The four-story building was rectangular and definitely upscale. Each apartment had two stories, and the corner apartments were taller with a rounded frame and roof, like a castle. Toni remembered when the apartments were first listed for sale at a paltry $1,200,000 a few years before. Villegas could not afford the place alone, not according to his tax records, and no one else was listed as a cohabitant. Villegas' apartment was in the southwest corner of the complex, and looked out to a large parking lot across the street, next to a twenty-four hour gas station. Beyond that, were restaurants, sandy beach and the Pacific Ocean. They parked to the right of the gas station behind the shrubbery.

The sky was still dark, though dawn approached. He saw light in Villegas' living room and a deck running around to the front entrance. A shadow hit the drapes while it moved across the room. What was he doing so early in the morning?

41

Toni turned to Lynn.

"He's been up since four? Let's get our stuff and get ready. I don't like this."

"You think he's getting ready to run?" Lynn asked. She put her hand on Toni's arm to stop him from opening the door.

"Could be, but that would mean he's been tipped off. Whatever it is, I don't want to wait and find out. Let's go get him."

"Wait," Lynn said. "Let's talk about this first. If he's running, maybe he'll go to the unknown, whoever is helping him."

Toni turned and faced Lynn. "Look, you're probably right. We could wait here and see where he goes, if he's going anywhere. Maybe the jerk is just up early to go for a jog. Randy Black said pick him up, so it's on him, not us. I didn't get up at five in the morning to change plans. We're doing what we're told to do, and that's that. I can't afford another screw up, Lynn, and I'm certainly not going to be the one to explain why we sat on our ass all day, because we thought he was going somewhere. Fuck it. Let's get ready."

"I'm just thinking out loud here. This could be our opportunity to find his helper."

Toni looked down. "I'm tired and I just want to get this over with today. It's Friday and I just want to spend a quiet weekend alone."

Lynn stared back at Toni. "I'm sorry. I know you've got a lot to deal with. Why don't you come over Saturday night and have dinner with me and Ken? It'll do you good to get out of that place. You can bring Bailey. She likes the back yard and needs to run off that energy of hers."

"I'll think about it. Now can we get this over with?"

Jeff and Steve had finished their coffee and were laughing hysterically. "Well boys, are you ready? What's so damn funny?" Lynn asked.

Jeff and Steve were both in their twenties and recently graduated from Quantico, the bureau's training facility. Assigned to Lynn as their training agent, they were as green as they get, but Lynn thought they were good kids and would some day be good agents.

"Sorry Lynn, Steve just told a joke is all. We're ready."

The four stepped from their cars and huddled behind them, putting on the usual gear, the bulletproof vests and windbreakers with "Federal Agent" emblazoned on the back. They checked their weapons to be sure they were locked and loaded. Toni took his Sig-Saur 226 from his holster. He pulled out his clip, slapped back the glide, popping out the seated nine-millimeter round. He slapped the loaded clip back in, armed the weapon, and slid it back in his

FIERCE LOYALTY

holster. He popped the clip out again and added the extra 9-millimeter round, and slid the clip back into his belt-holstered weapon. He was ready to go, the caffeine-driven adrenaline coursing through his body. Steve would stay with the cars and make the call to the local police. He would wait for the radio call from Lynn to bring the car into the complex after Villegas was arrested. If anything happened before she called, Steve would call for help, drive into the apartment complex, and back the three agents up.

Toni, Lynn and Jeff walked across the street and entered the complex through the main gate, which the security guard opened after Toni badged him. Villegas's apartment was in Building A, first on the left. Toni pointed to the stairway to the second floor, where Villegas' apartment was. He looked at his watch – 6:16 A.M. Dawn had arrived and morning light infused the typical San Francisco overcast. Light drizzle fell, misting the air. As Toni and Lynn had agreed, the new agent, Jeff, would arrest Villegas. Toni would clear the residence and keep neighbors or visitors away.

Toni started up the stairs, Lynn and Jeff following. Toni pulled his weapon from his holster. At the top was a hallway about twenty feet long, with no windows. At the end of the hallway, the front porch opened up on each side, Villegas' place on the left, a neighbor to the right.

As Toni reached the opening, he pressed against the wall and looked to the right. No one was there. He did a quick peek to the left where Villegas' front door was ten feet from him. To the left of the door was a window, something Toni did not like. A vulnerable spot if someone was inside the window. He noticed a space to the right of the door, big enough to hide in, but nothing else. Beyond that, was the street where they had watched the apartment. He remembered an open deck on the other side of the wall. He saw a well-camouflaged door in the wall, leading to the deck.

Toni decided his best position would be right where he was next to the window. Lynn and Jeff would have to go to the door, back-to-back or side-by-side, and make the arrest.

6

Ricardo and Juan Miguel Contreras were brothers. Born a year apart, they rarely went anywhere without each other from the time they were children, growing up in the barrios of Bogota until now. In their late thirties, they grew up in the drug business, and became known within the cartels as los dos diablos, the two devils. They were killers. When the two devils came to your neighborhood or your door, death followed, though usually not as quickly as the victim wished.

They started out slowly in the killing business, their first kill was a Colombian government official, Jorge Espinoza, who teamed up with the Americans to help rid the country of the drug cartels. Then the Ruben Cartel called upon Ricardo and Juan Miguel to show their loyalty, an initiation to the family. When the job was done, what Ricardo and Juan Miguel did, gave the cartel leader a chill. Instead of shooting Espinoza dead in the street, they broke into his home in the middle of night and tortured him and his family to death — Espinoza, his wife and two young children. The brothers became legends. Their loyalty never questioned, and the Colombian governments position on the drug trade changed.

Ricardo and Juan Miguel's trademark became nighttime house break-ins and torture, so sneaking into Dr. Jose Villegas' apartment was no problem. The brothers watched Villegas for three days, picking up on the FBI surveillance after only two hours the first day. Villegas had been involved in many business projects in Mexico, and had approached the Ruben Cartel in Mexico with an offer to traffic their drugs into the United States.

Villegas, under the assumed name Jorge Padilla, and a partner built storage warehouses south of the border near Nogales, Arizona, where the cartel

FIERCE LOYALTY

could ship and store drugs. Villegas and his partner, a Mexican named Francisco Posada, kept all their work well out of the sight of U.S. law enforcement officials. Villegas dug a five-mile tunnel under the border and into a storage facility on the U.S. side, where drugs could be quietly moved underground. In addition, Villegas helped the cartel launder drug money through his storage facility business, which eventually got him in trouble. He got greedy, and began skimming money from the Ruben Cartel to the tune of about ten million dollars, enough to be noticed. Los dos diablos were called to do the dirty work.

At 3:30 A.M., Ricardo and Juan Miguel climbed the back wall of the apartment complex, well out of the sight of the two FBI agents stationed in front. They had considered the problem if they stumbled onto the agents that morning. If need be, they would kill them too. It took Ricardo only seconds to pick the locks on Villegas' front door. Both entered, Ricardo holding a silenced .38 special he bought from a street dealer in San Diego.

Juan Miguel stood next to Ricardo with a backpack over his shoulders, rope in his left-hand, and a ten-inch knife in his right hand. They walked to a hallway where four doors led to what they presumed were bedrooms or bathrooms. They opened three, finding no one. Ricardo opened the fourth door and ran to the bed where Jose Villegas lay asleep. Ricardo jumped on Villegas, the .38 pointed at his head.

"Don't fuckin' move, shithead," Ricardo whispered, his left hand over Villegas' mouth.

Juan Miguel took duct tape from his backpack and slapped a strip on Villegas' mouth. He tied the rope around his neck like an animal collar and yanked it downward, throwing Villegas out of bed. Juan Miguel dragged Villegas out of the bedroom, then knelt down and whispered, "You fuckin' bitch, I hope you say prayers, you piece of shit, cause we gonna teach you some lessons, show you to obey, you piece of garbage. You try somethin', I gut you like the pig you are."

Villegas was choking and turning pale as air was slowly cut away from his lungs. He began to sweat. Tears broke from his eyes. His hands grasped the rope around his neck as he lay on the floor.

Still pointing the gun at Villegas, Ricardo kicked his forearms, breaking his hold on the rope, then stomped Villegas' hands, crushing them under the heel of his boots.

"You tell us where the dinero is, amigo, and we kill you like a man, not like a chicken."

The brothers looked at each other and laughed. They dragged Villegas to the living room, tied him to a chair, and took turns beating him nearly unconscious. Villegas knew he was going to die if he didn't do something fast. He had planned for it. He knew if the cartel learned he was skimming money, they'd kill him. He always slept in a long sleeved shirt with an eight-inch knife blade that would flip out under his wrist.

The intruders tied his hands behind his back and sat him upright on a kitchen chair. He had hidden three guns and several other weapons in his apartment. A .22 pistol hidden under the couch was closest to him. His head throbbed from the beating and he felt several loose teeth. He tasted the sweetness of his blood from open wounds in his mouth. His left cheek felt swollen. His left eye was almost closed.

His attackers took a break. One drank a beer from the refrigerator. The other peeked out the window. Villegas looked at the clock: 6:15 A.M. He worked his hands loose enough to jerk his right hand back. The blade jutted out from under his wrist. He began slowly to cut the rope.

From the window, Juan Miguel saw the two cars parked at the gas station. Four people putting on equipment he recognized as police gear. One pointed toward the apartment. He watched three of them begin walking toward the complex.

"Ricardo! Get the shotguns. We got company"

"What's happening?" Ricardo asked, looking toward the window.

"It's those cops we saw. They're coming this way, three of them. They're in the complex, and headin' to the stairs below. Get the fuckin' guns, Ricardo!"

Ricardo opened the backpack and took out four pieces. He linked them into two shotguns and began loading them. He threw one to Juan Miguel, and they went through the apartment to a side room, Villegas' office. A window looked out to the front door and the entry. Juan Miguel opened the blinds just enough to see the entry. They didn't have to wait long. Two of the three they watched, came into the complex. Ricardo and Juan Miguel knew they had to dispose of the cops and get away, as fast as possible. They took aim at the male and female cops that stood in the front entry, and almost simultaneously they pulled the triggers.

Click.

Click.

7

After surveying the area, Toni looked back at Lynn and Jeff, and whispered, "Clear." He waved them to the door. The window blinds were closed, but a light came through a slit in the blind. No light came from the window onto the front porch. He heard no noise from the apartment.

Lynn and Jeff passed Toni, Lynn nearest to the door, Jeff behind and to her left. Toni readied himself for trouble, his weapon pointed forward and down away from his two partners at the door.

Lynn looked back at Jeff and nodded, then at Toni to see if he was ready. At that moment Toni heard two clicks, then the familiar sliding and cocking sound he'd heard a thousand times. The sound was at his left ear and came from behind the window. Toni didn't hesitate.

"Get down!"

Toni leaped at Jeff hitting him below the shoulder as if tackling him, just as the shotguns blasted through the window, showering lead and glass. Lynn had turned after Toni yelled, and stepped right into Jeff's path. They toppled her over. Her head hit the ground squarely, as they all flailed to the ground.

Toni landed on top of Jeff, whose eyes were wide-open but without recognition. The sound of shotguns reloading met Toni's ears. He felt for his weapon, rolled off Jeff's back, spun into a combat stance, and instinctively fired off two rounds at each of the hazy figures in the darkened window. They fell backward, hands releasing their weapons, and flailing in the air. Death found them with Toni's nine-millimeter rounds.

Toni smelled the powder in the air while his eyes focused on a cloud of smoke emanating from the gun barrel. He looked at Jeff, his eyes now closed, blood trickling from his right arm and ear. Lynn also lay face down, motionless.

Sweat beaded down Toni's face, eyes wide, his ears buzzed. His left shoulder hurt like a raging forest fire.

Toni surveyed the area, but all he saw were bodies and glass everywhere. He got to his feet and tried to look into the window, but nausea and dizziness stopped him. He felt pain at the back of his left leg. Blood puddled below him, as it dripped from his pants.

Toni collapsed to his knees, then to his hands. The walls began to spin, and he fell to the ground. He saw the face of a child peeking out the neighbor's door. He smiled as he thought of Chloe, but the child looked scared and started to cry. He wanted to get up and comfort her, but he couldn't move. Was he dying? He tried to focus on Chloe, but realized he didn't recognize the crying girl. Darkness fell upon him, and her face faded. His last memory was the wail of sirens in the distance.

8

An Asian man wearing a black gown with a yellow dragon embroidered on the sleeve introduced himself as Simi, as he met Jamal and Mohammed at the door. They hadn't seen him before, a servant of their boss, Gideon, they believed. Simi opened the door and led the men to a room just off the entrance.

"Please sit," Simi said. "He will be with you shortly. He insists I take the package. Please, give it to me."

Jamal looked at Mohammed, who nodded in agreement, and handed Simi a large briefcase-sized package. Simi bowed and smiled thinly, then slipped out the sliding glass doors, and scurried away. Jamal and Mohammed sat in the waiting room area of the desert palace owned by a man known as Gideon, though land records would show the palace was owned by a French biotechnology company, Geneon Systems. The company had offices all over the world, including Israel, the United States, South America, and other European nations. They swore allegiance to the man who summoned them, but they had yet to see his face.

The palace was in Megiddo, a city they entered with false identification as French citizens, employed by Geneon Systems. They changed their looks to appear more French than Palestinian – shaved their beards and got short haircuts. Hand-picked by their leaders, Jamal learned French as a child growing up in France. His family lived in Paris until he was eleven, then his parents returned to Palestine to give their children a chance to know their ethnic background, and learn their people's ways. The Israelis jailed their father, claiming he was a terrorist. Jamal never saw his father again. Their mother was detained for several months, and Jamal, his younger sister and brother were left to fend for themselves.

49

Eventually, Jalal Amaseh, a man with connections to the rebel terrorist group Hamas, took them in. Jamal was taken immediately to a training camp in Pakistan near the Afghanistan border. There he met Mohammed, twelve years old, and they became inseparable. They trained until they were prepared to strike out at their Zionist enemies and Israel. They were brothers in arms and both ended up in the Gaza Strip, and knew only one thing: hatred for the Jews and their henchmen, the United States.

Twenty-six years old and members of Hamas, they were sought by Israel and the United States. Eight months before, their Hamas leaders called them to work with an organization known as The New Jihad whose leader was known only as Gideon. The Hamas did not like the fact that they could not see Gideon's face, but soon realized it was not necessary. Gideon planned and executed the kidnapping of two Israeli military commanders, and allowed Hamas to kill them. The two groups wanted the same thing, the destruction of the western world, but Gideon needed forces – something Hamas had – and Hamas needed the resources, money, and weapons, which Gideon seemed to have. Since Saddam Hussein and Osama Bin Laden had been put out of commission or forced to hide by the western crusaders, money had gotten tight for Hamas.

Deep inside the palace, Gideon sat peacefully on a deck overlooking the desert. In the distance was the ancient city of Megiddo. He thought how easy it was to gain control of his guest's minds, as well as their leaders in the Hamas. Crude, malicious, violent creatures he thought, "perfect for my plans".

Gideon had big plans to infect the United States with enough smallpox to wipe out half of the population. He did not want the Hamas or any of his other allies to know about the plan, because he also intended to infect the entire Middle East, as well.

These Middle Eastern countries, according to Gideon's intelligence reports, would lose ninety percent of their population, because vaccine was almost non-existent there. Israel would mobilize much faster, and save between forty and sixty percent of their populace. No Palestinians would survive, nor would their terrorist leaders. All part of Gideon's plans was to eliminate all potential future enemies, even the ones he called allies.

He intended to take over the oil producing nations of the region, the majority of OPEC, and control the world's major oil supply. There were still South American and African countries in OPEC, but they would hardly be a problem when he threatened them with genocide. He aimed to control India and Pakistan also, gain access to their nuclear arsenal, and unify the region,

FIERCE LOYALTY

becoming the most powerful nation in the world: Babylon. He would have to reckon with the United States, but with half the population sick and dying, they would be in no position to do anything. The U.S. would be in chaos.

The plan was going well until someone infiltrated his underground chemical holding facility and stole a vial of the virus he got from the Russians. His security officers picked up the infiltrator's trail and traced him to Jerusalem. Gideon called in his Hamas allies to do something in return for his generous contributions.

Gideon knew of Jamal and Mohammed, and requested them by name. They had done well in Jerusalem, so well he asked them to take another assignment in Rome, where they flew immediately to follow the Catholic priest, John O'Brien. It was a simple task – follow the priest when he left Rome, and at his first stopover, break into his room and steal all his belongings. He figured the priest would stay at a church, but something went wrong, and they killed the priest.

The overriding factor in his decision to send Jamal and Mohammed was the small chance they could be caught, and he didn't want to risk losing even one of his men. He never considered they would kill the priest. The thought enraged him.

"Stupid, stupid, stupid! Fucking stupid!" Gideon whispered.

In retrospect, their decision was appropriate. The priest left a clue leading the police away from his organization, and had they been caught, neither would have said a word, knowing they would face much worse, if they talked. Their time would come anyway, very soon.

A knock at the patio door startled Gideon. He saw Simi, a man that Gideon had known and trusted his whole life. Simi, in his sixties, was Vietnamese. He came to France with Gideon's family in the 1960's when the French abandoned Indo-China. Simi practically raised him and taught him many things. He respected the old man, something he always wanted to tell him – but a servant? How would he react? He raised his arm and motioned Simi to come in.

"Sir?"

"Yes, Simi? What can I do for you?"

"Your company is here," Simi said.

"Did they bring the priest's belongings?

"Yes. I have inspected the contents and put them in your study."

"Is everything in order?" Gideon asked.

"It is, sir."

"Very well then. The coin on the table, Simi," Gideon replied.

51

"It is time to decide, is it not, sir?"

"Yes, Simi, it is. What is your impression of our two visitors?"

"My impression, sir?"

"Yes, how do they look to you? Are they scared? Are they stealing anything?" Gideon prodded.

"Sir, they seem very comfortable and wish to be paid for their mission. They may be a little nervous, since they were not summoned here after their initial work. I believe, sir, after they spoiled the mission in Venice, they should not be paid. They should be thrown into the snake pit, where they will almost certainly end up anyway."

"Oh Simi, never short on words, are you? That's why I keep you with me. You know what people think even before they do. Well, what should we do with these two? Kill them? Or pay them?" Gideon asked.

"The coin. Shall I flip it, sir?"

"Yes, Simi, take the coin and flip it. Heads, we kill them, and Tails, we have Bruno take them down to the workout room, and give them something to think about," Gideon replied.

Simi took the coin from the table and flipped it. Gideon looked straight out into the desert, not at the coin.

"Well, it seems we have to kill them, Simi," Gideon said without looking at the coin. "We can't trust them to keep quiet."

Simi bent to pick the coin up inspecting both sides. He knew why his master did not even look. The coin had heads on both sides. A decision had already been made for the guests. Simi put the coin back on the table, but noticed another coin under the envelope filled with American money. The coin showed the golden feathers of an eagle, the tail side of the coin. He looked at Gideon, who stared aimlessly to the desert behind the dark sunglasses he wore to hide his eyes.

"Yes, sir," Simi said. "It will be done in the usual manner if that is what you wish?"

"It is, Simi. Make it happen," he said, without feeling.

"Will there be anything else, sir? Something to eat, perhaps?"

"No, Simi. Nothing else is required. Leave me."

Simi left the room as quietly as he had entered.

Gideon stared silently into the desert. He rose from his chair and walked to a place where he could see another building below. He watched Simi open the building's unremarkable door and stand aside as Jamal and Mohammed went in. Simi followed them and closed the door. Gideon knew their fate and

FIERCE LOYALTY

smiled as he thought how Simi would show them to the stairs into the buildings below ground, with a workout facility with a gym at one end, and a shooting range at the other end. Simi would show them down a hallway and tell them to go through a door leading them into the sights of Gideon's security personnel, who would open up on the two Hamas terrorists. What angered Gideon was that he planned to use Jamal and Mohammed in case someone else meddled in his affairs, as did the infiltrator just a week before. There were others he could use, though, and Hamas would not find anything out, until it was too late for them to retaliate.

Gideon went to his private office, and sat behind the desk. He thought he heard muffled automatic weapons firing, then smiled as he found the package Simi put in the 'IN' basket. He opened the envelope, and read the information he needed to execute his plan.

The final piece of the puzzle was now in place. The plan should go off without a hitch. He had planned everything carefully, and his goal was becoming reality. He could feel the power of holding the world hostage. No one could do anything about it. Not even those bastards in the United States. He picked up the phone and pressed a pre-programmed button to the laboratory. The line was picked up immediately and Gideon heard the voice of his chief biologist, Dr. Francois Laurent. "Yes?"

"What is your progress?" Gideon asked, curtly.

"The virus is almost ready. Another twenty-four hours, and it will be ready for shipment."

"Excellent, Doctor. And the antidote, when will it be ready?"

"The antidote will be ready in another forty-eight hours. Do not worry. We will have enough for one dose each. We will infect ourselves first, and then take the antibiotics after we confirm we have been infected. That will take another seventy-two hours, then another seventy-two hour recovery period. Because Dr. Langlois and I will be infected first, we are really ten to twelve days from starting shipment. Duplication and refining will take another few weeks, maybe a month, depending on the labs in the U.S."

"Well, we're within the time frame. Don't worry about the U.S. labs. They'll be ready," Gideon said.

"I won't then, but they..." Dr. Laurent started.

"You need not worry, Doctor. Just do not fail me," Gideon interrupted. "You will regret it. You have given yourself little time for mistakes. My men must be ready to go within two weeks. We are only eight weeks away from the planned infection dates. This is the most difficult piece of our plan. Those

53

bastards must be blamed. The infections must occur in the U.S. first."

"I said we'll be ready, and I mean it. Now, let us get back to work here," he answered, irritated.

"I will tell you when I am through talking, Doctor!" Gideon screamed into the phone, "and I am not through with you, yet."

"I understand, sir," Dr. Laurent said shakily, "but I am extremely busy here. The work is delicate and takes all my concentration. The virus will be ready. You can count on it."

"Yes, Doctor, I am counting on it. You will feel my wrath if you fail. Do you understand me?"

"I understand you, Gideon, more than you know," he replied, as the phone went dead on the other end.

9

Toni smiled at Chloe, knelt to her height, and kissed her forehead.

"Love you, little one. Be good, and we'll get ice cream later, Okay! When I pick you up."

Chloe smiled back at her daddy, "Ice cream, yummy! I'll be a good girl, I promise. I wuv you daddy."

Toni rose to his feet, "Okay, three o'clock sharp."

Turning to Veronica, Toni laughed at their daughter's brightness. Veronica looked at him as if she didn't recognize him. Coldness came over him. He tried to call out Chloe's name, but no sound came from his mouth. He saw only the vapor of his breath. No words came with it. He watched Veronica and Chloe walk away holding hands in a silvery white mist. Chloe turned and waved, then disappeared in the haze that seemed to cloud his vision. As she disappeared, his voice came back, "I'll be back, Chloe. I'll come for you."

His lips were parched. His tongue felt like a swollen fish in the hot sun after being hooked by an angler. Toni opened his eyes and the white hospital world exploded into his aching brain, an earthquake on his skull.

He tried to focus on the lowered voices in the room, looking around to find where they came from. He tried to position himself, but stinging pain and soreness hit him. His eyes fell on someone recognizable, his boss Alex Fox, and an unknown man who looked liked a doctor, as well as another man and a woman he didn't know. He looked at the clock, and saw it was a few minutes past nine, but he didn't know if it was day or night. 'How much time had passed?' was his first thought.

"Hey, can you guys keep it down?" Toni said, in a wretched voice.

All four people turned and looked at him. Each silenced by the mumbled words. The man who looked like a doctor, put his hand up to the others, and they all stopped in their tracks.

"Mr. Brazil, I'm Dr. Farnsworth. How are you feeling?"

"Like a Mack truck ran straight into my head, stopped, then backed over it again."

Alex and the other two laughed.

"That's to be expected after what you've been through," the doctor said. "How many fingers do you see?"

"All five," Toni replied dryly.

"Good. Do you know where you are, Mr. Brazil?" Dr. Farnsworth asked.

"Well, if I had to guess, even though I see my boss over there" – Toni nodded toward the back of the room – "I know I'm not at my office. I'd say, a hospital, Dr. Farnsmouth."

"Farnsworth."

"Whatever. Can I have a drink of water?" he asked hoarsely.

"Of course." The doctor put a plastic cup to his lips, and gave him three small sips.

"Thanks Doc," Toni said.

"Do you know why you're here, Mr. Brazil?" Dr. Farnsworth asked.

"Sorry, Doc. Why don't you fill me in?"

"Well, you've been in a light coma for about three days. We weren't sure if or when you'd pull out of it. Your injuries are another story. You were shot in the left shoulder from behind, right about here." He pointed to Toni's shoulder. "Tore up your rotator cuff pretty bad. You were also hit in the left leg, and punctured your femoral artery. You'll be sore for a few weeks, and we'll need to change your bandages every day, but you'll live."

"How long am I gonna be laid up?" Toni asked, tiredly.

"I'd say six to eight weeks including rehab, maybe longer depending on how fast you heal. Your leg isn't that bad, but your shoulder. We had to put it back together. Frankly Mr. Brazil, I've heard what you did, and I have no idea how you did it in the shape your left shoulder was in, when they brought you here," he said smiling. "I'm finished here. I'll see you tomorrow."

He stopped at the door to look at Alex and the other two people, and said, "He needs his rest. Don't keep him too long, understand?"

"Toni," Alex started, "I don't know what to say, but thank God you pulled through, buddy."

"Thanks. How are Lynn and Jeff? What happened to them?"

FIERCE LOYALTY

In an unusual professional tone, Alex said, "I think I'll let these two tell you. This is Lisa Carlyle, Special Assistant to the President of the United States on drug policy, and this is Thomas Trimble, Deputy Director of the FBI."

Carlyle and Trimble stepped forward to shake Toni's hand.

Carlyle went first, "It's nice to meet you, Special Agent Brazil."

"Please call me Toni, Ms. Carlyle, and you too, Mr. Trimble."

"Well, if we're going to be on first name basis here, then, it's Lisa," Carlyle said in a sweet southern voice.

Lisa Carlyle was a thirty something southern belle, with blonde hair and icy see- through blue eyes. She was pretty, Toni thought, but a Washington politico and that meant anything that came out of her mouth was probably a spin on what she wanted Toni to believe.

On the other hand, Toni knew who Thomas Trimble was, and what his friends in the FBI believed. He had never seen a picture of Trimble, but just looking at him, he understood why everyone said he is just another political backstabber. Tall, slim, and dark haired, he looked slick, never unshaven, his gleaming face looking like he stepped from a shower fifteen minutes before. Trimble worked his way up by brown-nosing his bosses, and taking credit where credit was due. One of Toni's good buddies, an agent in Southern California, broke a case interrogating a would-be terrorist, but Trimble, the supervisor, stepped in to take the credit.

"It's nice to meet you both, but could you tell me why you're here?" Toni asked. "I'm tired, my head is killing me, and will someone please tell me how Lynn and Jeff are doing?"

Trimble looked over at Carlyle for permission to talk. "Lynn and Jeff are both fine. Lynn was not hurt badly, except for a concussion. She hit her head after you tackled her. She's been released. Jeff was shot in the right hand and grazed on the temple. He was knocked out, when he hit the ground. He's also been treated and released."

"That's good news. Thank you."

"Well, we should be thanking you, Toni," Carlyle said, standing by Toni's bed.

"How do you mean, Ms. Carlyle?" Toni asked, suspiciously.

Carlyle nodded for Trimble to continue.

"Toni, you killed two very bad guys, Ricardo and Juan Miguel Contreras. Brothers – they were known as 'los dos diablos' in the Ruben Colombian drug cartel. They were two of the most feared hit men in the business. We've seen their dirty work before, and it's not pretty. They've tortured and killed children, mothers, fathers, cops, or anyone to get their point across," Trimble explained.

"What the hell were those guys doing in Villegas's apartment? What are you telling me?"

Then Carlyle spoke. "Let me answer one of those questions. Villegas was involved in drug smuggling. Your actions three days ago brought that out in the open. You saved Villegas' life as well, not to mention the lives of two FBI Agents. The President of the United States has decided you are going to be this country's number one hero. You might be thinking that the Colombians might retaliate, and we were a little concerned about that too, but we decided that putting you in the national spotlight, might make the cartel think twice about coming after you, or your family."

Toni wasn't sure what was going on, but it didn't smell right. He looked at Alex, who was half smiling. Just then, the phone rang. He picked it up.

"Hello."

"Hey hero!" the voice on the other end said.

Toni recognized the voice. "Bo!" It was his friend, FBI Special Agent Jeffrey Bodakis, known to his friends as Bo.

Jeffrey Bodakis was in charge of the New York City Field Office for International and Domestic Terrorism. Bo and Toni went back fifteen years when they were assigned to a health care fraud task force in Los Angeles. They were both young field agents at the time, and teamed up on the case that catapulted both of them into promotions within their agencies.

"Let me guess," Bo said, in his usual upbeat voice. "Trimble's in your room right now, along with a pretty young lady by the name of Carlyle."

"Yes, and how do."

"I just heard you woke up," Bo said.

"News travels fast. How'd you get put through to the room?"

"I told the operator I was your brother," Bo said laughing. "I wanted to call and congratulate on your Hero-ship, and give you a heads up."

"Thanks, but what do you mean? Heads up from what?" Toni asked.

"Toni, be careful with those two. I don't trust either of them. Rumor has it they're fucking each other, and plotting scenarios to make themselves look good. Know what I mean?"

Toni looked at his three guests. He knew the history between Bo and Trimble. "I hear you. Thanks for the call. How you been?" he asked, changing the subject.

FIERCE LOYALTY

"Not bad. We should talk about this later when you're feeling better. Have you turned on the news? Man, you are all over the television. I'm getting sick of seeing your ugly face every time I turn around," Bo said, laughing again.

"Just jealous, aren't ya, buddy?" Toni said, chuckling, but hurting at the same time. "You're right. Let's talk when I'm feeling better. Thanks for the call." He hung up the phone.

"Who's going to tell me why those two thugs were in Villegas' apartment?"

"Look, Toni," Trimble started, "Villegas was beaten pretty bad. You guys must have walked into the middle of the brothers killing him."

"I figured that out already Trimble. Are you saying Villegas is dead?"

Trimble answered, "No," shaking his head. "Villegas is not dead, but as far as anyone else is concerned, he was found dead three days ago. I hope you understand my point here," Trimble said, smiling no more.

"What the hell is going on here? Did you guys put him in witness protection or something?" Toni asked skeptically. "Alex, what's going on?"

Alex stood back, listening to the song and dance, but he knew the plan Carlyle and Trimble had reluctantly told him about wouldn't work. Alex Fox wasn't stupid. He looked at Carlyle and Trimble, shook his head, and said, "I told you he wouldn't fall for the hero crap."

"Here's the way it is Toni," Alex said. "These two don't want you to know that you're in danger. They've already received threats against you. Your case against Villegas is history. They believed the less you knew about his fate, the better. They don't trust you, even though you saved two FBI agents' lives."

Visibly upset, Toni said, "Why is my case against Villegas over? That's two years of my life away from my family, and you're telling me I have to give it up? Because you want him to work with you to make you look good?"

"Wait just a minute, Agent Brazil," Trimble said, holding up his hands. "Two of my agents were hurt. This is the Bureau's case too. Remember, you asked us for help. Beside, we have a plan, and a damn good reason for doing this. Just let us explain."

"No!" Toni said, more controlled. "I don't want to hear your explanation, Trimble. Whatever it is, it's just to make you look good. Isn't that what you do best?"

"Well, how," Carlyle started.

"No, Ms. Carlyle." Toni cut her off. "I'm not sure I trust what you're going to tell me. Alex, please, would you finish?"

Alex shook his head and said, "Truth is, Toni, their plan to put you in the

59

national spotlight is probably the best thing for now. I doubt the cartel will try anything. They'd be risking too much, and we could use some good press, too. So," he continued, "you're going to Washington in ten days for a ceremony at the White House, where you will receive the Congressional Medal of Honor."

Looking irritated, Toni said, "Congressional Medal of Honor? Ceremony? Do I have to go through all of that?"

"It's for the best, Agent Brazil," Carlyle said. "Alex, please let me explain the rest. Toni, I understand where you're coming from, with Villegas. As for your safety, I'd be scared to death of retaliation, too. I lost my husband because of some drug deal gone bad. He was an undercover DEA agent, and I was scared the drug dealers would come after me, but they didn't. Time passed and things cooled off. The Villegas thing has got to go our way. He's too valuable to the government, and your case has been taken into consideration. He's agreed to pay back the money as part of a deal we made with him. You'll seize it as part of your case closure."

Toni was seething, but knew whatever he said would be for naught. They would do whatever they were going to do, and he couldn't stop it. "Okay, Ms. Carlyle, go ahead, explain why I have to give up two years of my life for you and Mr. Trimble."

"After you killed the two Colombians, Villegas was found tied up in his apartment, beaten to a pulp."

Trimble, nodding along with her, continued where she left off. "He was still conscious and apparently babbling about drugs and the Ruben Colombian Cartel. After he was brought to the hospital, he begged for our help. He was scared to death. We agreed that in exchange for information about the, who, what and where of the flow of drugs into the United States from Columbia through Mexico, we'd hide him. The plan was simple. We tell the media that he was found dead at the scene, along with the Contreras brothers, and the Colombians think the brothers finished their work before you killed them. It's a good plan, Toni and, considering your case was a white collar crime, this was just too good to pass on."

Toni realized Trimble had come clean, and was right about the drug case being more important than his case. But he was curious what deal Alex had made. He knew there was more, and that Alex would tell him later. Still, he wanted to hear it from Carlyle and Trimble, so he decided to make them work a little harder for what they would get from Villegas.

"Well, I don't mean to burst your bubble," Toni started, "or tell you how to

FIERCE LOYALTY

do your job, but how do you know the information Villegas has is good? Just what did he tell you, anyway?"

Trimble looked at Carlyle again, and she nodded her approval. "Look, Toni, you've been out of it for almost three days now. We've confirmed what he told us. Villegas had an A.K.A. of Jorge Padilla, a name he used in Mexico. He bought land on both sides of the border near Nogales, and built storage warehouses on both sides. He told us the cartel dug tunnels under the border, and smuggled drugs into the United States through the tunnels. We've already confirmed the name, the land purchases, and warehouses. We set up surveillance on the storage facilities. We've also found evidence of the tunnels. The information is good."

"I think we deserve something in return for this," Toni said, looking at Alex. "After all, you'd have nothing if it wasn't for what happened, and my case."

Alex smiled, knowing exactly what Toni meant, and said, "We got some concessions, Toni. When they approached me with their plan, I told them it wouldn't work because we were not going to drop our case against Villegas, unless they gave us something in return."

"And what did we get?"

"Protection for you and your family, which I agreed to from the start!" Trimble responded, defensively.

"And funding for twenty-five new field agents, I might add," Carlyle said, looking at Alex almost defiantly. "You proved yourself rather well, Agent Brazil. It opened our eyes to your talents, and your agency's needs. You'll be well taken care of, believe me. Your protection was never an issue Toni."

Toni looked at the three people standing before him, and said, "Well, I guess too bad for Villegas. I mean, if I had just gotten there five minutes sooner. He might still be alive."

10

After six weeks, Toni's rehabilitation was going well. He no longer used crutches to walk, and rarely used his cane. His shoulder progressed better than the doctors anticipated, and he could drive himself around. It was midday, when Toni drove into the lot and parked. The parking lot was situated directly across the street from the building he called home. The sun lit a cloudless September day and gave off the type of heat of mid summer. A typical, San Francisco Indian summer.

The street was remarkably quiet for this time of day, but Toni felt like he was being watched.

"One of these days I'll see them," he said to himself. Toni knew his "Protectors" were watching him, and Ms. Carlyle told him they would not be obvious. Toni wanted it that way. He wanted his privacy and agreed his protection assigned would be out of sight.

Toni lived in the lower Market Street area of San Francisco where he and Veronica moved ten years earlier. The view of the bay from his apartment was fabulous.

Toni entered the building and walked the staircase up to the eighth floor. His left leg hurt with each step, but he decided to speed his rehabilitation by walking the eight floors up and down.

Toni opened the front door and went in. The glare of the sun came through the windows to his left that faced the bay. As he tiptoed toward the kitchen a sudden low ruff from within the apartment startled him.

"Can't get by you, can I, Bailey?"

Toni patted Bailey on the head and scratched her face. "Hey girl, are you mad? Sorry I'm late. Did Dana walk you?"

FIERCE LOYALTY

Toni went to the kitchen, opened the refrigerator, and grabbed a cold Anchor Steam. He looked out the kitchen window and saw the beginnings of the fog rolling in. The weather was cooling off. He took a long swig; relieved he was off the medications so he could drink again. He realized how quiet the house was without Veronica and Chloe. He wondered what his daughter was doing, who she would call Daddy, and why they hadn't visited him in the hospital. He wanted just to see his daughter, but Veronica wouldn't bring her.

Toni thought of the morning six months earlier, when he said goodbye to his wife and daughter. He didn't know it would be the last time he saw them. He remembered the note Veronica left.

"There's so much to say, but I'm not sure you'll hear it, or understand anyway. It's best for both of us to be apart for now. I'll call you when we're settled. I'm sorry Toni, but I can't be second to your work anymore, and it's not fair to Chloe."

Toni resisted the urge to let go, and to get angry. Holding back gave him a sense of sanity, kept his mind together, and he couldn't let go of that. He had to function, keep up the front. He had some hope that Veronica and Chloe would come back some day, soon. It was a fantasy and he knew it. She was in a new relationship.

Toni took another swig from his third beer and turned his thoughts to work. Another week of rehab and he'd be ready to go back to the job. Everything else in life felt surreal. He didn't know what to believe and not to believe. A Catholic, he always believed in God, but Toni wasn't so sure what was out there anymore. His faith in life was gone.

Toni returned to the couch and sat down. Bailey lay her head in his lap, looking up at him with her sad, watery eyes.

"How about a little TV, Bailey?" Toni picked up the remote and tuned in CNN.

"This is Gail Roberts, CNN News, Atlanta. Our top stories for Thursday, September second. Three bodies were unearthed yesterday in Fontviel, a village in southern France five Kilometers, north of Arles."

Toni looked down at Bailey. "Guess that's not good news, huh, Bailey?"

"The unidentified bodies were found after torrential rains ravaged the surrounding areas, causing mud slides. French authorities say the three men appear to have been dead for at least a month. Their teeth had been pulled out, and they were stripped naked."

"Well, definitely not good news for them," Toni said.

"No identification was found on, or near any of the bodies. Authorities said identification will be nearly impossible and that they are checking the surrounding areas and Interpol for missing persons."

"In other International News, Italian authorities are no closer to identifying who was behind the brutal killing of a Catholic priest six weeks ago in Venice. Father John O'Brien was shot four times in the chest, and his throat was cut during the brutal slaying. The Italian government believes more than one person participated in the murder. The killers left a note, but the contents have not been released. Vatican authorities released a statement indicating that Father O'Brien was visiting Venice for a brief vacation, before returning to his parish in Dublin, Ireland."

Toni looked back at Bailey. "There's just no good news any more, nothing." He had read about Father O'Brien's murder in the newspaper and thought about the hotel, Palazzo Dei Dogi, imagining what the crime scene looked like.

"What has this world come to, people killing each other, for what? Race? Religion?"

Toni's eyes were heavy, blinking as he stared at Bailey. A nap was a good idea. Bailey decided she would follow his lead. She rested her head on Toni, and closed her eyes.

11

"Who is it, Larry?" Margaret asked, standing next to her husband on the front porch of their two-story white Cape Code farmhouse.

"I don't know, honey. Are you expecting a delivery today?" Larry Tunney replied to his wife of forty years, as they watched the dust from a white van approaching from a distance.

"No, of course not. Deliveries come on Tuesday, not Friday. Should I call someone?" Margaret asked.

"No, I reckon it's just someone lost. I'll take care of it. You go get the dog and tie her up in the back yard so she don't come attacking anybody," Larry replied.

Larry and Margaret Tunney were life-long farmers. They grew up in Marysville, California, where their parents owned and operated chicken farms. Forty years before, they announced their wedding plans to their families, who were delighted. So much so, they merged their farms into one, and called it Sunshine Farms.

Over forty years, the farm became the largest producer of farm fresh eggs in Northern California. Twenty years earlier they began raising pigs and dairy cows. Larry thought it was the most natural of combinations. People eat eggs and bacon for breakfast and wash it all down with milk. The idea turned their little farm into a money machine.

Larry and Margaret had four children and sent all four to college. They bought their parents out of the farm and retired them in Florida. Sending the kids to college, retiring their parents, and remodeling the old house used up their savings, and at fifty-eight, Larry was worried about their own retirement. He had some money in a money market mutual fund, but the year before, he had to take some out to pay for their daughter's wedding, and two years before that, his wife's surgery. Larry hadn't considered selling the farm, but then lately he thought it might be the only way out of the financial situation they were in.

The farm would run at a profit for a few more years Larry believed. However, to retire at sixty-five, Larry and Margaret knew their four children would have to help out. How was he going to tell his children? They had three sons. Chad, a lawyer, worked in San Diego; Larry Jr. was a software engineer in Seattle; and Tucker, a professional baseball player in the minor leagues in Eugene, Oregon. Their daughter, Chantel, a veterinarian, had just married and lived nearby in Yuba City.

The van turned into the driveway. Margaret tied up Ben, the German shepherd, and came up behind Larry putting her left arm inside of his right arm. Larry could see two men inside the van as it parked next to his 1994 GMC pickup.

Larry approached the van. He could see the writing on the side, Geneon Systems. The doors opened simultaneously. A man in his early forties wearing a fitted double breasted green suit with a tan shirt, and a light green tie stepped from the van. He stood motionless looking at Larry and Margaret through dark sunglasses. The other person joined him, a woman in her thirties, wearing a black skirt and a white blouse. She was attractive and had nice legs. The man took off his sunglasses and smiled.

"Hello there! Are you Larry and Margaret Tunney?"

Surprised the man knew his name, Larry stopped, unconsciously stiffening, squeezing Margaret's left arm tight.

"Who wants to know?" Larry replied.

The attractive woman approached Larry and Margaret, and stretched her right hand in a greeting.

"Hello. My name is Bonny Savard," she said.

Larry shook her hand but said nothing.

"And this is my partner, Phillip Lowe." Her partner approached and held out his hand.

"How do you do?" Margaret said, shaking Bonny Savard's hand. "You'll have to excuse my husband. We don't get too many visitors out here."

Larry spoke up. "Yes, yes, I'm sorry. My wife is right. What can we do for you folks? How'd you know who we are?"

Bonny sensed trust. "Well, Mr. Tunney, everyone knows who you are. Sunshine Farms, I mean."

FIERCE LOYALTY

"Oh, oh, I see. Yes, Sunshine Farms. Just what can we do for you two?"

"The real question Mr. Tunney, is what we can do for you?" Lowe said. "Bonny and I are with a company called Geneon Systems. We're here to discuss a business proposal. Here's my business card." He thrust out a card and handed it to Larry. "Do you mind if we sit down somewhere, so we can explain in more detail why we're here to see you?"

"Well, sure," Margaret said. "Why don't I get us all some tea, and we can sit on the porch." She waited for her husband to agree. "Okay, Honey?"

"Yes, sure, I think we could do that," Larry replied. He eyed the card, and they walked to the porch.

A few minutes later, Margaret joined them on the porch, pouring each person a cup of tea. She sat next to her husband and asked, "Well, you two said something about a business proposal?"

"Yes, ma'am, that's right," Lowe replied. "Our employer is in the business of gene research and is currently looking to buy a dairy farm. We'd like to discuss your dairy farm."

Surprised at the proposal, Larry said, "Gene research? What kind of research do you have in mind, Mr. Lowe? Are you talking about research on animals? Because if you are, well you can forget it."

"No, no, no Mr. Tunney," Bonny interrupted. "We don't do research on animals. It's the product, primarily milk and eggs, and their effects on the human body. No, the animals would be safe, Mr. Tunney, " she said smiling at Larry and Margaret.

"Oh, the product is all," Larry said, relieved.

"Mr. Lowe, Ms. Savard," Margaret said. "We haven't thought about selling the farm, and we've lived here all our lives. We love it here, and I just don't think we're ready to sell."

"Look, Mrs. Tunney," Bonny began, "our employer is prepared to pay you and your husband a fair price for everything here – the livestock, the house, the land and anything else. We're even prepared to offer you money for the name Sunshine Farms, as well."

Larry looked at his wife. He raised his eyebrows and she raised hers. "Would you continue to sell the produce on the market?" Larry asked.

"Oh, of course," Lowe replied. "The product name will continue, and we would take over your contracts with your buyers. In fact, along with the purchase price, you'd also receive a fifteen percent share of future revenues for the use of the product name. We plan to use only a tenth of the produce for research. The rest would be sold."

"I see," Larry said.

"Mr. and Mrs. Tunney," Lowe started again, "you are only our first stop today, but you're our first choice. If we don't buy your farm, we'll buy another one somewhere near here. I'd hate to see our second or third choice get rich." He smiled.

Larry knew they needed the money. Could this be the solution he prayed for? He asked, "What kind of offer are you talking about, Mr. Lowe?"

Phillip Lowe leaned forward, and took a sip of the tea. He had their attention. "We've done a complete analysis of your farm's current holdings, and we determined its worth to be . . ."

12

Phillip Lowe and Bonny Savard shook hands with Larry and Margaret Tunney. They got into their van and sped off the farm. Bonny opened her briefcase and took out a cell phone, then dialed the number given to her weeks earlier, for the boss's location that day. The phone was picked up after two rings. The voice on the other end was unmistakable. Gideon spoke.

"Has your mission been accomplished?"

"Yes. It's done. Tomorrow, we'll deliver the cash to the Tunneys and sign the papers." Bonny said.

"Any trouble convincing them?" Gideon asked.

"None at all," she replied. "Once they heard the amount we were willing to pay, and offered an extra hundred grand to be out in five days, they jumped at it."

"Yes, I get it. Farmers are all the same. You and Lowe have done well. You bought all nine dairy farms without a hitch. The plan is ahead of schedule. You'll have two weeks to get the farm outside of New York City, ready. What is the status of the equipment?"

"The equipment has arrived, and is in storage," Bonny answered. "We're just waiting for the Tunneys to move out in one week. The place will be ready when the package arrives. Dr. Geron will be here in three days to get this place ready. Phillip and I will finish tomorrow and leave for New York."

"Very good. Anything else, Savard?" Gideon asked, nastily.

"No," Bonny replied, coolly.

"I suspect not. I expect . . . Never mind." Gideon sounded angry, and hung up.

Bonny Savard took a deep breath and put the phone back into her briefcase.

She exhaled, relieved for the moment.

"That's it then," she said. "He's satisfied. One more to go."

"Are you sure he's satisfied?" Lowe asked. "If he even suspects we've lied to him, he'll have someone on us like flies on shit. Did he say anything suspicious?"

"No, he started to say something, but he stopped and hung up."

"Damn. Damn. Damn, Bonny!" Lowe cried. "If he finds out we've undercut him for the five million, he'll have us killed, not to mention our plan to tell the FBI about this shit."

"Stop it! He doesn't suspect a thing, Phillip!" Bonny returned.

"How the hell do you know? Just how the fuck do you know he hasn't got someone waiting for us in New York, or watching us already?" Lowe replied, angrily.

"Calm down, Phillip! If he has someone in New York waiting for us, we'll have to do what we think is best. Kill them if we have to," she said.

"Are you ready to kill, Bonny?" Lowe asked, sarcastically.

"We've already decided we'd do what we have to do," she replied quickly, her eyes beginning to water. "If he had any clue, we'd probably be dead already. He probably plans to kill us, anyway. We're liabilities! We know too much! Have you ever thought of that?" Bonny whimpered.

"Yeah. I've thought of our liability status altogether too much," Lowe responded, calmly. "Let's just remember who got us into this."

"It's my fault? Is that what you want me to say?" she raised her voice. "You can leave if you want. I didn't know Gideon had this in mind. Yeah, I slept with him. Is that what you want to hear? Remember, we agreed I'd do it with him so I could steal the precious product information for those jerks you got involved with. And you forget I agreed to do this, after I was caught to keep you and me alive. How the hell was I supposed to know I would find out about this crazy plan? You'd better be prepared, Phillip, because you bet your ass he's got someone on our tail. You think he trusts us out here alone? If you want to leave, go ahead. Let's see how far you make it."

"All right. All right. I'm sorry," Lowe replied, sheepishly. "No ones leaving anybody here. You're right, I was wrong. I just wish I knew who was watching us. I haven't seen anybody following us."

"I know," Bonny said, taking a deep breath. "It makes me nervous, too. But, we're doing the right thing. We buy the farm outside Albany, the third one on the list. He's expecting us to go to the first one. We buy the farm and call him. We ditch the van, drive to New York, get the hotel room, call the

FIERCE LOYALTY

FBI, and wait a few hours. We make our deal and get the fuck out of town with our new looks and identities, and Gideon's five million. The feds won't know what we really look like, nor will Gideon's people. The plan *will* work. Just keep calm. It will work. It has to." She brushed a tear from her cheek.

"I hope so, baby. I fucking hope so." Lowe said, watching the rear view mirror closely.

13

Toni shuddered as he woke to the pounding that echoed inside his head but came from the front door. He had fallen asleep on the couch with the TV on. The story of the slain priest was being told again. Bailey was no longer next to him. He looked at his watch. Four-thirty, he read and contemplated ignoring whoever was at the door. He wasn't expecting anybody. No one stopped by his place without calling first.

The pounding started again, but this time a voice yelled, "Toni, come on man! Open up."

He thought he recognized the voice, but couldn't place it. Bailey began to bark. She barked only when she knew the person outside the door. Otherwise, she growled.

"Come on Toni, open the door! I know you're in there. I saw your car across the street! Open up!"

"I know that voice," he said to himself.

Toni went to the door. He never installed the peephole he intended to, for years, and now had no way of knowing who was on the other side.

"Toni! Are you in there!" the voice shouted, again.

"Okay! Okay! I'm coming. Hold your horses. Who is it?" Toni yelled.

"It's Bo!"

"Bo?" Toni opened the door, "Bo! What the hell are you doing here?" Toni peered at his longtime friend.

Jeffrey Bodakis was one of Toni's best friends. The day Toni was discharged from the hospital; Bo flew from New York City to accompany him back to Washington, and to the White House awards ceremony. Toni had not expected that, and appreciated his company more than anything. His

72

FIERCE LOYALTY

personal life in tatters, he needed a friend and Bo stepped to the plate.

They had known each other for fifteen years, and had worked together in Southern California. Toni and Bo teamed up on many investigations, early in their careers. They became friends. Their backgrounds were also similar. Toni's father was Portuguese and his mother German; Bo's father was Greek and his mother African American. They both tried to fit into the community they most resembled, but never knew the feeling of being accepted.

"It's about time you opened your door," Bo said. "I thought the neighbor was going to call the cops. Dana remembered me and said she saw you come home a few hours ago, so I knew you were here. What's going on, buddy?"

"Come on in, Bo," Toni said. "I was sleeping, taking a nice afternoon nap."

"Must be nice," Bo said, as he walked past Toni into the hallway. He bent down to pet Bailey, whose tongue was out. Bo walked into the living room, and saw the three empty beer bottles and the television on CNN. "You been drinking, Toni?"

"I had a few beers after my rehab visit. It went well after lunch. I fell asleep watching the news. What brings you out this way, Bo? Terrorist commies here in San Fran or what?" Toni changed the subject.

"Since when do I need an excuse to come check up on my friends? But it is San Francisco. Plenty of whacko's out here." They both laughed. "You got any beer left?"

"I should. Bought a twelve pack on the way home this afternoon."

"Bring one. No, bring two for me, and why don't you have another one with me?"

Toni brought the beer to the living room where Bo was petting Bailey.

"Here you go, two for you, one for me," Toni said.

"Bailey looks happy. You taking her on walks, yet?" Bo asked.

"No, not yet. Dana still comes once a day, usually in the morning, but Doc says next week I can start walking a little faster. I just can't take that long stride yet. Damn leg hasn't healed as fast as we thought it would. I must be getting old."

"We're getting' old," Bo replied, taking a swig of beer. "It's a fact of life, you know, first birth, then death. Can't do anything about it. So, you hear from Veronica?"

"Yeah. We talk once a week, so I can talk to Chloe." Toni lowered his voice. "She started school."

"That's great. Have you seen her?"

"No, and I don't expect to until the divorce is final," Toni responded. "I'll have her part of the summer next year, I expect. I won't be able to travel as much."

"How've the media been? They still bothering you?" Bo asked, taking another swig.

"Hell, yeah. I get a call about once a week now, but I signed the non-disclosure agreement with Uncle Sam. Can't talk about an ongoing case." Toni rolled his eyes. "I did get on Leno, and a couple of morning shows. That was fun. Some guy called me who wants to write a book, and the local television is following my recovery."

Bo took a long pull on his beer. Toni watched, as Bo ordinarily didn't drink much without food around. Maybe he'd had a long flight.

"What's up, Bo?" Toni asked. "Why you here? You're all dressed up, got your weapon on, but you're drinking. That's not like the Bo I know. You didn't come three thousand miles just to shoot the shit. Lisa finally leave you or something? Come on. Give it up," Toni prodded.

"You haven't changed a bit. No, Lisa hasn't left me, at least, not yet," Bo replied, and took another long drink. He looked at the empty bottle and put it on the coffee table.

"Toni," Bo said. "I had to come here on business, and something came up. I figured it would be best to tell you in person. Don't know how to say it."

"What's bothering you, Bo? What the hell's going on?"

"There's no easy way to say this. It's your brother. He's dead." Bo watched Toni take the news. He blinked twice as if the words hadn't hit him yet.

"What?" Toni said, finally. "Which one?"

"Your brother Bobby," Bo replied, calmly.

"Bobby?" Toni's voice trailed off. "I haven't seen Bobby in over ten years. How'd it happen?"

"Bobby committed suicide, two nights ago."

The words hung in the air. Dismayed, he shook his head, Toni asked, "Suicide?"

"I'm sorry, buddy."

"I knew it would happen some day, but suicide. I never would have believed it. Drug overdose, yes. Car accident, yes. But suicide, no way." Toni looked away. "Bobby and I lost touch over the years. I knew the day would come, and I thought I was prepared for it. It still hits hard. Suicide . . . Where'd it happen?"

FIERCE LOYALTY

"Inside a Catholic Church in Montreal."

"A Catholic Church? Montreal? Canada Montreal?"

Bo shook his head in affirmation.

Toni sat; his thoughts crisscrossed his brain as fast as the electric currents could pulse. "How did Bobby end up in Canada, of all places?"

"Toni, I came to tell you the Canadian authorities have invited you to come to Montreal and claim Bobby's remains."

"What do you mean, 'Invited'?" Toni asked.

"They found your business card in Bobby's belongings and since you're known all over since the Villegas case, they wanted to invite you."

"You mean this is official?"

"Yes. They called my boss who called the President. Then my boss called your boss, and they all agreed you should go."

"Why didn't Alex call me?"

"There's something else I haven't told you, yet," Bo answered, "but before we discuss that, your boss will call you tonight. They wanted me to tell you personally. The Bureau believes we owe you the respect. The Canadians are paying for the trip."

Still stunned, Toni said, "Well, if it's official business. I'm not ready to go back to work for another two weeks, but I'd go anyway for Bobby," Toni said. "What's this other thing about?"

"I have a friend on the Montreal police force. He's been assigned to take you around when you arrive. He called me because he knew we were friends." Bo finished his beer and took another from the table. "My friend's name is Kelly Primeau. He's a homicide detective, a good man and a good cop. Kelly and I have worked together on a few things, and I can vouch for him."

"Bo," Toni replied, "What are you trying to tell me?"

"Kelly will show you where Bobby was living," Bo answered. "You're there to take care of Bobby's stuff only, that's all. Don't poke around in their business. You have no standing or authority."

"What are you talking about? What would I poke into?"

"I'm getting to it," Bo replied. "Kelly believes there are some suspicious circumstances surrounding Bobby's death. He wasn't involved in the investigation, so he's speculating."

"Did your friend tell you the circumstances he thought were suspicious?"

"No," Bo answered.

"Where was Bobby living?"

"At the basilica in Montreal, with the priests," Bo replied.

"Well that's suspicious in its own right."

"It was kind of a big deal, Toni," Bo said. "A church official, Father Michael Chason, called the police when it happened and asked if they could keep a low profile. Apparently, Bobby's suicide happened *inside* the basilica, where they say mass. That's all I know. Kelly will fill you in when you get there."

Toni stood up and turned to look out his living room window to a view of buildings and the San Francisco Bay. What had happened to Bobby over the past ten years? How did he end up in Montreal? He'd lost touch with his brother and always believed that he'd see Bobby again. Bobby was dead and it hadn't sunk in, it didn't feel like reality. He raised his bottle and whispered, "cheers."

"I don't think I can believe it," Toni said. "Living at a church? The last thing I would have expected would be for Bobby to be anywhere near a Catholic Church."

"People change. When's the last time you heard from Bobby, anyway?" Bo asked.

In a whisper, Toni replied, "Funny you should ask."

"What do you mean?"

"I just remembered. Bobby called me, about five, six weeks ago. He left a cryptic message. Said he needed my help, or something like that," Toni said. "I thought he wanted money. I wrote down the number, but never got a chance to call him back, not that I would have anyway. The next morning was the Villegas shooting. I forgot all about Bobby calling."

Bailey now joined Toni near the window. She was a dog, but she knew when her owner wasn't right. "I loved my brother, Bo, but he left me little choice."

"I know, Toni," Bo replied, somberly. "You took care of him best you could."

"Yeah," Toni replied. "Well, you gotta go?"

"Nah. I was hoping I could stay here," Bo said. "I got a plane ticket for you. Figured we'd just go to the airport together in the morning."

"Sure. Not a problem," Toni responded. "Thanks."

"Let's grab some food," Bo suggested.

"Good idea. We can go to Mo Mo's down the street."

"Sounds great. But I'll need your office for an hour or so. Got a surveillance going north of here. Just need to be on-line with the agents for awhile," Bo said.

"Have a shot at it. I need a shower anyway." Toni picked up the empty

FIERCE LOYALTY

beer bottles, and dumped them in his garbage.

Toni thought of Bobby and how alone he must have felt. Maybe suicide wasn't so far-fetched. Life was testing him again. His brother's death was sinking in.

"I'm sorry, Bro," he whispered. "I won't fail you again."

Toni let his emotions finally take over.

14

"Team 1, Team 1. Come in Team 1. Can you read me? This is base camp, Alpha."

"This is Team 1. We read you Alpha."

"Where are the targets, Team 1?"

"They just left the farm and are headed to the highway. Looks like they're headed to the hotel."

"Excellent, Team 1. Call in when they get to the hotel. Base out."

"Roger, Alpha. We also intercepted a call from Targets cell phone. We'll advise later. Team 1 out."

"Team 2, this is base camp Alpha. What's your 10-20?"

"Alpha, this is Team 2. We're at the farm. Everybody's good to go here. Tunneys are Okay. "

"Very good, Team 2. Call me on a hard line and advise. The number is 4 – 1 – 5 – 2 – 2 – 9 – 2 – 3 – 7 – 9. Did you copy Team 2?"

"Team 2 copy, 4152292379."

"You got it. Alpha out."

"Team 2 out."

The phone rang in Toni's office, "Bodakis."

"Bo, its Velarde."

"Randy. How are the Tunneys?" Bo asked.

"Well, they really don't know what to think," Senior Special Agent Randy Velarde responded. "I think they're a little shocked, but they've agreed to cooperate. I had to let them keep the money though."

"That's fine. We knew it would probably have to be that way. The sale is legal," Bo said.

FIERCE LOYALTY

"Yeah, but they have to be out in five days," Velarde replied. "The targets are returning tomorrow with the money and paperwork. Guess how much they got for this place?"

"No idea."

"Two-and-a-half million in cash, fifty thousand shares of Geneon stock, plus fifteen percent of future sales," Velarde said almost jealously.

"Wow!" Bo said. "Well, at least they got some cash. That stock won't be worth crap when we're through with Geneon Systems."

"That's what they said. They asked if they could sell the shares after the sale is complete. Mr. Tunney already knew the stock was trading at thirty-six dollars a share," Velarde chuckled.

"Funny what money does to you," Bo responded. "Hey, Randy, are the Tunneys the parents of Tucker Tunney?"

"You got it. They said Tucker is going to make the big show this year with the Giants."

"He's good enough," Bo replied. "Randy, it's your show here. I'm heading back to New York tomorrow with Toni. Let's hope those two stick to their schedule as well as they have, so far."

"How's Toni doing anyway? How'd he take the news?"

"As good as could be expected," Bo replied. "They were pretty close years ago, but had a falling out, lost touch the last ten years. Toni said his brother called him out of the blue and left a cryptic message. Now he's dead. I don't think it's a coincidence. In fact, I'm sure it's related, but I couldn't tell Toni a thing until we get a closer look. He's the only chance we have to make the connection to Gideon."

"Primeau's boss still blocking him?" Velarde asked.

"Oh, yeah. Kelly believes it was staged to look like a suicide," Bo said. "It just doesn't smell right, you know. As much as I hate to say this, I hope Toni's brothers' death was homicide. If we can stop this thing before it starts, we may be able to connect Bobby Brazil's death to Gideon."

"I hear you, Bo, but Toni can take care of himself. You gave him the little push we discussed?"

"Yeah, and I'm pretty sure he'll start causing problems right away," Bo answered.

"If I know Toni Brazil, he'll get in someone's face real fast if he sniffs foul play," Velarde laughed. "You trace the anonymous call, yet?"

"Traced it to a pay phone at the Dallas Fort Worth airport, the last place Bonny Savard and Phillip Lowe were, the day it came in. Things are happening fast, Randy, and we have to be ready to move, as soon as we know how the virus is being smuggled in, if all this is true. The information we've got has been checked out so far. We confirmed that Geneon Systems bought a large amount of laboratory equipment, enough to set up eight to ten labs."

"Info sounds good. You think it's those two that called?"

"It sure looks that way," Bo answered. "The disguised voice was female. My gut tells me it was Bonny. I'd bet my pay check on it."

"One more thing, Bo," Velarde said excitedly. "Jack just called from Team 1. He's pretty sure someone was following the targets. They caught sight of another vehicle, and they're running the plates. They pulled off the surveillance, once they noticed it. Jack said he noticed it when he saw the same car parked across the street from the hotel, with two guys in it. On the way back to the hotel, he noticed the same car behind them and the same two guys. They pulled off and the car went on. It's parked at a hotel across from Savard and Lowe's hotel again."

"All right. I guess Gideon is raising the stakes," Bo said. He took a deep breath. "Let's call in more agents, Randy. Start a twenty-four hour surveillance on our second vehicle."

"Plate goes back to Hertz rental, Bo," Velarde answered. "Rented at the San Francisco airport, same day Savard and Lowe came to town. Looks like we have a tail on the targets," he said. "Jack says there are two men in the car. They got out and went into room 214 at the Holiday Inn. Jack says they look Arab."

"I want them watched around the clock," Bo said. "I want agents in the rooms next to them, above and below. I want to know who they call, everything. I'll get the warrants. When the targets return the van to Geneon Systems, I want that van looked over for transmitters, bombs, anything. I want to know how sophisticated these guys are."

"You read my mind," Velarde said. "We'll confiscate the tail's van when they return it to Hertz and go over it with a fine tooth comb."

"Be careful, Randy. Keep in touch. I want to know exactly when Lowe and Savard get on that plane to New York. And if the two unknowns try anything crazy, take them down."

"You got it, Bo. Talk to you later."

"Good luck, Randy. And good job."

Bo hung up the phone and leaned back in Toni's office chair. He took a file from his briefcase, opened it, and looked at a picture of Bonny Savard. She was pretty: shoulder length brown hair, brown eyes that looked innocent,

FIERCE LOYALTY

and nice tanned skin. She was born in Montreal. Parents divorced, and at twelve she moved with her father to California. She was a cheerleader at Linda Vista High School in Cupertino, California, and then graduated from Stanford in biology. She spoke four languages other than English fluently – French, Spanish, Italian, and Russian – and worked for Geneon Systems in international relations.

Bo wondered how she could be mixed up in the case, and hoped she was the anonymous caller. He could deal with her; maybe help her out of the mess. The FBI tech told Bo the voice was female, but the equipment used to disguise the voice was top notch, the type governments use to scramble communication signals and voice recognition. That disturbed Bo. He didn't want to believe the woman was a traitor or a spy working for another government.

The caller said the smallpox virus had been obtained outside the United States and would come in through Montreal. Then the voice became garbled – something about Catholic priests. He didn't know what that meant until Detective Kelly Primeau of the Montreal Police Department called to tell him about Bobby Brazil. Kelly said he believed Bobby's death was a cover-up and he couldn't find out why. Kelly's boss, Alexander Savage investigated the case himself and concluded that Bobby Brazil died of a self-inflicted gunshot wound to the head. Kelly suspected otherwise.

Kelly told Bo that he didn't like what he saw, because Savage never conducted death investigations. New to the department, Savage transferred from immigration and was put in charge of Kelly's squad. Kelly was being strong-armed away from the Bobby Brazil case by a superior who had never investigated a death case before. When Kelly said Bobby died in a Catholic Church, Bo remembered that the anonymous caller said the virus would be smuggled in by Catholic priests.

The case was coming together, Bo thought, as he considered why Father Chason, the priest in Montreal, wanted to keep the investigation of Bobby Brazils death out of the media. Was this the Catholic priest connection Savard spoke of? If it were all connected, his best chance to find out what was happening in Montreal was Toni Brazil.

He wanted to tell Toni everything he knew, but the powers would not allow it, specifically, Thomas Trimble. He thought about sending Toni into the case without warning. He could get his friend killed. Bo couldn't tell him, his career hung in the balance. Trimble threatened to demote anyone who leaked anything outside the FBI. He knew it was wrong, but what could he do?

81

Trimble didn't like Toni. After the Villegas shooting, Trimble was furious because an agent outside the bureau made the FBI look bad. Trimble wanted Toni brought up on charges of endangering the FBI Agent's lives, but that went nowhere. No one told Toni that story, but Bo considered it.

"Hey, you look like you got some bad news?" Toni said, as he walked in. "You look like death warmed over. Your surveillance go bad or something?"

"No. Everything's fine. Just a little tired. You ready to get a bite to eat?"

"I called down to Mo Mo's. They've got a table waiting for us," Toni said.

"We'll talk on the plane tomorrow about the Montreal thing, but I wanted to remind you how sensitive the French Canadian guys are," Bo said, wanting to tell Toni about Trimble.

"What's the problem, Bo? You afraid I'll stick my nose in where it doesn't belong?"

"Yes and no. I want to keep my contacts in good standing, is all," Bo replied.

"I'll do whatever Detective Kelly Primeau says. But know this too. Bobby was my brother, and I loved him. I know who my bother was. I've been thinking about what you said, and I don't believe he committed suicide. If I believe they made any mistakes in their investigation. I'll do whatever it takes to prove otherwise," Toni said.

"Okay, Toni. I can appreciate that," Bo replied, letting out the air held in his lungs sighing.

Bo started down the stairs, but noticed Toni hadn't followed him. He turned to see where he was.

Toni was staring at a picture on the wall of himself with his four brothers, lost in thought of another time.

15

"Come on, Bobby, get up! Get up, dammit!" Toni yelled, kneeling next to his brother. Bobby lay on his stomach, his face down, his right arm folded under his body and his left arm jutting out at a forty-five degree angle.

Blood flowed from under his head. A few feet away, the 357 revolver still smoked. He shook Bobby. "Come on, Bobby, please, get up." A tear dropped onto Bobby's jacket. "I'm sorry, Bobby, I should have been here." He reached down and closed Bobby's eyes. "I'm sorry, Bobby. I hope you can forgive me."

"Excuse me, sir. Sir, excuse me."

Toni awoke in a panic. He looked up from his reclined chair in first class. A pretty blonde woman in a blue uniform smiled at him. She shook Toni gently.

"Sir, please wake up," she said again. "We are in Montreal."

"Oh, yes, thank you," Toni said, as he shook himself awake.

"Are you all right, sir?"

"Yes, I'm fine, just a little groggy," Toni replied, sleepily.

Toni and Bo had taken the 8:00 A.M. flight from San Francisco to JFK, a five and one half hour flight. The Canadian government made all the flight arrangements in advance, so Toni had nothing to do except get on the plane. From JFK, he took a six o'clock flight to Montreal, and arrived at 8:00 P.M.

Toni thought how little Bo talked on the flight from San Francisco. Bo was not usually quiet. Toni had sensed something wrong and believed Bo would tell him what was on his mind eventually. He never did, to his surprise.

83

SCOTT A. REZENDES

Toni thought of his brother and the dream he had, just moments earlier. He knew it was the guilt he felt after the way he treated Bobby the last time he saw him. Would Bobby be alive now if he hadn't pushed him away?

He took his bags from under the seat in front of him and stood. He was the last one off the plane. Bo told him Detective Kelly Primeau would pick him up at the airport. He zipped through customs with no trouble, showing his passport and getting the green light, and a stamp on his book.

Toni approached the open door that led into the airport concourse. His eyes found Kelly Primeau. Bo described Kelly as a tall slender man with blond hair. He said Kelly was also a good dresser and wore a tie everywhere. As Toni approached the man, he realized the man's eyes were closed.

"Excuse me, Detective Primeau?"

The man grunted and looked up at Toni. He stood abruptly.

"Monsieur Brazil?"

"Yes," Toni replied with a smile.

"Oh, I'm sorry. I fell asleep waiting," he replied.

"Are you Detective Primeau?"

"Yes, I am me. I mean, yes, it is me. Please call me Kelly, Monsieur Brazil," he said holding out his hand.

Toni shook his hand. "Nice to meet you, Kelly. Bo's told me a lot about you. Call me Toni."

"You wish to see your brother now?" Kelly asked, in slight accented English.

"Can we?"

"Well, we could, but I planned to take you to your hotel first, and take you to see your brother in the morning," Kelly said.

"That sounds reasonable. Let's go," Toni replied.

"But if you wish, we can make arrangements for you tonight," Kelly answered.

"Relax," Toni said. "Tomorrow is fine. I can see we've both had a long day."

"Yes, I wouldn't mind getting home," Kelly said. "Toni, I would like to ask a favor of you?"

"What can I do for you?"

"I would be honored if you would come to dinner at my home. My son is a very big fan of yours. He watched you on the television – Leno. I would be honored if you'd be our guest."

"Kelly, I would be happy to have dinner with you and your family. Thank you."

84

FIERCE LOYALTY

"Tomorrow is good?" Kelly asked.

"Tomorrow is fine. My arrangements are open ended, so I can stay another night," Toni said.

"Your travel is being paid by the Canadian government. You are welcome to stay as long as needed," Kelly responded.

Toni and Kelly walked out of the Airport terminal. At the curb, a Montreal Police car awaited to take them to the hotel.

"No horses?" Toni asked.

"Are you disappointed, Toni?"

"A little."

The drive to the hotel was short. Toni had never been to Montreal, and was surprised how the lights sparkled off the St. Lawrence River. The car pulled under the lanai and Toni opened the door as the car slowed to a stop. There had been little conversation between Toni and Kelly, but Kelly chatted with the driver in French.

"Monsieur Brazil, I will be here at nine. Is that okay?"

"Nine is fine, Detective. Thank you for picking me up. I'll see you in the morning."

"Please be in the lobby, Monsieur. Good night."

Toni grabbed his bag and got out of the car. Kelly got out to hold the door open.

"My reservation, Detective?" Toni asked.

"It's in your name. Please make yourself comfortable, order room service, anything you want," Kelly said, and shook Toni's hand again.

"Thank you for your hospitality," Toni said.

"You are welcome," Kelly responded, with a courteous smile.

Kelly got back in and the car immediately sped off.

Toni looked up at the multi floor hotel in front of him. He took a deep breath and entered the hotel lobby. Toni was met by white with gold speckled marble floors and the music he recognized as Bach playing on the piano.

A man in a blue suit walked up, "May I help you, Monsieur?"

Toni looked over the tall overweight man, "I need to check-in."

"Excellent. This way please." The man took Toni's bag in his right hand and escorted him to the check-in counter.

"I have a reservation," Toni said to the woman behind the counter. "It should be under Brazil." Her nametag read Monique and Toni thought she was attractive.

She tapped the computer in front of her. "Yes, Monsieur Brazil. I have

85

you for five nights, yes?"

"Five nights?"

"Yes, It is not correct?" she asked.

"I don't know. If it says five nights, then five nights it is, Monique,"

The woman smiled back at him, "Your room is prepaid, Monsieur Brazil. Anything you want, just let me, huh, us here at the hotel know."

Toni detected a slight reddening on her cheeks as she fumbled her words. She handed Toni the card key. "Your room is 735 Monsieur Brazil. Please let us know if we can do anything for you."

"I will," Toni said.

"This way, Monsieur." Toni heard a voice from behind him.

Toni turned away from the woman behind the counter and walked to the elevator directly behind him. He noticed the mirrored walls and caught Monique staring at him. He'd seen the look before and she embarrassingly looked away to do something else. He stepped on the elevator where the Porter waited holding his bag. The doors shut. Toni looked over at the tall Porter and hit the number three button.

"Why don't you let me take my bag? Here's something for your trouble. I can handle it from here."

The elevator door opened and without a word Toni took his bag from his escort. The porter stepped off the elevator, appearing dumfounded at what just happened. Moments later, Toni reached the seventh floor and stepped out into the hallway. The sign listed sections of room numbers pointing in opposite directions. His room number pointed him to the right, and Toni began his stroll down the beige carpeted hallway. He reached his room and went in. Toni dropped his bag and found the light switch. The lights illuminated a bathroom, and a bedroom through French double doors.

Once his things were stowed away in his room, Toni decided to relax with something from the in-room refrigerator bar. He reached in and got a Heineken, plucking off the cap with the bottle opener on the wall. He took a long pull, turned and found the room service book on the desk across the room. He opened the book to the dinner menu.

"What's this?"

From within the room service book, he took a white letter size envelope with his name on it. An adrenaline rush zoomed up his spine; the hairs on his neck prickled. He looked at it long and hard. He sat down in the desk chair, and held the envelope to the light on the desk. He could see something inside. Who knew he was in Montreal? Only two people knew his location, Bo and

FIERCE LOYALTY

Detective Primeau. The envelope could be from one of them.

Something protruded from within the envelope, something hard and grainy. Toni reached into his pocket and found his Swiss pocket tools. Carefully he cut the top of the sealed envelope. With the tweezers, he took a necklace from the envelope. Toni immediately recognized a Saint Christopher he gave Bobby ten years earlier, the last time he saw his brother. Toni remembered wrapping the medallion in a fifty-dollar bill, before he gave Bobby some money. The guilt panged in his stomach. He was surprised Bobby kept it. Bobby needed it more than he did.

Looking back into the envelope, Toni saw a piece of paper folded. With the tweezers, he took it out and unfolded it without touching it with his fingers. What he saw took his breath away. On the left side was a photocopy of his own business card. On the right side was written: *Bobby's death was no suicide.*

The note was unsigned. Someone had taken a risk to put the note in the room service book, knowing he would open it sooner or later. He ordinarily ordered room service the first night he stayed in a hotel. Who knew that? Was it just a guess? Why take such a risk? Why not tell the police? Whoever left the note believed Toni could do something about it, and had access to Bobby after his death, the Saint Christopher attested to that.

"It doesn't make sense," he said out loud. "Why tell me and not the police?" He decided to keep the note to himself. He would poke around tomorrow, and look for a hole in the police evidence. He would be able to think more clearly, then. Toni picked up the phone and hit the room service button.

"Room Service, May I help you, Monsieur Brazil?" said a young female voice.

"Yes, a Caesar salad, some bread, and three Heineken beers."

16

The next morning Kelly Primeau picked Toni up at nine exactly. Toni ate a light breakfast of pastry and coffee at the lobby café, which looked out to the hotel lanai. Toni sat drinking his coffee, as Kelly came into the lobby alone. He saw Toni in the café.

"Good morning, Toni. How are you this morning?"

Primeau had dropped the formality of the day before. He wore a very sharp dark blue double-breasted Armani, a matching tie, and a perfectly pressed white shirt.

"I'm fine. Detectives must make pretty good money," Toni said.

"We Canadians pay enormous taxes on their incomes. Why?"

Toni knew the suit cost over five hundred dollars. Bo said Kelly could be trusted, so he put it out of his mind. He had invited Toni to dinner that night, and perhaps his wife prodded him to make a good impression.

"It's your suit."

"Yes. My wife, she tells me what to wear." Kelly said. "Are you ready?"

"Yeah, Let's go."

They walked to Kelly's unmarked brown Taurus. As Kelly drove, Toni saw the city in the distance, tall gray buildings reaching upward, blocking the sun. It was a beautiful day; sun bright, a few puffy clouds floating by. A reflection off the water caught Toni's eyes. The city struck Toni as not American, but more European like Paris.

They were silent for most of the trip. Toni broke the silence, as they crossed over the bridge leading to downtown.

"Beautiful day, isn't it?"

"It is indeed. You are familiar with Montreal?" Kelly asked, politely.

FIERCE LOYALTY

"No. Only that the language is French. I've never been here, but I must say, I feel like I'm back in time, somewhere in an old European city."

"Yes, many say that about the city. It was colonized initially by French peasants. They wanted to get away from the King and Queen's rule. The city has been transformed many times since. Many immigrants have come here, such as the Portuguese, Jews, and Italians. You are Portuguese, correct?"

"Yes, that's right." Toni looked at Kelly.

"We have many Portuguese people here. They have wonderful celebrations with parades," Kelly continued, never taking his eyes off the road.

"We called them festas when I was a kid," Toni said. "We were always celebrating as a community and as a family. We're very proud people. I haven't been to a festa in years, though."

"Yes," Kelly replied. He looked at Toni out of the corner of his eye. "I'm sorry about your brother. I'm sure it was a shock."

"More than a shock, Kelly. Completely unexpected," Toni answered, bluntly.

"How so?" Kelly asked.

"My brother was no saint. He had a lot of problems – drugs, alcohol. He was alone and homeless. I haven't seen or heard from him, in ten years."

"I see," Kelly said.

"I know people change, but Bobby," Toni continued, without prodding. "I expected he would die, but not suicide. Drug overdose, car accident, you name it. I could see that, but suicide? No, I'm having some problems with that." He peered at Kelly to see his reaction.

"People change in ten years," Kelly said. "I met your brother more than once. It is hard for me to believe he killed himself too, but people's lives change. They become unbearable, apparently."

"Yeah," Toni countered, "but unbearable would have been his wife's death twelve years ago. I took care of my brother when she died, and he was a mess. I thought he was going kill himself then, but not like this." Toni paused momentarily to catch his breath, then started again. "Back then, he was drinking himself to death and trying to kill himself with drugs the slow way."

"It must have been hard on him," Kelly commented.

"But shooting himself, no. He never thought of that, then. I remember one night he was so bad, so drugged out he couldn't move, but he told me that no matter how drunk or high he was, he couldn't take a gun to himself or jump off a building. He didn't have the balls."

"Maybe he found them this time," Kelly said.

"Maybe," Toni said. "Bo said you'd fill me in on something suspicious about Bobby's death. What did you find?"

"I didn't do the investigation, Toni," Kelly started, "so I don't know anything really."

"That's not what Bo said," Toni shot back. Kelly's face flushed red.

"Oh?" Kelly said. "What did Bo say to you?"

"Only that you didn't agree with the findings of the investigation," Toni replied, matter-of-factly. "He said the person who did the investigation didn't have any experience, something like that."

"Well," Kelly began, "I may have mentioned a few things like that to Bo, but my new boss conducted the investigation. You will meet him at the morgue, so please do not mention my observations to him. Do you understand?" Kelly turned to look Toni in the eyes.

"I understand," Toni responded, his voice tightening. "Something happened here you guys don't want me to find out about. Am I getting close, Kelly?"

"I do not know," Kelly replied quickly. "I was assigned to meet you and drive you wherever you want to go. I was told to help you with anything, funeral arrangements, anything."

"Kelly, your boss, he . . . " Toni started.

"His name is Alexander Savage. Commander Savage," Kelly interrupted.

"Okay, Commander Savage. He did the investigation of my brothers death himself?"

"Yes. I would have done it," Kelly started, then cleared his throat and began again. "It was my turn to catch the case, but he interceded and took over."

"Isn't that unusual? You said he was new, didn't you?" Toni inquired.

"Yes, on both accounts," Kelly replied. "He's new, and it is very unusual for a commander to do actual case work. They usually oversee investigations."

"Had he worked a death case before?"

"To my knowledge, he has never investigated a death before this," Kelly replied.

"How do you know that?"

Kelly looked slightly aggravated at Toni's interrogation. "He came from Customs and Immigration just a week before your brothers death. He beat me out for the job. We both applied, but he had been a commander over at C & I, and I think he also had a connection."

Toni could see his questioning irritated Kelly. Was he hiding something? Bo said Kelly would fill him in, but he had said nothing suspicious about the

FIERCE LOYALTY

investigation or the evidence.

"Sorry, Kelly," Toni said. "I didn't mean to hit a sore spot."

"No problem," Kelly replied. "Anyway, I read his application. I know what your going to say, but it was just sitting there when I turned mine in. Curiosity got to me. No matter, he had no death investigation experience that I read."

"What happened to your last boss?" Toni continued.

"Commander Koty?"

"Koty?"

"Yes, he took a lot of grief for his name," Kelly said, "but he was a good man. He was injured in a car accident and almost died. He retired on disability. I was made the acting commander, but I knew I'd have to apply for the position on a competitive basis, instead of just being interviewed and promoted."

"Is that unusual, too?" Toni asked.

"Yes and no. Maybe not," Kelly said. "But I learned later that Savage lobbied the head of the police and the mayor for the position. Savage and the mayor were classmates in college. He had the connections."

"Politics," Toni replied. "I'm sorry you lost, but I don't understand why the guy butted in if he had no experience?"

"He said he needed to get the experience, first hand. He took a junior detective as his partner on the case."

"Junior detective?"

"Yes, a junior detective, the lowest level," Kelly answered.

"Let me get this straight," Toni said. "Savage, who's never investigated a death case, takes the case from you out of the blue, and insults you by partnering with a junior detective. At least tell me, did they found a suicide note?"

Kelly said nothing to Toni's question, while he pulled over to the curb in front of a tall gray cement block building.

"There was no suicide note that I'm aware of. Anyway, I can't answer what I don't know. I risk my career if I ask too many questions. You, however, have a right to ask questions."

Kelly smiled and nodded. Toni wondered if he were giving him a push. If that was the case, he didn't need one. He'd ask questions, anyway.

"We're here. My boss is in that building and my tone will change. I will speak French and will be very formal to you. You do the same. Don't mention our conversation. Be careful with Commander Savage, Toni. He is an intelligent man, despite his lack of experience. He will have an answer for every

91

question," Kelly said. "I know one thing about Savage: I don't trust him."

"Answer this if you can," Toni said. "Did Savage do a good investigation? Did he do everything he could? "

"The answer to that is simple," Kelly said aggressively. "No!"

17

Kelly and Toni entered the building saying nothing and took a private elevator down to the morgue. The stainless steel room was chilly and still. Kelly pulled open an unmarked drawer and showed Toni his brother. Toni viewed the body, confirmed the identity, and silently wished he'd passed up the viewing. It wasn't how he wanted to remember Bobby. The memory would be stenciled forever in his mind.

The whole showing took less than five minutes. They walked the lifeless halls of the freezer room. Not much was said during the journey. Toni focused on the echo of his shoes clanking on the smooth hard tiled floors. There wasn't much to say anyway, except "it's him", and when Toni heard his voice bounce around the walls; it was as if someone else said the words. Toni followed Kelly to a different set of elevators and they were bound for the eighth floor.

The coroner's office was on the eighth floor, where Toni would meet Commander Savage, the man who ruled Bobby's death as a suicide. Someone didn't agree with those findings, Toni thought, as he considered the note he found in his hotel room the night before. After seeing Bobby's body in the freezer room, the bullet hole in his temple, he admitted it looked like Bobby might have done it.

Kelly walked slightly ahead of Toni and stopped at an office where a nameplate read "Claude Chugay, M.D." with French words. Kelly interpreted to mean Chief Coroner under the name. The office was large and rectangular with a dark walnut desk to the right. A window was behind the desk and an oval conference table with six chairs occupied the left side of the room.

Two men inside, speaking French stopped their intense conversation, when

SCOTT A. REZENDES

Toni and Kelly entered. A short man in a white coat went behind the desk and picked up a file. He was bald and wore thick, black-rimmed glasses. Toni thought he looked just like what he pictured, a guy who cut up dead people – scrawny, but scary too. His nametag read Dr. Claude Chugay. He looked up from the file without moving his head, peering at Toni from above his rims. The other man approached, and put his right hand out to greet Toni.

"Monsieur Brazil," the man said.

Toni immediately disliked him, his smile showing coffee and tobacco stained teeth. He was fat. Toni figured he couldn't close his jacket, which was wrinkled and worn. He looked unprofessional. Not what he expected.

"Yes, that's me," Toni responded. "You must be Commander Savage."

Savage looked straight back at him without wavering, and Toni thought he could read, "Don't fuck with me," in his blood shot eyes.

"Please, sit down, Mr. Brazil. That's Dr. Claude Chugay," Savage began motioning to the scrawny man. "He is chief of the coroners office, and our best at determining cause of death."

Dr. Chugay walked from behind his desk and shook Toni's hand silently. All four men sat down at the conference table.

"How was your trip, Mr. Brazil?" asked Dr. Chugay meekly in perfect American English, laying the file on the table before him, as he sat.

"Thank you, Doctor, it was fine." Toni answered. "The time difference back East always messes me up."

"I hope your accommodations are acceptable." Dr. Chugay said.

"They are more than adequate," Toni replied, nodding politely.

"Good, then. I guess we should start," Dr. Chugay said. "My analysis is that your brother died of a self-inflicted gun-shot wound to the temple. I believe he died instantly. We have ruled the death a suicide," Chugay paused, as if waiting for a reaction. When none came, he continued. "Do you have any questions? We will be glad to answer them."

Toni sat back in his chair peering at Savage, who stared back. Toni wondered if he always looked like a bull dog with its jowls lumbering downward.

"Doctor, the bullet entered Bobby's left temple, correct?" Toni asked, calmly.

Dr. Chugay opened the file. "It says here it was the left temple."

"You didn't perform the autopsy, Doctor?"

"Yes, I did, Mr. Brazil, but I do so many, I can't remem . . ."

"You can't remember?" Toni interrupted. "You performed the autopsy, when? Two days ago?"

94

FIERCE LOYALTY

"Please, Monsieur Brazil, calm down," Commander Savage said. "Dr. Chugay is a very busy man. I chartered him myself to do the autopsy, because he is the best. I investigated your brother's death myself. I know it is difficult to accept, but he committed suicide."

"Oh, really, Commander?" Toni said, turning his attention to Savage. "And how did you determine that? Find a note? Talk to his family? Friends? Did you know his background?"

"Please Monsieur," Savage replied, coolly, "I know it is difficult, but I did everything I could. The evidence at the scene was very convincing." He turned to Chugay. "Doctor? The file please."

Chugay passed the file to Savage. He took out ten photographs and handed them to Toni. "Look at them if you wish. I believe you will find these as convincing as I did." Savage passed the photographs to Toni and added, "The toxicology report indicated your brother had a .21 alcohol level."

Toni took the photographs and looked at the first one. Bobby lay partially on his right side and his back, his lower body twisted and his left arm across his chest. Toni looked at Bobby's face; there was enough to recognize him. The deep burgundy colored blood puddled where he bled after the gunshot blew him over. The gun lying on the ground was a 38 Special. It apparently fell from his hand and came to rest next to the body, near the knees.

Toni paid attention to Bobby's face. He had a beard but had trimmed it. His hair was short, but sported a frizzy curl. Though he hadn't seen his brother in ten years, he thought Bobby looked good. "What happened here, Bobby?" Toni thought. The next picture was a close-up of the gun, the 38 Special. An attached report sheet noted the weapon's serial number had been scratched off and could not be traced. Convenient, Toni thought.

"Monsieur Brazil?" It was Savage. "Are you all right?"

"Yes. I'm fine," Toni replied, as he wiped his eyes. "Commander, is your determination of my brother's suicide based solely on this crime scene and Dr. Chugay's autopsy report?"

"For the most part, it is," Savage replied, as if offended by the question. "There was no note, and we did some interviews and analyzed the fingerprints on the gun. The information we received was consistent with suicide. His fingerprints were found on the gun and the interviews were consistent with a man who was suicidal."

Toni wondered who he'd interviewed. He called his brothers and his parents before he came to Montreal and no one in his family had been called. He peered up from the photographs. Savage stared back emotionlessly.

"Who did you interview?"

"His friends," Savage replied.

"What information in those interviews was consistent with suicidal tendencies, Commander?"

"Look, Monsieur Brazil, I know it is difficult to . . ." Savage began.

"What exactly, Commander, was said to you that makes you believe my brother was suicidal?" Toni raised his voice.

"Now, look here," Savage said, standing up. "I know you're a big shot hero in America, but you are nobody here. This is my . . ."

"This is your what, Commander?" Toni faced Savage across the table, "Your jurisdiction? Well, you can take your territorial bullshit and go shove it."

"I will not stand for this from you!" Savage yelled.

"You will take this from me!" Toni retorted, face to face with Savage, "What the hell do you know about my brother, Savage?"

Doctor Chugay got up and backed away from the table. Kelly stood and put his hand on Toni's left shoulder, not holding him back.

"I performed the investigation, and I'll stand by it!" Savage exclaimed.

"Did you call his family and ask any questions?" Toni asked.

"His family!" Savage exclaimed. "You should know best Brazil. You abandoned your brother! That's what the interviews told me. You and your family abandoned him! I know all about you. Your brother's friends and family were those priests and clergy. They told me everything I needed to hear!"

"You son-of-bitch, you don't know what you're talking about!" Toni yelled, and jabbed his finger into Savage's chest.

Savage looked down at Toni's finger. His face turned red, anger brimming from his lips, but his face suddenly settled and he smiled. He sat down in his chair, taking out a handkerchief to brush off his clothes.

"Don't ever touch me again," said Savage, calmly. "I'll have you thrown into one of our jails until the winter. And the winter gets cold here, Brazil. Not like California."

Kelly put pressure on Toni's shoulder to hold him back. He sat down, and Savage continued.

"Don't have much to say? I don't know what I'm talking about? Well look here. If you don't agree with my findings, ask the people yourself." Savage slid the file across the table at Toni.

Toni slapped his hand down on the file and in one motion shoved the file right back. It hit Savage in his protruding stomach and flew open with papers flying everywhere.

FIERCE LOYALTY

"I don't need your garbage, Commander," Toni shot back. "If you two had done your job, you'd know my brother couldn't have killed himself. I can see that just looking at the pictures."

His words took everyone by surprise. Savage just looked back at Toni with disgust in his face. He believed Toni was bluffing.

"What are you talking about?" Dr. Chugay asked, nervously.

"Did you do a complete review of my brother's body, Dr. Chugay?" Toni asked.

"I did."

"Did you note the scars on his body, Dr. Chugay?"

"I believe I did, but . . ." Chugay looked down at the mess of papers on the table. He spotted what he was looking for, picked up a stapled mass of papers, and flipped through them. "Let's see, review of systems. Yes. Here it is. He had a scar on his upper right thigh consistent with major surgery. X-ray showed a rod was placed in his leg to stabilize the femur," Chugay read.

"Keep reading, Doctor, but go to the left shoulder," Toni said.

"Yes, it's here. Major atrophy is apparent in the forearm, upper arm, and shoulder. A scar on the top of the shoulder indicates a surgical procedure, possibly to secure the rotator cuff. Three other scars on the shoulder and one around the elbow, which appear to be . . ." Chugay read.

"That's right, Doctor," Toni interrupted. "Pretty good analysis. I mean the rotator cuff surgery. You're right." Toni looked back at Savage, "Did you read this report, Commander?"

"I read it. So what? He had surgery on his shoulder and elbow."

"Did you note in your report how old the scars were, Dr. Chugay? Or at least, guess?" Toni asked.

"Let me see. Yes, it's here. I stated the one scar on his shoulder was relatively new, within the last three to five years, and the other scars . . ."

"That's enough, Doctor," Toni said. "Pretty good guess. Three years ago he had shoulder surgery, the fourth in the last twelve years. Want to guess how I knew that, Commander?" Savage returned Toni's glare, but said nothing.

"That's right. Say nothing, because you don't know, do you?" Toni said. "Well, Commander, I asked! I picked up the phone, called my family, and asked them, something you neglected to do, Commander." Toni emphasized on the word neglected.

"My investigation is finished, Brazil," Savage said angrily. "Your brother committed suicide! He was a drunk and you haven't told me a damn thing to change my mind."

"No, I haven't, but I will," Toni replied calmly.

"This meeting is over," Savage said, starting out of his chair.

"Come on, Commander," Toni said coolly. "It's just getting interesting. Don't you want to know my secret? The information that will change your findings?"

"No, Brazil, I don't."

Savage stood up. "Now let me tell you something. Don't fuck with me. You'll wish you never came here, you ungrateful jerk. When we learned who your brother was, it was my idea to call you and bring you here out of courtesy. Just don't get in my way, Brazil," Savage said, and abruptly walked around to the door. He yelled something in French at Kelly, who followed him into the hallway.

Toni looked at the mess on the table. He would need the autopsy report and photographs to study them further. He wasn't a homicide detective, but Primeau knew what he was doing. He needed Kelly's help and hoped he was still assigned to him, after the argument. Then Toni's thoughts were broken by the voice of a frightened man.

"What secret information, Mr. Brazil?" Dr. Chugay asked.

"What?"

"What's the secret information you have?" Chugay repeated the question, as the door opened and Kelly Primeau came back in.

"I'm sorry, Doctor," Kelly said. "We have to leave. We are expected at the basilica to meet Father Chason. Please, Monsieur Brazil, let's go."

Toni looked at Dr. Chugay, then at Kelly, who stood at the door stone faced.

"Doctor, may I take this mess from you?" Toni asked, pointing to the papers on the table.

"Yes, it's yours," Chugay replied politely. "Please help yourself. I have another copy."

Toni put the papers in a manila folder as quickly as he could. Toni then stopped abruptly at the door and turned back to Dr. Chugay to answer his question.

"My brother had no use of his left index and middle fingers, Dr. Chugay. If you believe he could have pulled the trigger on that double action revolver, that's fine. But I don't believe he could have done it with his left hand. It stands to reason that if Bobby wanted to kill himself, why not use his right hand? You think about that, Doc."

Kelly stood at the door as Toni passed by him. He looked at Dr. Chugay, shrugged his shoulders, and turned to follow Toni down the hallway to the elevator.

18

Kelly Primeau drove away from the building. Toni said nothing to him after they left Dr. Chugay's office, and he felt the tension between them. He wondered how to break the ice with Toni, so he spoke the first words.

"I see our mutual friend was right about you," Kelly said lightly.

Toni was studying the file he took from Dr. Chugay's office. He knew Kelly probably got chewed out, or was given orders to take him to the airport or worse, baby sit him even more. His gut told him there was something wrong with the picture surrounding Bobby's death. It was the same feeling he got when he was on the chase of a good investigation. Bo had vouched for Kelly, so Toni decided to give him some latitude.

"Did you get chewed out?"

"It's none of your concern, Toni. I expected what happened up there," Kelly said.

"What do you mean?"

"Bo told me you don't hold back, and if you know something's wrong, you'll say it. I guess the surprise was when you got in the commander's face. He ordered me to baby sit you twenty-four hours a day."

Toni chuckled. "I don't trust that son-of-a-bitch. Something's not right here."

"Well, I haven't seen that file," Kelly replied. "Why don't you bring it to my house tonight? After dinner, we'll take a look at it."

It was just what Toni wanted to hear. "Bo was right about you, too. He said he trusted you and you were a stand-up guy. Why didn't you pull me off your boss, sooner?"

"Because, I wanted to see how the commander would react to your dispute

99

of his investigation."

"And what did his reaction tell you?" Toni asked.

"He's covering something up," Kelly kept his attention on the road.

"Yeah, I got that same feeling," Toni said quietly.

"No. I don't think you understand," Kelly said. "He knows something else. He cut you off too fast without hearing you out. He walked out. We can talk about it later."

They drove on through the city streets in silence, until Kelly interrupted. "Was it true about your brother's left hand?"

Toni looked at the driver. "Yes. Well, at least it was ten years ago," Toni replied.

"What do you mean, it was?"

Toni looked down at the file. "Bobby had a motorcycle accident twelve years ago. His wife was killed. He lost the use of his left hand. He rehabbed it and regained some use of his thumb, pinky, and a little bit of the fourth finger, but not the index and middle fingers. Bobby was a mechanic and I knew he still worked on cars. It's possible he could have regained some use of his fingers, but I doubt it."

"Interesting," Kelly replied. "I noticed once, your brother never took anything in his left hand. In fact, I remember thinking it was strange, because I saw him smoke a cigarette with his right hand, put it down, then pick up a glass of water. And I thought; why not just take the glass in his left hand. That's why God gave us two hands."

Toni didn't know what to think about Kelly's story. He'd seen the same thing after Bobby's accident. "Yeah, and why not use his good hand to shoot himself," he said, then his eyes widened as a large gray church came into view. "Wow! That's a building," Toni said pointing to the neo-gothic twin towered structure.

"That's our next stop," Kelly said. "The *Basilique deNotre-Dame*. This is the epicenter of the city's old town. It is beautiful?"

"Reminds me of Europe," Toni responded. "This is where Bobby lived?"

"Not exactly. He lived at the seminary next door. You are Catholic, are you not?"

"Yes, I am," Toni answered.

"The seminary is the oldest building standing in Montreal today," Kelly said. "The gardens are beautiful. Your brother helped keep them."

"Saint Sulpice," Toni mumbled.

"You are aware of the history?" Kelly replied.

FIERCE LOYALTY

"I did some reading last night. The Sulpician seminarians came from Paris and took charge of the parish around 1663 or 1664, I believe," Toni answered. "It was the goal of Jerome Le Royer de la Dauversiere to found the mission here in Montreal, or Ville-Marie as it was known. The Basilica Notre-Dame was finished in 1829. Interestingly, the Sulpicians chose a guy named James O'Donnell, a protestant, an architect living in New York, and he designed the building. He later converted to Catholicism so he could be buried beneath the church. The organ in the basilica is a Cassavant that dates back to 1891 if my memory holds true. Shall I continue?" Toni looked in awe at the huge Church.

"Well. That was impressive. You know your history."

"I'm a religious history buff," Toni replied. "My wife called it an obsession, but I learned a long time ago that to understand a society, including the criminal aspect, we have to know the history as well."

"I will think about that," Kelly replied, stopped, and parked behind the building.

"What is really interesting, Kelly is that throughout history, the crimes we see today have changed very little," Toni paused to see if Kelly was listening. "For example, there have always been homicides, even serial killers, all the way down to swindlers and frauds. History lesson's over. Can we go in?"

"Yes. Father Chason is waiting for us I'm sure," Kelly said, as they left the car. "Bo said nothing of this hobby of yours."

"Doesn't surprise me," Toni answered. "He hates to hear this shit from me. Makes him feel inferior."

19

Inside the Basilica hallways was like entering another world. The stone walls were five feet thick. Toni dragged his hand along the surface to feel the strength and texture endured for the past 200 hundred years. He and Primeau walked through a long, arched hallway, where the only illumination came from the scented candles. Every twenty feet or so were unmarked mahogany doors, no nameplates, nothing to reveal what was behind them, yet Kelly seemed to know where to go.

They turned left at an intersection only to find the same doors on the right and left sides, of the hallway. Toni saw a glowing light from the end of the hallway and reckoned it must lead outside, but guessed that if this was the original design, the clergy must have wanted it to look like they were entering heaven. As the light grew stronger, Toni saw that the corridor opened on a garden, the gardens he'd read about. They were larger than Toni had pictured, at least two football fields side by side, he thought. Manicured Italian ferns decorated the paths, marked with pink, red, and blue flowers sprinkled on the ground like lights. Toni detected the scent of roses, but he saw none in the vicinity.

Kelly broke the silence. "Can you smell them?"

"Roses?"

"Yes. The priests say the scent never leaves the grounds, even in the winter. I've never been here in the winter, but I have no reason to doubt it."

"The Virgin Mary," Toni said.

"Yes. They believe she is here to guide them in their work," Kelly replied.

"And what do you believe, my son?" asked a voice behind Kelly and Toni. They turned simultaneously, and Toni's eyes came to rest on a slight man

FIERCE LOYALTY

about 5'4" tall in a typical priest's black cassock. He looked to be in his sixties, hair graying on the sides, a matching beard and mustache, and bald on the top. His ice blue eyes were bloodshot.

"Father Chason. I wish you wouldn't sneak up on me like that," Kelly said smiling.

"You must be Toni," Father Chason said as he looked up at Toni, with a genuine smile.

"Yes, Father, I am," Toni replied.

"I'm sorry for your loss," Father Chason said, shaking Toni's hand.

"I appreciate that," Toni replied.

"You'll have to excuse me, Toni. I've known Kelly here since he was an alter boy almost thirty years ago. Since he became a police officer, I have taken it upon myself to outwit him, keep him on his toes. I don't want to see harm come to such a good man," Father Chason said.

Toni smiled. "Well, someone has to keep him on his toes. It's a pleasure meeting you, Father. I've heard good things about you."

"And I can say the same, my son," Father Chason replied. "Your brother spoke proudly of you. He was a good man. Why don't we walk in the gardens and talk? After all, your brother kept this garden for many years, as if it were his own." He turned to Kelly. "Why don't you wait for us in the church, Kelly. You'll have time to go to confession while Toni and I talk."

"I just went to confession two days ago, Father," Kelly replied, hurt by his dismissal from the conversation.

"Well, I'm sure you've sinned, since then," Chason responded. "Toni, this way," he said, pointing Toni away from the doors he walked through only moments earlier. He and Father Chason started down a path toward the opposite end of the gardens. Toni understood why his brother stayed here – peaceful, a place of reflection, exactly what Bobby needed.

"Do you smell it, Toni?" Father Chason asked.

"Yes. She's incredible, isn't she, Father," Toni replied.

"You believe then," Father Chason said, stopping momentarily to look up at Toni.

"I've had experiences that would make a believer out of most, no doubt," Toni answered.

"Yes indeed. Many have. You are a Marian then?"

"I'm Catholic, Father, no particular belief or sect. I believe Mary is present in the world today guiding us, or warning us of our shortcomings. But lately I've been having doubts."

103

SCOTT A. REZENDES

"Hmm. You and Bobby are . . ." Father Chason started, paused to clear his throat – "were a lot alike. I'd like to discuss that further with you some day."

"Sure, but we have other . . ." Toni started. Father Chason interrupted as if he hadn't even heard him.

"You know, I've been here forty-five years. When I first arrived, the gardens were as you see them. Not much has changed as far as the plant life, only the people who tend them." He looked around the gardens. "During my time here, we've never had roses in this garden. Not then. Not now. About eight years ago your brother came. He was desperate, had nowhere to go. I took him in and we conquered his evils, his drug and alcohol addiction. I invited him to stay as long as he wanted, but I told him he would have to work for his meals. He agreed. He really wanted change in his life, Toni, very badly."

They continued to walk, as Father Chason was silent for a moment as if trying to formulate his next words carefully.

"Bobby began to work in the garden to pass his time, probably more to take his mind off his troubles, but he was good at it. We decided that tending the garden would be his job." He paused again. "Do you see that statue over there?" he asked, pointing to a statue of the Virgin Mary holding the baby Jesus in her arms.

"Yes," Toni replied, after a few seconds.

"Shortly after Bobby got here, I found him lying before her, crying." Father Chason turned to Toni. "He was drunk, mumbling prayers. I walked over to him and that's when I smelled them the first time, the roses. The aroma was overwhelming and everywhere. It has not left since. Bobby recovered and never fell back again. Not once in the last seven or so years did he drink alcohol, except for the blood of Christ at communion. She never left him, Toni, and now she remains to protect Bobby's legacy here."

Father Chason showed Toni a bench near the statue. "Bobby sat here many days, staring at the grounds. He said that if anything ever happened to him, he wanted to be buried here. He never wanted to leave here. I want to fulfill his last wish. I'd like your family to let me bury Bobby here."

Father Chason's teary eyes pled, and now Toni understood why they were bloodshot. They had become friends and unlikely confidants. Toni wondered if Father Chason knew what really happened to Bobby. He thought of the note in his hotel room again and wondered if Chason was its author.

"Are you all right, Toni?" Chason asked.

FIERCE LOYALTY

"Yes, I'm fine," he replied. "Father, I believe we can accommodate you. My family would be honored to have Bobby buried here, but there is a problem."

"Problem?"

"Well . . ." Toni started.

"His wife," Father Chason interrupted. "Yes, Bobby spoke of her. Arrangements to bring her remains have already been made many months ago."

"What arrangements?"

"There is something you don't know. Bobby had lung cancer. We found out twelve or thirteen months ago. The doctor told him he had a fifty-percent chance of beating it. Bobby sat down with me and made out his will. We discussed everything. I have it with his belongings," Father Chason said.

Toni was taken aback. He sat on the bench and slumped over, putting his face in his hands, and Father Chason joined him. He wiped his eyes and straightened up. "Father, I think you've done as much for my brother as anyone has in his life. I'd like to pay you."

"Pay? Nonsense. I don't . . ." Chason replied harshly.

"A donation then," Toni said breaking in …"At least for the spot of land where Bobby and his wife will be buried."

"Well. A donation? I don't…"

"Father!" Toni insisted.

"Very well. Agreed. Bobby was right about you. Stubborn."

Toni chuckled. "Father, I need to ask you a few questions."

"About Bobby's death, no doubt?" Chason answered.

"How was Bobby acting the days before his death?"

"The police asked the same questions. Are you sure you want to talk about it?"

"I'm sure," Toni replied calmly.

"The truth is, Bobby had been acting a little funny for some time. He was beating the cancer, and the doctor told him if his treatment continued to be positive, he believed the cancer would go into remission. But Bobby looked tired. At first, I thought he wasn't beating the cancer, but I found out otherwise. Then I suspected he had been drinking, but he denied it. I believed him. We talked about his behavior a few weeks ago, and he assured me that he was fine. He just wasn't himself."

"Did you think he was suicidal?"

"Not then." He paused momentarily. "But after we found Bobby that morning and I started talking to the police . . . Well, he just wasn't his usual self, Toni. It went on for weeks."

"How were Bobby's left shoulder and hand feeling?"

"He had surgery three years ago here in Montreal," Father Chason replied, "and his shoulder was better. He lost most of the use of his left hand and fingers."

"Did you tell the police that?" Toni pressed.

"Yes. I told Commander Savage myself. I remember, because I wondered how Bobby could have shot himself with his left hand."

"Did Commander Savage say anything?" Toni asked, more interested.

"Well, in fact he did. He said when people want to kill themselves, they find ways to do it. He searched through Bobby's belongings, his room, very thoroughly, but took nothing. They seemed to be looking for something. I'm not sure what, though." He paused. "Commander Savage asked about Bobby's Bible, and I gave him the one on his desk. He just opened it up, then closed it and put it back. He gave no explanation."

"Bobby leave a note?" Toni pressed.

"No note was found to my knowledge, but Bobby loved to write," Father Chason responded. "He'd sit in the garden and write in his journal. He had several journal books and updated them daily. I'll take you to his room and I'll show you. He had them all in order, numbered, dated, everything. I think they'll give you insight into Bobby's life the last eight years." Father Chason took a square wrapped object from within his cassock. "I believe you'll want these. I found them as I was going through Bobby's belongings. They had your name written on them." He handed Toni the package. "I think he finally found peace, Toni, but the last several weeks, he just was different."

"When did the change start?"

"I don't know, Toni. Let me think. I'm old, as you can see, so the memory fades at times," he replied.

"Take your time, Father," Toni said.

"When were you shot, Toni?" Father Chason asked.

"It's been almost eight weeks. Why?"

"It started before that. It was a few weeks after our new priest arrived from France, Father Chigall. I remember the news about your shooting. He was concerned about you. Your father called to let him know you were okay, and he calmed down a little. Still, he was distant and he just looked tired, like he was staying up all night."

"My father called here?" Toni was surprised.

"Yes, he called every week," Father Chason replied casually, as if that

FIERCE LOYALTY

were a normal occurrence.

Toni was dumbfounded to learn his father knew Bobby was in Montreal. His father never said a word to him about it.

"Did Bobby tell you he called me the night before I was shot?" Toni asked.

"No," Father Chason said. "He wanted to go see you, but he couldn't take the chance of crossing into the U.S. He said there might be an arrest warrant out for him. He asked me to keep that to myself, and I have not told anyone."

"You're sure Bobby wasn't drinking any more? His blood alcohol was .21 Savage claimed."

"I'm positive, and I don't care what the toxicology report said. I spoke to Bobby at dinner the night before he died, and he wasn't drinking," Father Chason replied.

"Who found Bobby?"

"Father Chigall," he replied. "He was the first to open the basilica in the morning and it was his duty to ready the place for visitors."

"Did the police talk to Father Chigall?"

"Yes, I believe so," Father Chason answered. "Look, Toni, I realize you are suspicious of the circumstances surrounding Bobby's death. I am too, but sometimes we cannot understand everything."

"Okay, Father, I understand. Enough questions. Do you think I could talk to Father Chigall?"

"Yes, I'm sure he would not mind, but he is not here today. He is doing missionary work this week," Chason said. "Now, let me take you to Bobby's room."

"Father?" Toni ventured.

"Yes?"

"Did Bobby have any friends outside the church?"

"Bobby was a gifted mechanic," Father Chason said. "You know that. He helped parishioners all the time, especially the poor ones who didn't have the money to pay a mechanic. The short answer is, Bobby had many friends in this community. There was one man he did see outside the church, Frank Tavares. Bobby and Frank met in our alcohol treatment program. I believe they were close friends. Frank was here many times."

As Toni and Father Chason stood up from the bench – Toni saw a priest running toward them calling for Father Chason. Toni felt a knot in his stomach. The priest looked alarmed.

"Father Chason?" said the dark haired priest.

107

"What is wrong, Father Corvo?"

"Father, you have a phone call. It's an emergency. There's been an accident."

"An accident? What has happened?" Father Chason asked.

"A car accident," Father Corvo answered, out of breath. "A man named Frank Tavares. He's at the hospital. The doctors say he's not going to make it."

"Frank Tavares?" Father Chason looked at Toni. "Oh, my God, I must go, Toni."

"I'm coming with you, Father," Toni responded.

"Toni, there is nothing for you to do," Father Chason said.

"This the same Frank Tavares?" Toni asked.

"Yes, Toni, I only know one man by that name."

"Then I'm going with you," Toni said, raising his hand to stop the argument he knew would come.

Toni thought Chason wanted to say something else, but he turned and walked away at a surprising speed. Toni followed him with his eyes. He could swear Father Chason was gliding above the ground.

20

The journey to the hospital was fast. Whether Toni was going to the hospital became a non-issue when he and Father Chason learned at the basilica that Kelly Primeau also heard the call. Commander Savage told him to drive Father Chason to the hospital as fast as possible. And since Kelly was assigned to watch Toni, he would come along anyway. At the hospital an emergency room nurse informed them that Frank Tavares had been in a one-car accident. He hit a telephone pole driving home and was thrown from the car. He was in critical condition. The nurse took Father Chason to the room where Frank Tavares hung onto life.

Kelly saw a policeman he knew and went over to talk to him. Toni sat in a waiting room, staring at the wall, wondering whether the accident was a coincidence or bad luck. Toni wanted to talk with Tavares, since he probably knew more about Bobby than anyone else. To add to the mystery, Savage's investigative report did not mention Tavares at all. He hadn't interviewed Bobby's best friend. Kelly came back and sat next to Toni.

"Well? What did the traffic guy have to say?" Toni asked.

"Unfortunately not much," Kelly replied, "but he did say Savage put an immediate gag order on this. No press, and worst of all, the scene was closed to everyone. He said Savage was on the scene within minutes, and most of the traffic division was ordered to keep everyone back. Savage and his crony were the only ones allowed at the crash scene."

"I don't like it," Toni said.

"I don't either."

"What's going on, Kelly?" Toni asked. "People are dropping like flies.

First my brother, now his best friend. Did you know Frank Tavares?"

"Yes," Kelly said, "and his wife and three children. He is a good man. They are very active in the church. His poor wife!"

"I have to talk to her," Toni blurted.

"Let's give her some time and see what happens with Frank," Kelly responded.

"You're right. Can we go back to the seminary? I'd like to go through Bobby's stuff. Father Chason said Bobby kept journals. I'd like to read through them. Maybe there's a clue about what's going on."

"It's three o'clock. The trooper said the accident was close to Frank's home. We can drive by the scene and see what's going on. I'm sure it's cleaned up by now, but you never know. There's nothing for us to do here except wait, so let's go," Kelly said.

As they walked through the waiting room door into the hallway, Toni spotted Father Chason emerging from behind a door, looking glum.

"Father Chason?" Kelly whispered.

Father Chason turned to see Kelly and Toni. He shook his head back and forth.

"I'm going to the chapel. You two boys will come to pray with me?"

"Frank's dead?" Toni asked.

"Not yet. The doctor says he's stable enough for surgery. Without it, he has little hope Frank will make it through the night."

"How's Belinda?" Kelly asked.

"She's not well," Father Chason replied. "She wants to talk to you Toni. Bobby and Frank were close, and she said something about them being in some sort of trouble. She's coming out soon. Frank is going into surgery. I'm off to the chapel." He turned to walk away.

Toni watched the small man in his black cassock shuffling down the gleaming hallway. He squinted; a bright light hit his eyes. He saw a bright multi-colored aura surrounding Father Chason, reflecting off the walls, as brightly as the sun in its morning glory.

21

Belinda Tavares was in her forties, small, with dark, smooth skin, and brown eyes that showed the stress. Her puffy eyes screamed desperation from her face, and Toni thought that fifteen years earlier she was probably a very pretty woman. She spoke broken English with a soft fluency and a slight accent. Toni noticed her hands were delicate, with manicured fingernails colored dark, bold red. She was a secretary at the Johnny Blue Jean Clothing Company, headquartered in Montreal. Now her life was turned upside down. She was a mess; was all Toni could think of as he watched her dab each eye with a tissue. She came out of the ICU as the hospital technicians wheeled her husband to surgery. She recognized Kelly and smiled courteously. She followed her husband to the end of the hallway, but stopped short at the swinging doors.

She returned to where Toni and Kelly were standing. "You are Toni? Bobby's brother, no?"

"Yes," Toni replied. "Father Chason said you wanted to talk to me?"

"That is correct," she said. "Kelly, you too, please."

They walked back to the waiting room, with its old fashion furnishings and dimly lit interior, and found it empty. Kelly closed the door and sat down next to Toni. Belinda's face was covered in tears, and Toni wondered how much she had already cried.

"Belinda," Kelly started, "we can come back tomorrow."

"No. No, please now is good time," she interrupted. "It will help take my thoughts off Frankie," she said, wiping away more tears. She turned to Toni. "I know your brother very well. He helped my husband get better from the

111

booze. After Bobby died, Frankie was really nervous and upset. I don't know why, but he was short with me, the way he was when he drank. But he was not drinking. I ask him, 'What is wrong Frankie?' and he just say nothing and walked away."

"When was that, Ms. Tavares?" Toni asked.

"Just two days ago, he was like that. I knew he was upset about Bobby. He went to the garage, I think to be by himself, but then he came right back in, holding a package, and he say, 'If anything happen to me, take this package to Toni Brazil,' and he gave me a book wrapped in a brown paper bag."

"What kind of book?" Toni asked.

"It was a Bible," she began, "but it had a hole inside it. At first, I don't even notice, but when I go through it, I see that a hole is in it."

"A hole?" Kelly asked.

"Yes, a hole," she repeated, "and the book was very cold."

"Was anything inside the hole, Belinda?" Toni asked

"There was a small box inside with writing on it. I don't know the writing. It was funny, backward letters," Belinda said.

"Backward letters?" Kelly asked.

"Where's the book now?" Toni interrupted.

"Frankie took it back to the garage. We have a freezer. He put it in there," she answered Toni.

"Did Frank tell you what was inside that little box?" Kelly asked.

She shook her head and said, "He just say it is dangerous and not to touch it or tell anybody about it. Toni and Kelly looked at each other in confusion.

Toni asked the next question. "Have you been home yet, today?"

"No. I came here from work."

"Has anybody been at home today?" Kelly followed.

"Just Frankie. He works the night shift. The kids go to my mother's, after school." She cocked her head. "Why you ask?"

"Belinda, may Kelly and I go to your house and get the book?" Toni asked, excitedly.

"Frankie wanted you to have it if anything happen to him," she sighed. "And now something happen to him" she said starting to cry. "Leave the key in the flower pot by the door." She dug into her purse and took out a lone key.

"Thank you," Toni said. "I'm really sorry about Frank. He's going to make it. I know it."

Belinda Tavares sat with her hands in her face. Toni stood momentarily at the door to look back at her, but felt powerless to help her, just as he felt now

FIERCE LOYALTY

about Bobby. He turned away to find Kelly waiting in the hallway.

Things were about to change, Toni thought. He didn't believe in coincidences, first Bobby, then his best friend. More was going on here than met the eye, and one man kept popping up everywhere bad things happened – Commander Alexander Savage.

22

At almost 5:00 P.M. Toni and Kelly left the hospital to drive to Frank and Belinda Tavares's house. There was still light outside, and the traffic slowed them as they drove through the city streets. The weather had turned sour, and rain clouds filled the sky. The lightening gave a nice show to the dwindling light of day. The rumble and crack of thunder drowned other sounds, and the rain came pounding on the man made objects all around. The bad news was anything left at the accident scene would be washed away for no one to find.

Toni knew that people smuggled drugs into the United States in whatever hiding places they could conjure up. A book with a hole cut in it was a favorite before drug-sniffing dogs found them. He wondered what Belinda meant by the backward letters. A Bible with a hole cut into it, a small box with backward letters on it, dangerous, and must be kept in a freezer?

"A penny for your thoughts," Kelly said.

"I have none Kelly. I can't fathom what's going on here. I was just trying to recall everything Belinda told us."

"Yeah, me too. I'm no expert, Toni, but we need to consider what has to be kept frozen. You have any ideas?"

"Frozen box with backward letters inside a book," Toni said. "If I had to guess, I'd say drugs? But what kind of drugs need to be frozen?" Toni paused, "Could freezing cocaine make it odorless?"

"I don't know about that, but I think it has to be drugs of some type," Kelly replied. "I think we have to consider other things too, like why was Savage at the scene? How did he get there so fast? The traffic guy told me Savage was on the scene within minutes, and his office is across town."

FIERCE LOYALTY

"I hate to say this, Kelly" Toni said, "but Savage is involved. Somehow."

"I think we have to consider that possibility," Kelly answered. "And if you think it offends me, you're wrong. What offends me is that he may be a dirty cop."

"Is there anybody we could talk to about Savage?" Toni asked. "Who's his crony?"

"His crony is a guy named Jacques," Kelly responded. "He's the one we should talk to. The little shit's been in trouble before."

"What kind of trouble?"

"A long time ago, when he first came onto the police force, a citizen complained that he was extorting money for protection in his sector. The complainant later recanted, and the charges were dropped. He was transferred to Immigration where he has worked under Savage for the last ten years. Savage brought him over to act as his assistant."

"Can we talk to your Internal Affairs people and get his file?" Toni asked.

"I'll have it by tonight. Someone owes me over in the IA Unit."

At 5:50 P.M., Kelly pulled the car to the curb.

"What's up?" Toni asked. Kelly was looking directly across the street.

"That's the accident scene," Kelly said, pointing to a steel light pole across the street, "and there's Frank and Belinda's house."

"What?" Toni exclaimed, "So what'd he do, floor the gas as he returned from running his errands and crashed into the light pole, a hundred yards from his front door?"

"I don't know? Jean said Frank was returning from the post office. So he must have driven past his driveway too fast, lost control, and hit the pole." Kelly theorized out loud.

"Jean say if there were any witnesses?"

"He said, Savage and Jacques were going to canvass the neighborhood, after they finished with the scene," Kelly answered.

"Can we get our hands on the accident report?"

"Depends," Kelly answered, "whether the report is finished. They have forty-eight hours."

"We can't wait that long," Toni said. "Frank's car, where would it be towed?"

"The impound yard at police headquarters," Kelly replied. "We can look at it tonight, before the evidence guys pull it apart tomorrow."

"Why would Savage investigate an accident like this?"

"If it causes a death, it automatically goes to Savage's division. When

115

SCOTT A. REZENDES

there are just injuries, it stays with Traffic."

"So, why is Savage doing the investigation?" Toni asked. "Covering up something, no doubt."

"Or, fixing a problem for someone?" Kelly suggested.

"Savage takes my brothers death case out of nowhere. Why? Then, three days later, he shows up to perform an injury traffic accident investigation of Bobby's best friend. Coincidence?"

"It's no coincidence, Toni," Kelly began, "but it may be premature to think Savage is covering something up. Maybe the mayor asked him to look into something we don't know about. Any other ideas?"

"You could be right," Toni consented, the air taken out of him by Kelly's thinking. "But, the way he acted at our meeting this morning . . . a box with backward writing . . . Bobby committing suicide . . . his best friend half dead in the hospital, and the commander doing investigations he's not trained for. It just doesn't add up." Toni paused. "Suppose Bobby and Frank found something. You said Savage and his crony, Jacques, came over from Immigration and Customs. What exactly did they do there?"

"What does your customs office do?" Kelly responded. "They worked at the airport dealing with customs issues. Well, well, well . . ." Kelly said, as if light went off inside his head, and then the same thing hit Toni.

"The Bible with a hole in it . . ." Toni said. "Savage ran the show at the Montreal airport customs division, didn't he?"

"You must have read my mind," Kelly replied. "Someone is smuggling something into Canada."

"But what? A dangerous box, with backward writing. What kind of language has that writing?" Toni asked.

"I'm not a linguist," Kelly said, "but, if we could find the box in the house."

"What did Bobby and Frank get themselves into?" Toni thought out loud.

"People stumble onto things, Toni. It's common," Kelly said.

"What do you mean?"

"I investigate homicides." Kelly paused. "Husbands, wives, friends, they stumble onto secret affairs, hidden assets, illegal activities, you name it. And they get killed for it, too. It happens."

"So Bobby and Frank stumble onto some smuggling ring, and now one is dead, and the other is hanging onto life by a thread. Is that your theory?"

"I don't know, Toni. I'm just thinking outside the box, as you Americans put it."

"Let's say Bobby stumbled onto a drug smuggling ring. How? He's at the

116

FIERCE LOYALTY

church tending to a garden."

"Yes, and the smuggling device is a Bible," Kelly answered. "Someone at the church is involved."

"Father Chason told me a young priest . . ." Toni started.

"Father Chigall," Kelly interrupted. "He's French, and I know that French doesn't use backward letters."

"He arrived just eight weeks ago," Toni observed.

"What are you saying?" Kelly peered at Toni. "That priests are smuggling drugs into Canada? I know I said I was thinking outside the box, but you Americans take it to a new level!"

"Far-fetched," Toni said. "I know, but Father Chason said Bobby began acting strangely, about eight weeks ago, just after Chigall arrived. Didn't four or five more priests arrive a few weeks, after Chigall?" Toni looked at Kelly for a reaction, but Kelly only smiled and nodded, looking straight ahead.

Kelly realized Toni was probably right. Something strange was happening at the basilica. He recalled Jeffrey Bodakis had told him that smallpox was being smuggled into Canada from somewhere. The Royal Canadian Internal Security Unit had asked him to assist them, with an investigation of Alexander Savage, which included allegations of taking payoffs to let drugs into the country.

Kelly wondered if the two matters were connected. There was no other explanation. Savage had something to do with what he believed was the murder of Bobby Brazil and the smuggling of a virus, one that could kill many people.

117

23

There was silence in the car. Toni wondered what Kelly was thinking about. They had been doing what investigators do best, throwing theories and ideas around to identify leads to pursue. His last idea caused a reaction in Kelly, and he wondered whether his new partner was telling the whole truth. His gut told him he was holding something back.

Toni felt a bit out of his league because of the type of crime: murder. Like his last case, Villegas, he didn't have a clue the man was smuggling drugs from Mexico. It almost got him and two other agents killed. Kelly seemed trustworthy, but not a lot of help. This was his territory, homicide. He should be leading the way. Maybe his hands were tied. Bo trusted him, so he must be okay. Toni saw Kelly's facial expression change.

"Look, that's Commander Savage's car parked up the street," Kelly said. "He and Jacques must be around here some place. Why don't you go into the house and find the package, and I'll look for Savage and Jacques. See what they're up to."

"Sounds like a plan. Let's get going," Toni said.

Rain was falling, but Toni didn't seem to be aware of it as he eyed the Tavares house, a three story brown brick building. The garage was for one car. Toni knew his search would start on the second floor, where he believed the kitchen would be, and then go down into the garage and basement.

"I'll meet you back here in twenty minutes, Kelly. This shouldn't take too long," Toni said.

"Twenty minutes it is then. Be careful."

They walked across the street together, and Toni stopped momentarily to watch Kelly stroll casually down the street, stopping briefly to look into Savage's

118

car. He shook his head 'No', signaling that no one was in the car. Savage and Jacques were out there somewhere, maybe even watching them.

Toni walked up the steps to the front door. He took the key chain Belinda Tavares had given to him from his pocket. He put the key into the lock and snapped it around counter-clockwise. He heard the lock click and snap. Turning the knob, he entered a dark entryway. He closed the door. No light came from anywhere. His eyes had yet to adjust to the dark. Remembering he had a small flashlight on his key ring, Toni reached into his jacket pocket again and pulled out the small object. He squeezed the handle and a small but concentrated beam lit the wall. He pointed it in all directions until he found the light switch next to the heavy front door.

He flipped the switch. A light came on high above, illuminating the elegantly decorated entryway, which led to the living room. As Toni walked forward, he saw an opening to his left that opened into the kitchen. To his right he saw the staircase to the third floor, where he would find the bedrooms. No reason to go up. Toni took a couple of steps backward and went into the kitchen. A window at the far end of the dining area let some light into the kitchen eating area. Toni's eyes started to become acclimated, and he saw a door to his left and reckoned it was the door down to the garage. It was ajar. Toni wondered why someone had not closed the door fully. Was Frank in a hurry? Or just careless?

Toni clicked the tiny pin light as he opened the door enough to see the stairway down into the garage. He pointed the flashlight through the door and downward. The stairs made a 90-degree zigzag. He found a light switch next to the door, and he flicked it. A light came on in the garage. He bent down and peered into the illuminated empty garage. He went halfway down the stairs, then turned in the opposite direction as he continued downward to the bottom. He stopped and turned slowly, looking for the freezer Belinda Tavares had described, but found nothing. He walked toward the garage door, but again nothing looked like a freezer. He saw a door against the back wall with a blacked out window. Another door in the far left was covered with a blind, but a small amount of light seeped through. That was the door to the back yard, he thought, which led him back to the other door.

"Why black out the windows?" He walked toward the door, and then stopped. He heard something move upstairs, as if someone were in the house. He thought of Kelly, but they agreed to meet at the car in twenty minutes. Barely five minutes had past. He approached the door again, but heard a slam. The door upstairs closed, and the lights went off. He heard something.

Suddenly, 'Slam', something hit him on the head, and knocked him to the ground.

Falling backward, Toni's head hit hard on the cement floor. Pain vibrated through his skull. He brought his arms around his face as tight as possible, keeping his elbows low, his knees coming up to his chest to protect himself from further attack. He heard a pounding on the stairs, then another slam, a door closing. He felt dizzy. No attack came, so he began to relax, but a strange fleeting blackness swept over him like a cloud. He felt a rush on his face as if G-forces were slamming him against a seat. A bright flash went off in his eyes. He couldn't move. Consciousness slowly dissolved.

24

"Toni? Toni?"

Toni's head was foggy. A hard throb hit him when he tried to lift his head. "Where am I?" In the dark he heard his name called again.

"Toni!"

A door opened and light came into the room. The glare hurt his eyes. He squinted at the stairs and remembered where he was. "Belinda Tavares," he mumbled. Someone ran down the wooden stairs and the voice came again.

"Toni! What the hell happened?" asked an alarmed Kelly Primeau.

He opened his eyes and saw a dark figure approach him. He tried to get up, but immediately got dizzy.

"Are you okay?" Kelly asked, kneeling next to him where he lay.

Toni hadn't spoken a word yet. He reached up, feeling for something to hold on to, but found nothing.

"If I could sit up. Just help me, Kelly."

"Sit tight, Toni. Your head's bleeding. I'm calling an ambulance," Kelly said.

"No. No. Don't," Toni replied, "I'll be fine."

His forehead was wet. Toni pushed himself off the cement floor with his elbows. His eyes stung with his own blood. He wiped his face and eyes with his shirttail, while feeling for the wall. He twisted his body against the wall and sat up. His hand felt the large knot on his forehead. He figured he had a concussion.

"How long have you been waiting, Kelly?"

"Do you remember coming here with me, Toni?" Kelly asked.

"Yes," Toni said, squinting his eyes in pain. "You went to find your two compadres, and I came in the house to look for the box Belinda described. Did you find Savage?"

"Yes," Kelly said. "In fact they were finishing an interview a block down the street. We talked about the accident. Savage said he was considering what you said earlier, and they decided to talk to Frank Tavares about Bobby. They were on the way here, when the accident call came in. They were two minutes away, so they got there first. I called dispatch to check their story. It checked out," Kelly said, looking concerned. "They called in that they were on the way here a couple of minutes before the accident call came in. Savage said there was one witness, but she only saw Frank Tavares speeding down the street, and hitting the pole without breaking. After I talked to Savage, he and Jacques took off. I went back to the car and waited. I thought I'd give you a few extra minutes before I came to get you. I waited and waited. It's been about thirty minutes since we parted ways."

"Thirty minutes?" Toni responded, taking in the information the best he could. "Did you tell them anything?"

"Like what, Toni?"

"Never mind," Toni said. "I've been here that long? Let's see. I looked around the house a little, and then came down here. Looked around some more, found nothing. Then I saw the door with the blackened glass. That's all I remember."

"What else?" Kelly prodded.

"What do you mean?" Toni asked, sullenly.

"The look on your face tells me there's something else, that's all," Kelly said.

Toni felt dizzy, but he wanted to stand up. He didn't want Kelly to send him to the hospital. His head hurt, and he needed something for the pain.

"Can you stand?"

"No. But if you give me a hand, I think I can get back to the car," Toni said.

Kelly took Toni's right arm and pulled him to his feet. Dizzy, and sick to his stomach, Toni brought his hand up to his face.

"Kelly, don't take this wrong," Toni said, "but I think I've had it for the day. Can we have dinner tomorrow?"

"I think you should go to the hospital, Toni," Kelly said, looking closer at Toni's head. "That bump looks pretty bad. You might have a concussion."

"I know." Toni paused. "But I don't want to go to the hospital." He clenched his eyes shut as pain shot through his temple like a lightning bolt. He opened

FIERCE LOYALTY

and closed his eyes until the double vision subsided, but everything seemed unsteady, not fixed. He leaned against a wall for support.

"Stay here Toni, and don't move," Kelly said, as he walked over to the door that was now open.

Kelly found a large white chest freezer against the wall. He opened it and peered in. He put his right arm inside, looking at something. Toni tried to walk to Kelly, stumbling like a drunk. The room spun from one side to the other, but he wanted to see what Kelly was looking at.

"Well," Kelly said, "they have some nice steaks in here but nothing else – and no frozen book."

Toni looked around the room and found a towel, a sink, and some aspirin. He turned the spigot and spilled four pills into his palm, shoved them in his mouth, and washed them down with a handful of water. He soaked the towel in water and wiped the dried blood off his face. He found a second knot on the back of his head and found more dried blood. He walked back over to where Kelly stood, and stared into the freezer.

"I'd feel ten times better if I could somehow blame your boss Savage and his partner, for this headache of mine," he now said, "but if they were with you, then who was in here to hit me on the head?"

"I watched them leave, Toni. They went the opposite direction, unless they doubled back. But this room is accessible only from inside the house. They couldn't have done it."

"There were two of them," Toni said.

"Two of who?"

"I remember the floor creaking upstairs, then boom, lights went out and so did I. They hit me fast and hard," Toni said, as his vision cleared.

"How'd they get out? No one came from the house through the front. There must be a back way out."

"Let's get out of here," Toni said, flinching in pain.

"Can you even walk?"

"I can take care of myself. I'm feeling a little better," Toni said. He was lying.

"Let me give you a hand up the stairs then." Kelly knew Toni was not telling the truth, but Bo said Toni was as tough as they come.

"I'm fine, Kelly. You go first, I'll follow," Toni answered. "Let's just go."

Kelly made his way up the stairs, and Toni followed, stopping momentarily half way up to gather himself. Upstairs, they went through the kitchen into the dining and living room, where the French double doors leading to a deck were open. Someone had left in a hurry.

Toni looked around the room. The chairs had been moved, and something caught his eye under one of them. He leaned down and picked up a business card. He turned the card over and read, "Alexander Savage." Kelly came over to see, and Toni handed him the card. Savage had been in the house, but the question was, when? The evidence mounting against Savage led only to more questions.

Toni went through the French doors onto the deck. The gate, left open, creaked back and forth in the wind. He saw the stairs that led down to the partially fenced back yard. Beyond the yard was an alley with parking. There was no doubt in Toni's mind that the person responsible for his headache escaped that way. He waved Kelly over and pointed beyond the fence to a rectangular dry patch on the wet pavement where someone had parked recently. He rubbed his face and cheeks between his hands, wondering if whoever hit him were a new player. But who? And why hadn't they killed him?

Toni noticed the humidity of the rain had departed and there was coolness in the air. Toni and Kelly said nothing to each other. They stood looking out from the deck. The wind whipped up into Toni's face, and he could feel it brushing through his short-cropped hair. He concentrated on the same invisible force hitting his face, its destination blocked, and he knew he had changed forever the direction of the wind.

Things were starting to make sense to Toni. He knew Savage was involved in Bobby's death and Frank Tavares' accident. Whatever the reason, he'd repay Savage the favor, no matter the cost.

25

Light from the hallway shone through the door briefly, illuminating the hotel room, but Toni's hands were full, and the door slipped from his hands and slammed shut. Pain vibrated through his skull. Kelly dropped him off moments earlier, and he came straight to his room holding the small briefcase with his personal belongings in one hand, and a bloodied shirt in the other. The briefcase was heavy as it held his nine-millimeter protection he brought to Montreal, and the package from Father Chason.

The room was dark, but with his head hurting from the pounding he took at the Tavares house, he didn't mind. His eyes were still sensitive to light. Toni reached along the wall to find a light switch. Suddenly a light came on behind him, making him jump. Everything in his hands flew away. He brought his arms up in front, expecting an attack, but instead saw a man sitting in the desk chair across the room.

"What the hell?" Toni yelled at the man who peered at him from across the room. "Who the fuck are you?"

The man wore a black suit with a white collar. Black hair with gray streaking gave way to a gruesome scar on the upper neck. He looked familiar.

"Maybe I should be asking you that question?" the man said in a thick Irish brogue, "but it is not necessary, because of course this is your room and I know who you are, Mr. Brazil." The man smiled at Toni.

"Look, I don't know what you want, mister?" Toni said aggressively. "You apparently have the wrong room."

"I don't have the wrong room, Agent Brazil," the man interrupted Toni. "Why don't you sit down, so we can talk."

"I think you need to tell me who you are," Toni said angrily. His head shook in pain as if his brain were loose and bouncing around inside.

"Are you all right?" the man continued comfortably. "You have a rather large bump on your head. And that shirt you threw at me is red with blood?"

"How do I know you're not the one who gave it to me?" Toni asked, confidently. "Now who are you and how do you know my name?"

"I'd be glad to tell you who I am, but please sit down. I'm not here to harm you."

Toni looked at the man siting in the chair. His hands were empty. He had no weapon he could see. Toni thought he recognized him, but couldn't place him. Should he leave the room? Should he get the weapon he brought just inside his bag? Had the Colombians hired an IRA assassin to take him out for killing the Contreras brothers?

"Why don't I just stand here while you tell me who you are? You look familiar to me. How do I know you?" Toni asked. "Are you a priest?"

"As I said, I'm not here to harm you. Please sit, and I'll explain. I promise. Do priests lie?"

Do priests lie? Toni thought. Considering the scenario he and Kelly developed about Father Chigall, he wasn't sure what to think about priests. The double doors leading to the bedroom were open, and he saw no one there, but he couldn't be sure no one else was in the suite. He looked into the bathroom and saw a man standing there, then realized it was his own reflection.

"Please, Toni, you can trust me," the man said. "Gino, you can come out." Another man stepped from behind a wall in the bathroom, also dressed in black with a priestly collar.

"All right, that's it," Toni said. He bent down to open his bag and retrieve his weapon. "I don't know who you guys are, but if you move . . . " He rummaged through his briefcase, his eyes on the second man. Then recognition hit him.

"I know you, don't I?" Toni said to the second man. "I met you today at the basilica."

"Gino, please come into the room," the first man said. The second man disappeared behind the wall, and came through the bedroom instead of walking straight at Toni from the bathroom.

Toni held the gun firmly pointing it away from the two men. Gino, whom he met earlier as Father Corvo, had nothing in his hands. Father Corvo sat on the couch, and Toni looked back at the man at the desk chair, across the room.

"Any one else I should know about?" Toni asked sarcastically. Both men

FIERCE LOYALTY

shook their heads 'No'.

Toni continued to stand holding his weapon safely downward. He was in control. He glared at the two men. "Well?"

"You can put that thing away, please," Gino said. Toni put the weapon gently in his belt holster.

Gino held his hand out to shake Toni's. "I'm Father Giovanni Corvo. You remember me?" They shook hands. "We have some business to discuss with you."

"Business?" Toni said. Then it hit him. He recognized the man behind the desk. He decided to be calm and see what developed. Something in Father Corvo's handshake made him feel they weren't here to kill him.

"What kind of business?" Toni asked, then slowly and carefully sat down, without taking his eyes off the two men.

"Thank you for sitting down," said the unknown man. "We have some important business to . . . "

"I know who you are!" Toni interrupted the man. "You're supposed to be dead!"

26

He sat alone in the parking lot watching the room from his car. He'd arranged for the room, making sure it could be closely observed. His underling dropped Toni Brazil and drove away quickly without much conversation. Primeau wasn't making any friends, which he noted, and decided Primeau might be trustworthy, but still needed to be watched. He sent his long time partner, Detective Grade Four Richard Jacques to follow Primeau and see where he went. He didn't want anybody snooping around his work. Too many things could go wrong, if he didn't pay attention.

He looked at his watch. Just past 9:00 P.M., "Jacques should be calling. Where is he?" he said out loud to himself. He sat alone in the car. He was anxious, waiting for Jacques to call. His leg twitched nervously, automatically. He felt his body shutting down, energy dropping, consciousness almost a sleep state. He began to sweat. Time for a jump-start. He took a deep breath to check his nostrils. Just a matter of time, he thought, before his nasal passages collapsed. He would never shoot the drug. He hated needles and could never bring himself to use one.

He reached over to the glove compartment and took out what looked to be a day planner, unzipped it, and opened it folding it outward like a small binder. On the left was a small mirror, on the right, a razor blade, plastic straw, and a small jar with a black screw top lid with a tiny spoon attached. He looked up momentarily to peer around the parking lot. He gazed up at the hotel structure and saw an illuminated glow coming from Toni Brazil's room. He could see a shadow of someone sitting near the window.

His hand shook as he held the small spoon. Sweat crawled down his forehead like an insect walking on his skin. He dug into the tiny jar, and moved the spoon filled with white powder slowly to his face. He wanted it with all his life, as if he

FIERCE LOYALTY

were in love. Nothing mattered to him but getting that pile to his nose.

The cell phone chirped. Savage jumped in his seat and dropped the spoon. He shuddered, tossing powder into the air. "Ah, fuck!" he yelled, fumbling for the phone.

"What?" he yelled into the phone.

"Savage? It's Jacques," said the voice on the other end.

"Jacques! Where the hell have you been? I've been waiting for . . ."

"Yes. Is everything . . ." Jacques started.

"No!" Savage yelled. "Where's Primeau?"

"He's at home," Jacques said meekly. "Is everything all right, sir?"

"What took you so long, Jacques?"

"I waited at the house to make sure he didn't go anywhere," he answered. "I'm sorry, sir."

"Fuck off, Richard!" Savage said. "Get your ass back here now. I need to do some other business." He flipped the phone shut.

He threw the phone down to the floor, and searched frantically for his jar. He looked down to his lap and felt a rush hit his body, as he spotted the jar in the day planner nestled on his lap. He took a deep breath and then let out a sigh of relief. There was enough cocaine in it for him to use now, but once he finished the pile, he was out and would have to get more soon. He quickly plunged the spoon in the jar scooping out the powder. He brought it to his nose and sniffed upward forcing the substance into his nasal passages. He exhaled out of his mouth, and drove the spoon back into the jar for a second time. He repeated the activity, until the jar was empty.

Savage sat back relaxed, smiling; beginning to chuckle to himself, feeling the kick of the Peruvian substance he'd taken off a smuggler, just two weeks before. He remembered the delight of the moment when he seized the substance from the idiot who tried to bring it through, in his clothes bag. He started to laugh aloud. He felt giddy, ready for anything. The power that came with the nose candy was incredible. No wonder he was addicted. Nothing could stop him when he was using cocaine – which was constantly.

Savage took a deep breath again, and looked up at Brazil's window. "You just mind your own business now, and this will all be over in a few days," he said, feeling invincible. He thought of Gideon, a man he'd never met, but made a deal with anyway. Gideon would make him rich. He could almost feel the money tickling his fingertips. Savage smiled, then shook in his seat as he thought about the future. "Soon. Just be patient," he whispered. "It's almost over now."

129

27

"Indeed. Obviously I am alive. You, as well, at the doorstep, Toni," the man said.

"Father John?" Toni started, but was interrupted.

"O'Brien," the unknown man said. "Yes. That's who I was. Who I am now is what matters."

"And who would that be?" Toni said, observing the pock marks reminiscent of stitches on the left side of Father O'Brien's neck, just above his collar.

"My name hasn't changed. Call me Father John. You've met Gino," he said, motioning to Gino.

"I followed your story on TV," Toni said. "It was sad to see a priest killed in Venice. It's a great city. Something that interests me, Father, is why are you alive while the world thinks your dead?"

"It's a long story," John answered, "one I can't tell right now. Let's just say I was lucky. Father Corvo here saved my life."

"Why have you two . . . Wait . . . How . . ." Toni stuttered.

"Too many questions will catch your tongue, Toni," John said smiling. "I know what you want to know. Why are we here? How did we get in? And since when do priests break into hotel rooms? Does that sum it up?"

"Well, it just about does, Father. How do you know my name? How'd you know what room I'd be in? Jesus Christ! How'd you even know I'd be here?" Toni asked.

"Toni, language please!"

"Sorry, but I've had a rough day," Toni said. "Someone took a pretty good shot at me, gave me this lump on my head, which is killing me, and you may be the one who put it there." He paused and caught his breath. "Then, I

FIERCE LOYALTY

found out my brother was murdered, and the police believe it was suicide. Something is going on here, I don't understand yet. I feel like shit and I'm hungry. Then you two show up, uninvited, scare the hell out of me, and I know you're priests, but I don't need you telling me what language to use, for God's sake! This is my room you're in, and, you broke in it! Now, you can answer some of my questions first, or get the hell out!"

"Okay, Toni, no problem. Calm down. Gino, why don't you order Toni some food, and get us all some coffee," John suggested.

"Coffee?" Toni said sarcastically. "Are you nuts? Gino, get me three beers. Heineken is fine. And I want pasta with chicken. If you guys want coffee, that's fine."

Father O'Brien nodded to Gino, who picked up the phone and ordered the meal Toni requested, except the coffee. "Forget the coffee," John said to Gino. "Have them bring a six pack."

"All right, then," John said with a sigh. "I'll answer any question you want."

"Well, first of all . . ." Toni started.

"We picked the lock. Neither one of us put the lump on your head, and we knew you'd be here because Detective Kelly Primeau told us."

"What? Kelly told you?"

"Not directly. He told Father Chason, who told us," John clarified.

"Where'd you learn to pick locks, Father?" Toni inquired.

"In lock picking class during adjunct training, after I finished seminary. Anything else?"

Toni smiled at Father O'Brien and shook his head. "I'm not going to get any straight answers about your spying, am I?" Toni did not expect an answer.

"Nope. I think spying is a harsh word, don't you think?" John answered.

"Nope!" Toni replied in kind, "But, I'm too damn tired, and my head hurts like hell. What business do you want to discuss?" Toni began to relax with his uninvited guests.

"Well, as it has to be, we want to discuss Bobby's death," John said looking at Gino, who'd been suspiciously quiet.

A knock came at the door. John nodded to Gino, who sprang to his feet and bolted to the door. Toni watched in amazement as Father Corvo pulled out a 9 mm Beretta.

"Who is it?" Gino called out, standing to the left of the door.

"Room service!" replied a female voice from the hallway.

John nodded at Gino, who changed sides and opened the door a crack.

"Room service," came the voice again, as Gino cracked the door.

"Just a minute," Gino said, looking back at John who nodded his approval.

Gino put his weapon away and opened the door. In walked a young blonde about nineteen years old, Toni thought. She was a little plump, her hair pulled back, and she spoke very politely with a French accent.

"Merci, Father," she said, as she wheeled in a cart. "Eh, Monsieur Brazil, please sign?" she said, and handed Gino the bill, who handed it to Toni, who signed it. After all, he thought, the City of Montreal was paying for it.

"Thank you," Toni said, and handed the bill back to the girl, who turned and walked out the door.

Toni pulled the cart to himself, took a beer, opened it and passed it to Father O'Brien. He opened another for Gino, and finally he opened one for himself.

"To Bobby," Toni said, raising his beer to John and Gino.

"Salute!" Gino said.

"You guys gonna kill me?" Toni asked bluntly. John and Gino both laughed.

"Why would you think that?" John asked.

"Gino pulled out that Beretta, and action like that says something to a cop like me," Toni said. "So what's the story here?" he asked. "Priests don't carry guns! Not the way Gino here does."

"Yes, not the way Gino does nor I, but that's a story for another time," John answered.

"Always a story for another time. I guess the words you use should make me feel more comfortable," Toni said taking a long drink of beer, finishing the bottle. He grabbed another beer and opened it, and sat back in his chair. "Father, why don't you tell me why you two are here."

"Gladly. We believe your brother was murdered, too. In fact, we may know who did it and why."

O'Brien spoke so matter-of-factly that Toni tried not to show his eagerness for him to tell who killed his brother.

"What evidence to you have that Bobby was murdered?" Toni asked.

"Toni, there are many things I cannot tell you for the protection of us all. However, I will tell you that Father Corvo and I are part of an organization within the Catholic Church that investigates things. I'm not sure how to . . ." John tried to explain.

"You're some kind of church detectives? Is that what your trying to say?" Toni asked, smiling at the thought of priest's acting like cops.

"Simply said," Father O'Brien replied, "yes. You said you followed my

FIERCE LOYALTY

story in Italy. Have you heard any other stories lately? Like the four bodies found in France?"

"I heard about it," Toni replied.

"They were found a month after I was attacked," Father O'Brien said. "Nothing in my room was missing, and the only memory I have was a light one, of my attackers standing near. They thought I was dead, but I could hear them. They were Palestinian, Hamas maybe. They spoke of a man named Gideon and a list I was carrying of graduating seminarians from many locations in Europe, including a small seminary in the south of France where the four bodies were found."

"What was the light you saw?"

"It was a portable copy machine," Father Corvo said. "I found John about five minutes later. I'd forgotten something in his room, saw blood seeping under the door, and busted the door down. I just missed them."

"What's this have to do with my brother?" Toni asked.

"Gino saved my life with a little help from a bullet proof vest," John began again. "In Italy, the church has a lot of influence. We cooked up the story of my death, because we believed there was a connection to the death of another friend of ours, in Israel."

"What connection?" Toni asked.

"A man named Gideon," Father Corvo answered.

"And my brother?"

"We're getting to your brother, Toni," Father John said. "Please be patient with us. It is important that you know this information."

Toni nodded in agreement, and Father O'Brien continued. "I was in the hospital for three weeks recovering. I was told to take some time off, so I went back to Venice to relax, while Gino looked for my attackers. A week later, the authorities found the bodies in France, just two miles from the seminary. I have a detective friend there. He called and asked us to help with something involving their case. We heard only what everyone else heard, that no evidence was found, the bodies were mutilated, and there was no way to identify them. When Gino and I arrived, we discovered the French did have one piece of evidence, but they had no idea what it was. My detective friend finally came to the conclusion that there may have been some religious connection since the bodies were found so close to the seminary. No one agreed with him, but he got the go ahead to call us and ask, four weeks after they found the bodies."

"What was it? The evidence, I mean," Toni asked.

"A tattoo," Gino answered.

"A what?"

"A small tattoo, Toni, like this," John answered as he rolled up his pant leg. He tugged down his sock and showed Toni a small, cross-shaped tattoo on the front of his ankle.

Toni crouched forward to see the tattoo, and was surprised when a second foot was paralleled next to John's with the same tattoo. Toni followed the second foot and saw Father Corvo staring back at him.

"You're telling me the man had the same tattoo as you two?" Toni said.

"That's right," John answered.

"The man was a priest," Toni said, as the light bulb went on in his head.

"Right again," John repeated. "All four men were young priests. I selected one of them to join my group."

"I'm still not sure what this all has to do with my brother. Can you guys speed it up?"

"The four priests were all headed to one place," Gino said.

"Where would that be?" Toni asked, his patience wearing thin.

"Right here, Toni," John answered. "Montreal. But, no one else knows what you now know, and you can't tell anyone. Do you understand?"

"Yes," Toni answered, "I do, but . . ."

"We reviewed the list of graduating seminarians who were headed to Montreal," Gino said.

"We found eight," John continued, "and six had already arrived in Montreal, and two more were enroute."

"We tried to find the last two," Gino said, "but they had disappeared."

"The trail leads here, Toni," Father John said. "We got here two days ago, the same day your brother was found dead at the church."

Toni slumped back into his chair and looked up at the ceiling, not knowing whether the priests were telling the truth or filling him with bullshit. He decided they were probably telling some form of the truth. After all, they were priests, although not the normal kind of priests Toni confessed to. He knew if the roles were reversed, he'd probably hold back information, but what would they hold back? He decided to see if they would show more of their cards.

"You're saying the Church was involved in Bobby's death?"

"Yes and no," John answered. "Six young priests came to Montreal. None of them match the pictures of the six who left the seminaries."

"Impostors," Toni said, not surprised. "They stole the list and saw how many were coming here. They killed the graduates and replaced them. The

FIERCE LOYALTY

question is, who is Gideon? Why did he go to the trouble of this elaborate scheme? And now, gentleman, what the hell does this have to do with Bobby's death?"

"Well, Toni," John said, "if we knew all the answers, we would tell you, but we don't."

"We don't know who Gideon is, but we believe he's smuggling something into North America. Again, no one knows what it is."

"It's hard to believe no one knows who Gideon is," Toni said.

"That's what I thought, too," Gino answered.

"Do you have an idea what he's smuggling?"

"We don't know," John answered. "But we believe Bobby got in the way, found out what was going on."

Toni picked up on a change in Father John's voice, and knew he'd just heard what he was waiting for. The priest was lying, holding a card. Why? Toni figured they wanted something from him, but what?

"What do you two guys want from me?" he asked.

"We want your help, Toni," John said. "Isn't that obvious?"

"No, it's not. I can't help you, if you won't help me?" Toni replied sharply.

"I don't understand your question," John replied.

"I think you're holding back information. You said at the beginning that you knew why Bobby was killed, but you haven't given me a clue."

"I told you there are things I can't tell you, but you're right," John responded. "The truth is, we're not sure what Gideon is smuggling."

"Do you think it's a mass destruction device?" Toni asked bluntly.

"We're not sure what it is. We do know that your brother was killed because of it. He found out what was happening, and we believe he may have taken something, some evidence, from one of the impostors. We need to find it. Will you help us find it?" John asked.

Sensing sincerity, Toni responded, "Okay, Father. I'll do what I can, but I want to be clear about this. Gideon, whoever he is, killed my brother. Someone was helping him. Who?"

Gino spoke first, "Impostors, Toni, just remember. They are not real priests."

"Chigall," John admitted. "He's missing, and we believe he may have helped kill your brother."

"Helped?" Toni caught the word. "Who else?"

"We don't know who is helping Chigall and the others," John said, "but there is a wild card here, someone we don't know about, yet."

Toni was silent, and took another drink from the now warming bottle of beer. They knew something else and believed they knew what it was Bobby found. They wanted it, and so did Toni. He was so close that afternoon – a dangerous box with backward writing.

Toni knew only that Bobby was murdered, that a man named Gideon was involved, and that no one knew who Gideon was – no one, Toni thought, but Savage. He would prove it, and confront him. He wouldn't let his brother's death be in vain.

28

"He won't be any more trouble, sir. I'll take care of him, just like we did his brother."

"Like his brother! You idiot, I don't want him killed! Not now anyway. Now listen to me!" Gideon said. "The only one who'll be killed is you if you botch something else."

"Yes, sir," he replied, sheepishly.

"Now is not the time to panic. Brazil knows nothing. If he has the package as you suspect, he won't know what it is, unless he has it analyzed. Where would he have that done?"

"I don't know, sir."

"Exactly," Gideon said. "New business. What's the progress on finding Bobby Brazil's journals?"

"Well . . ."

"As I thought. No progress!" Gideon stormed. "If Brazil finds his brother's journals, then he might know what we're doing. I want them found!"

"Yes, sir."

"You will die if you fail me!" Gideon threatened. He could feel the fear coming through the phone. "Just go about your business, and stay out of the way. Two more of my men are coming. They'll be arriving in three days. Just be at the airport to help them. Do you understand me, Jacques?"

"Yes, sir, I do," replied a shaken Detective Grade Four Richard Jacques.

"Their arrival date and time will be sent the same way. Now what's that asshole Savage up to?" Gideon pressed.

"He's watching Brazil, as we speak," Jacques responded quickly.

"I don't trust him, Richard," Gideon said in a calmer voice. "You keep

137

your eye on him. Is that understood?"

"Yes . . . I . . ." he stammered.

"Good then," Gideon said. "Now, don't call me again, you shit head, unless you find Brazil's journals." He slammed the phone down considering the possibility of another Brazil messing with his plan.

Gideon looked up from the phone to see Simi at the door. "Bring them in," he commanded.

"Yes, without delay," Simi replied, in the usual peaceful voice.

Gideon marveled at how Simi could be everywhere and anywhere without being heard and wondered sometimes if Simi listened to him think out loud. Simi seemed always to be there just as he decided he needed something. His thoughts returned to the phone call. He hated having to trust the people he bribed to do what he needed, but that was a risk he had to take. He usually disposed of them, anyway.

Gideon now thought about François and Michael, his 'Angels of Death', the carriers of the plague. They were trained and ready, and he would have to dispose of those liabilities, as well. He heard them coming up the stairs. Simi appeared at the door.

"If it pleases you, sir, François and Michael are here," Simi said elegantly.

"Send them in immediately." Gideon turned his chair to face the window.

Simi opened the door. Gideon watched the reflection in the window. Simi nodded, and the two shuffled through the door and stood at attention, in front of the desk.

"At ease, gentlemen. Please sit down," Gideon said. He turned to face them, and took them in as if they were prizes. Both were dressed in perfectly ironed camouflage uniforms with black beret caps. They were cleanly shaven, and Gideon could see that he had picked the best two for the last shipment. They would have to be the best. They would have to do more than the previous messengers.

"I have your orders," Gideon said, searching their eyes for weakness. "Are you ready?"

"Yes, sir!" they said in unison.

"Good," Gideon responded. He opened a desk drawer and took out two sealed nine-by-twelve envelopes. He passed one to each of the two men. They took them, but did not open them.

"You have twenty-four hours to get your affairs in order, starting when you leave this office," Gideon said. "Use them wisely. Simi will have your written orders and a package. The envelopes I have given you hold ten thousand

FIERCE LOYALTY

dollars, each. You will need that for expenses during your mission. When you get to Montreal two men will confront you in customs. Don't be alarmed. They will escort you through customs. After that, François, you will give them your envelope. They will open it and complain, since they expect more. The envelope also holds instructions how these men can get their final payment. Those instructions include a meeting in Washington, D.C., where you will kill him, his partner, and anyone who gets in your way. Specifics are in the orders you will get from Simi. You will also meet your comrades in Montreal. They have been waiting for you. You will all accomplish your mission together, just as you trained. Are you with me?"

"Yes, sir!"

"Good," Gideon repeated. "There is just one more thing I need from you two. We had another intruder and lost a package. I need you to retrieve the package and kill the man. I don't care how you do it; just get it done, discreetly. He has our package, or will soon. His picture and location will be in your orders. His name is Toni Brazil. Michael, your envelope also contains ten thousand. Split it between the two of you for expenses. Are there any questions?"

"No, sir!"

"Good." Gideon recalled with a slight smile that the last soldier who asked him a question about his orders was dead. "All your travel arrangements have been taken care of. Everything you need will be supplied. You have come far. You've been chosen by God to perform these tasks. When you leave here, you are to consider nothing but our cause, our plans, and your destiny. Protect the package with your lives. It must reach the last two cities, San Francisco and New York City. You may go now." Gideon saluted them.

They stood and returned the salute, turned about face, and marched in unison out the door. Gideon watched his soldiers leave. He had watched them train and knew their capabilities as soldiers. His soldiers had to be able to kill at will with many techniques, including their bare hands.

Gideon turned his chair to look out the tinted window toward the desert. In one week, he would leave the compound and go to his estate near, Nice. There he would wait, order, and watch, as the once great United States fell to his plague, his hidden army, and his will. He would watch the rest fall, too – the Middle East, Russia, and the European Union. One more farm had to be bought and should be up and running in the next five days, one last farm in New York State. Duplication would be ready within another week, and the virus inserted into the eggs and milk. Genius, Gideon thought. The bubble he and his brother developed in the lab would hold the virus, so small; the human eye could not detect it. It kept the virus alive and multiplying, until broken open. A fine mist spread the pestilence into the air, where it would float for hours until it found its intended human target.

Gideon thought of the secret test carried out in a lab in France. It was perfect. Ten people locked in a soundproof room, observed by a camera for ten days until they were dead. Then Simon found out, and all hell broke loose. He walked away from me, again. He didn't understand. Mother and father, killed by the Americans, stupid fucking Americans. Their dirty war in Vietnam killed my mother. They did it. They will feel my pain soon. Yes, very soon, as Simon did. Fucked with the wrong person, Simon. How could you tell on me? I had to do what I did Simon. Oh, Simon, you never understood, my poor little brother. No!

He looked at the wall where several clocks told the time in different places around the world. He looked at New York. Nine in the morning. Savard and Lowe would be on their way to New York soon, where they would finish the work they promised, and meet their fate. He thought for a moment about Bonny Savard. What a waste, he thought; she was a good piece of ass. Faithful too, until Lowe came into the picture. He wished he could kill Lowe himself, but he knew keeping him alive meant Savard would do what he wanted.

Gideon also knew they were liabilities, especially since Bonny made that phone call at the Dallas-Fort Worth Airport. He wondered what she was up to. Did she call the FBI, CIA, or someone else? He thought not. His two soldiers watching Savard and Lowe reported nothing through the chain of command, and the telephone records showed nothing, but a call to her home. It was probably nothing, but he could not dismiss it. She had to die, anyway. He laughed as he realized that Bonny Savard and her lover had about forty-eight hours to live.

29

"Director Mahoney," said Jeffrey Bodakis as he shook the hand of the FBI director. "It's nice to see you again, sir."

"Yes, Jeffrey, it is. You know my deputy, Tom Trimble, and this is Lisa Carlyle."

"It's a pleasure to see you again, Ms. Carlyle," Bo said.

"Yes, it is, Agent Bodakis," Carlyle responded with a sweet smile that appeared genuine.

"Jeff," Mahoney said. "I didn't know you two had met. That's good news."

"We've met, sir, but I'm not sure why she's here."

"I can clear that up," Tom Trimble said. "She's the newly appointed White House Assistant Chief of Staff for International and Domestic Terrorism. She's got the president's ear, Jeff."

"That's Agent Bodakis to you, Trimble," Bo said, clenching his jaw.

"What?" Trimble replied.

"I said . . ." Bo said, more assertively.

"Come on, you two!" Mahoney interrupted Bo, angrily. "We've got business here. You two and this feud have got to stop, and I mean now! Let's get down to business. Ms. Carlyle was promoted after her work with Trimble on the Ruben Colombian Cartel case."

"What happened to Phil Leoni?" Bo asked, as he looked around the table.

"Phil retired about eight weeks ago," Carlyle answered casually. "I thought you would have been notified." She realized Trimble did not notify Bo as he should have.

"All right," Mahoney said. "Jeff, fill us in on what's happening with this case of yours."

"Yes, sir," Bo answered, a little embarrassed by his exchange with Trimble. He looked at the three people in his New York City office waiting for answers he did not yet have. "Sir, I believe we should put the military on alert."

"What?" Trimble said with a laugh. "What the . . ."

"Shut up, Tom, and let Jeff tell us what he means," Mahoney said.

"Sir, in the last four days since the anonymous call, my team has dug up some interesting facts. Let me start with the phone call. We received an anonymous call on the live hotline with a voice de-scrambler. The hotline agent recognized that, and hit the tracer mechanism, which traced the call to an apartment here in New York. The apartment is rented by a woman, Bonny Savard, and her live-in boyfriend, Phillip Lowe. I sent two agents to the apartment within an hour of the call, but no one was home. The agents spoke to the apartment manager, who said that both Savard and Lowe told him they were on an extended travel work assignment and would be gone indefinitely. According to the manager, they have been gone for over a month. He said that they paid three months rent in advance, and he is the only one with access to the apartment."

"Who made the call, Jeff? The manager?" Director Mahoney asked.

"My agents thought the same thing, but he denied it and let the agents search the apartment complex, his apartment, as well as Savard and Lowe's. When they searched Savard and Lowe's place they found out what happened. A call-forwarding device was connected to the phone. We traced all incoming calls to that phone and found the original call was made at a pay phone at the Dallas-Ft. Worth airport. My agents found another coincidence. The caller said Geneon Systems was involved at the very top of the organization in a plan to spread smallpox virus throughout the United States and the EU. Well, Savard works for Geneon Systems."

"I see," said Carlyle, interrupting, "but did the caller mention who at the very top of Geneon Systems was responsible?"

"I'll get there, Ms. Carlyle," Bo answered. "The caller said Geneon Systems is involved in researching dairy products. The company is buying dairy farms, setting up labs, where they plan the spread of the smallpox virus," Bo said, pausing for the questions he thought would follow. When none came, he continued. "That's all the caller said. The problem is where the virus came from. We know the Russians didn't destroy their cache, but there is no evidence they are selling the virus to terrorists."

"But there was that . . ." Mahoney began.

"Incident," Bo interrupted. "That's right, sir."

FIERCE LOYALTY

"Incident?" Carlyle questioned.

"Yes. About three years ago, a Russian general was caught trying to smuggle virus out of their lab during a routine search," Bo said. "We found out when a Russian scientist defected. The Russian government assured us they recovered every bit of the stolen virus. Our intelligence sources told us otherwise. The general's finances were seized by the Russian government, except for one Swiss bank account we found under one of the many aliases the general used. The account had $2.5 million in it. No one knows where the money came from, except, of course, the Swiss," Bo said.

"We couldn't get the Swiss to tell us?" Carlyle asked.

"No, the Swiss have those swell bank privacy laws, and they're anal about them," Trimble said.

"So we believe the general may have sold some of the virus?" Carlyle asked, refocusing the discussion.

"We've been waiting for intelligence on any smallpox virus out there on the black market, but nothing has come up, until now," Bo said.

"The phone call from the Savard woman," Carlyle said. "What about the Lowe guy?"

"Lowe works for the same company, Geneon. He just started. He worked for a competitor before, Chesapeake Pharmaceutical," Bo said. "We picked up Savard and Lowe in San Francisco where they flew from Dallas."

"Where have they been the last four weeks?" Mahoney asked.

"Eight other cities, not including San Francisco and New York City, which is where they are heading next. The cities are..." Bo looked at a list, "Washington DC, Pensacola, St. Louis, Des Moines, Seattle, San Diego, Denver and Dallas."

"What have they been doing in those cities?" Trimble asked.

"They've been buying dairy farms mostly. Every farm they've bought has at least cows and chickens, and some have pigs." Bo waited for someone to ask, why dairy farms? But no one asked. "They've spent over $15 million so far."

"I'm sorry, this might be a stupid question, Jeffrey," Carlyle said, "but what am I missing? Dairy farms, and the smallpox virus? How do they mix?"

"Very well actually, Ms. Carlyle," Bo answered. "My team believes they are manufacturing more virus at the labs and will insert it into the dairy product somehow. If they've found a way to insert the virus into food, we're in big trouble. That could spread the virus throughout the country. The entire world could be affected."

143

SCOTT A. REZENDES

"Oh," Carlyle said, sounding a little panicky.

"Did you eat eggs, or drink milk for breakfast, Ms. Carlyle?" Bo asked with a wry smile.

"In fact, I eat eggs once a week," she answered. "I drink milk every day – you know, for the calcium," smiling back at Bo, sensing he was being facetious. "Am I in any trouble, Jeffrey?" Carlyle asked.

"Not yet. My team has checked into Geneon System. They have bought enough lab equipment within the last six months to build and supply at least fifteen labs, maybe more. The supplier said they have delivered lab building and supply equipment to farms in the EU, Switzerland, Russia and the Middle East," Bo said checking his list. "Also, India, Pakistan, and Hong Kong. Geneon Systems has offices in all of those countries."

"What about this company, Jeff? Have you found out who's behind this?" Mahoney asked.

"It's French owned. The founder, president, CEO and chairman was Dr. Simon Picard, a Stanford trained bio-technologist."

"Was?" Carlyle asked.

"Yes," Bo said. "Nice catch, Ms. Carlyle, you're good at this. He died last year in a diving accident off the Great Barrier Reef. His body was never found. People assumed he was eaten by sharks."

"Do you believe it?" Trimble asked.

"I've asked our office in Sidney to check it out. They're tracking down the investigating police officers. I've also talked with French officials. Dr. Picard had a brother. They didn't have a current photo. He hasn't been seen in public for some time."

"I'm not following you, Jeff?" Mahoney said, looking around the table at the other confused faces.

"His brother," Bo said, "Thomas, has not been photographed since he was a child. He spent some time in a hospital for the insane. Apparently, only one man has seen him as an adult, a long-time servant. No one knows what happened to Thomas, after Simon Picard's death. He just vanished – with a fortune too, my French counterpart told me."

"You still haven't answered my question, Jeffrey?" Trimble said. "Do you believe – that he's really dead?"

"I don't know what to believe, Tom," Bo said. "People try to fake death all the time, but they do it for money. Picard was a multi-billionaire, so I doubt it was money reasons. I've thought a lot about why someone like Picard would fake his own death. The only reason that makes any sense is, if you're

144

FIERCE LOYALTY

dead, you can hide and reappear later. If he's still alive, he's our main target."

"What do we know about him, other than he was rich?" Mahoney asked.

"He was French, born in 1955," Bo started, looking at his notes. "So far we've verified that his father was Dr. Jerome Picard, the French ambassador to South Vietnam in the 1960s. The elder Dr. Picard died in a 1967 ambush in a village during a survey of alleged North Vietnamese atrocities. He was surveying the area with other American dignitaries, and protected by American troops. The French blamed the U.S. for his death."

"Are you working on a theory?" Carlyle asked.

"Our theory right now," Bo began, "is that Dr. Picard, if he's alive, and from thirty to fifty others would have to be involved to pull the labs off. It's possible the regular workers at the labs wouldn't know they were working with a biohazard."

"Why?" Carlyle asked. "What's his motive?"

"Why, and his motives, aren't questions I'm exploring right now, Ms. Carlyle. We could speculate on his motives for hours, including the obvious, that he believes the U.S. is at fault for his father's death. All I know right now is that he has the means to spread the virus if he has it. He could kill half the United States population. And the farms he's purchased are all suppliers to military bases. He could take out our military without them knowing what happened. For example, if just one egg infected with the virus breaks open in the kitchen of an aircraft carrier, the ships ventilation system would spread the virus to seventy-five percent of the personnel, within seventy-two hours."

Everyone at the table went silent.

"Are any of the labs up and running?" Mahoney asked, breaking the silence.

"We've begun surveillance on the locations we know of within our borders, but we have yet to scratch the surface. We don't know if the virus has been brought to the labs or how the virus is coming into the country," Bo said.

"What's your plan to find out if the virus is here? And what about the labs outside of the country?" Trimble asked, sensing his nemesis was finally without answers.

"I wasn't finished, Trimble!" Bo responded. "Surveillance has turned up guards at each farm, but they don't look like rent-a-cops. We've checked with local security companies, and none have been contracted. Each farm is set up similarly with a large steel building close to the main farmhouse. The guards are stationed all around the house and building. We've seen no weapons, so there is no probable cause to enter for a search. We're set up on the farm near San Francisco, and the former owners are cooperating. We can put our

145

agents in place of their farm hands. We should get a pretty good idea of what's going on as that lab is built, and gets up and running."

"We need to get probable cause any way we can," Trimble interjected.

"I don't want to do a search warrant at just one farm," Bo started, "and hope to gather enough evidence to search the others. It's too risky. They could accelerate their plans at one of the other labs, and that's all it will take."

"I agree," Mahoney said. "We need enough evidence to go into all of the labs at once. Ms. Carlyle, what do you think the president will want to do about the international implications?"

"I'll recommend that the president inform the leaders of each country where the labs are and let them take care of the problem," she replied. "It's all we should do, unless they ask for assistance."

"Jeff? What about this Cain and Abel thing you mentioned in your faxed report last night?" Mahoney asked.

"Oh, Yeah," Bo replied. "We got a break while surveilling Savard and Lowe. Our SOG team picked up another tail on them. We've had them under surveillance for two days now. They are definitely tailing Savard and Lowe and have been doing so, at least since Dallas. We believe they've been on them the whole time. We sent a tag and bag team to fingerprint and gather other evidence from their hotel room this morning as soon as they left."

"That is a break," said Mahoney. "When this is over, Jeff, I want the names of every agent who worked on this case with you. They deserve recognition."

"Right, but let's just hope we catch this before the plan is hatched. Now, what about the military?" Bo asked.

"Ms. Carlyle?" Mahoney prompted.

"I'll recommend an alert on all dairy products delivered to military installations during the last month, and new deliveries will be quarantined immediately for testing. I'm also leaning toward recommending we start vaccinating military personnel immediately as well," Carlyle answered.

"I agree," Mahoney said, and nodded to Bo. "Are we done here? Anything else we should know before we brief the president? Carlyle and I have to catch a plane to DC and fast. Trimble, I want you to stay here, and take over Jeff's other collateral duties, case complaints and so forth. He'll need to concentrate on this. Clear?"

"But . . ." Trimble started.

"Is that clear, Tom?" Mahoney asked again. "You're going on vacation in two weeks anyway, so take it easy. This will be over by then, and you won't

146

FIERCE LOYALTY

have any of the clean up to worry about."

"Yes, sir," Trimble said glumly.

"Where you going to be, Jeff?" Mahoney asked.

"I'll be working with the team that's set up to tail Savard and Lowe, along with Cain and Abel."

"Let me know if you find anything new, Jeff," Mahoney said.

"Good luck with the president – and you too, Ms. Carlyle," Bo said as they all got up from the table.

"Thank you very much. I usually get my way with the president. I think he'll see my point of view. Nice seeing you again," Carlyle said. They all filed out the door, leaving Bo alone in his office.

"Likewise," Bo said. The three walked through the hall, Trimble yapping in the director's ear.

Bo felt tired and worried. What if he failed? He sat on his office couch and rubbed his face with his hands. He knew only time would tell now whether he succeeded, or failed.

30

The next morning, Bo was startled awake by his ringing telephone. He didn't know where he was at first, but soon recognized the couch in his New York City office. He remembered calling his wife, telling her he'd be late. That was the last thing he remembered. He answered and heard his colleague and good friend for many years at the FBI, Randy Velarde, calling from the San Francisco FBI Office. He and Velarde became friends at the Harvard Law School, before either joined the FBI. When they met, they realized they shared aspirations of working for the FBI and became best friends.

When he hung up the phone, his head began to ache. The stakes were getting higher, the stress of the game settling in. He considered what Randy Velarde told him about the two unknowns, dubbed Cain and Abel. Apparently Cain and Abel received a phone call early that morning, after which they cleaned the entire room, wiping down everything, and leaving abruptly. Velarde thought it was funny, so he didn't follow them out. Instead, he called his teams set up along the main highway from Yuba City to San Francisco to watch for their vehicle. If a team saw them, they were to report location and time. Cain and Abel drove straight to the San Francisco airport and left on a 7:00 A.M. flight, not to New York, but to Dulles International Airport.

Bo concluded they were tipped off, but by whom? The phone records showed the only call to their room was from a pay phone in Washington at 2:23 A.M. If they were tipped off, someone in the FBI might be working for Gideon, someone high up. Bo recollected who knew about Cain and Abel, and the only people were the agents on his team, Director Mahoney, Trimble, and a variety of staff and other agents – maybe the director's secretary or White House staffer, like Carlyle. As many as twenty to thirty people had

FIERCE LOYALTY

access to the information he'd sent to the director's office yesterday.

And what of Savard and Lowe? Was someone else watching them, or would they be met at JFK and followed from there? Part of the game, Bo thought – cat and mouse. Every case was like that at some point. He would tail Cain and Abel from Dulles Airport, tail Savard and Lowe from JFK, and hope for the best. He called his counterpart in the Washington field office and asked them to detain Cain and Abel, if they got on an international flight from Dulles. It was well thought out, he thought. Detain Cain and Abel and send two agents in their place to the destination. Bo called the CIA. They were glad to supply support, no matter the destination. The plan, if it worked, would give Bo extra time to solve the case, as well as two subjects to interview.

Bo thought again about Toni Brazil. He wondered if Toni had made any progress in Montreal with Kelly Primeau, but since he'd heard nothing, he figured they probably hadn't done too much in the one day Toni had been in Montreal. While he considered calling Toni, the phone in his office rang.

"Jeff Bodakis," he said.

"Bo, it's Randy again. The tag and bag guys found a print on the doorknob in Cain and Abel's room. We reviewed the video we got in the room, and guess what?"

"What? I'm under some stress. Just tell me," Bo said, excited but irritated.

"I think you'll like this Bo. Cain took his right glove off to wash his hand, but he didn't put it back before he and Abel left. Cain opened the door, Bo. We got a clean thumb and index. We downloaded it directly to the DC finger print guys and got a hit. Cain's real name is Saied Al Muhammad, a known member of Hamas. We found his partner too. Abel is Yassir Al Abib Haqi, another member of Hamas. They're Palestinian terrorists, Bo, both linked to Hamas!"

"Great work, Randy," Bo exclaimed. "Finally, we get a break."

"We got lucky Bo, real lucky. Oh, before I forget, I'll be on a plane to New York a few hours before Savard and Lowe's plane. I'm at SFO now, and we're boarding in about ten minutes."

"Okay, Randy. See you in about five or six hours. We'll be ready for you," Bo said, ready to hang up.

"Bo?" Randy said. "You still there?"

"Yeah. What you need?"

"The only way Hamas is behind this is with the support of someone much bigger, like a Bin Laden. I think we should consider this Gideon guy as just an alias for him."

"It's worth more consideration, Randy. Now have a good flight," Bo said, and hung up.

Bo sat looking out the window across to New Jersey, considering Randy's last words. He was right. Hamas had no way of pulling such an operation. They had nothing to gain and everything to lose. Someone bigger was behind this, and Bo would have to find the answers fast.

31

Toni woke to what he thought was an alarm clock but soon realized it was the phone in his hotel suite. He looked at the clock as he struggled to locate the phone. It was 8:15 A.M., and he didn't remember falling asleep the night before, after Father O'Brien and Corvo left. He saw the bottle of Excedrin P.M. and the four empty beer bottles next to the phone. In a hoarse voice he couldn't recognize as his own, he said, "Hello."

"Toni? Toni Brazil?"

"Yeah. Who is this?" "It's Father Chason. I'm sorry to disturb you, Toni. I can call back," Father Chason said kindly.

"No. No, Father, it's fine," Toni said. "Is everything all right, Father? Frank. Is Frank okay?"

"Well, Frank is still alive, but he's unconscious. Toni, the police are here again to ask more questions. Commander Savage said he was re-evaluating Bobby's death and wanted to search his belongings. I wanted to call and ask your permission," Father Chason said.

"You mean Savage is there now?"

"Yes, standing right next to me in fact."

"Are you okay, Father?" Toni asked. He noticed stress in Father Chason's voice.

"Yes, I'm fine," Chason replied. "Commander Savage wants to speak with you. Here he is."

Silence came on the line and Toni heard something in the background, a sound like someone hitting something. He heard Savage say something in a muffled voice and realized that Savage hand must have been covering the telephone receiver.

151

SCOTT A. REZENDES

"Mr. Brazil?" Commander Savage was on the line.

"Yes, Commander. What can I do for you?"

"I'd like permission to search your brother's belongings for evidence," he said. "I need you to come down here and release your brother's belongings to me. It is the only way."

"And what do you expect to find, Commander? A match box with a phone number on it?" Toni asked, sarcastically. "Have you reconsidered your pathetic handling of the investigation, Commander? Just trying to find another hokey reason to back up your original assertion of suicide?"

"Mr. Brazil, I'm trying to do my job. You pointed out some reasonable issues at our meeting yesterday, and with the Tavares accident, I'm reconsidering what happened to your bother," Savage said, professionally.

Toni considered his next words carefully. "You can search, but only with me present."

"I wouldn't do it any other way, Mr. Brazil. It's done then. I'll have someone pick you up immediately and bring you down here," Savage said, almost too quickly.

"Don't bother. Detective Primeau will be here in fifteen minutes to pick me up. He'll bring me," Toni said.

"Yes, you are right. It is done. I'll see you in one hour, Mr. Brazil." Savage gave the phone back to Father Chason.

"Toni?" said Father Chason.

"Father? Make sure he doesn't touch any of Bobby's things until I get there."

"Yes, I understand."

"I'll see you in one hour," Toni said.

"Very well, then. Hurry, would you?"

Toni walked to the bathroom and looked at the bloody bandage wrapped around his head. He changed the bandage, carefully taking the old one off. The mark wasn't as bad as it felt yesterday, light bruising around a small cut, nothing a regular band-aid wouldn't cover. If only people shaved their foreheads, it would look as if he cut himself shaving. He wet his hair and put some hotel shampoo in it, dunked his head under the running water, and stood up. He looked at himself in the mirror. He was unshaven for two days, and had dark circles under his puffy eyes. "You, my friend, look like shit," he said, wanting to take a shower. He didn't have the time.

It was almost nine. He made coffee with the hotel in room coffee machine and poured himself a cup. He thought about his visitors the night before,

152

FIERCE LOYALTY

especially Father O'Brien, the supposedly dead priest. They talked about someone named Gideon, who kills young priests. It seemed a little surreal.

Toni believed they had not told him everything. He wasn't even sure if they were really priests. Father Corvo handled himself more like a bodyguard. One thing stood out: Father O'Brien's insistence that he trusted no one and watched his back, all the time. They said Gideon used international terrorists to take out anyone in the way, and that's where Bobby came in. According to Father O'Brien's theory, Bobby stumbled onto something at the basilica, and told Frank Tavares about it. The priests were looking for the same thing he was – a box with some strange letters they believed Bobby had taken. They hadn't a clue as to where it might be. Father O'Brien wouldn't confirm Toni's suspicion that the box was some kind of mass destruction device.

His thoughts turned to the conversation with Savage. What was Savage up to? Was he really re-opening the investigation into Bobby's death? Why not just get a search warrant for Bobby's belongings? Surely the Canadian justice system required a search warrant. Why ask his permission? If things were reversed, he wouldn't ask permission. He'd get the warrant signed by a judge and go for it. Savage was up to something, he thought, but what?

There was a knock at the door. "Toni!" He heard in the familiar voice of his driver. "Toni! It's Kelly."

"Be right there, Kelly." Toni opened the door to the well-dressed detective.

"How is your head?" Kelly asked immediately.

"It's better. Thanks for asking. You ready?"

"I'm ready," Kelly replied.

"Change of plans this morning, Kelly," Toni said, as he walked into the hallway.

"Yes, I know. To the basilica," Kelly replied. "Savage called me ten minutes ago and told me to bring you directly to him at the basilica. He was very clear."

"Wait a minute," Toni said, as they arrived at the elevator. "What exactly did Savage tell you?"

"Nothing. Just that he had spoken with you and I was to take you to the basilica where he would meet us," Kelly replied plainly. "Why?"

"You have search warrants here in Canada, don't you?" Toni asked.

"Of course. Very similar to your search warrant, I believe. Maybe a little tougher to obtain than in your country even. Is there a problem?"

"Didn't Savage say anything to you about searching Bobby's belongings or why you are taking me to him?" Toni pressed.

"No, I don't know what you're talking about. He's already searched Bobby's belongings, and he would not need your permission since Bobby is the victim, not the suspect," Kelly responded.

Toni looked back toward his room. He had his weapon, even if it were illegal. Father Corvo wore one concealed and so would Toni, especially after their warning. Was there something in his room someone might want? He remembered the package from Father Chason. He hadn't thought of it before.

The elevator opened, and Toni considered his next move. He looked at Kelly who held the elevator door open and looked at him confused.

"Is something wrong, Toni?"

"No," Toni lied. He wondered what Father Chason said yesterday about Bobby's journals. Did Father Chason tell him that he told the police the last journal was missing? He needed to know. His next move depended on it.

"Let's go," Toni said to Kelly as he stepped on the elevator, and pressed the lobby button. They reached the lobby and walked towards the front door.

"Where'd you park?" Toni asked as the doors opened to the outside driveway. He stopped and stood looking around the parking lot.

"I'm right here, Toni," Kelly said, pointing to the only car in the driveway. "You don't remember what my car looks like? You sure your head feels better?"

"Oh, here you are, right in front of me," he said in obvious surprise. He laughed as he walked to the car, opened the door, and climbed in, "Drive," Toni said, "and go where I tell you to go."

"What?"

"Just do what I tell you. Now drive around the parking area like you're leaving." Kelly pulled away from the curb and directly to the exit. He turned left and drove straight ahead.

"Now turn left here," Toni said, pointing to the cross street.

"But . . ." Kelly started.

"Kelly, damn it, just do it. Check your rear view and look for a tail," Toni said.

"Would you at least tell me what we are doing?"

"I'll tell you in a second. Turn right here, then take the second left. Keep checking your rear view."

"Nothing. I don't see anything. I don't think we've been tailed. What's going on?

"Are you sure about that tail?" Toni asked, looking in the side mirror.

"Yes," Kelly said, and took another right. "There, no one. Are you

FIERCE LOYALTY

satisfied?"

"Okay, now head back to the hotel."

"What are we doing?" Kelly asked, irritated.

"Just go back to the hotel and park where I tell you," Toni said, smiling at his confused partner.

Kelly turned the car around, and they returned to the hotel, and parked next to a car Toni had seen before, a blue Taurus, the car Savage and his partner Jacques drove. Kelly looked at him. "What's going on? Can you let me in on the joke now?"

"It's no joke, Kelly," Toni answered. "Savage begged me to meet him this morning at the basilica to search Bobby's things. I kept wondering why he wanted to search Bobby's stuff, but then I remembered that Father Chason told me the police had already searched everything. I asked myself why not get a search-warrant? Then you said nobody needed one. Something didn't add up. Then I remembered something else." Kelly listened intently. "I guess I forgot about it after I got hit on the head. It just didn't register."

"What?"

"Father Chason gave me a package. My bet is that it's Bobby's last journal. Father Chason said he found it hidden in Bobby's room, but he told the police it was missing," Toni said, as if talking to himself.

"So? I don't understand." Kelly said.

"I can't believe I didn't see it before."

"What? See what?" Kelly urged.

"How does Father Chason speak to you, Kelly? Directly, or does he test you?" Toni asked.

"That's easy. He's always testing me," Kelly replied.

"Exactly. He was telling me something but not straightforward. The information flew right by me. He was testing my hearing or something. I don't know." Toni said.

"Well? Tell me, what did he say?"

"He gave me that package so discreetly, I just didn't think about it. So the police, more specifically Savage, must have asked him for Bobby's last journal and Bible after they searched through his stuff. Yes, that's it," Toni exclaimed.

"What's it?" Kelly inquired.

"Kelly, why would Savage search Bobby's belongings?"

"Maybe to look for something to substantiate his own suspicions, such as a suicide note," Kelly replied.

"Okay," Toni answered. "What else would you search for? Journals?

Things like that?"

"Well, yes, but only if there was no note," Kelly replied.

"What about someone's Bible?"

"Well, I've never asked for anything like that," Kelly said.

"I thought he was rambling, not making sense. He's old," Toni said. "Frank Tavares's wife described a Bible with a hole cut out of the middle. Damn, Kelly, I've had it all the time, at least one of them."

"You mean you have what we were looking for yesterday at the Tavares house? Then what was going on there? Just a robbery you walked into?" Kelly theorized.

"No," Toni said, "either Bobby and Frank created a decoy or there's more than one package with funny writing on it."

"Bo said you . . . Wups!" Kelly stammered.

"Bo? What does Bo have to do with this? Fuck, I knew there was something he wasn't telling me. He needed something, didn't he?" Toni demanded, as he looked straight at Kelly.

"Wait a minute, Toni," Kelly started. "We'll talk about Bo later. Right now we've got to deal with this. The package is in your room?"

"I think so," Toni said, annoyed at Bo and Kelly, "and Bobby's last journal. But how'd they find . . . Oh shit!" Toni exclaimed.

"Father Chason!" Kelly said. "And Savage has him."

"That means Savage's crony is here," Toni replied.

"Jacques!" Kelly said. "And that's his car."

"Let's go get him," Toni said, anger boiling to the surface. "He knows who killed my brother!"

Kelly peered over at Toni, his insides turning with adrenaline and his eyes burrowed in on the man sitting next to him. Toni's anger had come to the surface, his contorted face showed a different person.

32

"What will you do with us?" Father Chason asked the man who sat in the corner of his office at the basilica.

Alexander Savage was waiting for Toni Brazil and Kelly Primeau to arrive. He hung up the phone with Brazil ten minutes before and knocked Father Chason out long enough to tie him up. He took out his new stash of powdery delight in the small jar with spoon device connected. He heard what Chason said, but his response waited until he juiced up, three times in each nostril. His body shook as he took the last snort. Letting out a long sigh, he closed his eyes, smiled, and felt the rush begin. Opening his eyes, he stared at Father Chason through a yellow film.

"Oh, Father, that's not for you to worry about. You should be concerned about yourself, don't you think?" an evil smile twisted his lips.

"That's what is wrong with society, Commander Savage. Everyone believes they should just be concerned about their own well-being. We've become a selfish society," Father Chason replied.

Savage laughed. "Father, Father, Father! Well, at least they'll say you preached to the end."

Father Chason sat at his desk, his arms tied behind his back, his ankles tied together and to the chair. He showed no signs of pain or alarm. "Your threats of death do not worry me, Commander. I am an old man and death is a daily ritual at my age. Kelly and Toni are another matter."

"Everyone dies, Father, you know that. They'll have an accident, just like Frank Tavares, brake failure or something like that," Savage said, matter-of-factly.

"You are an evil man, Commander, and I believe that garbage you put into

SCOTT A. REZENDES

your nose is the reason for it," Father Chason said with disgust. "I ask you – no I beg you to stop and repent your sins now, before it is too late."

Savage laughed again, his stomach bouncing around, his shoulders slumping downward as he tried to contain himself. "Sometimes, Father, good or evil, people do what they believe in, whether it's right or wrong in society's view. Whether I kill you, Brazil, and Primeau now or not, you'll all be dead soon, anyway. If anything, I'm doing you a favor. Just think of it as mercy killing." Savage laughed again. "You believe in that stuff, right? Mercy?"

Father Chason closed his eyes, bowed his head, and began to pray.

"That's right, Father! Pray! You're going to need it," Savage giggled.

Father Chason opened his eyes to look at Savage, whose eyes bulged, red fluorescent. "I'm praying for your soul, Commander Savage." He bowed his head, and softly closed his eyes.

33

Toni pulled out his gun in the car. He dropped out the clip in his hand, and racked the 9-mm Sig-Sauer back, popping out the seeded bullet. He slapped the clip back in, and quickly racked the chamber, loading the first round in the chamber, then re-holstered. He popped out the clip again, then re-inserted the missing bullet, and placed the clip back into the weapon. He was loaded and ready. Kelly just watched, not saying a word.

"Are you ready, Kelly?" Toni said.

"Not as ready as you are. How did you get that in?" Kelly asked.

"You're the one who got me through customs. You should know," Toni replied.

"Never mind. Let's just hope you don't need it."

"You've got one, don't you?" Toni asked.

"Of course," Kelly answered. "I just don't pull it out like that."

"Just making sure it was loaded."

"Why don't we just wait for him here?" Kelly said. "It might be easier to take him here."

"Yeah, you're right, but we need to take him somewhere out of the public eye. I've seen no back up, so why make a public spectacle? We should do this quietly. Beside, we may need to squeeze some information out of him. I don't want some Johnny Public to see us and call the police. I want him alone."

"You Americans," Kelly said. "How do you want to work it?"

"We'll wait outside the door. When he tries to leave, we'll stick our guns in his face. He's not expecting us."

"Geeze, Toni. But I . . ." Kelly started.

159

"Kelly!"

"All right. Sounds good, I guess," Kelly replied.

Toni and Kelly got out of the car and walked to the hotel entrance, hitting the automatic doors in stride. At the elevator, Toni looked at Kelly, and said, "I'll meet you on the seventh floor."

"What?"

"I'm taking the stairs," Toni said. He jogged to the sign at the end of the hallway marking the stairwell. He hit the door running, and started up the stairs. Arriving at the seventh floor, he noticed for the first time his leg didn't hurt.

At the landing, Toni checked the door, opened it a crack and peeked into the hallway. Clear, he heard the elevator 'ding' down the hall and Kelly walked toward him. Toni entered the hallway, seeing Kelly he nodded. They took out their firearms and crept slowly towards Toni's room, about halfway between the elevator and the stairs. Toni put his ear to the door, and then stepped away. He nodded to Kelly, confirming sounds coming from the room. Toni signaled Kelly that he would take Jacques down, and Kelly nodded. The knob turned, and the door began to open inward.

"Hold it right there!" Kelly yelled, holding his gun straight out in front of him.

Jacques wasn't looking up as he walked out the door with a bag in one hand. Surprised, he jumped backward and threw his arms up in the air. The bag flew back into the room. He brought his hand up toward a shoulder-holstered weapon, just as Toni Brazil slammed his left foot into his chest. Jacques crumpled to the floor.

As if they'd worked together for years, Toni and Kelly grabbed Jacques, each taking an arm, and dragged him into the room. The door closed behind them. They threw him into a chair. Toni slammed his left forearm into his face, stunning him, and pointed his gun at his head. Kelly cuffed Jacques' arms behind him, and patted him down, finding two weapons, one in a shoulder holster, the other in a pant leg. Kelly picked up the bag and pulled out two books – a Bible and Bobby Brazil's journal, dated the month of his death. Jacques' nostril bled where Toni hit him. He didn't know what hit him, Kelly thought, and now he wanted to hit him, too. Toni held his weapon to Jacques' head.

"Wake up, motherfucker!" Brazil said. "Wake up!" Toni stood, and backhanded Jacques across the cheek with his left fist closed.

"Toni!" Kelly exclaimed, "Take it easy."

FIERCE LOYALTY

"Yeah, come on, take it easy," Jacques cried.

Toni sensed Kelly behind him and set up a good cop-bad cop scenario. "If you don't start talking and I mean now, I'll beat your face so bad, your mother won't recognize you," Toni said, with a wild look on his face.

Jacques looked at Toni and saw he was serious, "Look, I don't know . . ."

Immediately, Toni slammed his open right hand across Jacques face again. "Don't fuck with me!" He got right into Jacques' face, spitting out his words.

"Toni!" Kelly said louder. "Come on, back off."

"Yeah, back off!" Jacques repeated.

Toni stepped back, and Kelly came forward with the books in his hands, "What the hell you into, Jacques?"

"Oh, fuck you, Primeau. Uncuff me and . . ." Jacques started but Toni backhanded him again. Blood splattered the wall. Jacques groaned.

"He'll kill you, Jacques, and frankly, I'm not sure I'll stop him after what you did to his brother and Frank Tavares."

That got his attention. "I didn't kill Bobby Brazil. It wasn't me. I swear, I don't . . ."

"Shut up!" Toni spat into Jacques face. "All I want to hear is the truth." Toni stood on Jacques' feet and pressed down on his thighs so he could not kick. Toni was right in his face. "You tell us everything you know, and God forbid, if you lie to me!" Jacques turned whiter. Toni stood and backed off.

"What's so important about Bobby's journal?" Kelly asked Jacques.

"Read it, and you'll find out. Brazil took notes on everything going on." Toni turned back to Jacques. "Okay, okay! You really have to read it. I did just now. He copied Gideon's men's orders completely."

"Gideon?" Toni responded.

Toni opened the Bible to the middle and found the white box, but there was no writing on it. He held it out for Jacques to see. Jacques eyes got big. Toni opened the box and pulled out a vial, with a label. Funny writing, just like Belinda Tavares said. Toni recognized it was Russian script. He brought the vial up to the light, and saw a clear liquid inside it. Toni brought the vial up to Jacques face. Jacques began breathing hard.

"What is it, Jacques?" Toni asked.

"You don't know?"

"What's that supposed to mean?" Toni said. "Tell me what's going on, Jacques, or I'll break this open right under your nose."

"Toni!" Kelly exclaimed. "Give him some room."

Toni took a step back. Kelly looked nervous. He found the couch and sat

161

down.

"Look, I'll tell you guys what I know," Jacques said, "but you've got to protect me. Please!"

"We'll do what we can, Jacques," Kelly started, "but . . ."

"Hey, Savage is expecting you guys any minute now. When you don't show up, he'll probably kill the priest and take off," Jacques said, excitedly.

Toni looked at Kelly. "You've got a cell phone. Call Savage and tell him we're stuck in traffic. I'll keep an eye on this one," Toni said, calmly. Kelly walked out of the room, leaving Toni and Jacques alone.

What's in the vial, Jacques?"

"I'm sorry about your brother," Jacques said. "You have to understand. Savage is a crazy man, and the man he works for is, too."

"What the hell are you talking about?"

Kelly walked back into the room and nodded at Toni. "I've given us a few more minutes, is all," he said, winking at Toni. "I also called ISU. They're coming to take over."

"What's ISU?" Toni asked.

"Internal Security Unit," Jacques said, his face relaxed. "I can't wait to tell them about how you two treated me."

"Maybe I should mess you up some more, Jacques?" Toni stood up from the couch. "It's time for you to start talking asshole!"

"Yes," Kelly said, "I agree, Jacques. I've lived up to my side here. You'll be protected."

Jacques looked at Toni, then Kelly. They stared back at him. He had no choice. It was time to talk and deal.

"Six months ago, Savage and I were approached by an Asian man. He called himself Tran. He knew everything about Savage and me, our families, where we were born. He didn't look like he could harm a flea, and . . ." Jacques stopped, considering his next words carefully.

"And what, Jacques?" Toni interjected.

"Savage and I. Never mind. We were taking money from drug dealers to let their runners in at the airport. This Tran knew it and threatened to turn us in if we didn't cooperate with him." He stopped again. "Can I have some water?"

Kelly got up, got a cup of water, and gave it to Jacques. "Anyway, Savage said no. He told the guy to go to hell."

"What happened?" Kelly asked.

"Tran, this old guy, broke Savage's wrist so fast I couldn't believe it. He

FIERCE LOYALTY

grabbed the hand that Savage pointed at him, and snap! We agreed then to do it, help him out, and shit, it sounded so easy, just do what we were doing."

"So what was the problem?" Kelly asked.

"Tran wanted to cut our fee in half, considering he wouldn't turn us in," Jacques said. "Well, Savage was pissed off, and Tran said he'd notify us when his first runner was coming. Time went by, maybe two months, and then Tran appeared again at an airport restaurant where Savage and I were having lunch. He handed us a key to a locker where people put luggage. He said our instructions and money were there."

"Then what?" Toni pressed.

"Savage went to the locker, got the instructions, which included a list of eight flights, dates, and times the runners would come, and where we were to take them. But Savage was still pissed off about the fee and his wrist."

"What he'd do?" Kelly prodded.

"The first runner came, and that's when Savage decided to kidnap him. He gave him a tranquilizer. When he fell asleep, he took him to an abandoned building, tied him up, beat the crap out of him. The guy never talked, but Savage found his package, just like that one over there." Jacques pointed to the Bible. "He was dressed like a Catholic priest."

There was silence. Then Jacques began again. "The runner had a beeper, and it went off at some point. Savage called the number and ended up talking to a guy named Gideon," Jacques said. "I couldn't believe it. Savage made a deal with the guy that would pay him a million and a half-dollars. I'd get five hundred thousand. It was too good to be true."

"Keep talking, Jacques," Toni said, now standing. "Where'd my brother come in?"

"I'm getting to it," Jacques answered, calmly. "We didn't know what the package was, but Savage found out, knew someone who happened to speak Russian. He told him what it was. I remember the moment well. Savage smiled as broadly as I'd ever seen. It was strange."

"What was the package, Jacques?" Toni asked.

"I . . . That vial over there is full of the smallpox virus." Jacques swallowed hard.

Kelly looked at Toni who returned his look of disbelief. Toni put the vial in the white box. He looked around for a safe place and decided to put it back in the Bible, which he put in the bar refrigerator. He did it smoothly without taking a breath.

"Then what?" Kelly prodded.

163

"Savage called Gideon and re-negotiated his deal to five million. Again, Gideon agreed. I couldn't believe it. Savage seemed over confident. I got scared. I thought we would be killed. It was getting serious, but Savage said he wasn't worried."

"Why?"

"Savage had decided to keep the package and the runner. We still have him. Savage moves him to a new location every two days." Jacques looked at Kelly. "Shit, Primeau, this thing is bigger than Savage and me. Did you believe we could handle this ourselves?"

"Who else is involved, Jacques?" Kelly asked.

"Savage has kept things, mostly favors on other people in government, Kelly. A lot of people owed him. Working in customs has its perks. Lots of people ask for favors, especially government officials. Savage always gets something in return. That's all I'm going to say on that."

"We'll talk about that stuff later. Now what about Bobby?" Toni demanded.

"About two months ago, maybe a little longer, the second runner came. He was supposed to bring Savage and me the first of ten half million dollar payments. He only brought a hundred thousand. I thought Savage was going to kill the guy, but he couldn't, because Father Chason was expecting him. This guy, Chigall, said Gideon only gave him the hundred thou, and the next runners, six in all, would bring the other payments totaling a half million each. Savage was really angry, but there was nothing he could do."

"Does Father Chason have anything to do with this?" Kelly asked.

"No, he has nothing to do with it, but the runner, Chigall, was expected at the basilica. I swear, it's all I know."

Toni looked at Kelly. Neither believed Father Chason was involved, but he must have caught on and Savage found out.

"Keep going, Jacques. There's more," Toni said.

"Savage had Chigall watched. It's where your brother comes in, Brazil. He stuck his nose where it didn't belong. He started watching Chigall, too. Why? We could only speculate, but he seemed to be writing stuff down all the time. Chigall was everywhere. He was looking to lease a building, we found out. Then one day, we noticed your brother wasn't around anymore. Chigall had leased space and went there every other day. Your brother was sly, though; he began watching us. We didn't know how he got on to us." Jacques paused.

"He was Special Forces. Fought in Vietnam, '65 to '67," Toni said proudly.

"Yeah, we found that out later. He found our prisoner and then found the

FIERCE LOYALTY

package. He knew what it was. He also found Chigall's package, his orders, everything. He copied it into his journal. It's all there. He took the package from Chigall's room at the basilica. Chigall came to us about the same time. That's when we figured out we had been robbed, as well. Your brother made one mistake."

"What was that?"

"He didn't leave town fast enough. We knew it was him. He was the only one it could have been. We caught him and held him hostage for a night. He didn't say a word. Chigall called Gideon, who ordered Bobby Brazil's death. In fact, as soon as Chigall told him he was a Vietnam vet, Gideon erupted, wanted him dead immediately. He didn't care what he had to say or not."

Toni was breathing heavy. "Who did it? Who killed Bobby? Dammit, tell me!" he screamed.

"Hey, it wasn't me! It was Savage and Chigall. They knew your brother had some history with alcohol and drug abuse. Savage forced him to drink it, and I mean he forced it down his throat. I'm sorry, I didn't want . . . Jesus, Chigall beat your brother unconscious, and then Savage found his gun. Then we searched his room, nothing. No vials. So they set it up to look like a suicide." Jacques started to weep.

Toni slapped him across the face again, first with his palm open and then with the knuckle side. This time a crack was heard. He broke Jacques nose. "And you watched, you piece of shit!" He walked to the bathroom and closed the door. In a few seconds, he came out with a wet towel in his hand. He put the towel over Jacques' face. Jacques gasped and cried, "No! No! Don't hurt me!"

Toni placed his hands over Jacques nose, one on each side, and jerked his left hand re-centering Jacques nose with a crackle. Jacques screamed. Toni pulled the towel away from his face. "Quit crying you bitch!" he said, wiping the blood off. He shoved two cotton balls into Jacques' nostrils. "Open your mouth."

"Why?" Jacques asked, whimpering.

"It's how you're going to breathe for the next few weeks, while your broken nose heals, Shit head!"

"What are you, Brazil?" Jacques asked, in his new nasal voice.

"Your worst fucking nightmare, Jacques," Toni replied. "Now, tell us about Frank Tavares. What did you guys do to him?"

Richard Jacques bowed his head. He'd already said a lot, and the magnitude of what he was involved in started registering. He was a murderer, he thought, and he began to feel sick. He thought how he had watched in horror as Savage and Chigall beat Bobby Brazil to death, while he did nothing. He turned his churning mind to Frank Tavares. Another of Savage's victims, and again, he watched.

"Savage and I went to his house yesterday morning," he began. "We watched his wife and kids leave the house. Then we forced our way into the house. Savage tortured him by forcing the corners of a business card under his nails. We asked him where the vials were, and Frank finally told us he had them hidden at his bank lock box. Savage didn't believe him, but he took us there. Chigall followed him. While we were inside the bank, Chigall cut his brake line. We followed him home, and he crashed in front of his house. We had to respond, but then two other cars showed up, so we couldn't just start searching his house for the package. We went through the motions, started canvassing the neighborhood for witnesses. We ended up interviewing this woman who wouldn't let us leave. You know the type? By the time we finished with her, Kelly showed up, and we decided to search Tavares' house later."

"Very good, Jacques. You're learning," Toni said. "Now, I want you to tell me everything you know about this Gideon piece of shit. If I don't like what you say, I'll break your nose again. Fix it up again, and break it again if I have too. Got it?"

"Yeah, yeah, I got it," Jacques replied, "but I've never met Gideon, and . . ."

Toni turned and brought his face within an inch of Jacques. "You will tell me everything I want to know!"

Jacques sat with terror in his face. His eyes began to water. A stream of tears erupted down this swollen cheek. Jacques was guilty of killing his brother. Toni wanted to exact his revenge, kill him right then and there. He considered putting his gun directly between Jacques eyes and as slow as possible, squeeze the trigger, then watch his head explode, not to be recognized. But, one look at Kelly, and he knew he wouldn't let him do it. Instead he slammed his right fist into Jacques' mouth as hard as he could. Jacques' head jerked backward, then forward. Blood gushed onto his shirt, and his head settled on his chest.

Toni bent down and leaned over to Jacques left ear. "Sorry about that, you might have to breathe from your fucked up nose after all."

He didn't look at Kelly as he stood, turned, and walked into the bathroom to wash his bloodied hand.

34

Two of Kelly's colleagues showed up minutes after Toni persuaded Jacques to cooperate with Kelly and the ISU squad. Toni even convinced him to tell everyone that he fell and broke his nose during the initial struggle. Jacques subsequently spilled the beans about Gideon's plan, and both Toni and Kelly were surprised by the revelation that Gideon had been paying Jacques to keep an eye on Savage and to keep him informed of his own soldiers' whereabouts.

With Jacques cooperation and Bobby's journal, Kelly and Toni felt pretty good about stopping Gideon and catching up to Savage. Kelly's ISU team found the warehouse where Gideon's men were holed up, awaiting their final orders. They were all dead, shot in the head while they slept. But they had other problems. Father Chigall, or whoever he was, vanished along with Savage's original prisoner, and there was no sign of the six remaining vials of smallpox virus. There was still the question of who took the virus from the Tavares house. Jacques claimed that neither he nor Savage took it, because Toni and Kelly showed up just as they were about to steal it themselves.

In addition, Alexander Savage took Father Chason hostage and disappeared. Had Chigall and Savage separated or were they together? One or both of them shot the six men at the warehouse and were on the run with the virus. They had to decide quickly if Jacques should contact Gideon. The problem would be coaxing Gideon out of his stronghold and into the open, where he could be nabbed. Since there were no known recent photographs of Gideon, and no one knew what he looked like, it was another problem. Over four hours had passed since Savage and Father Chason left the basilica. Kelly's cell phone chirped.

167

"This is Detective Primeau."

Toni eyed Kelly. He didn't say a word, just the perfunctory grunts, and then he hung up.

"That was Tatum at the customs office on the border, near Phillipsburg," Kelly said.

"A U.S. Customs agent let Savage through the border into Vermont about two hours ago. He said he was with an old and young priest. They showed him pictures of all three, and he confirmed it was Savage, Chigall, and Father Chason. They all had passports. It looked normal to him, so he let them through. He guessed they're heading down Highway 89 towards Burlington. My guess is they're already there, maybe half way to Albany, and probably headed to New York."

"What are they driving?" Toni asked.

"Dark SUV. Looks like a Ford Explorer," Kelly answered. "Video got the plate, Quebec 325 UVM. All points bulletin went out fifteen minutes ago. U.S. Customs has contacted the New York State police. We should call Bo." Toni looked up from Bobby's journal.

"Yeah, Bo," Toni said glumly. With Savage in the United States and with the State police notified, the FBI would be involved before long. Toni hoped they could reach Bo first.

35

Saied and Yassir knew the phone call meant they were compromised, and when they heard the one-word code, they put an alternate plan of action into motion. They always had multiple escape plans and the code word determined the plan. As many as ten other people might be contacted, or just one. Depending on the number, some knew more than others, but most would be paid to perform a task. They did not need to know more. Gideon knew that Americans always looked to make a buck, legally or illegally, so long as they weren't caught. Capitalism at its best. He counted on it. The code words were just numbers, and that morning was thirteen, not a good number. They knew they were being watched. Every move had to be perfect if they were to escape undetected.

They reached San Francisco airport just forty-five minutes before United Flight 302 to Washington boarded. A rental car was arranged at their destination. They boarded the plane and sat in the last row. The airplane was crowded, but not full. They picked out the two FBI agents riding with them. One was sitting ten rows up to the right; the other twelve rows to the left. They awaited their opportunity; patiently as the plane filled and the doors were closed.

"Good morning, ladies and gentlemen. This is Captain Morley, and I'd like to take this opportunity to welcome you to our daily non-stop to Washington Dulles International Airport. On behalf of the crew and myself, I invite you to sit back and enjoy the flight."

The time had come. Yassir pointed to his left as the truck approached. They waited.

"Ladies and gentleman, this is the captain again. I apologize, but it looks like we'll be delayed just a few minutes here. I've been informed that we tried to depart San Francisco without your breakfast onboard the aircraft. I'll be powering down here just for a few moments. Don't be alarmed. The crew will open the rear hatch and, I've been told it will just take a few moments. Thank you for your patience."

Just as the captain finished his speech, the plane came to a stop, and two young ladies in airline uniforms came down the walkway as the truck drove up. Yassir made eye contact with one of them; she winked back at him. He put his arm on Saied's to signal the time had come. The attendants unlocked the hatch, and two men walked onto the plane pushing a large cart. One positioned himself to block the walkway. He looked at Saied and Yassir, and nodded.

Saied looked forward just as one FBI agent turned forward, looking away from Saeid. Only the head of the other FBI man was visible. Saied and Yassir dropped to the floor and crawled to the rear of the plane. They stood and put on overalls that matched those of the two men who pushed the cart onto the plane. Those two, in turn, took their overalls off and crawled quickly to the seats Saied and Yassir left vacant, dressed as ordinary travelers. The whole swap took just forty-five seconds.

Saied and Yassir left the plane and drove the truck back to its station. While Saied drove, Yassir shaved his head and trimmed his beard. When they stopped, Saied did the same, and within fifteen minutes they re-entered the airport with new looks, new identification, and tickets on a flight to Baltimore, a thirty-minute drive from Washington.

36

"Jacques! I thought I told you not to contact me again! What is your problem?" Gideon yelled into the phone.

"I'm sorry, but the shit has hit the fan here."

"What are talking about, Richard? And what is the matter with your voice? It sounds nasal as hell," Gideon replied. "Are you sniffing that shit with Savage?"

"No. I've caught a cold, and . . ." Jacques started.

"Is that what's bothering you? A cold? My last two men are on their way, Jacques. They're a day early. Didn't you get the message?"

"No," Jacques replied.

"No? They'll be there in two hours, you shit! You and Savage better be there!"

"Look, Gideon," Jacques started, his voice pitched high, "Savage went off the deep end. He killed all your men, stole the packages, and took off. The police here believe he's on his way to New York City."

"What? I hope your not bullshitting me!" Gideon yelled.

"I'm not, sir. You pay me for information; now you're getting some. Why are the last two runners coming early?" Jacques asked, changing the subject.

"Why are you still alive, Richard? They have a job to do. I've ordered them to take care of Toni Brazil. You will make the arrangement, just as you did with his brother," Gideon said. "Now, you haven't answered me yet. Why didn't Savage kill you?"

"It's not for the lack of trying," Jacques replied, his voice shaking. "Savage just missed me. Look, I'm playing dumb. The Royal Canadian Internal Security Unit's been asking me questions all day, but they believe I know nothing of

171

why Savage went crazy, and they don't know about the virus."

"Good," Gideon replied, calmer. "What about Brazil's journal? You find it?"

"Good news here too, sir. It's been recovered, along with the missing package. I have them both safe and secure," Jacques replied, confidently.

"Richard, you surprise me for a Grade Four Detective. You've shown some smarts." A long pause. "So, all my men are dead?"

"Yes. I have pictures, if you want proof," Jacques replied.

"That won't be necessary. I have people who will check it out, and if you're lying, you know what will happen. What else do you know?"

"Savage took an old priest hostage, and I'm told Chigall is with him. Nobody knows if he's a hostage or helping Savage," Jacques said.

"Well, that's interesting, Richard. We have a problem, but I believe we can take care of it. It shouldn't delay the plan too long, so long as we recover the six packages. I have just the man to do it, too," Gideon said slyly.

"Who, sir?"

"You, Richard. Who else?" Gideon replied, almost joyously. "It's time you got your hands a little dirtier. I want you to find Savage. You know him best, and I have a feeling you will know where to find him. Now, you pick up the last two runners in two hours and take them to Brazil. Is that understood, Richard?" Gideon said, evil but calm.

"But, I've got these guys on my butt. I can't do it. How can I? Okay . . ." Jacques said. The two men standing in front him – Toni Brazil and Kelly Primeau – told him to accept Gideon's offer.

"I knew you'd agree with me, Richard. Now here's what I want you to do," Gideon began.

37

"What do you mean, they're not on the plane?" Bo said into his cell phone, as he stood in the FBI's security office at JFK. It was 3:00 P.M., and Jeffrey Bodakis and his team were setting up surveillance positions at the airport when the call came in from his counterpart at the Washington field office.

"Look, your agents got on the plane with them," said Assistant Special Agent-in- Charge Frank Thomas. "When they got off, they weren't there. They never left the plane. We searched it, nada. No one was there. I'm sorry Jeff, but we lost'em."

"Have any clue how they did it?"

"Apparently, a little boy said he saw two men crawl to the back of the plane and then two men crawl to the seats before take off. Sounds like a wild story, but apparently the flight was delayed because they forgot to put food on the plane. Your targets were sitting in the last row, and they loaded the food at the rear of the plane. They had help, but no one saw a thing other than the kid. We're locating the crew to interview," Thomas said.

"What about the two impersonators?" Bo asked.

"That's another thing. They must have changed their clothes and looks before they got off the plane. No one saw them leave, and there was nothing left behind, no masks, clothes, nothing. They must have stuffed their gear in bags," Thomas explained.

"Well, that's just great!" Bo responded, not believing what he had just heard. "They had help, no doubt about it. Frank, let me know what you guys find out," Bo said. "See ya."

"Okay, Jeff, I will," Frank replied, and hung up the phone.

"Un fucking believable," Bo said, as he put the cell phone back on his belt.

173

"What's up, boss?" asked Special Agent Larry Turnbull. "Everything hunky dory?"

"Not exactly, Larry. Would you go get Valarde for me? And take his place. Randy will be with me the rest of day."

"Oh, yes, sir, boss," replied Turnbull. He turned and hurried through the door leading into the terminal.

In the security camera Bo watched Turnbull exit into the terminal and run through the airport to Velarde. Bo liked Turnbull, but he was from Atlanta, and Bo couldn't take the southern drawl today. The news that just came in wasn't good, and Bo knew it meant the subjects could be anywhere. He saw Velarde making his way through the terminal. He was grateful that Randy came to New York at the last minute to stay with the case, especially with the recent news. He wished Randy had taken the same flight as Cain and Abel.

Bo knew Randy wouldn't be happy about the news either, since the young agents who lost the pair were under his supervision. The news told him that he had underestimated the men, maybe the whole group he was dealing with. Bo buzzed Randy through the security door and greeted him with a smile.

"Hey Randy," Bo said glumly.

"Turnbull said you wanted me. What's wrong? You look like you just got hit by a train," Randy said.

"Your boys lost Cain and Abel," Bo said plainly.

"What? How?"

"They just walked off the plane after they got on it," Bo said.

"I don't understand, Bo. What are you talking about?"

"We underestimated them, Randy. They had help. Somehow, they switched places with two other guys or something, and pouf! They were gone," Bo answered.

"Damn! I'm gonna shit-can those two when I get back to SF," Randy said, enraged by the mess up. "Damn it!"

"Yeah, you got that right," Bo replied, disappointed. "They're young, Randy. Easy assignment turned into something over their heads. Watch out. You might be the one criticized. I suggest you chalk this one up to experience. Beside, when's the last time you were burned on an assignment when the targets had inside help like that?" Bo asked.

"Ah, shit, Bo," Randy replied, head down and silent. "Yeah, you're right. I hear you. What do we do now?"

"Well," Bo started, "I think we assume the worst. Cain and Abel are here in New York City with new identities and looks, watching Savard and Lowe.

FIERCE LOYALTY

It's the only thing that makes sense. We'll have to keep our eyes open. We should assume they know we're on to them as well." Bo looked at Randy with raised eyebrows.

"Yeah. Okay, man," Randy answered. "I'll put the word out to everyone else." He pulled out his cell phone, which doubled as a walkie-talkie.

"I doubt we'll even see them close to Savard and Lowe until later. I think Cain and Abel are here to kill them. We've got to be prepared to take them down," Bo said seriously.

"Look, Bo. We know where Savard and Lowe are staying tonight and tomorrow. They're not going to their apartment, which probably means they're planning to run after they finish here. I say we hook them up tonight in their hotel room," Randy said.

"Patience, Randy," Bo replied. "Patience never killed the cat. I'll give it some thought, though, if we spot Cain and Abel. Otherwise Savard and Lowe are the best bait we have right now. We can't afford to act hastily."

38

Upon orders from his superiors, Kelly flew to New York City with Toni Brazil, and took the newly stitched and bandaged Richard Jacques in tow. Gideon ordered Jacques and the last two runners to fly to New York, where they'd receive further instructions where and when to meet Savage, who Gideon believed would contact him and demand more money. He would agree to pay more and set up a meeting place for the delivery. All Jacques had to do was wait for the call from Gideon and then send the runners to kill Savage.

But other plans were in the works as well. In New York, Toni and Kelly would make contact with Jeffrey Bodakis, and hand over evidence of the scheme to the FBI, along with Richard Jacques for questioning. Jacques would be prosecuted in Canada for his part, but Toni persuaded him to cooperate, and maybe earn a reduced sentence. Toni tried to contact Bo. He was out of the office on an assignment and could not be reached. Bo's secretary offered to put Toni in touch with his temporary replacement, Tom Trimble. "No, Thanks," Toni said.

While working out the final details of their travel, Kelly received two phone calls. The first informed them that the body of the first kidnapped runner had been found dead, dumped in a back alley behind Alexander Savage's home, a bullet in his head like the others. The second call was better and came just as they were leaving for the airport. Vermont police found Savage's car parked at the airport in Burlington. They inquired at the check-in gates but found no one fitting the description of Savage, Chigall, and Father Chason. They checked the rental car station, which produced a break. Savage, Chigall, and Father Chason rented a blue Dodge minivan two hours earlier.

The Vermont and New York State police stationed unmarked cars at all

176

FIERCE LOYALTY

major highway intersections and bridges between New York from Vermont. They would be found, but the plan was not to pick them up, but rather to find out where they were going. Neither police department liked it, but Toni asserted federal jurisdiction, since there was a potential health risk to all Americans. Toni knew he was walking a fine line with his authority, but it was risk he had to take. He wanted Savage first.

Since Toni's hotel was near the Montreal airport, he and Kelly swung by to pick up his belongings, and then onto the airport for the short flight to New York City. The Royal Canadian Police called ahead that they were coming into the country with a prisoner, so they'd be escorted through customs without delay. Yet, Toni felt they were not alone. His intuition told him someone was watching his every move, but he wasn't sure who.

Toni left Kelly and Jacques in the car and again felt watched while they were dropped off at the departure gates. He'd seen no one suspicious and no unusual cars, but Toni knew his gut. Something wasn't right. He'd wait for their move.

Earlier in the day Jacques helped Kelly and the ISU take the last two runners into custody. Anyone reporting to Gideon and watching the airport wouldn't have seen a thing. Kelly and Toni drummed up a plan to have two ISU officers take the place of the runners after a short disappearing act at the customs office. The Royal Canadian ISU had twenty-five volunteers at the airport within an hour, and Toni and Kelly matched two officers with the runners.

Dressed like Catholic priests, the runners were easy to locate when they came into the customs area. Jacques escorted them to a closed room, where the Royal Canadian Police took them into custody, and began an interview. Neither man would talk, and Toni believed they were wasting precious time trying to make them. They were loyal to Gideon, and all that mattered to them was their mission. They did however, have four vials that matched the vial Toni found in Bobby's belongings, which were taken to a Canadian government lab for testing. All four vials were 'hot' with the virus. It was for real. Toni, Kelly, and everyone in the ISU who participated in the take down were shaken.

Toni knew why Bobby was killed, and he thought about his call for help, remembering the desperation in Bobby's voice. Why hadn't he called Bobby back that night?

Toni turned his thoughts to Richard Jacques. Even though he helped take down Gideon's runners, Toni knew he also helped kill his brother. One false move by Jacques, and he'd kill him with his bare hands, if he had to. He'd rather see them all dead for their part, but being in his line of work, he'd keep his thoughts to himself. He'd wait for an opportunity to exact his revenge. There had to be an avenging Angel, and Toni wanted to believe he was that person.

The airplane landed at JFK International Airport 3:30 P.M. Toni reached down to turn on his cell phone. He looked at Kelly, who had Jacques handcuffed.

"Can you get my bag, Toni?" Kelly asked.

"Sure thing," Toni replied, as they all stood. Toni's cell phone chirped. "Voice mail," he said to no one in particular as he dialed into his voice mail.

They started through the jet-way, Toni behind Kelly and Jacques, listening to the message.

"Shit!" Kelly and Jacques turned simultaneously. Toni slowed to a stop as they entered the terminal.

"What's going on?" Kelly asked.

"Ask him," Toni said, pointing to Jacques. "He knows."

"What?" Jacques replied. "Me? I don't know what you're talking about?"

"Well, if you want to be that way Jacques, I'll call Gideon and let him know what you're really doing," Toni replied.

"You wouldn't, Brazil."

Toni opened his cell phone and took a phone number from of his shirt pocket, while staring at Jacques. "Country codes," he said into the receiver.

"Wait!" Jacques exclaimed. "Okay! Just hang up you crazy son of a . . ."

"Let's get one thing straight right now, Jacques," Toni said. "If you fuck with me, I'll put you down. I'm not on duty, asshole. I will put you down so fast."

"What's going on, here?" Kelly interrupted.

"Okay," Jacques began, staring at Toni. "I'll tell you, but I want protection from these guys. They can kill me, fine, but I've got a wife and two kids."

"That's not the issue, Jacques," Toni said. "Kelly's ISU already assured their safety."

"Toni? What's happening?" Kelly asked again.

"Savage isn't going to New York," Toni said bluntly.

"Where's he . . ." Kelly started.

"Washington," Jacques said glumly.

"We've got another flight to get on," Toni said. "It leaves in an hour, but Jacques here has some explaining to do first." He took Jacques firmly by the upper arm.

FIERCE LOYALTY

"Where we going?" Jacques asked.

"There!" Toni pointed to a bathroom.

"Wait," Kelly said. "We have to contact Bo. This thing has to be brought to the federal authorities. You know that."

Toni shoved Jacques into a chair. "Stay!" He turned to Kelly. "You call him. Jacques and I will discuss his future on this earth." He tossed the phone to Kelly.

"No!" Jacques interrupted. "You can't leave me with him, he's crazy!"

"Shut up, Jacques!" Kelly said with a hint of anger in his voice.

"We'll try Bo before we leave, and I'll try his home in case he's off work. But I think Jack here owes us an explanation," Toni said.

"What do you mean?" Jacques squawked.

"That call I got, Kelly, was from your old boss, Koty. He said the New York police picked up our guys as they crossed over to New York from Vermont, but they bypassed New York City, went through Albany, and they're in Pennsylvania, headed for D.C. They've got us on a flight to Washington in an hour."

"Jacques," Kelly said, "I'm starting to lose my patience with you. Now start talking."

Jacques looked resigned and began to talk immediately. "Savage called me last night after he killed Gideon's men. That's when he came up with the plan for me to search Brazil's hotel room. He said he had his own plan with the virus, and he'd call me from his boat."

"Where's his boat?" Toni asked.

"Somewhere in Virginia," Jacques replied.

"Where was he going to call you, Jacques?" Kelly asked.

"Home. He's got a cell phone, and he said if I didn't hear from him by tonight, to call him. He said he was going to need my help. I told him he was crazy, but he threatened to kill my family, if it was the last thing he did."

"Oh, Jacques. I'm sick of your fucking lies and excuses," Toni spat into Jacques' face.

"You don't understand, Brazil," Jacques blurted. "I believe him. You forget, I've seen him do a lot of things. He's the one who decided to kill your brother the way they did it. Chigall went along with him." He paused, his eyes watering. "Gideon should be calling soon. He'll know Savage is headed to Washington, soon enough. I wasn't trying to hide anything. This whole thing is crazy."

"I won't argue with you, Jacques. Either you're going to help us right now, or we're going to drop you off at a New York police station where they'll hold you in one of their drunk tanks. You ever see one of those cells, Jacques?" Toni asked.

"I know his cell phone number, but I don't know what kind of boat he has, only that he moved it to Virginia a month ago," Jacques said urgently.

"Let's go, Jacques. We're taking you to the FBI. We'll catch another flight," Toni said, in a lighter voice. He took Jacques shoulder to lift him off the chair.

"One more thing," Jacques said. "There is another person involved with Gideon's plan."

"What?" Kelly asked.

"Savage mentioned once that the Americans wouldn't know what hit them, because there was someone helping from the inside, and . . ." Jacques swallowed.

"Inside what, Jacques?" Toni asked.

"The U.S. Government," he replied. "There's also another plan to circulate the virus."

Toni turned without a word and steered Jacques through the terminal. He looked for the sign for outside transportation, but realized they had to consider what Jacques had said. He felt sick that someone inside the government could be in on Gideon's plan, the plan that had ultimately led to Bobby's murder. He couldn't decide whether to go to D.C. or find Bo and get rid of Jacques, first. His job was almost done, he thought, and he wanted to put his brother to rest. But he couldn't drop the ball and run. That would be too easy.

Toni decided what to do. He knew who killed Bobby, but many more were at risk. He wouldn't rest until it was over, until Savage and Gideon were stopped. He was on a mission now, and he knew what he had to do.

Journal entry: May 18, 2001

It's my little bro's birthday today. I wish I had the guts to call him. Well, happy b-day little bro. I could sure use your help today. Father Julius Chigall arrived only two weeks ago, and I already know he's not a priest. Why would a priest have three different passports, with three different Ids', all with his face, some with a beard, some without and short or long hair. I found them by accident the second day he was here, while returning his clothes from the laundry. I looked further and found a weapon I recognized as a semi-automatic nine-millimeter Makaroff, Russian made pistol. I'd seen them in Vietnam used by the Viet-Cong.

FIERCE LOYALTY

I continued my search, and found what appeared to be maps and other paper work. They were written in French and I began to copy them on the pages following. They appeared to be instructions, maybe orders. I don't know. I finished copying them in two hours. I'm having them translated tomorrow by a friend at McGill University. More disturbing was what I found in Father Chigall's Bible, which was in a drink cooler placed in the back of his closet. The cooler was very cold and had what appeared to be dry ice inside it. I retrieved my leather garden glove, reached in and picked up what appeared to be a book, a Bible, though it was different. I opened it, and I found a compartment inside where there was a box with Russian writing on the outside of it. I copied it down in the following pages. I'm having it translated as well, at the University. I think it is some kind of biohazard. But whatever it is, I'm scared. I'm afraid this guy is some kind of terrorist, and I've stumbled onto something. Maybe I'm just crazy, imagining these things. I don't know. I've decided to keep my cool, and continue to watch Chigall. I want to call Toni so badly, but I don't think he'll talk to me.

BB

39

The phone rang breaking his daydream as he watched the New York countryside move by. He found the cell phone and lifted it to his ear. "Bodakis," he said.

"Bo! Thank God I found you," said the voice on the other end.

"Frank, is that you?"

"Yeah, Bo, it's me," replied Special Agent Frank Thomas. "I've got some good news for you on Cain and Abel."

"Well, I can sure use some. What ya got for me?" Bo said, and Randy Velarde, who was driving, began to show interest in the call.

"Your two principals flew into Baltimore on another flight. They boarded the flight under two new aliases. They landed three hours ago. We're trying to find out if they caught another flight, rented a car, or were picked up," Thomas said.

"That is great news, Frank. How'd you find out what happened?" Bo asked.

"Velarde's guys in SFO hit the pavement. A check-in clerk at U.S. Airline identified them. They were traveling under the names Benny Cisco and Juan Franco. The clerk said she spoke Spanish fluently, but they weren't speaking Spanish. She said they had short hair, almost buzz cuts. We altered their photos for her, and Bingo! Unfortunately, they landed in Baltimore about the time she made the ID, but we're only two or three hours behind them. The Baltimore airport is small, so we should know any time now," Thomas said.

"Fantastic, Frank, let me . . ." Bo stated; now feeling the adrenaline starting to flow.

"Wait! My other phone is ringing. Hang on Bo!" Frank interrupted.

182

FIERCE LOYALTY

Bo looked over at Velarde, at the wheel of the white nondescript van that was part of the six-vehicle team following Savard and Lowe.

"Bo? Are you there?" Frank asked.

"I'm here, Frank. You're breaking up a little, so hurry. What's up?" Bo said.

Frank's reply was too garbled to be intelligible.

"Frank? Frank?" Bo yelled into the phone, but it was dead. "Shit! These damn things." He looked at his phone. It had run out of power.

"What happened?" Randy asked.

"My phone ran out of power. I lost him," Bo replied. "They found Cain and Abel. I heard that part, but that's it."

Bo paused. The distinct chirp from the phone attached to the console between the seats startled them. Bo reached over to pick it up, when something caught Velarde's eye, the vehicle they had followed for the last hour.

"Oh shit!" Velarde said. Bo looked up and saw Savard and Lowe's vehicle was pulling over to stop.

"What now?" Bo sputtered as they passed and the car stopped on the side of the road.

183

40

Toni suddenly felt the presence he knew was around. He stopped abruptly and turned around but recognized nothing and nobody. He peered through the crowds but saw only the faces of people he did not know.

"What's wrong, Toni?" Kelly asked.

"I don't know. I keep feeling something, like someone is following us. I can't explain the feeling. When I look, there's no body I recognize."

"I've had the same feeling," Kelly said.

"You didn't say anything?"

"Nor did you, until now," Kelly answered.

"If we're both feeling it, then I'm believing it more. If someone is following us Kelly, who would it be? Someone helping Jacques maybe?" He looked at Richard Jacques.

"I'm dead, I know it," Jacques said, upset. "It's Gideon's men."

"Shut up Jacques!" Toni said, loud enough so that people walking by them heard his remark.

"I can't think of anyone, but it's possible Jacques is right. It could be Gideon's men," Kelly replied.

"We need a plan, Kelly. What are we doing? I can't seem to get through to Bo, and I don't trust Trimble. We have to get this thing to Bo. He's the only one I trust," Toni said.

"Well, we know the secondary plan to distribute the virus is Gideon's only hope at putting his plan to work," Kelly concluded. "I'd bet they're going with the four-corner theory – D.C., Dallas, Chicago, and Los Angeles. That's where they'll release the virus. He'll want to infect as many as possible and fast. So he has everyone going to Washington. What we don't know is if Savage is a part of the

FIERCE LOYALTY

second plan."

"Not bad. Kill the evidence, and go to Plan B," Toni concurred. "Where'd you learn about that four-corner theory?"

"Saw it in a movie," Kelly said. He and Toni broke out laughing.

"I can't believe Gideon knew Savage would take his guy hostage. It's my guess that Savage knew he was disposable and decided to put a kink in it. Instead he took Chigall hostage, and killed all his men. Savage is greedy, but smart. He wants more money," Toni theorized, "and he has what Gideon needs, the virus."

"I believe you are right," Jacques inserted. "Savage isn't part of Plan B. He would have told me. I'm sure of it."

"Well, then, we all agree. Savage is alone, and he's the person we have to find, especially if we can't get to Bo," Kelly concluded.

"I have a plan," Toni said. "Let's assume Jacques is clear, and neither Gideon nor Savage knows he's cooperating." He looked at his watch. "We have thirty minutes to catch our flight to D.C. I need to make one phone call before we board the plane. Let's go, Jacques. You're going to be our bait."

Journal Entry: May 25, 2001

Today I followed Chigall to a vacant building, where he was met by a real estate agent. He was not wearing his collar and dressed in a business suit. The RE agents name was listed on the 'For Lease' sign on the building, Francois Greico, 514-714-2252. Building location 2292 Chamois Way. I am not sure what he's doing here, but it's definitely not church business. After they left, I entered the building. I can still pick a lock. It has eight large rooms, two stories, four rooms on each level. Full bathrooms with showers. I believe the building used to be a gym. I followed Chigall back to the basilica. I heard him on the phone in his room. He sounded panicked. He spoke French, so I couldn't understand what he was saying. Something is wrong, and I don't know what. I had to re-schedule my meeting at McGill with the bookworm, Father Chason wanted me to move some storage items to make room for four new priests visiting next week.

Who else can I tell about this? Father Chason? I'm not sure anyone would believe me anyway, except maybe Frank. But, I'd rather not involve Frank, unless I have to. He's a good friend, but he's got a family and his shit together now. Neither of us have had a drink in four years, thirteen days and about 14 hours.

BB

41

"Hello Bonny," said the familiar voice through the cell phone that rang moments earlier inside a briefcase. She knew who it was before she answered. The voice always made her shudder.

"Gideon," Bonny Savard answered nonchalantly. "We haven't gotten to the farm yet, so there's nothing new to report."

"Good, because there's been a change in plans," Gideon said.

"A change?"

"Yes. There's a problem, and there is no need to buy that last farm. I want you to turn around immediately and drive to Washington. There is a room reserved in your name at the Marriott Hotel in Crystal City, Virginia. Are you writing this down, Bonny?"

"Yes, Gideon, I'm writing," she replied, looking at Phillip who was driving the Geneon System company van. He looked back at her in confusion. She shrugged her shoulders in return.

"Good. I've checked the bank account we set up. You have five million left. I've arranged for you to pick up a million in cash at the Bank of Switzerland on 14th and Pennsylvania tomorrow at 11:00 A.M. When you have done that, return to the hotel and wait for further instructions. Do you understand?" Gideon asked.

"Yes, but why are we . . ."

"No questions, Bonny. You just do as I say. If you refuse, I will have you killed. The van you are in has an explosive device and some other electronic surveillance devices. It's very high tech, so if you think you can just walk away from the van, you're wrong. It will explode before you can open the door. When you get to the hotel, call me before you get out of the van. Press

186

FIERCE LOYALTY

the # 3 button on the phone. It will dial me, and I can turn off the device," Gideon said. "Oh, and if you believe you can run once you've reached the hotel, I'd think again. You'll be watched. One wrong move, and you are history."

"When can we go, Gideon? I'm starting to think I'd rather be dead. You've locked us up in a jail," Bonny said, beginning to cry.

"I promised you that I'd let you go, didn't I?" Gideon said, raising his voice. "You distrust me? You question me? You bitch!"

"No! I don't trust you Gideon," Bonny whimpered. "Why should I, you bastard!"

"I've let you live this long, have I not?" Gideon asked, calmly. "It didn't have to be like this. It could have been different for us. You know that, don't you, Bonny?"

The line went silent and she could hear him breathe. Before she could answer, Gideon hung up.

"Yes," Bonny whimpered back into the phone. Silence was the response.

Philip Lowe looked at Bonny. He didn't know what was said on the phone, but saw tears streaming down her face. He put his hand on her arm. Her face said it all. They were dead, unless they did something soon.

42

Gideon and Simi had been at the estate in Nice a few hours. Gideon sat looking out from his balcony over the Mediterranean. The sun was bright, and the air was warm, perfect, he thought. His plan went awry because he trusted Savage, maybe underestimated him. He knew Savage was a wild card and believed he could use him for his own purposes. He had a back-up plan, just in case. He had started paring the operation down, closing all but two farms in the United States. He sent two of his scientists to his offices in Dallas and Chicago, where Geneon had smaller, less sophisticated labs, but capable of duplicating the virus.

The focus shifted to recapturing the virus and delivering it to the labs, where it would be painstakingly duplicated and released into the air conditioning system of the airports in Dallas, Chicago, and Washington. From those three locations, it would spread throughout the country within a day or two. The plan's one major drawback was its failure to spread the virus directly to the U.S. military. However, he bought two other dairy farms secretly in the beginning to test the original plan. He had those facilities getting ready for the virus to be delivered. They would be his final plan if the Dallas and Chicago labs didn't work. He also believed Brazil knew about the virus and would notify the authorities, who would begin inoculating the military anyway. The U.S. wouldn't know what happened or who was responsible, until it was too late. The plan would work subtly, infecting hundreds of thousands of people.

The Middle East would be a different story, as well as Russia, India, and Pakistan. He'd have control of their nuclear arsenals soon, and the U.S. would either negotiate with him or invade those countries. Impossible with the job they'd have in isolating the virus at home. Massive confusion would

FIERCE LOYALTY

reign around the world, as all the research and development he and his brother did over the years came to fruition in the European Union countries, Russia, China, and the Middle East.

The stakes were higher though, if anyone found out. The outbreak could be linked to his company, and not to the United States, maybe even to who he really was, something he didn't want. His plans for Europe, Asia, and the Middle East would be delayed while the virus was disseminated simultaneously before any one country found out what was happening. More importantly, the initial outbreak had to occur in the United States, and then spread to the rest of the world to appear as if the U.S. government had an accident with the virus. Nothing else was acceptable. The blame had to lie with the U.S.

"Yes, Simi, what is it?" he asked, as his servant appeared on the balcony.

"You have a phone call, sir."

"It is Savage?"

"It is, sir," Simi replied, in an unusually tense voice.

"Is there a problem, Simi?" Gideon asked. "Please, tell me your thoughts."

"Sir, I believe Savage is no longer needed, and I'd be grateful if you'd allow me to honor you with his death warrant," Simi said.

Gideon smiled. "You will have your opportunity. Now give me the phone and prepare yourself for a trip to Washington."

"Thank you, sir," Simi replied, handing him the phone. Gideon hit the mute button on the phone and put it to his ear.

"Well, well, well. I presume we have a negotiation to undertake, you and I," Gideon said.

"Gideon! Is that you?" Savage replied aggressively.

"It is me, Savage. Now what have you done with my product?"

"I see you've been told about my work back in Montreal," Savage said.

"I have, Savage. I don't have time for your antics. What do you want?"

"It's not what, Gideon; it's how much to return your product and keep me alive and quiet," Savage replied cautiously. "Since you already tried to kill me once, this will be on my terms. Is that understood?"

"Of course," Gideon responded graciously, "your terms. I've got a million in cash waiting for you, and I assume you're on your way to Washington. Just let me know where to drop it off. You can leave the product with Chigall."

"I'm afraid you don't understand, Gideon, a million is not what I had in mind," Savage replied. "You see, I know you have billions, and I know who you really are, Gideon – or should I call you Simon?" Savage asked, pausing for effect.

189

Gideon laughed and stood up, amused by Savage's use of the name Simon. He would have to do away with Savage. He thought before, he could use him, the wild card, to kill Bonny Savard and Phillip Lowe, but no more. He would have Simi kill Savage, which would please his old friend. He took a deep breath. He heard Savage breathing strangely. He was coked up by the sound of his nasally voice.

"Oh, Alexander, you are just too good for me," Gideon said. "Are you still using that nasty nose candy?"

"None of your business, Gideon." Savage retorted. "Stop playing games."

"You are right, of course," Gideon replied. "How I could have underestimated you, I'll never know. How much will it take for us to come to terms?"

"Well," Savage said, feeling more in control, "you and I are very much the same type, Gideon. I've done more than my share of research on you. I also know who your brother is." He hit Gideon with a moment of silence. "I was thinking more like twenty-five million."

Gideon laughed, holding back the anger. The money was no problem. There was more of that than he needed, but with the mention of Simon and his brother confirmed that Savage was the fool he thought he was. Savage thought he knew the truth, but the truth eluded him. But he knew Savage wasn't bluffing, and he needed the virus. He thought more about his next step and broke the silence with a calmness and control that kept Savage in doubt.

"Savage, you are very cunning and deceitful. You've been a busy man. Since you are in charge, how would you like the money delivered?" He would let Savage make the plan and he'd work around it. "What is your plan?"

"Do you have a pen?"

"I do." Gideon picked up a pen from the glass table.

"Then write this down: Bank of Switzerland AIS 9-9-2-5-8-4-6-3-2. You get it?"

"Very good, a Swiss bank account. Aren't you the smart one?" Gideon replied.

"Of course," Savage said. "I want the twenty-five million in the account first, and then I want the million in cash you offered me, too. As soon as I know the money is in the account, and I've picked up the cash, I'll tell you where your product is, within twenty-four hours."

"Consider it done," Gideon replied. "Call me in twenty-four hours. The money will be in the account." He hung up before Savage could say another word.

FIERCE LOYALTY

"Simi! Simi!" Gideon yelled. Silently as a cat on the prowl, Simi returned to the balcony where Gideon sat, calmly staring out at the water.

"Yes, sir."

"Make arrangements for Washington," Gideon said urgently.

"I have, sir," Simi replied.

"I need you to make arrangements for me. I am coming with you," Gideon said, without feeling.

"Do you believe that's wise, sir?" Simi asked.

"No, Simi. It is not wise, but it is necessary," he replied. "I want you to call the bank." He handed Simi a piece of paper. "Transfer twenty-five million into this account."

"Will that be all, sir? Do you want me to pack you a bag for the trip?"

"No. I will take care of it myself, Simi. You are dismissed for the day." Gideon said, as he held up a glass of water and drank it swiftly.

43

Simi turned and walked back into the house and down a long hallway, which overlooked the three stories down to the front entrance. His walk became quicker as he reached his room, and closed the door behind him. His demeanor had not changed. He sat on a wooden chair at a desk. He found the piece of paper Gideon gave him. He considered what he was doing, waiting for an opportunity to reveal itself. He believed it had finally come, and he was ready to take advantage. He opened the drawer, took out his personal phone book, and turned to the back page. He found the number to tap into his laptop to dial the bank.

"This is the Bank of Switzerland automated teller. Please enter your account number," the recorded voice instructed him.

Simi punched in the account number and the password. After a few seconds, the screen gave its approval. He requested a transfer of funds. He knew the money was for Savage, to be sent to the account Gideon wrote down, but today would be different. Simi punched in his personal account number, where he would transfer the twenty-five million. He had set up accounts under several business names and aliases for almost twenty years, waiting for the chance. Finally it had come. He would move the money among the more than three hundred accounts he controlled, and only then direct it to his personal consulting account, named T&T Enterprises. Anyone trying to trace the money would take years to find it. By then the money would be gone.

Simi had been silent through the years. The Picards had underestimated him, even though he warned them to never underestimate anyone. At first, he wanted to test them, but as time went on, and he'd seen Thomas and Simon

FIERCE LOYALTY

change, he saw he couldn't stay. Thomas Picard had killed Simi's son, and when he returned from the mental hospital, he saw that Thomas would kill him if he said anything or left. He planned an escape. At first he wanted to kill Thomas, but he was stuck. He had nowhere to go. He'd have to endure and take care of the bastard who killed his son. It hurt every time he looked at the man, but Simi knew it would do him no good to kill him. He developed the plan that would hurt him most. He would spoil his plan to infect the U.S. with smallpox, take his wealth, and find the son taken from him almost thirty-five years before.

Over the years, he took whatever turned up. A hundred thousand here and there wouldn't be missed, but he knew he'd have to gain Gideon's trust, as well as access to his money. As it turned out, that was the easy part. When the moment came, he would vanish with all of Picard's money he could get his hands on. He set up accounts and developed a computer program of automatic withdrawals, so chunks of money would move around among various accounts within forty-eight hours of the initial transfer. Then every day for the next six months, the money would move again to accounts all over the world in many different banks. He tested the scheme at least once a year when Gideon asked him to transfer large sums. It worked so well, the accountants never questioned it.

Simi hit 'Enter' after his account number. Savage would be either dead or on the run within forty-eight hours, and Gideon could only hope his death would be painful. He considered approaching Toni Brazil to do the deed he'd wanted to do for so long. It was payback time. Simi knew he'd help Brazil kill Gideon if the opportunity arose.

Simi logged off the on-line banking program. He looked at the piece of paper Gideon gave him, crumpled it, and tossed it into the garbage can beside the desk. He put the address book back in the drawer. He reached in and pulled out a picture of himself standing with his wife and twin boys. He remembered the day in Vietnam, August 30, 1967, two weeks before his life was turned upside down. His wife dead, then a few years later, his son murdered. Thinking of them made him go cold. He thought of his other son, Tommy, still alive and living in Washington. He hoped he could catch up with him and explain his life, and that Tommy would understand. If not, he would die. There would be no reason to go on living alone. Death would be his new beginning.

Simi smiled, rubbed the picture with his left hand, and put it on the desktop. He reached into the drawer again, and took out an envelope, gazing at the

193

return address from T. T. Carlyle. He could barely make out the date of the postmark, 1985. His son Tommy wrote the letter seventeen years earlier, but he never answered it. Simi watched him from afar, knowing where he was all the time; waiting for the day he'd escape the Picard prison. That day was coming tomorrow.

44

"Sir, it's Stan Jacobs in our Australia office. I got the lead for the Picard accident case file. Is the information still relevant to your case?" he asked Jeffrey Bodakis.

"Yes, Jacobs. I'm just in the middle of something here," Bo replied.

"Should I call you later? Your secretary said you'd probably want this report ASAP and an update about what is happening here," Jacobs continued.

"Yes, yes, you're right, Jacobs. Now is a good time. Tell me what you've found out about Simon Picard's accident." Bo peered at Velarde whose eyes never strayed from the road. They were not sure at first why Savard and Lowe turned around, but it was clear they were not aware of the surveillance. A phone call came in on Savard's phone. They were able to triangulate the call made from overseas, probably France.

"I faxed my report to your office, sir, but to give you a short overview," Jacobs said, "the authorities here investigated a diving accident after a call came in from a dive tour operator about a missing passenger identified as Simon Picard. They determined he was dead. Picard was on the tour by himself when they got to the dive area. Everyone dived for a couple hours, but Picard never came back. They never found his body, although two days later they found some of his gear. It had Picard's blood on it. They also found shark teeth in his gear and shark's blood. They believe he went off on his own, something went wrong with his equipment or he had some kind of accident, and shark's attacked him."

"How long before they noticed he was missing?" Bo asked.

"Over four hours, sir. Everyone had come back. They did a head count before leaving for another spot for a short dive and noticed he was missing."

"Any other boats in the area, that day?" Bo asked again.

"Oh, yes, sir, there were two other tour boats, but no one reported seeing Picard," Jacobs replied.

"Any thing else, Stan?"

"Well, yes. A privately owned boat was seen in the area and identified by one of the tour boat Captains, Jesse Bohannon. He noted the boat in his log, as he always does for insurance purposes. The police traced the boat to a local man named Luther Franks, who rented it to an American-Vietnamese man on vacation with his wife and two sons. The guy's name is Thomas Bui Tran. The police interviewed them, but they didn't see anything," Jacobs said.

"Thomas Tran?" Bo asked. "Name's familiar."

"Yes, sir, it might be. Mr. Tran was an extremely reliable witness. He works for the Federal Bureau of Investigation," Jacobs said, with some conviction.

"Right," Bo said. "I thought that name was familiar. Tommy Tran. I think he works at D.C. Headquarters."

"I ran him, sir. You're correct. He's at HQ. In fact Tran gave his address in Alexandria, Virginia," Jacobs reported. "That's about everything. Will you need anything else from us?"

"Did you contact Agent Tran?" Bo asked.

"No, sir. When I located him at HQ, I figured I'd give you the option of re-interviewing him," Jacobs replied.

"Thanks, Stan. Just one more thing, what squad is Tran assigned to?"

"Intel," Jacobs replied quickly. "International."

"Thanks, Stan. You did a fine job."

"Thank you, sir. Let me know if I can assist further. Gud'ay as we say in Australia!"

"Gud'ay, Stan."

Bo dialed another number. "Jamie?" Bo said, as his secretary, Jamie Stone, picked up after one ring.

"Hello, Jeffrey," she replied.

"Thank God, you're still in the office," Bo said with a sigh of relief.

Jamie Stone had been his secretary for six years. A tall African American woman in her early forties, she worked her way off welfare as a trainee, when she and Jeffrey Bodakis met. Shortly after, Bo was promoted and told to hire a secretary, and he already knew who he wanted, Jamie Stone. She was tough, intense, and Bo trusted her to do things right.

FIERCE LOYALTY

"Your orders! Don't you remember, boss?" Jamie responded brightly.

"Of course I do, Jamie. I need you to do one thing for me, and then you can go home to your family," Bo said.

"Whatever I can do for you so I can get out of this place."

"Sorry, Jamie. Trimble been driving you nuts?"

"Oh, forget him. He left hours ago, went back to D.C. That's what he told me anyway!" she said.

"What? He went to DC? Why?"

"You think he was going to explain that to me? I know I run this place, but he walks to a different beat. You know that!" Jamie replied sassily. "I probably just ignore him, anyway."

"Shit!" Bo yelled.

"What you want, Jeffrey?"

"Call personnel at HQ and have them pull the official personnel file of Special Agent Thomas Bui Tran, as well as his background investigations from the last . . . Oh, get all of them. Tell them I will pick up the files at nine tomorrow morning," Bo said.

"You going to D.C. too?" Jamie asked.

"Looks that way, Jamie," Bo said. "If any one asks why I want the file, just tell them he's being considered for a promotion."

"What if Tran's OPF is in storage?" Jamie asked.

"Where's storage?"

"Boyers, Pennsylvania."

"Then tell them to send a new agent to pick it up," he answered.

"Can I quote you on that?" Jamie asked, without a quiver in her voice.

"You ask me that every time." Bo replied.

"I know, but the first time I don't ask. I'll get in trouble. Is there going to be anything else?"

"No, that's it, Jamie. If I need anything else, I'll call you at home. Have a nice night."

"I sure will, Jeffrey. You too," Jamie replied. "Oh, I almost forgot. Your friend, the one whose brother died, has been calling – three times in fact."

"Toni Brazil?"

"Yeah, that's him, Toni Brazil. He said if I talked to you to give you his number, and tell you to call him as soon as possible," she said.

"Toni's been calling? Anybody else?"

"No, just Toni. He did say it was urgent, but I was under your orders not to give out your cell phone to anybody, and . . ."

197

"Yes I remember, Jamie. Give me his number," Bo replied, and she gave him the number. "Thanks, Jamie. If he calls back, give him my car phone and cell phone."

"You be careful out there, Jeffrey," Jamie replied. "I'll hurt you worse than anyone else you know."

"I know that," Bo retorted smiling.

"Tell Velarde I said the same. Good night, boss," she said.

Bo hung up and thought about Special Agent Tommy Tran. There was no doubt Tran had access to every report sent to Director Mahoney's office regarding his case and countless others. It was time to meet Special Agent Tommy Tran, Bo thought, and sooner rather than later.

45

Toni, Kelly and Richard Jacques boarded the short flight to Washington's National Airport. Toni started his career in the nation's capitol fifteen years earlier, and visited at least once a year since his relocation to San Francisco. They were seated at the rear of the plane, which suited Toni just fine since it afforded some privacy to question Jacques further. It would be almost 6:00 P.M. when they arrived in D.C., just about the same time Jacques would check his messages at home to see if Savage called.

"So, Jacques, tell me about Gideon . . ." Toni said, stopping mid-sentence as he saw what he'd been looking for the last several hours, a man he made a mental note of on the flight from Montreal to New York. The man wore a baseball cap, but Toni saw his head was shaved as he lifted the cap off his head. He was short, stocky, no facial hair, with a scar on his left cheek that gave him away. Toni remembered the scar.

"What's going on?" Kelly asked.

"I believe I've found what we were feeling earlier, Kelly. Nine rows up on the left, green baseball hat."

Kelly peered forward and sighted the man. "I'll keep an eye on him. Let's change seats."

They got up and moved to other seats, which caused enough commotion in the airplane cabin to turn heads, which gave Kelly a chance to observe the man. He, too, recognized the face.

"I've seen him before," Kelly whispered, "our earlier flight to New York. It's too coincidental, Toni. He's our tail."

"What do you think?" Toni asked. "The guy who hit me at the Tavares house?"

199

"It's possible. But who is he?"

"Maybe Jacques here knows," Toni said, "or maybe he works for Gideon." Jacques was sweating, and more nervous. "You'll be fine Jacques. Whoever he is. He won't try anything until later."

"What? How do you know that?" Jacques stuttered.

"Just a gut feeling, Richard. Now relax," Toni said. "If this is your last few hours alive, may as well enjoy it. I'll even buy you a drink."

"Thanks. I could use one," Jacques said, breathing heavy and trying to calm down.

"We need to discuss what you'll say to Savage when you contact him tonight," Toni said, his voice becoming serious.

"I know. You have to believe me when I say that I'm sorry about your brother. Savage threatened to do the same thing to my family, if I said anything or went against him," Jacques said.

Toni could see he was scared, but shrugged off any sympathy. He didn't care what Jacques felt. It wouldn't bring back his brother. "What makes you believe I care? Your family is still alive, and they're being protected. Remember what happened to my brother, or is that just a distant memory for you?"

"Did you find the note in your hotel room, Brazil?" Jacques asked.

Toni wanted to choke him. He gripped the St. Christopher medal around his neck he found inside the envelope with the note. Anger stewed inside Toni as he stared at Jacques. He gathered himself deep inside, deciding not to pursue the matter of the note. Though he was convinced Father O'Brien put the note in his room. But Jacques brought the note back into the forefront and only confused the matter more. He took a deep breath trying to calm his nerves. He changed the subject.

"I need you to set up a meeting with Savage sometime late tomorrow afternoon. It's what Gideon wants anyway. He thinks you're with the last two runners, so he'll probably want us to kill Savage and maybe Chigall. Gideon will call you, and soon," Toni said, considering his next words carefully. "There's a place in Old Town Alexandria, the Torpedo Factory, near the water on King Street. It's public enough, plenty of places to blend in." Jacques nodded his acknowledgement.

Toni continued. "There's a places for Savage to dock his boat. My guess is he's docked either at the main D.C. marina or somewhere on the Alexandria side of the river. We can't watch every marina, and he won't arrive until late tonight. If we're lucky, we'll find him before our meeting tomorrow. Regardless, we'll take him out on his boat. I'll have to get Bo involved, and fast."

FIERCE LOYALTY

Toni bore in on Jacques. "Whatever you do, Jacques, don't try to escape. You'll be killed for sure. I'll make sure of it." He almost wished Jacques would try to escape. He wanted Jacques to squirm, just like his brother did when Savage, Chigall, and Jacques beat him to death. He didn't care about the note any more. It was a little too late.

Journal entry: June 3, 2001

Today I found out what the package with Russian writing is all about. It says 'Small Pox Virus', 'Danger', 'Danger', 'Danger'. It was shocking and my friend at McGill University wanted to know where I'd found these words. I won't mention her name, but she knows me, and I have a nickname for her, Bookworm, cause she's always in the library doing research, at least that's where I always find her. I had to tell her that I was reading an article about the virus and Russia, and I was curious. Chigall is up to something wicked. I now know that. I noticed that Chigall's been nervous lately, he knows his stuff is missing, so he's been asking around if anyone's been in his room. It's only a matter of time before he figures it out that I'm the one. I'll do what I have to do.
BB

Journal entry: June 16, 2001

Today, while following Chigall, I noticed someone else following him, too. There were two of them, and I wrote down the license number, Quebec 550-6LNO. I recognized one of them, the driver had been at church before, and I remembered Father Chason told me he was a cop. If they're cops and I could trust them, maybe I should talk to them. Something about the passenger though, I didn't like the way he looked. When have I ever trusted cops, anyway?
The French writings I copied from Chigall's books were translated. They turned out to be instructions with dates of departure and the location of where Chigall was to travel. He was to depart on September 1, 2001 driving to a location near Arlington Virginia. He was the last to leave, there were six scheduled departure dates, all listing teams or individuals and the locations, cities and states, though no addresses. I don't know why. There was a map of the United States that listed military bases with arrows leading from the cities to the bases. The locations listed are Dallas,

201

TX, Pensacola, FL, San Francisco, CA, Chicago, IL, Arlington, VA and New York City, NY.

The writings were military type orders and signed by a 'Gideon'. Who is Gideon?

The bookworm wanted more information from me, she's suspicious I know, but I had to tell her it was just some research I was doing. I considered telling her, but would I be putting her in danger? I think so. I didn't say anything. I have to tell someone, but whom do I trust – Toni? Will he even talk to me? If he does, will he believe me? I'll call Toni, and send him the info if I have to prove to him that I'm not crazy. I don't know who else to contact and if he'll just let me explain to him what I found, he'll know what to do. I wonder if he knows how badly I feel. He's my little brother, he's blood, he'll talk to me, he has to: I'll make him.

BB

Journal entry: July 2, 2001

Today, I decided to call the RE agent listed on the for lease sign on the building, Francois Greico, 514-714-2252. He told me the building was leased to a company named Geneon Systems, a French company. I called Toni, my brother, last night, but he wasn't home. I could only leave a message. My dad called later, and told me Toni had been shot. I'd seen the news about the shooting, but the news didn't release anyone's name. Shit, I wish I could be there for him now. I'd do anything. Dad said it was bad, but he's stable for now, and not to come unless his condition changes. Man Toni, you can't die on me, not now. Who can I tell about what's going on. I want to be there for you Toni, and I will be somehow, some way, but I can't cross the border, not right now, I just can't take the chance. Love you Bro, I'll say a prayer for you.

I spoke with the bookworm, and she did some research for me on Geneon Systems. It's a biotech company that develops medicines for the aids virus, or at least that's the company line. She told me the company was owned by a Dr. Simon G. Picard, whose middle name was 'Gideon'. He was a leader in the research sector on viruses, but recently he died in a diving accident in Australia. The company and assets were left to his brother and sister, Thomas Picard and Melissa Picard, but the sister wasn't a part of the company board of directors or leadership team.

FIERCE LOYALTY

Thomas was the Chairman of Board, and President of the company. He was also acting CEO, as he had recently fired the last one a few months ago. There were no known photographs of Thomas Picard for the last 20 years. He was a recluse and there was a $1 million bounty for a picture of Thomas Picard issued by The International Inquirer. Apparently, no one knew what this guy looked like.

The bookworm told me about an article she read in an Australian Newspaper. It mentioned a witness from America who just happened to be a FBI Agent, Thomas Tran, who just happened to be vacationing with his wife and kids in the area. He worked in Washington DC. What did that mean? Was Picard under investigation by the Fed's? I might be able to call in an anonymous complaint to the FBI, but would they investigate in Canada?

BB

46

"Jacques? You sound under the weather," Gideon said, the laptop telephone device in his lap. The device helped divert signals away in case someone was tracing incoming calls. He had to be careful now. He was getting personally involved against his own better judgment.

"I'm fine," Jacques replied, "just a little tired."

"Good then. You and your guests will be heading to Washington immediately," Gideon said. He looked around the airplanes first class compartment. Everyone was sound asleep. "Your orders are to take care of two people, a Bonny Savard and Phillip Lowe. They will meet Savage at a yet to be determined location."

"Yet to be determined? Who are Bonny and . . ." Jacques started.

"That is not your concern, Jacques," Gideon said, calmly. "You and your guests are to simply take care of them. Is that understood, Jacques?"

"But," Jacques mumbled nervously.

"But what, Jacques? What is your problem?"

"Savage has already contacted me, and . . ."

"He what?" Gideon shouted, as quietly as he could. A head popped up from two rows in front of him.

"Savage called me. He wanted my help. He wanted to meet tomorrow at a place in Alexandria, Virginia, the Torpedo Factory," Jacques said, as if reading from a script.

"What is the matter with you Jacques?" Gideon asked, irritated.

"Nothing, sir. I just thought, well, I knew you'd want to . . ." Jacques stammered.

"Spit it out, Jacques!"

FIERCE LOYALTY

"I just thought you wanted us to take Savage out, so I agreed to help him so I'd know where to find him."

"Yes, Jacques, you were right. You continue to surprise me, Jacky. But too many things have gone wrong and time is of the essence here. I can't have any more mistakes. What time is the meeting?"

"Two-thirty. I needed time to get there, and flights were full," Jacques replied.

"Okay, Jacky, two-thirty it is then. Are you near a fax machine?" Gideon asked.

"I . . . Yes . . ." Jacques replied and gave a number Toni wrote down.

"I'll send you a picture of Savard and Lowe. They will meet you at two, at this Torpedo Factory, King and Union Street, I see. There appears to be a restaurant there," Gideon said. He punched instructions into the keyboard of his laptop, which displayed a picture of the building and restaurants at the Torpedo Factory. "The Chart House. They will meet you there, and you will approach them. They will give you a bag you will then give to Savage. Your guests will take care of them after they leave. Is that clear, Jacky?" Gideon asked, excitedly. His plan seemed to be coming together even better than he had hoped.

"Yes, sir," Jacques answered. "What about Savage?"

"Savage is my problem, Jacky. I will take care of him personally."

"I understand, sir."

"Good boy, Jacky. You do your part and walk away," Gideon said quietly, knowing he was lying, but giving Jacques a false sense of security.

"Walk away?"

"I never want to see or hear from you again, Jacky. Is that understood?" Gideon said.

"It is," he said. "Just one thing, Gideon."

"And what is that?"

"My guests want to know what their orders are after they take care of Savard and Lowe?" Jacques said.

"Nice try, Jacques. That's a Grade Four Detective question. I still don't trust you," Gideon replied, cautiously. "They already have their orders."

"The money will be transferred to my account then, as usual?" Jacques asked.

"It's already there, Jacques," Gideon said, and hung up the phone.

Gideon looked to his left where Simi sat, his eyes closed. He noticed Simi's arms lay flat with palms up, the fingers brought together at the tips

205

barely touching. Simi sat cross-legged on the first class chair. He was meditating, not sleeping.

Simi taught him to fight using Tae Kwon Do, and then taught him to respect nature and acquire wisdom; but meditation was a procedure Gideon did not have the patience or personality for. Simi claimed that meditation cleansed his spirit of the shame and dirt of everyday life. Meditation was an opportunity, not a task, to be practiced daily, not only when needed or desired.

Simi breathed in deeply and then exhaled slowly, a clear signal that he was finished. His eyes opened. "You are watching me," he said, cautiously.

"Yes, it is my wisdom to watch you and learn, but it is also time to discuss our plan," Gideon replied.

"Our plan does not matter, sir. Our actions will determine our fate," Simi responded gently.

"Yes, Simi, you are correct. We must be stealthy and sleek, or we will not succeed. I do not trust Jacques. His loyalties are not in line with our future. He must not survive. I believe he is a weak link," Gideon said. "He may be cooperating with the police."

"Yes, my inner spirit agrees. My sight has seen his demise, as well," Simi replied.

"The alternate sites will be ready in forty-eight hours. I expect Savage will have at least two alternate plans for his escape. He has a boat, and I have arranged for a boat in case he tries to escape that way, which he most certainly will. Saied and Yassir will pick us up at the airport. They will take us to the boat, and we will move it to the docks at Old Town Alexandria in the morning." Gideon said.

"I want to terminate Savage on my own terms, sir," Simi said tonelessly.

"Yes, Simi. He is your responsibility and yours only. It should be taken care of before he meets with Jacques at 2:30 P.M. tomorrow. Therefore, it is imperative you find Savage first; terminate him, the old priest, and Chigall. Yassir and Saied will be at your service. Savard, Lowe, and Jacques will be terminated by Mikhail and François," Gideon said.

"I have no need of Yassir and Saied, sir. I will take care of Savage and his companions myself. It is wise for you to have the protection of the two Hamas agents. But I want to ask you if you've considered Toni Brazil?"

"Ah, Toni Brazil," Gideon started. He shuffled through some papers and took out a picture of Toni. "His termination should be done soon. I've ordered Mikhail and François to take care of him, the sooner the better." He paused, a smile forming on his lips. "And you are correct. I will keep Yassir and Saied

FIERCE LOYALTY

with me. I see your point. I may need the protection."

"Yes, this is a wise decision," Simi agreed. A slight, almost unrecognizable sliver of a smile parted his lips. For the first time in almost sixty years, Simi felt freedom at his doorstep. It was almost time to break free of his lifelong jail sentence.

47

Toni walked through the gateway into Washington National's concourse with Kelly and Jacques in tow. As he eyed his surroundings, he spotted what he was looking for, but the man was well ahead of them. Toni knew the tactic well, and knew his tail wasn't alone. There would be a trailer; someone hanging back that Toni had not spotted yet. Toni doubted they would make a move on Jacques in the crowded concourse, if he was their target. They would wait to get on the road, but Toni had a surprise waiting for them outside at the curb. Toni called his boss and trusted friend, Alex Fox. As they reached the escalator, he could still see the tail ahead of him. At the top, he headed straight for the doors to the main passenger pick-up area.

Toni looked back and forth but did not see their tail. "Where in the hell did he go?" he said. Toni pushed forward to the automatic doors, and they opened as he walked through. He looked right, and there was Alex Fox next to his black Chevy Suburban, waiting right where Toni asked him. He started a slow jog to the car, Kelly and Jacques following in a fast walk.

Seeing Toni, Alex got in, and Toni heard the engine rumble to a start. A horn behind him startled Toni into looking back, and he began running again. Kelly and Jacques followed, also running. Toni reached the car and opened the rear door first. He looked back as Kelly and Jacques arrived and jumped into the back seats. Toni slammed the door, gave one last look around the outer concourse. He saw nothing, opened the door and jumped in the front passenger seat. "Let's get out of here!" Toni exclaimed, slumping into his seat. The truck lurched forward with the accelerator punched to the floor, "We've got a tail."

"I take it you're in some kind of trouble," Alex said, checking the rear

FIERCE LOYALTY

view mirror. "You must be Kelly Primeau."

"Yes. Toni has said only good things about you, and you're right. We're in a bit of spot, sir," Kelly replied.

Alex realized Toni and Kelly had been through a long day, and decided not to chide them. "Toni, your gear is in the bag at your feet. What can I do to help?"

Toni considered the offer, but knew he wouldn't accept. "You are helping. Drop us off at the Holiday Inn in Old Town Alexandria. Get your family and drive somewhere safe, until you hear from me. This isn't your fight."

"I don't know what's going on here, but it sounds like something for the FBI. I think you should . . ." Alex started.

"Alex, we've been trying to contact Bo, but no luck. I don't trust anyone else at the bureau. They'll just bring in the brass, which can't be trusted at this point," Toni responded assertively.

"Look, Toni," Alex said quickly. "I've spoken to the guys at the office. We all want to help. You're going to need some backup for whatever you're into."

"You've already done your part, Alex. I don't want to involve you or the guys any more than what you've already done. Did you have any luck at the marinas?" Toni asked as they turned onto the George Washington Parkway.

"Matter of fact, I did," he replied. "Four weeks ago, a thirty foot slip was rented at the Potomac Marina on Daingerfield Island by a Canadian." Alex found a notebook and shuffled through its pages. "Here it is. The guy's name was Richard Jacques."

"What?" Toni looked back at Jacques, who looked just as surprised.

"What? It wasn't me! No!" Jacques whimpered, breathing in and out heavily.

"Relax," Alex said. "The harbor master had a copy of the guy's passport photo in the file, and it isn't that guy in the back seat."

"Lucky for you, Jacques," Toni responded.

"Who's the guy in the back seat? And what happened to his face?" Alex asked.

"He's the real Richard Jacques," Toni replied, "and he fell, to answer the second question."

Alex found the picture as he drove. "Here it is. Here's the picture of the guy." He handed the picture to Toni.

"It's Savage," Toni said, and handed the picture back to Kelly.

"Who's Savage?" Alex asked.

209

"He's our main problem at the moment, and a guy whose life is coming to a tragic end." Toni said, then changed the subject. "What kind of boat was docked?"

"A forty-foot Bayliner, the Juliet. It's at Dock C, Row 28. Sleeps four, full galley, shower, and bathroom. Has directional capabilities, two four hundred horsepower engines, and holds fifty to sixty gallons of fuel. It's seaworthy, but I doubt anyone would want to take it too far out. That kind of boat is shore to shore," Alex explained.

"What do you mean, shore to shore?" Toni asked.

"You don't want to take it too far from the shore. Fifty gallon's of fuel will take you only so far. There are refueling areas along the eastern seashore and inlets. Whatever this guy's doing, he'll only be able to go so far, at any one time. That could be advantageous, but my guess is that when he goes, he plans on not being found out. In other words, whatever he does, when he leaves the area, he believes he won't be identified for at least a week or two with a boat like that," Alex said.

"How long did he lease the space for?" Kelly asked, from the back seat.

"According to the harbor master, this Jacques or Savage guy explained that he just wanted temporary docking, and he'd be down within the month with his family. They'd be heading southeast of Florida to the islands. He gave him three months rent plus something extra, so they agreed to a short term rental," Alex replied. "This something to do with your brother, Toni?"

Toni contemplated whether to say anything. "Alex I know you want to help, but the more I say, the more risk I give to you. I can't do that. Thanks for doing all this. It's been very helpful."

They headed down Washington Street to Old Town Alexandria, one of Toni's favorite places. He lived there while he worked at FHA headquarters, and made regular visits for dinner when he visited. The hotel was right in the center of Old Town on King Street, a perfect vantage point, Toni thought. At the hotel drop-off, Toni noticed the dark blue Ford Taurus parked across the street and recognized Alex's wife, Julie, in the driver's seat. She smiled and waved at Toni, who waved back.

"You sure you don't need anything else, Toni?" Alex said, getting out of the truck.

"There is one thing you could do," Toni began. "There's an FBI agent named Thomas Tran. I need to know where he lives. You still have that contact over at the bureau?"

"You need to know where an agent lives? I'm gonna need to know why,

FIERCE LOYALTY

Toni," Alex replied, a little irritated.

"Can't tell you. If you want to help, find him for me," Toni replied.

"I'll do what I can, but no promises," Alex replied. "You sure there's nothing else I can do? Something a little easier?"

"Yeah, find Tran's address, and get out of town."

"What about Jeffrey Bodakis?" Alex asked.

"Can't get in touch with him. He's out doing something important," Toni replied. Then as his boss walked away, "Alex?"

"What, Toni?"

"Thanks for trusting me. When this is over . . ." Toni started. "Never mind! Just get out of the area for a few days, and tell everyone else you can think of to do the same."

Toni moved over to the driver's seat and drove to a parking area in front of the hotel. He got out, and Jacques and Kelly also left the back seat. They stood at the entrance, watching Alex Fox walk to the car where Julie waited. Toni knew he needed help, but couldn't ask. Alex looked over at Toni, then turned away and sped off.

48

The Lincoln Town Car waited at the curb of the main terminal at Washington National Airport, exactly where it was expected. The name 'Greenberg' was posted on the passenger side window. The bearded driver, in a black suit and red tie, stood at the rear door holding a sign with the same name. A second man sat in the driver's seat, waiting to pull away as soon as his partner packed the trunk and the passenger was seated.

The driver saw three men run to a black truck two hundred yards or so ahead. To his right, two men, one short and bald, the other of normal height, ran to the car. The short man said, "I'm Greenberg. Let's go!"

The driver readied the engine, and the two men rushed into the back seat. The door opened on the front passenger side and the second man got in after closing the trunk, and sat next to the driver.

From the back seat, the short bald man barked an order. "Follow that black truck up there! Now, go you idiot!"

The driver revved the engine, but waited for his partner seated next to him to put his seat belt on.

"Follow the black truck, you idiot," said the short bald man again from the back seat. He leaned forward to look at the driver and his partner in the front seat. The passenger was rubbing his face. What is he doing? Then the man in the front passenger seat turned to face him.

"Oh, for the love of God!" The short bald man said.

"Yes, Yuri," the man next to the driver said. "Getting closer to God is a good thing for you," said a smiling Father John O'Brien.

"John and . . . is that you, Gino?" asked Yuri Barhak, as he twisted to see the driver, who peered back at him in the rear view mirror. "Yes, it is you. You

212

are interfering in Israeli business. I could have my understudy arrest both of you."

"You wouldn't do that, would you?" John asked, pulling a long face.

"You know these two, sir?" the young man next to Bahrak asked.

"Yes, unfortunately, I do," he replied, sitting back and grinning slyly. "It looks like we are at the mercy of these two. May as well introduce you. Meet Father John O'Brien and Father Giovanni Corvo, the most unusual priests you'll ever meet," Yuri said. To the priests he said, "My understudy, Mika Revel."

"It's a pleasure, Mika. I hope you stay wary of your partner," John responded. Mika nodded and said nothing in return.

"Mika," Yuri started, "you should take note that we are speaking with a dead man. John died. How long has it been, John? Two months?" Yuri asked sarcastically. "They are nothing to worry about, Mika. They are friends." He put a hand on Mika's arm, stopping its movement toward the weapon tucked under his jacket.

"Can't blame him for trying, Yuri," John said. "You must have trained him well. I didn't notice his arm moving at all."

"John, would you tell us where we are going?" Yuri asked.

"Certainly," he replied. "We already know where Toni Brazil is going, but we'd like to know why you are following him. I thought you got what you came for," John said wryly.

"What do you mean, John?" Yuri asked, with a straight face.

"Yuri, please. I know all about the incident at the Tavares house. We know you and Mika took one of the two missing packages," John said, turning to face his Mossad counterparts. "I'd bet Toni Brazil would like to know who hit him on the head. I hear he's got a bad temper."

"I see," Yuri responded curtly. "I won't ask how you got that information. You priests amaze me though, not just with your faith, but also your cunning. You see, Mika," he continued, "these two priests are not your ordinary men of the cloth. This is your last lesson. It is good to have friends in all places, even those on the opposite end of the spectrum. The opposite does not always equal the enemy."

"You are wise, Yuri," John exclaimed. "I hope we can become friends, Mika. I'm sure we can help each other. Yuri knows how to contact me. You may leave my information with him, Yuri, if you wish."

"Now, John, I insist you tell me. Where are you and Gino taking us?" Yuri asked.

"A little bird tells me everything Brazil, Primeau, and Jacques say. They will meet us at the Potomac Marina in approximately twenty-five minutes, unless they decide to eat first." John responded jovially.

"I see you're using more sophisticated devices these days. I presume if Brazil is headed to the marina, then Alexander Savage will be there too?" Yuri asked.

"You are a smart one, Yuri, but Mr. Savage won't be joining us for at least another two or three hours," John said. "Your surveillance techniques need some work, Yuri. Toni picked you up in New York."

They arrived at the turn-off to the Potomac Marina and Restaurant, and followed the short driveway, to the almost empty parking lot. The L shaped two-story structure was round on the right side by the Potomac, with a beacon light at the top. The restaurant below glowed in the darkening surroundings of the marina grounds, covered by green grass and tall pines, birch, and weeping willows. Fall was in the air and nature's colors were abundant. Gino circled the parking lot, eyeing each vehicle as he passed slowly by. They parked in the front row, overlooking the main marina and the larger boats. The water glistened with lights reflected from the sidewalk and the few boats whose sails were lit and cabins aglow. At the end of Dock C, slip 28, the Juliet glittered in the faint light spiraling from a pole at the slip entrance.

"There she is, Yuri," Gino said, "and Juliet is her name."

"We wait then, and we agree to make our move together," Yuri said.

"No," John said. He raised his hand, which held a miniature canister pointed at Mika. He smiled at the confused expressions of the two Mossad agents in the back seat, obviously surprised and wondering what was happening. John sprayed Yuri and Mika with the sleep agent and stopped them cold.

"No, Yuri, we do not agree to move together. I'm sorry for the inconvenience, but we can't have you interfering with church business – nor obtaining the virus," John said.

Yuri and Mika's eyes went wide as balloons, and then just as quickly they closed. They slumped together. Gino hit the buttons rolling both rear windows down. "Let's go, Gino. We have only thirty minutes," John said.

Simultaneously, they jumped from the car, opening the rear doors and dragging Yuri and Mika to a twenty-eight-foot sailboat at Dock B, Slip 21, - The Marian. Gino looked at his watch. It was almost 8:00 P.M.

49

At 9:10 P.M., they passed the sign on the freeway, Harrisburg 15 Miles. Bo looked at Velarde, who sipped the coffee they'd picked up five minutes before when they stopped for a quick break and the other surveillance teams took over. They were doubtlessly headed for Washington, and Bonny Savard and Philip Lowe had not a clue they were being followed. Bo seemed lost about why they were going to D.C. A change of plans was the only explanation, but what was the change and why?

They considered pulling Savard and Lowe over, taking them down, and finding out what was going on. She talked once on a cell phone, or that's what they believed. Bo had a gut feeling they should be patient, and see where they'd go. The decision was his, and he hoped he wasn't making the wrong one. He tried twice to call Toni Brazil, but apparently Toni's phone was out of the service area. He decided to call him the next morning. The van was quiet as he and Velarde sped to catch up to the surveillance party. The silence was broken by the phone ringing inside the cab.

"Bodakis," he answered sluggishly.

"Yeah? Jeffrey Bodakis?" the voice replied.

"Yes, you got him. Who is this?"

"This is Agent Robert Pears, DC HQ Security Division. We've got a file on Agent Thomas Tran for you. Your admin said it was urgent. I looked you up, found out you were on surveillance, and wanted to know if you needed me to fax the file to you," he said.

"Fax the file to me? I'm in a car," Bo replied.

"Yeah, I know. Vehicle ID New York FAF223 is the license plate number and should be noted in the glove box," Pears responded.

SCOTT A. REZENDES

Bo opened the box and found FAF223, then replied, "I found it, and it's confirmed. Are you going to tell me there's a fax machine installed here somewhere?"

"Absolutely. All surveillance vans have them now. We installed them six months ago in your division. Look in the rear behind the driver's seat. You should see a metal box. Lift the lid, and you should find the equipment inside. The fax is coming through, according to my information here," Pears replied.

Bo looked behind Velarde's seat. There was a box, and he could hear something inside. He found the knob, lifted the handle, and there it was – paper flowing out of an HP fax machine.

"I take it you found it, sir?" Pears replied.

"Yes, Pears. Hey, thanks a lot," Bo responded. "This is unexpected."

"Sure thing. Your admin said Tommy's up for a promotion. I didn't know he put in for a supervisory position," Pears commented.

"You know Agent Tran?" Bo asked.

"Sure do. Tommy's good folk, good agent, and a smart guy, too," Pears said. "He's out on leave though. In fact, we had lunch today. He's leaving in the morning for Florida with the wife and kids."

"Shit!"

"Something wrong, sir?" Pears asked.

"No, Agent Pears, nothing at all. I just planned on speaking to him tomorrow about his application. Now I'll have to wait. Did Agent Tran tell you when his plane left?"

"Plane? That's not his way. Tommy's an avid sailor. He's got a boat out at the DC Marina, - The Drifter. She's beautiful. He's probably on her tonight doing last minute prep, if I know Tommy. He loves that boat," Pears said.

"Agent Pears, you're the duty agent tonight?" Bo asked.

"Yes, sir. Is there something else I can do for you?"

"Pears, I'll meet you in two hours at HQ, front gate. I need you to take me to Agent Tran's boat," Bo said urgently.

"Tonight? Why?"

"Because it's a matter of national security," Bo responded. "You've just been assigned to me the rest of the night. I'll take care of everything."

"I thought he was up for a job promotion?" Pears said, curious.

"That's not what I said," Bo responded.

"Is Tommy in trouble?"

"I'll tell you more when I get there, Pears."

"Okay. Two hours it is then, eleven o'clock. I'll be waiting, sir," Pears

216

FIERCE LOYALTY

said.

"Thanks, Pears, you've been a great help." Bo hung up the phone.

He reached over to the fax machine and pulled off the next two hours of reading material.

"What was that all about?" Velarde asked, looking back and forth from Bo to the road.

"We're breaking off the surveillance in DC. It's late. Whatever is going on, these two will have to stop at a hotel sooner or later. We'll wait and approach them early in the morning. You and I will be working late. We're meeting an Agent Robert Pears at eleven who will take us to Mr. Tran," Bo said, looking at the paperwork he took from the fax.

"Anything interesting in that file?" Velarde asked.

"Thomas Binh Tran, AKA Thomas Carlyle, was born in Saigon, 1967, the adopted son of an American Colonel, Franklin Carlyle, and wife, Jasmine Remy-Carlyle," Bo read. "Carlyle? Interesting coincidence."

"What coincidence?" Velarde asked.

"Carlyle's the name of the president's new White House Assistant Chief of Staff for International and Domestic Terrorism, Lisa Carlyle," Bo said.

"I don't believe in coincidences, Bo."

"I don't know, Randy. What are the chances? Carlyle is a fairly common name," Bo said.

"How much you know about her?" Velarde asked.

"Not much, to tell you the truth. Anyway," Bo said, "says here he changed his name to Tran in 1985, eighteenth birthday, after his adopted parents died in a car crash. Joined the Army Special Forces. Was assigned to a DEA unit in Colombia, drug war. Earned his college degree by 1988 and has an IQ of 198. Served in Desert Storm, then joined the bureau in 1993, was assigned immediately to Intel and been there ever since," Bo read on, then stopped, "Oh my God!" he then exclaimed.

"What? What you find?" Velarde asked urgently.

"Has an adopted sister, Melissa Carlyle!" Bo read, growing flustered. "Damn you and your coincidences."

"I told you. No such thing as a coincidence," Velarde said smiling.

"Says here that Tran hasn't seen her since he joined the Army in '85. Is that possible?"

"Anything's possible. Hell, he had to take a lie detector test too, didn't he? He's either a real good fibber, or he's telling the truth," Velarde said.

"Here's something interesting," Bo said. "Tran says his sister was adopted

SCOTT A. REZENDES

by the Carlyle's too, about a year after he was adopted. He didn't know who her real parents were, but the information was left in the Carlyle's will in case they died, so the kids would know who there real parents were. Tran says he has never met his father, who was half Vietnamese and half Laotian. His name was Binh Tran Simivong, and his mother's name was Truoc Vu Tran. When he decided to change his name, he used Tran, because both his parents had Tran in their name, and Binh was his father's birth name. According to his adoption and birth records, his mother was killed by the Viet Cong in 1965, and his father worked for the . . ." Bo said, then went silent.

"What? Worked for who?" Velarde asked.

"His father worked for the French ambassador to South Vietnam, Jerome Picard. He was the kid's nanny!" Bo said.

"The same Picard that died in that raid in 1967?" Velarde asked.

"The very same," Bo said. "Simivong disappeared after that and hasn't been heard from. No one knows what became of him."

"So let me get this straight," Velarde began. "Our Tommy Tran is the son of this Simivong fellow, who was the nanny for the Picards, the French ambassador to South Vietnam in 1967. Two years ago our Tommy Tran shows up in Australia where the son of Jerome Picard, Simon, is allegedly killed in a diving accident?" Velarde stopped, stymied. "Coincidences, Bo. They just don't happen like this."

"No, they don't, do they? We need to talk to Tommy Tran, and soon. Pull over!" Bo picked up the phone.

"What? Why?"

"Because I'm calling in for a helicopter pick up. We don't have two hours!" Bo said. "We won't be getting any rest tonight Randy."

"Great. Just great," Velarde said under his breath, as he read the freeway exit sign, State Police – Next Exit.

50

Toni felt tired and considered the next step in his plan. He could use some help, and he knew it. He recalled Alex Fox's offer. He'd been curt with Alex, maybe a little harsh. He was on the George Washington Memorial Parkway headed to Daingerfield Island and the Potomac Marina. He closed his eyes, trying to muster strength as he waited at one of many stoplights on Washington Street. He wanted to turn back and sleep, get up early in the morning. But he had to see the boat and its location before the morning. He'd changed his clothes and was wearing the all black garments Alex brought. He looked into the gym bag and found the night vision equipment, binoculars, eyewear, and camera lens. He'd need them to see the boat from where he would set up his surveillance position.

Toni knew the marina, how it was situated next to a park and wooded area. A paved running and biking trail ran through the parking lot and driveway into the marina. The boats were all to the left of the driveway, which gave way to a square parking area next to the harbor master's quarters and a restaurant. Toni knew of a smaller parking lot behind the restaurant where he parked the truck.

The dry dock was full of boats stored or waiting for repair, perfect cover for a surveillance spot in a wooded area just beyond the dry dock on a hill, well out of sight of anyone. Kelly wanted to accompany him, but then the problem became Jacques, and what to do with him. They considered cuffing him to something in the room, but there was nothing permanent. They'd have to gag him too, because once they were gone, he'd make noise, and eventually escape. To Kelly's dismay, Toni decided to check out the boat until Savage arrived. He smiled as he thought about what he'd do to Savage when he caught up to him. He wanted him first, and get some pay back for what he did to Bobby. The only problem was Chigall - Was he cooperating with Savage or being held hostage like Father Chason? That question would be answered when Savage arrived. In any case, Chigall had a hand in Bobby's murder, too. Toni would put them down one by one.

Toni thought about FBI Agent Thomas Tran. Kelly wanted to know why he wanted Alex to locate Tran. He explained that he had read the name in Bobby's journal, and that Tran was in Australia when Simon Picard disappeared. Both agreed it was probably no coincidence that Tran was there. They had discussed whether the FBI Tran was the same man Jacques said approached Savage and Jacques a few months earlier. Jacques described Tran as an older man. If it was the same person, Tran would be close to retirement. He knew he'd have to find Tran to find Savage, especially if Savage didn't show up at the marina.

He slowed the car, turned into the driveway, and slowly coasted down to the parking lot. In the restaurant to his left, people were eating dinner. He wished he could do the same, but wondered what would happen if the virus was broken open. Everything would change, and no one would be eating dinner at a restaurant. Many would die.

Toni drove to the row of parking spaces that faced the marina and parked in a space overlooking the entire area of floating boats. He looked for Dock C, Slip 28. It was just to his right, and housed one of the bigger boats in the marina. He backed out and drove to the parking spot shielded by the restaurant, where Toni eyed a young couple in their late twenties. He noticed how she looked at him with a sexy smile. She was attractive, Toni thought, with her long brown hair that fell on her tanned shoulders. She picked up her glass of wine, took a sip, never taking her eyes off the man across from her. He took a bite of his food. He didn't even notice the look in her eye at that moment. He'd missed it, the moment gone forever. Toni wondered if Veronica had ever looked at him that way. He didn't know, too busy to notice. He had to change his thoughts and forget about Veronica and Chloe. It was time to move on.

Taking the gym bag, Toni stepped out of the truck and broke into a run to the woods behind the dry dock. He ran up the hill, the forest growth grazing his face and arms. It was dark, but his eyes adjusted. He slowed to a walk, and found a small opening that looked down on the main parking lot. As good as it would get, he thought.

Toni unzipped the bag, and took out the equipment, including a folding

FIERCE LOYALTY

chair. He sat in the chair, and arranged the equipment. He put the camera on a tripod looking down at the marina, then raised the binoculars and saw the boat perfectly. Even though there were many trees around, he'd found a view straight to The Juliet riding calmly in her slip. The binoculars were good and he would be able to make out who was who on the boat. If he had a long-range rifle and scope, he could take Savage out. That was one piece of equipment he couldn't get from Alex.

Toni looked around the marina at the other boats. Something caught his eye on a sailboat across from The Juliet, a man walking up from below the main cabin. He thought he recognized him, but was unsure. He adjusted the focus on the binoculars, and followed the man around the outer deck where he sat down in a chair facing Dock C. Toni picked up the camera with the 300mm night vision telephoto lens. He brought the camera up to his right eye and brought the man's face as close as possible. Toni recognized him, took the camera away from his eye briefly, then looked again to see if his eyes were deceiving him. He'd met the man once, but had seen his face many times on television over the past two months. It was the face of a ghost, most would believe. The man was alive and well, and Toni wondered whether he was friend or foe.

The name on the boat fit perfectly – The Marian. The man was Father John O'Brien. Toni knew O'Brien wouldn't be alone, and expected that Father Giovanni Corvo was aboard as well. How did O'Brien know where to find Savage? Toni remembered when they met in the hotel room in Montreal. What did O'Brien say? Father Chason gave them information he'd obtained from Kelly Primeau. With Father Chason held hostage by Savage, who was helping O'Brien? Kelly? Maybe, but he and Kelly were together all day, and most of the last three days. It had to be something else, Toni thought, good surveillance techniques maybe, or electronic surveillance? Was it possible? Were they using electronic surveillance? Whatever it was, the plan was changed, and he'd have to wait to make his move. He would watch and see what O'Brien did when Savage arrived. He would then figure whether O'Brien and Corvo were friends or enemies. Toni looked at the sky. A half moon floated overhead. "Give me strength," he whispered.

The headlights of a car pulling into the driveway brought Toni's attention back to the marina. He couldn't see what type of vehicle it was. He brought the binoculars up to his eyes. The vehicle circled the lot and finally slowed to a stop. Toni homed in and saw it was a blue Dodge minivan. He hit the night vision button, and moved in closer to check the license plates. It was the van

Savage rented. He leaned down and took a knife from the bag. He sheathed it in its grooved pocket tied around his ankle. He took the binoculars again and started back to a sitting position.

A blast of light, so bright, hit him that he had to cover his face with his left arm. Toni felt the heat of fire. The blast shook him off the chair, and he bounced and rolled over, then looked down at the marina and watched as The Juliet exploded in a ball of flame and smoke. A second explosion erupted as a boat next to The Juliet blew also, throwing him to the ground again. Pieces of the boat began dropping around the marina, onto the parking lot and the other boats. Fires broke out on several other boats, and he barely noticed Savage driving away. The taillights left the marina and turned right onto Washington Parkway, heading toward downtown Washington.

Toni took the binoculars and watched Father O'Brien, Father Corvo, and two other men running along the dock to the parking lot. Father O'Brien was helping one of the men, a short, bald, bullish man who Toni recognized from the plane and in the airport. Who was he? Why was he with Father O'Brien? All four men jumped into a black Lincoln and drove away. Toni knew he had to leave too, and fast. He didn't want to be held for questioning when the police arrived. He couldn't afford to be detained, not now.

Sirens blared in the distance. The police would arrive soon and begin questioning the restaurant patrons. Toni scrambled to pick up his gear. He didn't have time to fold the chair. He took a detour to the right, near the river, and dropped the chair down the hill. It tumbled down the hill and fell into the river. "Perfect," he said and sprinted to the truck.

From the edge of the wooded area, he saw his truck and the restaurant patrons standing outside in the parking lot. He pulled the keys from his pocket and hit the button to unlock the door. The lights blinked, and he started a sprint to the truck, running low. He got there in seconds, quietly opened the door and jumped in. He saw a dirt road leaving the dry dock area and remembered that Marina Drive continued to the south side of the Island, but he wasn't sure where the road led.

Fire engines began arriving at the driveway with lights flashing. There was fire everywhere, and he couldn't leave through the front entrance. He decided to try the dirt road and see where it took him. He backed out slowly without headlights. He found the night vision goggles, slipped them over his face, and turned them on. He heard the buzz of the battery, turning his view into a green glow. He released the brake, and the truck lurched forward slowly, beginning the drive into the unknown.

FIERCE LOYALTY

To his right, Toni saw a faint glow through the woods. He followed the dirt path and found what he was hoping for, a paved road leading to the back of a large building. Light began to reach his eyes, and it became difficult to see. He took off the night vision gear, looked around, and immediately knew he had found the back maintenance road of the Alexandria Power Station. In one direction was the Parkway; the other was blocked by thick chain swinging between metal poles.

Toni breathed a sigh of relief. He put the transmission in park, opened the door, and jumped out. He opened the rear door and looked around for the equipment that came standard on many police vehicles, bolt cutters. He found them, walked to the chain gate, and cut it. He drove through the gated area, stopped, and returned to the chain gate. He picked up the chain and re-hooked it, using a space he'd left in the chain link. No one would know the difference. He put the truck in drive, and moved out. He reached a second street, this one paved. The street sign read Slaters Lane. He knew where he was. Turning right, he found the safety of the Washington Memorial Parkway. He turned right again, and headed for the Capital city.

Toni wasn't exactly sure why he headed for Washington and questioned himself thoroughly, but there was only one place he could think of to find Savage, the Washington, D.C. marina. He drove the speed limit and looked to his right as he passed the Potomack Marina where firemen scrambled to put out the blazing inferno. Savage must be going to the DC marina. Why would he blow up his own boat, unless he was trying to throw someone off the trail? Did he find out about Alex's inquiries? Or was it his plan all along? Just then, the cell phone rang.

"Yeah?" Toni answered.

"It's Alex."

"Alex! What did you find out?" Toni asked, excitedly.

"I just heard on the news about an explosion at the Potomack Marina," Alex said. "You know anything about it?"

"Not a thing," Toni replied smartly.

"We're gonna sit down . . ." Alex started.

"Alex!" Toni blurted. "You have anything else for me?"

"Yeah," he said, clearing his throat. "I found Agent Tran."

"Where?" Toni looked for a pen to write down the information.

"He's at the DC marina," Alex said. "He's on a boat called The Drifter, Row 2A, Slip 22. I called security. They're expecting you."

"Funny world," Toni said.

223

SCOTT A. REZENDES

"What do you mean?"

"I'm already headed that way."

"Whatever you're up to, Toni, you shouldn't be doing it alone," Alex cautioned. "Why don't I meet you there?"

"It's personal, Alex. Thanks anyway. Beside, you should be headed out of town." Toni hung up before Alex could argue more.

Journal Entry: July 14, 2001

Picard's name was familiar to me, and when the bookworm told me Dr. Simon Picard was the son of the former South Vietnamese French Ambassador, Jerome Picard, killed in Vietnam, it all came back to me. Funny how life makes a full circle. Simon, the kid from the jungle that day, and now he was dead too, just like his Father and Mother. I'll never forget the look on the mother's face when we returned without her husband. I later read in a newspaper she had been pregnant at the time of her husband's death, and gave birth to a little girl. But then about a year later, I read again where she committed suicide. It was sad. The kids were separated, the boys went with Picard's brother and the girl went with the mothers' sister who lived in the U.S.

It occurred to me that Simon's middle name was Gideon, and the orders Chigall had were signed by a Gideon. What did this mean? Was it the same person? Was Simon really dead?

BB

Journal Entry July 29, 2001

Today the two cops following Father Chigall visited the church and had a private meeting with Chigall. I could hear them yelling in a room, but couldn't make out what the conversation was about. The noise alerted Father Chason, who came and got me. He didn't know what was going on either, but became concerned and asked me if I knew anything about what was happening. He was concerned that Father Chigall had gotten in some kind of trouble.

Later after the cops left, Father Chason told me that Chigall had acted very strangely when he asked if there was a problem with the police. But Chigall had simply said there was no problem and that he was counseling the one identified only as Commander Savage for his

224

use of alcohol. He explained that Detective Jacques had brought him by to discuss the problem, and Mr. Savage got upset.

The Bookworm called. She had done some research on the FBI Agent, Thomas Tran. She found out he worked at FBI Headquarters in Washington, DC. She wants to know what I'm really doing. She called the FBI to locate Mr. Tran. The phone was transferred and answered by someone saying 'Intelligence Room'. I might write a letter to him. I have to do something.

Later today Father Chason told me privately that he was unsure whether Father Chigall was being truthful. I didn't tell Father Chason what I knew, but I knew he was right: Chigall had not been truthful. The two cops had been following Chigall all week, and I didn't believe Chigall was aware of it. Father Chigall had gone to the office space he leased for Geneon Systems everyday and spent all day there. I asked Father Chason what Father Chigall was supposed to be doing everyday. His reply was that Chigall was visiting hospital cancer wards. I knew then that Chigall was a fake, nothing more than a drug runner, but one that was dealing in the type of poison that could kill a lot of people. The question was, what should I do next? Will anyone believe me? I think they'd just arrest me.

BB

51

The helicopter arrived within fifteen minutes of Bo's call and the ride to the J. Edgar Hoover FBI Building took another fifteen minutes. A few minutes before they landed at 10:00 P.M., a call came in reporting an explosion at the Potomack Marina in Alexandria. After Bo and Velarde were dropped off, the chopper took off immediately for the scene. An early report said a boat exploded, and the FBI's bomb squad had been called out.

Agent Robert Pears met Bo and Velarde on the helipad, and escorted them to the elevator at the north end rooftop. They talked little, except for Agent Pears said he called Tommy Tran's house and spoke briefly with Tran's wife, Mimi. She confirmed that her husband was on the boat preparing for their departure in the morning. Pears ran a key card through a device connected to the elevator panel, hit the number five, and punched in a code on another device.

As the door opened on the fifth floor, Bo realized that in all the years he'd worked in D.C., he had never been on the floor. The fifth floor was Special Operations Division, and you needed an access key. A security officer in military fatigues met them, asked for their identification, and signed them in. They entered an aisle, where they seemed to walk and walk. Bo wondered how Pears found his way. No one said a word, until Pears opened a conversation Bo wished he'd started as soon as he met them.

"Tommy Tran's a good guy, sir. I'm sure you'll like him when you meet him. He's a popular guy around here tonight as well," Pears said.

"What do you mean around here tonight?" Bo asked.

"Oh, a friend of mine called asking for Tommy just an hour ago, just after I spoke with you," Pears replied.

"A friend of yours? Who?" Velarde asked, suspiciously.

FIERCE LOYALTY

"He's a big wig at FHA-CID, Alex Fox."

"Fox?" Bo exclaimed, looking at Velarde, and then back at Pears.

"Yeah. Alex and I were both park police. Then he went to FHA, and I came to the bureau. Known Alex for twenty plus years. You know him?" Pears asked.

"Yes. I know him. But why was Fox asking for Tran?" Bo asked.

"Wanted to know where Tommy was. He said it was important. Had something to do with his boat. They both moor at the DC Marina. Like I said, I've known Alex . . ." he started again.

"I know, I know, for twenty years," Velarde interrupted, irritated.

"Something wrong with that?" Pears asked, abruptly.

"No, Agent Pears," Bo responded, "but we'd better get going if we're going to meet Tommy Tran tonight."

"Oh, almost forgot. Deputy Director Trimble wants to see you two," Pears said.

"Trimble's here?" Bo said.

"Yeah, he called from his office, said he wanted you in his office when you get here."

"How'd he know we would be here?" Velarde asked.

"Had to get approval when you called for the helicopter. He's the one who gave the approval," Pears responded.

"Shit!" Bo spat. "I believe we're going to skip it, Pears. We don't have the time to listen to Trimble spout off."

"But, look, I'm the one who . . ." Pears started.

"Look, Pears," Velarde interrupted, "this is national security. Trimble knows all about it. Now you're either with us, or you're with Trimble – who doesn't give a crap about national security," Velarde said. Pears eyes grew wide.

Velarde noticed Bo was silent too and flicking his eyes. Randy realized he'd opened his mouth once too often. He turned around, and saw Trimble looking at him, red faced. He could almost see the steam coming from his ears and nose.

"I don't give a shit. Is that it Velarde?" Trimble said, in a controlled voice. "Why don't you two come to my office, and we'll talk about what I do give a shit about."

Trimble stood looking directly at Velarde, and held his arm out to let Velarde and Bo pass. Pears started to follow, but Trimble put his arm up. He smiled at Pears and said, "You can stay here and wait for these two. They'll be back when I'm through with them."

227

52

Toni was amazed at the size and number of boats docked, as he peered out the window at the marina. He wondered which was The Drifter and whether Tommy Tran was a good agent or corrupt. He didn't think it mattered. He would approach him as if he were on the wrong side. He learned long before to be prepared for the worst.

Toni stopped for coffee to gather himself together, after what happened at the Potomac Marina. A half an hour passed before he started for the DC marina. He drove down the street fronting the marina, looking for the security office Alex described, and just as he said it would, the square white building soon came into sight. The security guard, a short man with a protruding stomach wearing a dark jacket with a plastic badge, and a baseball cap stood beside the office door as if waiting for him to arrive. Toni had to find the two vehicles he saw at the Potomac Marina, the blue minivan driven by Savage and the black Lincoln O'Brien and Corvo and the two other men escaped in. He'd written down the license plates, so he could identify them, but as he drove through the surrounding streets, he did not see the vehicles.

Toni turned his attention to finding a spot to park, close enough to the marina to walk or run to, but far enough, away not to be noticed or look out of place. The parking lots across the street from the marina were empty, except for the few vehicles parked by residents or visitors. They were too obvious, and not only would he not use them, neither would Savage or O'Brien. He found a large hotel complex with cars parked all around the outer perimeter of the building, one space just waiting for him, and just two blocks from the marina security gate.

The marina was rectangular. A long cement walkway in front of the gated

FIERCE LOYALTY

area led to the wooden decks of the slips. During the day, people on their way to the marina could stroll on the walk and gaze at the boats, then eat at the restaurants on the opposite side overlooking the boats. Everyone, however, had to go through the security gate. Toni looked at the boats as he came toward the guard waiting near the white, boxy building and the wire gate.

Toni felt for his weapon. He approached the man in his late fifties or early sixties with the round stomach Alex described.

"You the guy to see Mr. Tran?" the guard asked, as Toni pulled out his badge.

"Yes, sir," Toni said, and held his credentials out to the man.

"Well, Mr. Fox didn't say you were a cop, too. Okay, Mr. Tran's boat is right over on Row 2A, Slip 22." He pointed to his left and showed Toni the area. "It's just three rows over, the one with the lights on."

"Thank you," Toni said. "By the way, how do you know Alex Fox?"

"Mr. Fox has a boat docked here, and he lets me stay on it whenever I want. And you can call me Jerry," he said as he unlocked the gate. "If you need anything else, just pick up the phone at the end of the dock and dial one."

"Thanks, Jerry," Toni said, as he walked through the gate. "I shouldn't need anything further. Did you tell Mr. Tran I was coming?"

"I assumed you called him before you came," Jerry said, somewhat suspiciously. "Is everything all right?"

"Oh, of course I called, but I didn't know if you called when you saw me arrive."

"Oh. Well, I didn't see you arrive, so no, I haven't called Mr. Tran," Jerry replied, calmly.

"He knows I'm coming. Has his wife shown up yet?" Toni asked.

"No, Mr. Tran is alone for all I know. He said his wife was coming tomorrow morning with the kids," Jerry replied.

"Thanks," Toni said, starting to walk away. Then he turned to Jerry, again and asked, "Anyone else show up yet?"

"No. Are more coming that I should know about?"

"No, not that I know of either. Thanks again, Jerry."

"All right then," Jerry said and closed the gate.

As Toni approached Tran's boat, he decided it would be in his best interest to get a look at the vessel from a distance and see if he could locate Tran on the boat. How he approached Tran would determine if he would cooperate. He still didn't know if Tran was corrupt or not, but he was sure he was about to find out. Toni thought about what Jacques said about Tran. Jacques said Tran was older, but he broke Savages' wrist without any trouble. If it was the same guy, Toni had to be careful.

As he approached Row 2A, Toni thought, things were almost too quiet. A dim light atop a pole on each row barely illuminated the area. Toni looked down row 2A and saw five or six boats with lights on. He wondered how anybody found the right boat at night. He walked down row 2A, trying to be quiet. He was still wearing the dark clothing he had on at the Potomac Marina, so he knew he'd be hard to see. The boat slip numbers were posted on wooden platforms. He passed the fifth slip, and stopped to look at the large boat on his right. He'd always wanted to live on a boat, and this one would do just fine, Toni thought, as he looked over the fifteen foot wide and fifty or so foot long boat. As he turned away from the boat, a shadow moved behind him. A voice spoke before he could react.

"I don't know who you are, but I do know you're not here for a nightly stroll," the voice said. "Don't move, don't turn around. Put your arms out in front of you where I can see them."

Toni complied and knew by the Asian sound of the voice that it was probably Tran. He didn't know what type of weapon was pointed at him. He was caught by surprise, and he was trying to be quiet.

"Who are you?" the voice asked, "and what do you want?"

"Tommy Tran?" Toni asked softly.

"Wrong answer. Who are you?" the voice responded, sternly.

"Okay. I got it. Name's Toni Brazil, and I'm here to see Tommy Tran," Toni replied, confidently.

"Don't know any Toni Brazil," the voice responded, "so I don't know why you want to see Tommy Tran. Why don't you fill me in, Mr. Brazil?"

"It's Special Agent Toni Brazil," Toni said, "and I need to talk to Tommy Tran about Simon Picard." He hoped the name would get the man's attention.

"You have your credentials?"

"They're in my back pocket."

The man took his wallet from a back pocket without a word. Toni was uncomfortable not knowing what the man was doing. He didn't want to be shot in the back, and not without seeing his reaper. He could only see a faint shadow of the person behind him in the dim light.

"I know what you're thinking," the voice said. "Move slowly forward. I'm sure you know the slip number. Don't make any sudden moves. I'll shoot you if you do. I know you're armed. I can make it look like you were here to

FIERCE LOYALTY

kill me."

Toni knew it was Tommy Tran. He had all but said his name out loud with the last statement - me. It occurred to Toni that Tran was waiting for him, and he wondered how Tran knew he was coming.

The Drifter was a beautiful forty-five foot sailboat, dimly lit from the inside cabin. Toni saw a shadow in a small window as he boarded the boat. Was he wrong? Was Tran inside? He realized he no longer knew, and momentarily doubted his gut feeling.

"Go ahead. Walk slowly to the rear and sit down in the deck area," the voice ordered.

Toni followed instructions and walked to the rear of the boat. He stood in front of a lawn chair looking out over the water and the marina. The city lights reflected off the Potomac. He wondered if that image would be the last thing he would see. He knew something was wrong; maybe he gave too much information. A door opened behind him. Someone else was there. Whoever it was had failed to take his weapon. He was ready to use it in a split second if he needed to.

"Sit," the voice ordered.

53

Toni turned around and sat down, but no one was there before him. He heard voices from the inside cabin, but could not make them out or see who was talking. He felt for his Sig, found it, and felt comforted. He put the 9-millimeter semi-automatic weapon on his thigh. He sat in the dark, and his dark clothing concealed the gun. They let him keep the gun, even after his captor acknowledged it. Why not take it? It didn't make sense. He realized that his captor or captors were probably friendly. Just then, three men, two of whom he knew, walked out of the cabin. Toni sighed in relief when he saw the two familiar faces. Father John O'Brien and Father Giovanni Corvo stood with an Asian man in his late thirties.

"Can I get you a beer, Toni?" Father O'Brien asked.

"Not tonight, Father," Toni replied. "You two keep showing up in all the right places. What are you doing here?"

"Maybe I should ask you the same question," Father O'Brien replied. "However, I believe you're here to ask questions of Mr. Tran, are you not?"

"Father," Toni said. "What were you doing earlier, tonight?"

"I'm sure you know the answer already," John O'Brien replied quickly. He nodded at Gino and Tommy Tran, if speaking in code. "Toni, do you think you could go to my van and get something for me?"

"Sure," Toni answered. "Does it have to be now?"

"No, no," O'Brien said, "after you two finish talking, in an hour or so, if you don't mind? I'm going to get some rest."

"No problem," Toni responded, and John flipped Toni his car keys.

"It's right on the front passenger seat." He and Father Corvo turned and walked back inside the cabin.

FIERCE LOYALTY

The two men stared at each other in silence. Tran made the first move and walked toward the boat's railing. "You can put your weapon away. I think you know none of us will kill you," he said. "We haven't been formally introduced. I'm Tommy Tran. I'm sure you know that. I know who you are, yet who doesn't?" He held out his hand.

Toni saw the hand, but ignored it momentarily as he took the 9-millimeter Sig off his leg and re-holstered it. He shook Tran's hand, as he smiled and nodded. He was confused as all hell. Tran was still a possible enemy, but he was with the two priests.

"How do you know the two priests?" Toni asked.

"It's a long, strange story. I could ask you the same. Maybe this is one question we can both answer later, after this is over," Tran replied.

Toni laughed, understanding his answer. "All right. Later it is then."

"Father O'Brien said to expect you, and soon," Tran said. "He asked me to cooperate with you. I think he wants to recruit you."

"What?"

"He's a good man. He's seen a lot. Give him a chance. I did," Tran said, smiling and remembering the day he met Father O'Brien. "I don't think you'll regret it."

"I think I already do," Toni replied. "Anyway, I didn't have a choice about meeting O'Brien. He just showed up."

Toni smiled looking out to the water as he stood against the rail to face the same direction as Tran.

"How long you been with the bureau?" Toni asked.

"Eight years. Recruited in 1993," Tran replied matter-of-factly.

"You know Jeffrey Bodakis?"

"I've heard the name, but never met him. He's the SAC in NYC, isn't he?" Tran asked.

"Yup," Toni replied. "He's a good friend of mine."

"You want to know about Simon Picard," Tran said, "and whether I'm a good cop or bad cop, right?"

"Well," Toni started, "I'm here to discuss Picard and your trip to Australia two years ago. But also some other matters."

"I can tell you that I didn't kill Picard," Tran said.

"Was your trip to Australia an official assignment?"

"You may infer what you want, if that will help," Tran replied.

"I don't care about inferences and shit like that," Toni blurted. "My brother's dead, these men killed him, you're connected somehow, and some serious shit is about to happen. You know that if you're here with O'Brien and Corvo," Toni said, looking straight at Tran to see if his face gave anything away.

"All right," Tran responded at length. "So this is personal for you, too," he said, and thought to himself about the personal side of his work he'd kept silent for years. He didn't believe anyone knew about it; he was sure Brazil didn't know unless Father O'Brien filled him in.

Toni picked up on Tran's words, as if they had been kept in for years. He said nothing and waited patiently for Tran to start talking.

"I was on assignment in Australia," Tran said, ending the silence. "CIA – FBI - DEA joint operation. I was assigned to follow Dr. Simon Picard. DEA said he was running drugs through his company, Geneon Systems, delivering them to the United States through Canada. DEA said he was dealing with the Colombians. But what the DEA didn't tell us was that Picard was cooperating with them in a sting op. My wife is a CIA specialist. She and I were supposed to follow him, and that was all."

The information took Toni by surprise. The DEA is a sister agency of the FBI, and work together on drug cases all the time. Toni knew many agents at the bureau, so he was aware of the cooperative environment. Not telling the bureau of the sting was curious.

"Why didn't the DEA tell you Picard was cooperating?"

"Never got an answer to that. The lead agent was suspended and transferred somewhere to the boonies after Picard disappeared. Then he popped himself. Someone on the inside leaked information, and I mean our inside, the bureau or the DEA. After his death, DOJ believed the lead agent was the leak. There was no further inquiry," Tran reported.

"What happened to Picard?"

"I don't know what you read, but Picard was killed by the Colombians. We found that out later. It was never publicized. It got buried, and I mean deep," Tran answered.

"How'd you find that out?"

"We, I mean the bureau, had an insider. We already knew Picard was working with the Colombians, and I'd been assigned the case a year before the DEA came to us. It happened fast, the joint OP effort, I mean," Tran said. "Our source was wired. We found out two months after Picard disappeared. This Colombian said Picard's brother, Thomas, found out he was working with the DEA and told the Colombians."

"So Simon Picard's own brother killed him?" Toni asked.

"He probably ordered the hit, along with the Colombian drug lords.

234

FIERCE LOYALTY

However, you'll be interested to know, the two Colombian brothers you killed a few months back did the hit. We proved they were in Australia at the same time Picard was there," Tran said, looking at Toni. "Glad they got what was coming to them, thanks to you."

Toni flashed on the Villegas brothers falling backward to their deaths after he shot them. He tried to shake off the thought, but the image of that day, haunted him. Toni looked at Tran trying to stay focused.

"Tommy," Toni began, "are you certain Simon Picard is dead?"

"Our source is, and I know how the Colombians work. I'm 99.99% sure Simon Picard is dead. They don't lie about things like that. No body was found, just his gear and blood," Tran answered.

"Why would Picard's own brother rat him out?" Toni asked himself out loud.

"Do you know anything about Thomas Picard?"

"I know his father died in Vietnam, and his mother committed suicide two years later," Toni answered, looking confused.

"Yeah, that's right," Tran said. "I was adopted by a Colonel James Carlyle and his wife. She just happened to be Ambassador Picard's sister-in-law," Tran said automatically, as if he'd rehearsed the history a thousand times over. "Thomas and Simon were brothers, and they have a sister, Melissa. They went to live with Dr. Picard's brother in France after their mother's death. Melissa was adopted by Mrs. Picard's sister and her husband, Colonel James Carlyle. The Carlyle's also adopted me. My father worked for Dr. Picard at the French embassy as a teacher for the kids. I was just a baby. After Dr. Picard's death, his wife moved to France and gave birth to Melissa, and a year later committed suicide. My father, my brother, and I accompanied Mrs. Picard back to France." He paused to take a drink from a glass he'd brought with him.

"Your brother?"

"Yeah, my brother. But I'll get to that later," Tran said, with a hint of anger. "Anyway, after her death, Dr. Picard's brother wanted my father to stay with them and help with the kids, Thomas and Simon. The condition was that he could take only one of us, me or my brother," he said sadly. "He refused at first, but Picard threatened him with deportation back to North Vietnam, so he agreed. He would have been shot as a spy if he had returned to that place."

Tran took another deep breath. "Anyway, Thomas Picard grew up hating his older brother, because he was always following in Simon's foot steps, that

235

kind of stuff. In fact, Thomas spent time in a mental hospital when he was around thirteen, after he tried to hit Simon on the head with a rock."

"What about the sister. You said her name was Melissa?"

Tran looked to the ground. He knew Toni needed to hear it all. "Melissa and I were both adopted by Colonel Carlyle and his wife. Her name is Melissa Carlyle. Does that name ring any bells, Toni?"

Toni nodded. Melissa Carlyle held a very high position at the White House. He remembered when he met her the first time, and again at the White House ceremony after he was out of the hospital. He liked her, but knew she was very political, another word for two-faced in Toni's view. He had said nothing, and there was silence for a while.

"I'm two years older than Melissa," Tran said. "I joined the army when I turned eighteen. Truthfully, she and I didn't get along very well, so we never communicated until our adopted parents died in the car accident. I'd been in the army less than two years. " He paused as if lost in a thought, then snapped out of it and continued. "The Carlyle's were good to Melissa and me, treated us like their own. The accident was suspicious."

"What do you mean, suspicious?"

"Melissa had some mental problems from the time she was about eleven. It was obvious I wasn't the Carlyle's real child, and they eventually told us we were both adopted. It crushed Melissa and made her angry that the Carlyle's wouldn't tell her who her real parents were, until we were old enough," Tran said. "It was for our own protection, as I see it now."

"Keep going," Toni prompted.

"When I decided to enlist, I was eighteen years old. Colonel Carlyle told me if he and his wife should die, the records would be unsealed when Melissa and I turned eighteen. He just wanted me to know that. He told me why they adopted Melissa and me, and then he told me about Melissa's two brothers. He kept an eye on them over the years, but what neither of us knew was that Melissa, who was fifteen at the time, overheard our conversation. She wanted to know who her parents and brothers were so bad, it took over her life."

"What are you trying to say, Tommy? That Melissa was somehow involved in the Carlyle's' death?" Toni asked, looking straight into Tran's eyes.

"The Carlyle's died in a car accident, killed by a reckless driver who cut them off and forced them off the Parkway into the Potomac. A witness got a partial license plate. The car was never found," Tran said pausing, and looking off into the distance. "But I found it."

"I think I'll have that beer now," Toni said, as he walked over to a cooler

FIERCE LOYALTY

next to his vacated chair. Toni opened the cooler, took a beer, and tossed one to Tran. "You were saying something about finding the license plate," Toni prodded.

"I found the partial plate on Melissa's boyfriend's car. The reason why DC and Virginia police didn't find it was because they only looked in DC, Virginia, and Maryland. His plate was from West Virginia," Tran said coolly. "The accident occurred one day before Melissa's eighteenth birthday. I confronted her, but she just blew me off, said I was crazy. The guy, her boyfriend, was a scum bag." Tran looked around his boat. "A few months later he went missing, too. He was never found, nor was his car. She later came to me and said she'd make big trouble for me if I said anything to the police. After that, I didn't speak to her for years."

"Until," Toni lead on.

"Melissa turned up married to the DEA agent assigned to the Simon Picard case," Tran said calmly. "She showed up at the first OP meeting, three years ago. She was working at the White House as the Assistant White House Chief of Staff for the Drug War back then too."

"What about you? Didn't she know who you were?"

"No. It had been a long time. I changed my name, and I was scrawnier back then. She acted like she didn't know or recognize me, and I said nothing to her."

"Then, you're saying that Melissa Carlyle has been involved in at least two homicides," Toni surmised.

"Four, if you count her boyfriend and ex-husband," Tran replied, bluntly.

"Her missing boyfriend," Toni responded, nodding his head. "That's right, she mentioned to me that her husband was a DEA agent. I could swear she said he died in the line of duty."

"I have no proof she killed anyone. It's just conjecture," Tran replied, "but she turned up at that OP meeting, and that's when I found out she was married to the lead DEA agent, Mac Thompson."

"Mac?" Toni asked, surprised. "He's dead?"

"You knew him?" Tran asked. "Mac died a year ago, self-inflicted gun shot to the head. It wasn't made public, I understand."

"Shit. I knew Mac through Jeffrey Bodakis. Mac was a contact for my agency on drug diversion cases," Toni said. "No one told me he was dead. No wonder I haven't heard from him."

"DOJ inquiry said he was the leak," Tran said.

"He wasn't the leak, no way. He was too good for that kind of bullshit."

237

SCOTT A. REZENDES

"Well," Tran began, "I don't know what to say. He seemed like a good guy, but I was only one of twenty-five task force members from CIA, FBI and DEA. My wife and I were assigned to do surveillance during the Australia trip. We had information that Picard was meeting with the Colombians. It never happened, and Picard turned up missing."

"Then Melissa Carlyle must have known that Simon Picard was her older brother. She had access to all the reports. She's the leak!" Toni blurted.

"That's what I thought, too," Tran said.

"But?"

"No buts. The DOJ investigated it and found Mac to be responsible," Tran replied.

"Didn't they question Carlyle? She was his wife for god's sake!"

"Of course. DOJ-OIG did the internal review. They questioned everyone, including me, my wife, and Carlyle. She divorced Mac shortly after the inquiry, and then he was transferred," Tran said. "We know what happened after that. I heard she left the White House to grieve or something like that, and then returned a week later. Now she's the new Chief of Staff for International Terrorism."

It was difficult for Toni to believe Lisa Carlyle was a killer, and probably a spy. She was attractive and innocent looking, but just as he thought the words, he concluded she'd be the perfect spy.

"What else do you know about Thomas Picard?" Toni asked.

"After we found out he was the one who ratted out his brother, we did a background investigation. My wife and I did," he said.

"On or off the books?"

"On the books, but only a few knew of it," Tran answered.

"What did you find?" Toni asked.

"We found a lot," Tran said, seeing Toni nod at him to continue. "After his two year hospitalization, he returned to school and apparently lived normally. He then went on to graduate from Stanford Medical School, hooked up with his brother Simon, and founded Geneon Systems in 1984. Then, a few years later, he quit without warning. Some said he was feeling unfulfilled in his work, but basically he dropped off the face of the earth for about ten years."

"What happened to Thomas during those ten years?" Toni asked.

"Some said he went off the deep end again, hospitalized secretly. I never found the hospital if that was the case. There were witnesses who said he and Simon were constantly arguing about the company," Tran paused, "but, as I looked further, I found that Simon was misdirecting large sums to a Swiss

238

FIERCE LOYALTY

account all that time. The Swiss later told us the account was in Thomas Picard's name and had been accessed by Thomas from Pakistan, consistently, over a ten-year period. A lead was sent to Pakistan to find out what Thomas was involved in there, but no one knew him or had seen him. We figured it was a misdirection."

"A misdirection?" Toni questioned.

"Yeah, the funds were drawn from Pakistan, but the bank employees did not recognize Thomas Picard's picture. After exhausting every lead, we drew the conclusion Picard sent someone to do the dirty work, in case they were caught," Tran explained.

"Did they describe the person?"

Tommy Tran looked away, anger in his face, "They made one mistake, the Picards, I mean."

"What was that?"

"There's a man who has watched their every movement, probably even changed their diapers," Tran said looking down, his eyes moist.

"That was your father, wasn't it?" Toni asked.

"Yes," Tran replied. "He was their slave basically. His name is Binh Tran Simivong. They call him Simi."

Toni realized that the case was personal for Tommy Tran, as well. His father took care of the Picard brothers. What they had done to him to make Tommy so angry was not apparent. Tran's father helped the Picards do the dirty work, but Toni said nothing and let Tran continue. He wanted to know what angered him.

"The Picards changed names and identification whenever they moved around the Middle East," Tran resumed. "Simon's nickname was The Ghost. He'd take a vacation, but no one would see him for days, sometimes weeks at a time. He was a master of disguise. My father taught him that!" he raised his voice, as if proud of his father's teachings.

"Where's this going, Tommy?" Toni asked.

"They sent my father to pick up the funds at the bank. They had photographs of him. They made him use his real name to sign for the money. Simon and Thomas Picard were bankrolling terrorists in Afghanistan, and my father was their cover man," Tran said seething. "They used my father as their fucking gopher!"

"Gideon?"

"Thomas Picard," Tran replied. "I heard some rumor through Intel lines about Al Gyden. People just called him Gideon for short. It stuck, you know.

239

Anyway, rumor had it Gideon bought some white lightning."

"White lightning?" Toni asked.

"Sorry. Russian slang for smallpox," Tran explained. "I went to my supervisor. He said he'd send it up the chain to see what they wanted us to do. You know, follow the lead. The answer came back an hour later that the CIA was going to handle it."

"When was that?"

"Just a few months ago, maybe six months," Tran replied. "I'd been on the Picard's like flies on shit for three years, following their movements. I assumed the word would come back to keep following the trail. But they said CIA, so I call my wife, because this is serious shit and she knows nothing about it. My wife's a supervisor at CIA HQ. She should have known."

"So you kept digging?" Toni asked.

"Gideon was Simon's middle name. I turned up an alias Thomas Picard used over ten years ago, John Gideon. Traced the passport used by Gideon, did some checking here and there, and it was a direct hit! Gideon was Thomas Picard," Tran said.

"What did you do then?" Toni prodded.

"I never met my father or brother. I just wanted to know if he was traveling with Picard," Tran said somberly.

"You've been tracking your father, haven't you?" Toni asked. He knew the answer.

"No one knows he's my father, except you and Father O'Brien," Tran responded.

"And Melissa Carlyle," Toni said. "What became of your brother?"

"Remember, I told you Thomas Picard was institutionalized at thirteen?"

"Yes, I do," Toni responded.

"You see, I was a twin, but not identical. When I was twenty, and the Carlyle's died, I got to open my adoption records. That's when I found out my father's real name was Binh Tran Simivong. I also found out that I had a brother, a twin. Everything I told you here tonight is a result of me trying to locate my brother and father. I found my father easily enough within four years, while I was in the military. I searched them out when I was off duty, or on leave. When I found my father and the Picards, my brother seemed to no longer exist," Tran said.

"I don't understand. What does it have to do with Thomas Picard being in a mental hospital?" Toni questioned.

"I learned my father was Thomas Picard's personal assistant, but I found

FIERCE LOYALTY

no indication my brother was around. Thomas Picard's disappearance was all just bullshit, Toni. The Picards got involved with Muslim extremists in Pakistan and Afghanistan, first to fight the Russians, then to get back at the Americans. Did you know they both converted to Islam at the same time? Just prior to starting Geneon Systems. The whole thing has been about getting back at the Americans for killing their father, and they believe, their mother. They blamed the Americans for their parents death," Tran said.

"What about Melissa? Has she ever met her brothers?"

"Yes."

"I still don't understand where your brother fits in," Toni persisted.

"Sorry, I got sidetracked," Tran said, taking a drink of his beer. "Simon wasn't the only person who'd been hit over the head with a rock. Thomas Picard killed my brother before he attacked Simon. They found him dead, his body dumped in a garbage can. His head bashed in."

Toni knew exactly how Tran felt and realized he had a score to settle too. They had more in common than Toni imagined. Then he recalled that Tommy hadn't said his brother's name, and he decided to take a chance. "What was your brother's name?"

Tran paused, took another drink, and looked back at Toni. "His name was Bobby." Tran downed the rest of the beer, crumpled the can, and dropped it on the floor.

Toni gasped silently and tried to change the subject. "What happened to your father? Did you ever meet him?"

"I never approached my father. I couldn't, with my job. I've been tracking him for years, never telling anybody he was my father," Tran replied. "But, after I found out about my brother, everything changed. I want to meet him, just once."

"Me too, but for a different purpose," Toni said. Tran understood.

"My father did not kill your brother," Tran said. "Thomas Picard did."

"Tommy, they got the virus," Toni said urgently. "If your father is traveling with Gideon or Picard, we can find him, and stop this thing."

Tran leaned forward, his hands over his face. He looked at his watch. It was 11:10 P.M. "His plane lands at Dulles in fifteen minutes," he said. "I checked the passenger manifest. He's sitting next to a man named François de Pescarde, one of Thomas Picard's many aliases."

Tommy Tran crossed to the other side of the boat, gazing across the space between his boat and a sixty-foot luxury yacht. A light was on inside the boat. "There's one thing I didn't tell you about Melissa," he said. "The Carlyle's

241

took us sailing all the time when we were kids. Do you see the Simon Says?" He pointed across the marina. "That's Melissa's boat. Believe it or not, I saw her there one night about a month ago having a dinner party. I checked the registration and marina rental guide. The boat's registered under her ex-husband's name, Michael Thompson."

Toni considered the dilemma facing them. He looked at the Simon Says. The cabin light was on and he wondered if Melissa Carlyle knew he was lying in wait, for her and her brother, Thomas Picard. Anger welled up as he thought about Melissa Carlyle's treachery. She betrayed him, and he wondered how she really felt when he killed the Villegas brothers. She had no conscience. She deserved anything that happened to her if she got in the way. He hoped she would.

"I just wanted to meet my father," Tommy Tran said.

"I know, Tommy. I have a feeling you'll meet him one way or another," Toni replied. He blinked and shook his head slightly. For a moment, he saw a four-year old Asian boy standing next to him.

54

"I wanted you to come by my office for a reason!" Trimble said, looking grumpily at the two FBI agents sitting at his desk. "I know you two don't like me. I know what you think of me, Bodakis, but when I say come to my office, I don't care if a boy on a bike delivers the message. I want you in my office! Is that clear?"

"It's clear," Velarde answered. "Let me just say . . ."

"Shut up, Velarde," Trimble replied, sharply. "I don't want your apology. You are such an asshole sometimes. You guys think I'm a dumb shit. Well, I'm not as dumb as you think. Now, you two have done a very good job, and I'm about to tell you something you don't know."

"Thanks for the compliment," Bo replied, "but what are you talking about?"

"About two months ago a report reached the White House about the possible purchase of smallpox stolen from the Russians. Melissa Carlyle told us that the report was sent to the CIA to check out the validity."

"Why wasn't I told about this earlier?" Bo asked.

"Let me explain," Trimble said, throwing his hands out and standing up. "We couldn't, Jeff. It could have compromised another case. The agent you were to see tonight, Thomas Tran, he reported the smallpox purchase. His wife is a supervisor at the CIA's foreign intelligence office, and he told her. She and her boss contacted Director Mahoney. We all had a meeting. The CIA heard nothing about the smallpox."

"I'm not following you," Bo said. "What does this have to do with another case?"

"Tran sent the information up the ladder. It ended up on my desk, and I took it to Mahoney, who gave it to Carlyle, who was to apprise the president during the daily national security briefing. I followed up on it with Carlyle, and she told me the president ordered the CIA to handle the verification. But, it never made it there. In fact, the information never made it to the president," Trimble asserted.

"How do you know that?" Velarde asked.

"Notes," Trimble replied. "Every morning, the president is briefed on national security issues, and notes are taken. There's also a report generated, but it was never disseminated to us. Carlyle is responsible for liaison with us, CIA, and the NSA, and she's responsible for taking notes and generating a final report. We're the only ones who didn't participate in the meeting that day. Carlyle asked Director Mahoney and me to handle another matter. She said there could be another leak inside the Department of Justice, and suspected it was Deputy Attorney General Greg Myers. At the time, we trusted Carlyle, and the DOJ-OIG had just finalized the case against Mac Thompson. We didn't want another black eye, so we took it seriously."

"So, what has been going on?" Bo asked, assertively.

Trimble, still behind his desk, began pacing back and forth. Bo looked at the desk. It was neat and orderly. He saw a yellow post-it next to the phone with a number written next to a name, B. A. Star. He didn't recognize the name. Trimble turned back toward him and Velarde.

"Jeff, after the meeting with the CIA, we knew if we asked Carlyle for the report she could generate one with the information and blame it on someone else. However, the vice-president gets the report and approves it, but it takes time to do all that. So we had to wait for that report to be generated and approved," Trimble reported.

"How long?"

"Thirty days if it is a non-emergency and twenty-four hours if it's crucial to national interests. Of course, we believed it would be considered crucial. The report didn't come for three weeks. The information wasn't there, none of it."

"What's been going on, since then?" Bo asked.

"We asked Tom Tran to keep doing what he was doing, along with his wife. I was assigned to Carlyle. We've been documenting everything and doing background investigations on her. We even found evidence that she planted evidence on Mac, murdered her parents, and is responsible for the disappearance of another person thirteen years ago. It just kept spiraling. We were about to indict her on murder charges, but we knew she was the leak, not Mac or Myers. So we waited, sealed the murder indictment, and got a

FIERCE LOYALTY

wiretap warrant. Then your case developed, and that call made to California to your Cain and Abel duo came from none other than Ms. Carlyle."

"Son-of-a-bitch!" Bo exclaimed. He stood and began walking around the office.

"You can see why we couldn't tell you," Trimble said calmly. "Carlyle was all over this. We had to tell her when the operation became nationwide. That call, Jeffrey, linked her to Hamas and whoever is responsible for your case – Gideon. Plus, we didn't know how, when, or where the smallpox was coming into the U.S," – Trimble paused – "or how they would disseminate it, at least until your case came to light."

"So why now?" Bo slipped back into his chair. "Why bring us in and tell us now?"

"A couple of things came up recently," Trimble said.

"This doesn't sound good," Velarde commented.

"First things first. Something we didn't know. Tommy Tran is the adopted brother of Melissa Carlyle," Trimble said.

"We know," Bo said.

"It's not what you think," Trimble said, reading the suspicion. "Tran's clean. He just didn't tell us everything. We think his real father is involved too, but that's another matter."

"What's the bad news?" Bo asked.

"Your target, Gideon. His Muslim name is Muhammad Al Gydin, hence Gideon," Trimble said.

"His Muslim name?" Bo caught the key word.

"Yeah, that's right. His Christian name is Thomas Picard, Doctor of Microbiology," Trimble stated, smartly.

"I should have been brought in on this earlier," Bo stood up and put his hands on Trimble's desk.

"You would have been, if we had known New York City was involved," Trimble answered.

"How long have you known Gideon's real identity?" Bo asked.

"I just found out a few days ago," Trimble said. "The wire tap on Carlyle's boat. She called Thomas Picard and used the Gideon name."

"So what's our next move?" Velarde asked. "Arrest Carlyle?"

"No," Bo said, "we wait." Trimble nodded in agreement.

"For what?" Velarde blurted.

"Well, I think our smarter-than-average deputy director is about to tell us," Bo said, winking at Velarde.

245

"That is correct," Trimble said. "Carlyle lives on a boat and Cain and Abel are meeting her there tonight, as a matter of fact."

"What else?" Bo asked. His energy rising.

"Something else might be going on. I have a team listening in on it," Trimble said.

"Tommy Tran?" Velarde asked.

"Oh, no," Trimble started.

"He doesn't know, does he?" Bo asked, looking at Trimble.

"Would you tell him after what you know?" Trimble asked sarcastically.

"You said he was clean. Why not tell him? You don't trust him a hundred percent, do you?"

"No, I don't," Trimble replied, letting his response float a few seconds. "Tran's been working the Picards for three or four years. He had to know about his real father working for them. He never said a thing to anyone. Bottom line, he held back important information from the bureau case file, which may have led to this very circumstance."

"Come on, Trimble," Bo said. "How do you know that?"

"We have a policy on this, Bodakis," Trimble replied. "Would you have continued investigating a case where your father was involved? Especially as a possible target?"

"Depends on whether I knew it was my father? And, Tran has never met his father according to his records," Bo rejoined.

"We don't know that," Trimble said.

"You're going to fire him, aren't you?" Bo asked.

"I don't see where we have a choice, Bodakis. What would you do?"

"I'd at least give him an opportunity to leave the bureau on his own, after what he's done. I sure as hell wouldn't ruin his career," Bo said, shaking his head. Trimble was still the asshole he thought he was.

"Yeah, well, that's why I'm here and you're where you are, Jeff!" Trimble said. "He's got to go."

"We'll see about that," Bo said sharply. "Where's the wiretap squad set up?"

"No. That's not where you two are going tonight," Trimble said confidently. "I've got something else for you to do."

"This is still my case, Trimble," Bo said, "and I believe . . ."

"Forget what you believe, Bodakis!" Trimble retorted. "The case has been turned over to me. I'm in charge now."

"The hell you are!" Bo shot back.

FIERCE LOYALTY

"Bo!" Velarde interjected. "Let's just do what he says."

Velarde's words and look confused Bo at first, but a split second later he realized Randy had something else in mind.

"You should listen to your partner in crime more often, Bodakis," Trimble said, glaring at Bo. "He's got the right attitude. I'll handle the wire tap squad tonight and call you if anything important comes up. I want you two to go over to Alexandria and check out the explosion at the Potomack Marina tonight. See if it has any connection to this case. Is that clear?"

"Yes it is," Velarde said, shaking his head at Bo.

"Let's get out of here," Bo said, holding in the anger.

"Call me as soon as you know anything," Trimble said.

Trimble stood with his arms crossed. Sticking it to Bodakis felt good, he thought. He chuckled as he thought how he had spoiled the case for Bodakis again, just like fifteen years before. He knew they'd be at the Potomac Marina all night long and out of the way.

"Oh!" Trimble called out to the departing Bo and Velarde. "I almost forgot. As soon as you two finish at the marina, you should try to get some sleep." He winked at them, and felt in control for the first time in months.

Velarde followed Bo out, but neither said a word. He saw Agent Pears standing by an office door, talking to someone and noticed Pears face had changed. He looked serious and confident as he turned and watched Bo approach. He knew then Trimble was using Pears as his errand boy. Pears began to smile as Bo approached, but stopped when Bo spoke.

"You're not coming with us, Pears. Just give me the keys to a car in the garage, and I'll be on my way."

"But . . ."

"But nothing, Agent," Velarde said. He eyed Pears suspiciously. "Give us the keys."

"It's fine, Agent Pears," Trimble said from down the hall. "Give 'em the keys."

Pears pulled the keys out of his pants and flipped them to Velarde. "Car's parked in the 'E' Section, space 303," Pears said, clearly unhappy. Bo and Velarde said nothing and found the door leading to the elevators.

Trimble eased slowly to where Pears stood watching the door close behind Bodakis and Velarde. "Good work," he said, putting his arm on Pears' shoulder. "Looks like they bought your anger."

"Yeah," Pears replied, "but I thought you wanted me to go with them."

"That's what I told you so you'd get pissed when they shot you down,"

Trimble said, slapping his shoulder and turning to walk away.

"Asshole," Pears said under his breath. He wondered why Trimble had taken him under his wing; now realizing he had just been used. He looked around to see if anyone in the office noticed. No one was around. They were all at the marina in Alexandria, investigating the fire. He was glad he wouldn't be running down leads all night, but he wondered what Trimble was up to.

55

Bo walked silently to the car in the garage of the Hoover building. He shushed Velarde and motioned him to get in the car.

As they passed through the security station, the silence built inside the car. Bo pulled out and turned left onto Tenth Street, then took a quick right onto a silent, but brightly lit Pennsylvania Avenue, as if going to Alexandria.

"You look like you could use some coffee," Bo said.

"Yeah, sounds good. It's going to be a long night," Velarde replied.

Bo reached Fourteenth Street and turned left, then drove into the tunnel at full speed crossing over to the Virginia side.

"There's a Starbucks right on the way," Bo said, "near Crystal City."

"Sure," Velarde replied, struggling to keep a normal conversation.

At Starbucks, Bo found a spot on a side street and parked the car on the curb with the passenger side tires on the sidewalk. He and Velarde exited and walked a short distance from the car, then stopped, turned around, and looked at the car.

"You think it's bugged?" Velarde asked.

"Bugged and tracked is what I think," Bo replied, "and if we can find the devices, I'm going to shove them up Trimble's ass when this is finished."

"Oh, would you let me have a crack at it?" Velarde said, and both men broke into laughter.

"He's all yours, Randy, once I'm finished." Bo walked back to the car.

Each took a side of the vehicle and began a thorough search of the inner body, under the bumpers and wheel wells. They shone flashlights under the car, along the drive train, into the engine block, and transmission. Bo flung himself under the car and checked the exhaust pipes, which were hot from the drive. He saw nothing out of the ordinary and decided that he'd have to wait and tear the insides apart to find what he knew was there. Bo worked his way to the rear of the vehicle and the gas tank. Again, there was nothing. Trimble knew where they were and would be suspicious if the car didn't begin to move again soon. He sent Velarde into Starbucks to get coffee, while he searched. He wondered why Trimble didn't want him on the case. Especially he wondered about the wiretap.

What was really going on? Trimble knew Pears faxed the Tran information to him, and knew that he wanted to talk to Tran. Why take him off that track? Why tell him about Carlyle? Cain and Abel would be at the DC marina, but Trimble wanted him away from where everyone seemed to be heading. Nothing made sense. Clearly Trimble was up to something, but what? He'd have to counter Trimble's plan with one of his own, a plan he would have to develop on the fly. But that's when he did his best work, he thought with a smile. Whatever Trimble was up to, he wouldn't get away with it.

Velarde returned with the coffee. Bo stood on the sidewalk, a short distance behind the car.

"We have to get going," Bo said, taking the coffee from Velarde.

"You find anything?"

"Nothing," Bo replied. "It's there, though, probably inside. He's a crafty son-of-bitch, that's for damn sure."

"Trimble? Yeah, he's a jerk. I don't care what information he turned us on to in his office. He's holding something back. I'm not even sure the info is good," Velarde commented.

"I agree," Bo said. "Hey, Randy?"

"What ya need?"

"Do you know anyone in the bureau named Star? First name starts with a B," Bo asked.

"B. Star," Velarde repeated looking at Bo from the passenger side of the car. "Name's not familiar. Why?"

"I noticed a note on Trimble's desk with a phone number, 202 area code, but the name stuck out B. A. Star," Bo said.

"Yeah, come to think of it, Trimble's desk was as neat as a pin! What a freak!" Velarde said. "I don't think I know anybody named Star. Why don't you call your guy in New York? What's his name? Jimmy? Jimmy Franks."

"Good idea," Bo said.

Jimmy Franks was the New York City office's most senior agent. Originally from California and an avid surfer, Franks had been around the bureau the

FIERCE LOYALTY

longest, and he knew everyone. Being the eldest of the bunch, he usually got to do background checks on new employees, judges, and other government officials. It was worth a call. Bo took out his cell phone while he and Velarde stood outside the car, drinking coffee. Bo had Frank's number programmed into the phone's memory. As he scrolled through the names and numbers he finally came to F, and Franks was the only one. He pushed the button. He heard the ring, and then a voice that sounded like a dead man's.

"This better be good, Jockety," Jimmy Franks said, not knowing who was at the other end.

"This ain't Jockety," Bo said, knowing he woke Jimmy up.

"Huh? Bo? Is that you, boss man?" Franks said in a tired voice.

"Yeah, unfortunately, Jimmy, it is."

"Is something wrong? Jockety's on call tonight, isn't he?" Franks asked.

"Nothing's wrong, Jimmy," Bo said, "but, I need a favor."

"Anything for you, dude," Franks replied.

"Do you know anyone in the bureau with last name of Star?" Bo asked.

"Ken!" Jimmy replied, with a jerky laugh. "Oh, no, he was that prosecutor dude. I don't think I know the dude, Bo-man. What's his first name?"

"Just have his initials, B and the middle initial is A," Bo said.

"Bad Ass," Jimmy replied. "Man I wish I had those initials." Bo sighed on the other end, so he got serious. "So it's B. A. Star?"

"You got it, Jimmy," Bo replied. "I hate to ask this, Jimmy, but . . ."

"Say no more, boss. I'll find out who the guy is. The name is familiar," Franks said.

"Thanks, Jimmy," Bo said.

"I'll call you on your cell in an hour or so," Franks said.

"Okay, Jimmy. I'll be waiting," Bo said. "Thanks dude."

"Over and out, boss-man," Franks said, and Bo's cell phone went dead.

"Let's go. He's on it," Bo said as he opened his door. Velarde followed him into the car.

Bo started the car and pulled away from the curb. The name was bugging him, as was everything else Trimble did and said. He turned right onto Eads Street, then turned left on Fifteenth. He took the on ramp heading South on the Jefferson Davis Highway. He hit the siren, and Velarde pulled the red flashing light off the floor and put it on the dashboard. He took the exit for Ronald Reagan National Airport, knowing that he needed to get to the George Washington Parkway to get to Daingerfield Island and the Potomac Marina.

Velarde sipped his coffee as if looking for life in the hot liquid. He turned off the siren, and kept the red light flashing in silence. Then another noise chirped. Bo looked at Velarde, who shrugged. It was Bo's cell phone. He thought of Jimmy Franks, but less than five minutes had passed. How could it be?

56

Toni stood next to Tommy Tran, who just stared at the boats in the marina. The heavy late summer air clung to their faces like a blanket, its humidity surrounding them with dampness. The sky spoke of distant lightning and the rumble of thunder. Rain was coming. Toni didn't know what to think of Tommy Tran, a man lost with no past. He thought it curious that Tran didn't go to the airport to follow his father and Picard, but Tran explained there was no need. Marina security was holding a key for two guests of Melissa Carlyle; their names were Simi and John Gideon. At 11:45 P.M., they would have to wait twenty-minutes for Gideon and Tran's father to arrive if they were on schedule. He thought of O'Brien and Corvo, and wondered why they were here. He needed to know more. He looked at Tommy Tran, who stood motionless, staring into the night, sad, as if he knew what was going to happen.

"So," Toni began, "what did you mean when you said Father O'Brien wanted to recruit me?"

"It's not for me to answer," Tran replied. "John . . . I mean Father O'Brien, he'll explain that to you when it's your time."

"Oh, I see," Toni said. "How do you know him?"

"I've told you a lot about me tonight, Toni." Tran turned to look at Toni, "all because Father O'Brien asked me."

"What are you saying? You're one of his warriors?" Toni asked, sarcastically.

"There's a lot you don't know, Brazil," Tran said. "A lot."

"Why don't you fill me in then?" Toni replied more seriously.

Tran looked at Toni, then at the cabin to his left. The door was closed, but the light was on. He could see O'Brien's legs through the cabin door window.

He turned back to Toni.

"There comes a time, Agent Brazil," Tran said carefully, "when you realize your career is probably over, not by choice, but because of something you did. My time at the bureau is borrowed. When they find out I held back information, I'm gone, and not quietly. I could end up doing jail time."

"I see," Toni replied.

"When this is over you will understand my predicament. I hope you'll see it my way."

"What have you done that's so bad? Looked for your father and brother? You don't think people will understand that?" Toni asked.

"I wish it was that simple," Tran said. "You're right though. If I was just trying to find them, people would understand. Maybe I'd be suspended or allowed to transfer to another agency. But . . ."

"But what, Tommy? You kill someone?"

"Not yet," Tran said anxiously. "I've put the country at risk though, and that won't be understood. My father, Picard, they're all criminals, and not just ordinary criminals, but terrorists. They won't understand why I held back information that linked them to killings, embassy bombings, and so on, just so I could pick the right time to meet my father."

"I can see your point. Jail time though," Toni mused. "You're wrong. Terrorists, shit. They would have found a way to do those things anyway, with or without your father."

"Maybe, but I've made up my mind," Tran said. "Tonight, it ends here."

"What about your family, Tommy? You have a wife, children. What about them?"

"They'll survive. That I know for sure," Tran said calmly.

"You're wrong, Tran. I know you're wrong. I hope you've thought long and hard about giving up your family," Toni said, shaking his head.

"I have, Toni. I hope it won't be necessary," Tran replied. He turned back to Toni. "It's time you got that package for O'Brien. He's parked near the hotel complex across the way. You know where it is?"

"I do," Toni replied. "I parked there myself, but I didn't see his car."

"He dumped the Lincoln. It's a white van he rented from Budget. Can't miss it," Tran said, smiling as if telling Toni something. "Good luck."

Toni felt around for the key O'Brien gave him and pulled it from a pocket. Sure enough, it had a Budget key ring, something he hadn't noticed before. He wasn't ready for the conversation to end, so he decided to keep pushing Tran. "You at least gonna tell me how you met O'Brien?"

FIERCE LOYALTY

Tran appeared to be in a trance. Toni figured that Tran had made up his mind to take Picard and his father out. But then what? Disappear? Kill himself?

"I met John about twelve years ago," Tran said. "I told you I was in the military right? Well, I was in the Special Forces, fighting the drug war in Colombia. I read an article about Simon Picard. I knew back then who my father was, and that he worked for the Picards."

"But?"

"The Carlyle's raised Melissa and me as Catholics. When on leave from the jungle, I'd find a church and go pray," Tran said. "I found the newspaper article with Picard's picture. It was 1989 or so, and I was called back to the jungle before they arrived. Then bad weather hit, and I got to stay put."

"Everything all right, Tommy?" Toni asked. Tran seemed lost in his own thoughts.

"Huh, oh yeah," Tran replied. "One day I went to a church and there was this visiting priest. It was John O'Brien. That whole day he kept showing up. It was weird, I thought at the time. Then about an hour before I was going to approach Picard, I was eating lunch, and O'Brien came over to me and introduced himself. Corvo was there, too. John told me why Picard was in Colombia."

"What did they tell you?"

"That Picard was a major drug smuggler, and he was there to meet with the Colombian drug lords," Tran said.

"Did you believe him?"

"I doubted him at first," Tran replied, "but he knew who I was, everything. He told me about my father, mother, the Picards, what they were up to. He knew everything. Then he told me about my brother and that Thomas Picard killed him. He proved it."

"So you didn't meet your father?" Toni asked.

"No. O'Brien convinced me the time wasn't right, and it would put my father in danger if I did. Then he asked for my help."

"Sounds familiar," Toni interjected, sarcastically. "So what did he ask you to do?"

Tran turned to face Toni. "Nothing, really. He was looking for some intel on a Colombian village I had been in."

"What'd you tell him?"

"The village wasn't a cocaine refinery, so I told him what I knew. He wanted the layout of the village."

"Then what happened?" Toni asked.

"Well, you're farther along than I was at the time. You've seen what he can do already, and how far he reaches in the community," Tran said, deep in thought and smiling, as if he admired Father O'Brien.

"Yeah, well, I've seen a dead man come to life," Toni said.

"Exactly," Tran replied, full of emotion. "You can never count him out."

"Did you ever find out why O'Brien wanted the layout of that village?"

"Yeah, the next day the news reported that a group of five missing nuns were rescued from a village where they'd been imprisoned by some anti-government extremist group," Tran said. "I was in that village with six other guys and we had no idea what was going on. O'Brien and Corvo went in there and got those nuns. No one was killed."

"What's he into, Tommy?" Toni asked lowering his voice.

"Over the years, John has shown up when I didn't expect it. He's got reach. We became friends. The more I learned about him, the more I realized we had a lot in common. It was like he picked me as one of his warriors. Like, I didn't have a choice." Tran paused, then said, "I've come to realize what O'Brien is dealing with, day in and day out, though."

"Oh, really and what is that?" Toni asked.

"Good and evil." Tran said, and turned away to focus again on the Simon Says.

Toni followed Tran's eyes. They changed when he looked at Carlyle's boat. Before long, Picard and Tran's father would arrive, followed surely by Savage. The guy just knew where to show up. Toni considered what he planned to do. With Tran, O'Brien, and Corvo present he would have to justify what he meant to do. They were all evil people. Were he, Tran, and O'Brien the good guys? Was it really that simple? Good versus evil. One thing was clear: Tommy Tran believed it was.

57

"Where the hell have you been?" Savage said into his cell phone.

"Putting the plan to work, Savage," the male voice replied curtly. "I think I should ask the same of you!"

"All right, enough," Savage retorted. "Have you pulled your people out of the way?"

"They won't be a problem," replied the man on the other end of the connection. "Nice plan at the marina. They'll be following leads all night and day tomorrow, probably for weeks."

"And Ms. Carlyle?" Savage asked.

"She'll either be dead by tomorrow, or in jail for a long time," came the reply, "and she has no idea that I'm involved – and listening in."

"Perfect!"

"What about the money?"

"It's all set," Savage responded. "Gideon will send it to the account by 2:00 P.M., tomorrow. Plus, another million in cash. I figured we'd split it, then meet in Switzerland as we planned."

"How'd you get the additional million?" the man asked.

"Gideon thinks I'm stupid, remember. It's what he originally offered for his worthless product. I decided to take it as well," Savage explained.

"Well, Savage, I'm impressed," the voice replied.

"We're in this together," Savage said. "You'll have to do the pick up. I'll be busy taking out Gideon's men, Cain and Abel I think is what you called them."

"Where's the drop?"

"You know the Torpedo Factory?" Savage asked.

SCOTT A. REZENDES

"Of course," came the quick reply.

"There's a restaurant called the Chart House," Savage said. "I'm meeting the gophers in the bar."

"Savard and Lowe."

"Who?" Savage asked.

"Two employees of Gideon, my people are watching. They're the gophers. That's why they turned around and headed to Washington."

"That doesn't sound good," Savage responded.

"Ye of little faith," the voice said.

"My apologies. You'll have to take care of it," Savage chided. "The boat ready?"

"She's ready. In fact, she couldn't be in a better location, docked right at the marina next to the Chart House."

"That's good," Savage said. "What about the IDs?"

"Look, I'm holding up my side of the deal," the voice replied, methodically, but irritably. "You just do yours. You won't be able to do squat without the IDs, and when we get to Switzerland, we each walk away with $12.5 million. You fuck up, and we lose it all."

"I'll do my part. Fact is," he said, "Cain and Abel will be taken care of within the hour. Got them in my sights right now," Savage said, while the blue Dodge Durango parked at Dulles Airport was in his sights.

Savage watched intently as Cain and Abel returned to the SUV carrying the luggage of two other men following a short distance behind, a tall white man and a short, older Asian man he recognized as Tran. Savage smiled broadly. He eyed Tran, and remembered when he broke his wrist. "Well now, looks like I'll be getting a little pay back as well."

"What?" the voice came back at Savage.

"Nothing, just thinking out loud, is all," Savage replied. The four men got into the Durango. "By the way, thanks for the info on the rental car for those two Hamas agents. It's seems to be paying off."

"No problem. How about your hostages? We can't leave witnesses."

"They're a little tied up right now," Savage said, laughing evilly. In the back of the van, Chigall and Father Chason lay bound and gagged on the floor. "Their fate is sealed, though. Don't you worry about that, Trimble."

58

"Bo?"

"No. It's Velarde. Who's this?"

"Oh Randy, it's Jake Owens. Man, I've been trying to reach Bo and you for the last half hour."

"Jake? Where you at?" Velarde asked.

"The Marriott, in Crystal City," Owens replied. "Savard and Lowe are here. They checked in fifteen minutes ago."

"Great, Jake," Velarde said. "Stay with them, and put two agents on their car and one behind the counter, in case they walk out."

"It's done," Owens said. "We got lucky too. Got a room next door to them."

"Things are turning our way. Bo or I will be in touch," Velarde replied. "Hold on Jake," Velarde said, holding the phone to his chest, noticing Bo waving at him.

"What?" he whispered to Bo.

Bo rolled down the windows as he slowed the car, then whispered to Velarde, "Tell him not to report it to Trimble, or anyone else at HQ. Keep it quiet."

Velarde nodded and raised the phone to his ear. "Jake, are you there?"

"Still here, Randy. What's that noise?"

"Nothing," Velarde said. "Look, don't call it in to HQ. Bo wants to tell Trimble and Mahoney himself."

"No problem, Randy. We'll keep it under wraps here," Owens replied.

"We'll call you in an hour or so, Jake. See ya." Velarde hung up.

At the Potomac Marina, Bo looked around and found fires on at least ten

259

boats. Fire trucks were all over and fire fighters were throwing water on the boats from the parking lot and the river from a fire engine boat. People stood outside the restaurant and police officers were taking information from the patrons and restaurant employees. Bo then noticed the suits, a lot of them, FBI. The whole night squad must have been there.

"What the hell is this?" Velarde asked.

"I don't know, Randy, but I don't like it," Bo replied, getting out of the car. "You never send the whole crew out, unless it's national security."

"This doesn't look like a national security matter," Velarde replied. They walked toward the standing suits.

"Nope, it doesn't," Bo said. "Who's in charge here?" he asked, taking out his credentials.

"I am," said a voice. "Jerry Garcia. Who are you guys?" he said, putting out his hand.

"Jeffrey Bodakis, New York City SAC, and this is Randy Velarde, SF Field Office ASAC," Bo answered.

"You guys are pretty far from home," Garcia said. "I'm the night supervisor. What are you guys doing here?"

"That's a good question, Jerry," Bo began. "We were wondering that ourselves, but Trimble sent us out. It might have something to do with a case we're working. What's been done?"

"Nothing yet," Garcia replied. "The locals got here first and seem to have it under control. They say it looks like a bomb was set off."

"They say why they think that?" Bo asked.

"One of the restaurant patrons saw some guy with all black clothes, running into the woods up the hill back here. I went up there, but found nothing. Then the patron told the locals that right after they saw the guy, the boats started exploding. The patron said the truck the guy drove up in suddenly was gone. They were trying to get out, you know, not paying attention," Garcia explained. "We got a description of the guy and his truck, but no plate."

"Okay," Bo said, "looks like we'll be following some leads all night."

"Yeah, we're just waiting for the locals to finish up," Garcia responded.

"Jerry, you have a car here?" Bo asked.

"Of course, what's wrong with yours?" Garcia inquired.

"Nothing, just low on gas, and I've got another OP going on," Bo said in a friendly voice. "Can we switch out and I'll return yours tomorrow?"

"Yours have enough gas to get back to HQ?" Garcia asked cautiously.

"Of course," Bo replied.

260

FIERCE LOYALTY

"No problem," Garcia said, reaching for the keys, which he flipped over to Bo. "It's the beige Taurus over there." He pointed to the parking lot.

"Thanks, Jerry," Bo replied. "Mine are in the blue one over there. I like your name, by the way. I'm a big fan."

"So I hear all the time," Garcia said with a chuckle. "What's your case about?"

"It's," Bo started, but his cell phone rang. "Sorry, I got to get this," he said smiling, happy to get out of explaining his case. "Bodakis."

"Boss-man, it's Jimmy."

"Jimmy!" Bo said. "You're early."

"You want me to call back?" Franks asked.

"No. No. What'd you find out?" Bo asked.

"Well, the name you gave me is not a person," Franks said.

"What? Say that again." Bo turned away, trying to block out the noise around him. He caught Velarde's eyes and motioned him away from the crowd.

"B. A. Star is not a person, Boss-man. It's a boat," Jimmy Franks said.

"A boat!" Bo exclaimed.

"What's wrong, boss-man?"

"Trimble. That's what's wrong," Bo said out loud. Heads turned at the mention the Deputy Directors name.

"Well, that's interesting, boss-man," Franks said, "because Trimble owns the boat."

The statement hit Bo in the face like a brick. "Jimmy," Bo said, swallowing a gulp of cold coffee, "did you say Trimble owns the boat?"

"Sure did, man, and it's a beauty. B. A. Star. Get it?" he said, as if telling a joke no one understood. "Be a star. It's Trimble's speech to the newbie agents when they come in to the bureau."

"You're shittin' me, right?" Bo said.

"Hell, no, boss man. I heard it myself straight from the horse's mouth," Franks replied. "She's a sixty-foot yacht parked at a place called the Old Dominion Yacht Club, Alexandria, Virginia." Again, there was no reply. "You okay, boss-man?"

"Yeah, Jimmy, I'm fine," Bo answered, "just writing down the info."

"Sorry, man," Franks replied.

"Jimmy," Bo said, "go to bed. I'll see you later. Oh, and thanks a lot, man."

Bo sought out Jerry Garcia back at the crowd of agents standing around talking, and drinking coffee.

"Jerry? Something's come up, and I've got to go," Bo said. "Thanks for your car."

"Sure thing," Garcia replied.

"Jerry, can you do me another favor?" Bo asked. "If Trimble calls down, would you tell him I'm busy doing an interview or something."

"No problem," he replied. "Anything else I can do for you?"

"As a matter of fact, there is. Where's the Old Dominion Yacht Club?"

"It's in Old Town Alexandria," Garcia said. "Take the Parkway south. Take a left at King Street and follow the road to the water. You'll run right into it."

"Thanks," Bo said, nodding at Velarde to follow him.

"Hey, Bodakis!" Garcia yelled.

Bo stopped, and turned to look at Jerry Garcia.

"Anything I can help with let me know. I don't think much of Trimble either." Garcia said, nodding at Bo.

"I wish I could, Jerry," Bo said. "Just being here now and covering for me is more than I could ask. Thanks." And Bo turned and walked to his new car, the Jerry Garcia G-car special.

59

Savage considered his luck. Two men walked behind Yassir and Saeid. The small one Savage recognized as Tran, the man who broke his wrist six months earlier, and set up the arrangement with Gideon. Tran blackmailed him and Jacques, into doing Gideon's dirty work. But things had changed, just as he planned, with a little help from the FBI and his Boston University friend, Thomas Trimble. The other man with Tran had to be Gideon, something he had not anticipated. Gideon took a risk to come out of hiding. Yet, for Savage's purposes, circumstances couldn't have been better. Still, he'd probably have to put off killing Saied and Yassir, at least for a few hours.

For now, he would wait and watch where they went. He'd figure out where to take them all out later. If the man were Gideon, that meant he might have to go through with meeting Gideon's gophers. He had a backup for that too, and the plan included Richard Jacques.

Savage followed the blue Durango that carried his targets from Dulles Airport. Within thirty minutes, they arrived at the Washington D.C. marina. They drove straight to the marina with no overt changes in speed or lanes, so Savage knew they missed his tail. They parked in an empty lot across from the marina security gate. Savage drove to a spot, a block behind the marina, near a hotel complex, and found a spot perfect for surveillance. He would wait and watch, pick a time to take action.

Savage had enough time to consider a plan, but he was feeling run down again. Time for a little juice, he thought. He reached into the glove box and found a vial of white powder. It was a dandy piece of equipment, he thought, as he screwed the top off. He dipped the tiny spoon in the powder, and raised it to his right nostril. He sniffed and rolled his head back. His eyes began to water, and let out a sigh of relief. He repeated it six more times and was ready. He smiled and peered back at his hostages. "Don't worry, my friends. The time is coming. You'll be set free just like the others." Savage laughed, as Chigall's eyes got bigger. He looked at Father Chason, who glared back. There seemed to be no emotion in Father Chason's eyes, no fear. Savage turned away, his smile, a scowl. He lay the vial in the ashtray, and looked where his 9-millimeter Glock 17 lay on the seat. From a bag, he took ammunition and loaded the gun, taking two spare fully loaded ammo clips as well. He was ready to go.

He looked out towards the street, as he shoved the ammo clip back into the handle of the Glock. Something outside the van caught his eye. He looked around the deserted street and sidewalk, but saw nothing, just a Dodge Durango parked in the lot across the road. A rush came over him, like warm sun invading his blood. The magic powder was kicking in. Savage felt his eyes getting wide. He shook himself, pounded the steering wheel in front of him, and grinned from ear to ear. Then it happened again! Something darted across his view. He looked about again, but nothing was moving. He shook his head, and slapped his own face, believing he was falling asleep, maybe just seeing things, an illusion caused by the cocaine. He stared out to the street, a silence came over him, nothing moved, and he saw nothing there.

Savage reached for the vial again in the ashtray. He started to panic, not knowing if he was seeing illusions. His mind was racing so fast, he could not comprehend his own thoughts. A wave of heat rushed through his body. He laughed out loud to himself, and dipped the spoon in the half-filled vial. He brought it to his nose, again, and then again. He caught himself in the rear view mirror. He looked at the image, scowling. His body felt as though he wanted to crawl out, and his eyes were so wide he thought they would fall out of their sockets. He brought one more pile of white powder to his nose. A flash of something outside startled him, and the powder flew into the air from his shaking hands. He dropped the vial. Wide eyed, he grabbed his gun off the seat. Something was happening outside, he just didn't know who, or what, it was. He looked behind him at his hostages.

"I'll be right back. Then it will be your turn," Savage said. He laughed. "I'll be back just for you."

Savage held his gun in front of him in both hands. He stared out the windshield for something, anything out of the ordinary. He took the Glock in his left hand, reached into the bag, and put his fingers around a cylinder. He brought it out and looked at it admiringly. "I'll need you tonight," he said to the

264

FIERCE LOYALTY

cylinder. He screwed it onto the barrel. "Mr. Silencer, good to see you again."

As slowly and as silently as he could, Savage turned the handle down, and the door popped open. He slowly slid off the front seat, his right hand holding the gun in his jacket pocket. Savage looked around. The Durango was silent, and he saw no one inside. His body started to tingle again. He felt ready to kill. He decided to inspect his weapon again, but it snagged on something in his pocket. He began to struggle, tugging with his right hand, but nothing happened. With his left hand, he tried to take hold of the pocket. It was dark where he stood, and he looked around for a light.

Savage heard the sound of feet running on cement. He looked to his right and saw nothing, then left. Before he could move a man dressed in black hit him full force. They fell to the ground. Savage's head struck the cement. He thought he felt blood gush down his scalp but wasn't sure. The man had him on the ground. He groped for his weapon, just as a fist crashed across his left cheek. He looked and saw a man he recognized. The punch didn't hurt his numbed face. He felt warmth where the fist hit, and then tasted blood in his mouth.

He smiled up at Toni Brazil, who stared back at him, controlled but serious. His teeth bloody, he spat, and tried to push Brazil off, but he was too late. A second fist crashed onto his other cheek, throwing his head left. He couldn't feel his face, but didn't matter, because Brazil brought his right elbow down toward his throat. He reached up with both hands and caught the forearm and triceps before the elbow crushed his throat.

"Come on, Brazil," Savage managed, struggling to hold Brazil's arm in check. "You can do it," he squeezed between clenched teeth, feeling the full force of Brazil's weight driving down on him. He saw the face of a mad man on top of him and he smiled. "I can see you in me, Brazil," Savage gurgled. Brazil said nothing, and put his left hand on top of his right fist, adding to the downward thrust.

Savage smiled at him as if he didn't care what happened. Brazil's sweat dripped onto him. He didn't have long before Brazil would break through. He looked to his right for his gun. He positioned his left leg, ready to knee Brazil, but Brazil was sitting too high on his torso. As fast as a cat, Brazil grabbed Savage's right arm and yanked it hard across his body, forcing him away from the gun.

Before Savage knew it, a fist slammed into his rib cage and again, faster and harder. Savage began coughing in pain. Toni's face came close to his ear. He whispered, "That's for Frank Tavares."

SCOTT A. REZENDES

Savage coughed out a laugh, waiting for more. Another fist hit the same spot, causing him to groan. He heard the crack of a rib dislodging from the cartilage on his right side, and for the first time, he felt the pain. Toni leaned closer. "And that's for Bobby."

Savage noticed his right arm wouldn't move when he tried to bring it down to protect himself. The pain was excruciating. He coughed and blood sprayed out on the ground. He knew it came from his lungs. He saw the shadow of Brazil's fist coming down on his head, causing his forehead to bounce against the cement. He grew dizzy, and what felt like a brick hitting his rib cage again slammed in. Brazil's elbow cracked another rib. He tried to catch his breath but couldn't. A broken rib had punctured his lung.

Savage could taste his own blood. He lay motionless. Nothing was hitting him. He couldn't move without horrifying pain shooting through his body. His breathing was shallow. He felt cold metal on his right forehead. Brazil pressed his own silenced weapon against his face. Then he heard the words.

"Is this what you did to my brother, Savage?" Brazil whispered. Savage felt the heat of Brazil's breath next to his face. "Or did you kick him around a little more before you killed him."

He tried to laugh at Brazil's attempt to scare him, but the pain was too much. He tried to speak, but he could only whisper between shallow breaths. "Kill… me. Go… on… shoot," Savage labored out, turning his head to look at Brazil. "I' d do… it… for… you."

Toni looked at the man sprawled on the cement. Blood trickled from his mouth and nose. He saw a tooth on the ground next to Savage's bloody face. He looked around briefly and pushed the guns barrel into Savage's temple. "We have a tradition in my family, Savage," Toni whispered. "We take care of our own. Don't you ever forget that, you piece of shit."

Toni stood up. He looked at the gun in his hand and pointed it at Savage, who was barely breathing. He sighted down the barrel, feeling a tear in his left eye. He aimed at Savage's head. "This is for you, Bobby."

60

"If you really want to kill him, this isn't the right place." A voice with an Irish accent hung in the air.

"I want to kill him," Toni answered, his weapon aimed. "You should go away, Father."

"I can't do that Toni," Father O'Brien replied. "He deserves it, all right, but if you let him live, he will suffer a long life in custody."

"Prison!" Toni shot back with a laugh. "Three squares, TV. I don't think so. It's too good for this filth. Besides, your student Tommy Tran, I bet he's getting his revenge about right now."

"Prison?" Father O'Brien replied. "Who said anything about prison?"

The words confused Toni so much, he began blinking. He looked at Father O'Brien, who was walking toward him.

"What?" Toni asked.

"There's a lot for you to learn about us, Toni Brazil," Father O'Brien replied.

"I have a feeling I'm about to learn something now," Toni replied.

"Oh, he'll end up in a padded cell, Toni. Crazy house, maybe one run by a Catholic priest, somewhere," Father O'Brien said, as he reached Toni and took the weapon from his hand. "You would have regretted it."

Toni looked away from Father O'Brien and nodded in controlled agreement. He released the weapon and walked toward Savage's van, seeing someone else standing there. Father Corvo nodded at him. "You fight good," Corvo said.

"What are you going to do?" Toni asked.

"We, Toni," Corvo replied. "It's what are we going to do?"

"Gino!" Father O'Brien motioned Corvo to come where he stood over Savage. "Come here and help me with him. Toni, open the van and untie Father Chason," Father O'Brien ordered.

Toni turned to the van and opened the back door. Father Chason was laid out and tied up with another body next to him. He reached into the van and took Chason's left arm, pulling the priest up and out. He un-gagged his mouth.

"Thank you, Toni," Father Chason said, licking his lips for the first time in hours.

"What about him?" Toni asked, pointing at the other tied man.

"Oh, no. He's with Savage. Hurry!" Father Chason said.

Toni stared at the drink cooler inside the van, then turned to Father Chason. "Is that the virus, Father?"

"Yes, but we'll leave it for the FBI. Now let's hurry," Father Chason urged.

"Hurry?" Toni said, under his breath. He looked around the van, and saw Savage was no longer on the ground where he left him. O'Brien and Corvo were carrying him to the security gate. As he watched, a hand fell on his shoulder. Startled, Toni jumped to the side but relaxed when he saw it was Tommy Tran.

"Sorry. I didn't mean to scare you," Tran said.

"It's all right," Toni replied. "What's going on?"

"Father Chason," Tran said, pointing to the red and white cooler, "grab the cooler, would you, and follow me."

"Sure," Chason said, as if he knew the plan all along. He picked up the cooler and carried it toward the security gate, across the street.

Toni was tired, and could hardly move. He wondered how a tiny man like Father Chason could go from being tied up for hours to carrying out a plan.

"Toni?" Tran spoke. "Help me with this guy would you? Grab his legs."

Toni took hold of the man's bound legs, and they pulled him out. He did not recognize the man, who looked at him with widening eyes.

"Stop," Tran said. "Put this over your nose." He handed Toni a cloth mask, which he put over his nose with his left hand. Tommy Tran took out a small aerosol can and sprayed the bound man's face. The man struggled at first, but quickly went limp.

"What the hell is that?" Toni asked.

"This?" Tran said, raising his eyebrows. "It puts people to sleep, usually a few hours. They wake up, but don't remember a thing. They have temporary amnesia for a few hours, and sometimes, days. Great stuff." Tran grasped

FIERCE LOYALTY

the prisoner's upper body. "Untie his legs, and I'll take him from here. You stay here. Close up the van."

"What about you, Tommy?" Toni stopped Tran in his tracks. "Where will you go?"

Tran turned to look at Toni, Chigall draped over his shoulder. "I'll be fine, Toni. My work is done here. In time you'll understand," Tran said solemnly. "You see, John and I have something in common. He seeks out those commonalties in people and helps them to find the truth. Some day you'll understand that you have something in common with John O'Brien, too. A fierce loyalty is what I'd call it."

Tran stood silently for a moment, then turned back and carried Chigall across the street through the security gate. Toni watched Tran walk through the gate and into the marina. He wondered what he was trying to tell him. He was tired and couldn't think straight. *What are they doing in there,* he then wondered. He decided to sit down on the curb next to Savage's van, and wait to see what happened next.

61

Toni waited, but no one returned. A half an hour passed, and Toni decided to walk across the street to the marina. As he approached the security gate, he saw Jerry, the guard, was in his seat inside the square white office, sound asleep.

"Toni!" A voice startled him, as he looked through the window at Jerry. Father O'Brien walked up. "He'll be fine. He's just sleeping."

"Won't remember a thing, right?" Toni asked, sarcastically.

"Yeah, it's great stuff," O'Brien said, with a smile.

"Got any extra? I could use some myself. I think I'd like to forget everything for a while."

"Not for personal use," O'Brien quipped. "It says so right on the can. Beside, I want you to remember everything you've seen and heard here tonight, Toni."

"What's going on in there, Father?" Toni asked.

"I'd prefer you call me John. What's going on in there? Well, you'll find out, just not now," O'Brien said. "By the way, Savage won't remember a thing, but we have to leave him."

Toni didn't know how to feel about Savage. He was an animal and deserved the worst. He'd have to wait a little longer, and Toni didn't feel good about beating him the way he did, even if he deserved it. Father Corvo approached and put his arm on O'Brien's shoulder, nodding to indicate that the work was done. Father Chason slowly walked up. He said nothing.

"Toni, we're outta here," O'Brien said. He turned to Father Chason and asked, "Did you call Kelly Primeau?"

"He and Richard Jacques are on the way here, right now," Father Chason

FIERCE LOYALTY

replied.

"Toni," O'Brien said, "I'm asking you not to go aboard Carlyle's boat, at least, not until the FBI arrives. You should wait fifteen minutes or so, no more, and call your FBI friend, Jeff Bodakis." O'Brien handed Toni the cell phone he dropped when he tackled Savage.

"Where you going?" Toni asked, putting the phone back on his belt.

"Sorry, we can't say," O'Brien said, "but I'll be in touch."

"You knew Savage was out here, didn't you?" Toni asked O'Brien, as he began to walk away. "I mean, when you asked me to get that package from your van, you knew, didn't you?"

"I don't know what you're talking about," O'Brien said jovially. "But think what you like."

Father Chason approached Toni. He hugged him genuinely, then pulled away. "I'll see you in a day or so, for Bobby's funeral, yes?"

"Of course," Toni replied. The small man looked tired. "Get some rest, would you?" Father Chason turned and followed John O'Brien and Giovanni Corvo.

Toni watched John O'Brien walk confidently to a white van. He got in, started the engine, and prepared to drive away. O'Brien looked up and caught Toni's eye. He nodded at him, and Toni nodded back. O'Brien looked away to check his mirrors and drove off. Toni didn't know where they were going, but something told him it wouldn't be far.

He turned to walk to his car, but suddenly heard an engine start inside the marina. He turned around and stepped inside the gate to watch The Drifter pull out of its slip, and move slowly away. He wondered what would happen to Tommy Tran, where he'd go. He wondered what made a man leave his life and family behind, everything he worked for thrown away.

For a small moment, Toni thought of running to Tran's boat and joining him. Disappear with him. Then he thought of his dog, Bailey. What would happen to her? At that moment Toni knew that he couldn't leave her. She was his family, and she'd have to go with him. He loved the dog too much. For the first time in a long time, he looked forward to going home.

Toni took a deep breath. He looked around the piers, then up at the night sky. He realized it was over. There would be no smallpox attack, and he had his revenge on Savage, even if he didn't kill the son-of-a-bitch. He knew it really didn't matter. An eye for an eye. Well, there was no satisfaction in it.

Toni reached for his cell phone and dialed the 10-digit number for Jeffrey Bodakis.

62

"Good morning, Washington, DC. It's 8:00 A.M., and I'm John Sinclair, KTV News. Our top story this morning is unfolding as we speak. What we know so far is, early this morning, the FBI arrested six people at the Washington D.C. marina. Right now the entire marina has been cordoned off to all traffic. For an update, let's go to Charles Fry at the scene. Charles, now to you."

"Good morning, John. As you said and can probably see behind me, the marina has been blocked off for two surrounding blocks. The FBI has evacuated all the residents. All the restaurants down here will be closed at least for today, and maybe longer."

"Charles," Sinclair interrupted, "do we know what the FBI is doing? Why have they blocked off the area and evacuated the residents?"

"All we know for sure is that some type of biohazard was found inside the marina, and, as you can see, the haz-mat teams are all over here. The FBI said there is probably no danger outside the area, where we are being asked to set up our cameras. Unfortunately the FBI has yet to tell us what the type of biohazard it is, or was. However, just a few moments ago a familiar face showed up, Special Agent Toni Brazil of the Federal Health Administration Criminal Investigation Division. Of course, Agent Brazil, as many of you know, was honored just two months ago at the White House for saving the lives of two FBI agents. He had no comment at this time."

"Charles?" Sinclair interrupted, again. "Early word from the FBI said six people were arrested. Have they released the names of the arrested yet?"

"Not yet, however . . . Hold on . . . Hold on. Okay, John, I've just been told that the FBI will be holding a press conference in just a few minutes. We are waiting for FBI Director John Mahoney to arrive. But to answer your last

FIERCE LOYALTY

question. The names of the six people arrested have not been released. Back to you for now."

"Thanks, Charles. We'll come right back to you as soon as Director Mahoney is ready. In other news, a fire broke out at the Potomac Marina in Alexandria last night, destroying seventeen boats. The cause of the fire is under investigation. Eyewitness reports indicated the boat fires were a result of an explosion on one of the boats. Police spokesman at the scene last night confirmed the report of an explosion on one of the boats, but the cause is still being investigated. Fortunately, no one was injured or hurt."

"I'm being told we need to return to the Washington marina where FBI Director John Mahoney is preparing to speak. And we return now to Charles Fry at the scene. Charles."

"Thank you, John. Rumors have begun to fly that something major has happened. Security here has been tightened. FBI spokesperson Angie Frickel arrived with Director Mahoney moments ago. She gathered all the news crews around and advised us that the president will make a statement at the White House following this news conference. She then said just this: a major terrorist plot has been foiled, and this news conference will air nationwide. And John, here we go."

"Good morning. I'm Angie Frickel. We'd appreciate it if you'd hold questions until after all three of the people behind me speak. I'd like to introduce them. Of course, FBI Director John Mahoney to my left; to his right is Dr. Mary Tomlinson, Director of the Centers for Disease Control; to her right is Secretary of Health and Human Services Matthew Dalton. To Mr. Dalton's left is Mark Vierra, Director of the CIA. We have a lot of information to share with you this morning, so now, the Director of the FBI, John Mahoney."

John Mahoney was a man of integrity. He knew the lives of thousands of Americans had been saved. He peered out at the News media staring back at him with eyes wide open in anticipation. He cleared his throat.

"Good morning. I've been asked by the President of the United States to give a full and complete statement of what has happened overnight, and to assure you that your government is working hard to protect you."

"With that in mind, it gives me great pleasure to announce that late last night, the FBI, working with the Federal Health Administration, the Royal Canadian Police Force, the CIA, and local law enforcement throughout the nation, has stopped a sinister terrorist plot to infect the United States government, Military, and its citizens with the smallpox virus." He paused. The press corps stopped breathing.

"Search warrants have been executed in eight cities this morning, and more are being planned and executed as we speak. Searches are taking place at homes, businesses, and storage facilities operated by a foreign owned company known as Geneon Systems. The company has offices throughout the United States, Canada, South America, Russia, Europe, Asia, and the Middle East. We have contacted all governments where this company has offices and or facilities, and advised them of the possible threat." He paused again, and took a drink from a glass of water on the lectern.

"I want to assure you that the FBI was made aware of these planned attacks, and an investigation has been ongoing for over two months. As a result of the investigation, late last night and early this morning, we arrested a total of eight persons in Washington and Virginia. Another thirty-three people have been arrested so far in six other states, including California, Texas, Illinois, Florida, Colorado, and New York. We expect more arrests in the United States and abroad in the coming hours and days."

"There is no indication – I repeat – no indication that the virus has been released anywhere within the United States. We believe the entire cache of the virus brought into the U.S. has been found, and isolated. We will be watching carefully for outbreaks over the next week in the areas where the virus was confiscated. CDC Director Tomlinson and HHS Secretary Dalton will discuss how to obtain a small pox vaccination in the coming days, for any citizen who wants one."

"Now, as for the people involved, those arrested this morning at this site, were two men identified as Saied Al Muhammad Hussein and Yassir Al Abib Haqi. Both have links to the terrorist group, Hamas. It is our conclusion that Hamas does not have the ability to perform an operation to this degree, and we believe they were working in cooperation with Osama Bin Ladin's terrorist network. They were carrying Canadian passports, though they are believed to be from Yemen. A third man arrested is identified as Anan Muhammad, a Saudi citizen, traveling under the assumed name of François Chigall. We will be releasing photos of all three men at the end of this news conference."

"In addition, also arrested here overnight was the president and CEO of Geneon Systems, Dr. Thomas Picard, also known as Muhammad Al Gyden. Dr. Picard is a French citizen, and we have notified French authorities of his arrest. Dr. Picard will be charged with murder, conspiracy to commit mass murder, and possession of an illegal biological organism. Dr. Picard's sister was also arrested, and along with the conspiracy charges, Ms. Picard is also being charged with a double homicide committed fifteen years ago in the

FIERCE LOYALTY

State of Virginia. She is an American citizen, and it gives me great displeasure to announce that Ms. Picard lived in the United States under the name of Melissa Carlyle."

"Also arrested was a Canadian government official, Alexander Savage. Mr. Savage was found badly beaten and taken to George Washington Hospital, where he is listed in stable condition. The Canadian government has already asked that he be extradited back to Canada where he will be charged with numerous related crimes. We are considering charging Mr. Savage with murdering a United States citizen abroad, as well as conspiracy to commit murder, possession of an illegal biological organism, and so on. The Canadian government has requested we extradite him to stand trial for the mass murder of at least eight other people found dead just two days ago in Montreal."

"Two others were arrested in Alexandria Virginia, this morning as well. I am not releasing their names at this time, since we are still investigating their involvement. They are cooperating fully with the FBI," Mahoney said, then paused and looked out into the crowd as if trying to locate someone.

"Finally, ladies and gentleman," he said, "I also stand here this morning, saddened by the news that FBI Deputy Director Thomas Trimble was found dead early this morning on his boat, of what has been described to me, as a self-inflicted gunshot wound to the head. Before you ask, we have yet to determine if it was suicide or an accidental shooting of some type. Thomas Trimble was my friend. I've known him for over twenty years, and on behalf of the FBI, I'd like to send my condolences to his wife, Carly, and his three children. He will be missed dearly by all his friends, here at the bureau. Now, I'd like to introduce to you Dr. Mary Tomlinson, Director of the CDC. She will give a brief statement. Thank you."

EPILOGUE

August 31, 2001 Journal Entry

*I found God in my heart, and when I found my heart, I found my soul.
It was then that I had faith. In the end, faith is all we really have.*
BB

Looking at the clock on the wall in the living room, I was amazed how fast time flew by that night. It was almost 6:00 A.M. I was up all night reading about Bobby's last few weeks. The sun was rising, and I noticed how the sky was almost purple before the sun turned it blue. It looked like it would be a clear day in the city by the bay. Next to me all night was Bailey, one happy dog, but what she didn't know was that I was happier to see her. She rested her head against my leg, her wagging tail, the only clue she was awake and wanted to be walked. I looked down at her, and she, with her endearing brown eyes, looked back with her tongue hanging out. I patted her head. "In a few minutes, Bailey," I said, and she put her head back down. She was happy to see me, and at that moment I realized someone loved me, even if she was a dog.

I finished reading Bobby's journal. The final passage gave me more insight into Bobby's life than his own words of the previous two hundred pages. They were his last words to sum up his life, and I was happy that Bobby had found God. In death, he was one step ahead of me. I closed the book like closing a chapter in life, but was it Bobby's life or mine? I wasn't sure.

I tried to imagine what Bobby's last days were like, not a nice thought. I could almost feel the pain myself. I knew Savage tortured Bobby before

FIERCE LOYALTY

killing him. The new coroner's report confirmed it. I missed a lot of Bobby's life, at least the last ten good years. He wrote a lot about his wife's death and how he lost his spirit afterward to guilt. He blamed himself, and I wondered if I tried hard enough to understand him back then. I wondered if he would have done what I did, give up. I didn't want to abandon my brother, but when the trust was broken, choices became limited. I wished I'd tried one more time. Would that have made the difference? I'll never know for sure. It was too late, and all I could do was read his journal.

It hit me at his funeral that I never said goodbye, never told him I loved him, or thanked him for being my brother. I believed that as Bobby was laid to rest in that graveyard next to his wife, he was smiling on us. That belief was all I had to hang my hat on. Bobby's death wasn't hard only for me, but for my mother and father as well. There face's carried their pain through their red eyes. It was transparent. You could see through them. Their pain was all I could see. Telling them about Bobby was the most difficult thing I'd done in my life, but what they felt, words could never describe. They returned to San Francisco with me for the time. My three older brothers followed them in a few days. Bobby's birthday was four days away, and we would celebrate it, one last time. The family was together again, and tried to comfort each other.

Although the last few days had dragged by slowly, I was glad to be home. I felt comfortable and relaxed for the first time in a long time. Everything seemed to calm down, except for the phone calls from the media. They were calling every hour or so, wanting interviews. The time, as I told one producer, was not right. I needed to grieve, then figure out what to do with the rest of my life.

The bad news was that I was put on paid leave from work. The good news was that I was too tired to care. I thought seriously about leaving the FHA. The bosses were not happy about my involvement in the terrorist case, but Alex Fox had calmed down the front office bigwigs, and I was getting paid. A meeting was scheduled in two weeks for me to explain myself. Why I was on a case they didn't know about? And while on personal leave from duty. Hell, it was the least I could do for Alex, who went out on a limb for me... again.

When I think back to the news conference, the one thing that comes to mind was how the government faced the music. The media soon recognized Melissa Carlyle as a White House staffer, and to the president's credit, he didn't cover anything up. Carlyle though, will also be charged with treason and face the death penalty. Mahoney named her as Thomas Picard's sister.

He couldn't hide her identity too long. The media and the politicians had a field day, as well.

Then there was the suicide of Thomas Trimble, completely aside from the terror plot. The governments cover up of Trimble's role in the terror plot; that I expected. However, the bureau doesn't like it when one of its own goes down by his own hand, and I thought they would fight the suicide finding. There was no fight. Perhaps covering up one aspect was enough, and I didn't know what his role was exactly, except that he was helping Alexander Savage. That alone was enough to make me happy he was dead, however his death came about – though I had a pretty good idea that Tommy Tran had a hand in it.

After the news conference, Bo took me to Trimble's boat, B.A. Star. It was located at the Old Dominion Yacht Club in Alexandria. The time of Trimble's death was estimated between one and two in the morning. The harbormaster reported that a boat named The Warrior, came in just past one, for a quick stop for fuel and a few other supplies. The on-call harbormaster described the occupants as two Asian men, one older and one young. They were met by a woman with two children. The Warrior pulled out at two. I knew it was Tommy Tran and his father. But I couldn't help wonder if Tran killed Trimble and set it up to look like a suicide, leaving evidence of Trimble's improprieties around the boat. It would be a mystery I'd let alone.

Bo said there were no other fingerprints on Trimble's boat. It had been wiped clean. He also said they found the wiretap equipment on Trimble's boat, and the transmitters on Carlyle's boat. He then told me the stereo was on when they arrived, and it was playing music from a CD called "The Holy Men." The name of the album was "The Drifter." I didn't say a word to Bo. That was the first time I held something back from him. I had no doubt Tommy Tran was on that boat.

Bo also told me that both the FBI and the CIA were quietly looking for Tommy Tran and his wife. Both submitted their resignations that day, cleaned out their bank accounts, and disappeared. There was no register of a boat named The Warrior, and there was the question of Tran's father, and what happened to him. He arrived with Picard, Saied, and Yassir, at Carlyle's boat, but he wasn't found there. He disappeared with over a million dollars wired from the boat to an account in the Cayman Islands. The account had been cleaned out only an hour before, small amounts wired to a hundred accounts around the world. Bo said they'd be tracing the money for months. I had a feeling that would take them nowhere. Tran was smarter than that. The money

FIERCE LOYALTY

was gone. I laughed at Bo when he told me over the phone. When he asked why I was laughing, I told him to let it go, Tommy Tran deserved to be left alone. He did nothing wrong.

And then there was Richard Jacques. He made a deal to cooperate with any government that would give him immunity from prosecution. Richard played the entire situation very well. He wired himself to record every conversation with Savage, Gideon, the Picards, and any one else you could think of, including me. I wanted to pound Jacques again. He deserved worse, but he was smart, and played the situation into his own hands. I knew Jacques would get his someday. He wasn't innocent, and I was glad I did what I did, which was let him live.

As it turned out, Alexander Savage was the lucky one. He didn't recover. His death was a surprise since he was in stable condition when he was taken to the hospital. They found loads of speed and cocaine in his blood, which resulted in severe convulsions, and his heart gave out. I didn't believe he had one, anyway. He was an evil man. With my anger gone, I decided forgiveness was a better fix than blame for Savage. It helped that he was dead, though. Nothing could bring Bobby back. Nothing could bring Savage back either.

The day before Bobby's funeral, I had dinner with Kelly Primeau, his wife, and two children. They invited my entire family. Bo was right about him. He is a stand up guy. He was patient with his kids, and it was impressive to watch him explain something to his son, John. At Bobby's funeral, Kelly told me Frank Tavares survived and came out of the coma that very morning. It was a little happiness on a sad day.

Kelly then introduced me to a young woman with an innocent face, who stood nervously next to her Scottish husband, who was a tall, slim man. Kelly introduced them as Elena and Mick Kennedy. Elena was the "Bookworm" Bobby wrote about in his last journal. It didn't dawn on me who Elena was until the church reception, where she explained her role. She and her husband met Bobby, one cold rainy day, when their car had broken down. Bobby wasn't the nicest and cleanest looking guy around, but he had a look of trustworthiness. That's how Mick described Bobby to me when he approached their broken down car. Bobby had fixed the car so it would get them home. He later fixed the car, and did it for free. It was something that stuck with the Kennedy's. They became friends with Bobby after that.

I was happy knowing Bobby's last years were good to him, and the church took care of him. He died believing in God, more than I could say for myself. I had lost my faith over the past months. I don't know when it happened. I could feel something new in me now. Maybe it was John O'Brien that made me start believing again. Father O'Brien appeared again, my last night in Montreal. He broke into my hotel room, again. I just laughed. We sat and talked comfortably for an hour or so, and he told me a little about his past. I asked him about Tommy Tran, but he said only that Tommy and his family had a new life in a safe place. He also told me that an Israeli Mossad agent named Yuri hit me over the head at Frank Tavares' house. I was too tired to deal with any loose ends, so I asked John to tell Yuri he owed me one. John laughed heartily, as the Irish do. I wondered whether I'd see John again, and in some strange way, I knew I would. A voice told me our meeting was already scheduled. I just didn't know when and where.

John then told me about his younger brother, and how he died. As he spoke, I sensed just how connected we were. John was helping others who lost family to violent nonsense. And I understood what Tommy Tran was talking about that night when he said that John and I shared something in common – a fierce loyalty to the truth.

Printed in the United States
93461LV00006B/247/A